ABOUNDING MIGHT

Book Three of The Extraordinaries

MELISSA MCSHANE

Night Harbor Publishing

To Aerin,
who might well be a Bounder herself

CONTENTS

CHAPTER 1

IN WHICH PRIDE GOES
BEFORE A VERY GREAT FALL

The mud, gluey and grey, stretched to the horizon and beyond. Tufts of filthy grass dotted it, trying to hold their own against the mud that sucked at them, pulling them down into the depths. Daphne crouched helplessly with her cheek pressed into it. It was gritty beneath the superficial softness, scratching her skin like sandpaper. She dragged air suffused with wet, stinking dirt into her lungs while the spots that filled her vision went away.

She could just see, above where her line of sight met the earth, the body of Major Branton lying where he had fallen, his chest a mass of— her vision clouded over, and she desperately sucked in air. She could still save him, if she brought him to an Extraordinary Shaper. She crawled, dragging her body through the mud, and with her eyes closed felt his mouth for breath. Nothing. It was too late. She had to rise, had to Bound away to let her commander know what had happened to the major. What she had allowed to happen.

She pushed herself to her knees, keeping her face well averted from the bloody corpse, and staggered to her feet. The roaring in her ears was replaced by the roar of battle, the pounding of the guns and the sharper crack of the rifles, the shouting and screaming of thousands of men all bent on doing to each other what had been done to Branton. She cried out, covering her ears like a small child experiencing its first thunderstorm, but her voice was swallowed by the din. Desperate, she Bounded—

light, a body like gauze, floating without air—

into the tent reserved for that purpose. An angular symbol of bold red strokes painted on the back wall of the tent provided a signature for ordinary Bounders to latch onto, to give them a focus for their instantaneous travel. Daphne, an Extraordinary, needed only her inner sense of what made up the location, its essence. At the moment, her greater ability seemed pointless.

She ducked out of the tent. Here, the noise of battle was reduced to the sound of cannons shattering the morning air. The screams of the dying were all but inaudible. Did it make it easier for the commanding officers to order their men into battle if they could not hear the screaming? Daphne felt the sound would echo in her ears forever.

Field Marshal Hagen stood a few yards away, conversing with one of his officers as if the battle were not raging around them. Daphne stumbled toward them. "Field Marshal, I am—Major Branton is dead."

Hagen turned his attention on her. "You were to convey him here. What happened?"

Daphne swallowed hard and tasted mud. "He was in the thick of the fight, and—Field Marshal, it is all entirely my fault, the major took rifle fire and I was overcome, I could not retrieve him—"

"Overcome?" It was an inquiry, but the hard, cold look on Hagen's face told Daphne he already knew the answer.

She stiffened her spine. "I lost consciousness. But it will not happen again."

"No," said Hagen, "it will not." He turned his attention back to the battlefield. "Report to General Omberlis immediately."

A sick feeling started in the pit of Daphne's stomach. "Yes, sir," she said in a voice quiet enough she was certain Hagen did not hear. Next to him, the officer tilted his head back in the attitude of someone Speaking to another, someone far distant. Likely someone in the War Office in Lisbon. Daphne could be anywhere she wanted in the space of a breath, but her shameful story would outrun her. She wiped mud from her face and Bounded.

The Bounding chamber in the War Office building was a tiny, cramped thing barely big enough for one person. Daphne had never Bounded there with a passenger and could not imagine ever doing so. She exited the chamber and trudged down the long hall to the marble stairs. It felt like a gallows march, all those people stopping what they were doing to stare at her, covered in mud and shame. She knew the latter was not visible on her skin, but it burned her nevertheless.

The marble stairs were far too grand for this rickety old building, one that had seen generations of inhabitants before the War Office had set up its headquarters there. Daphne stopped at the landing to look out over the city of Lisbon, its sea of rust-red roofs extending all the way to the banks of the Tagus River. She had Skipped to its shore the first day she had arrived in the city, four months before, and breathed in the smell of salt-tinged water, so different from the sour-sweet odor of the Thames. How eager she had been. How unspeakably foolish.

She continued up the stairs and down a second interminable hallway to General Omberlis's antechamber. Two armchairs stood unoccupied in the center of the space despite the men and women thronging it. They stood in groups of three or four, talking in low voices, and ignored Daphne in a way that told her they all were conscious of her presence, though they could not know of her shame. She stood alone among them, longing to sit but aware it would look like weakness, and she could not bear to be thought weaker than she was.

Three doors led off the antechamber. One of them, Daphne knew, was the door to the Seers' chamber, where the Extraordinary Seers attached to the War Office had Visions of the battles. Daphne's cousin Sophia had been one of these once. Another door led to the hall that ended in a larger room for the Speaker corps. The third was General Omberlis's office. Daphne watched this door warily. Perhaps she was wrong, and Hagen had not sent word ahead. Perhaps she was not doomed yet.

The door opened. A slim young man dressed in the black-on-black of the War Office uniform stepped out and surveyed the room. His gaze stopped on Daphne. "Lady Daphne," he said, "the general will see you now."

So short a phrase to convey her doom. She held her head high and walked at a stately pace through the door, which the functionary shut behind her, leaving himself outside. Daphne was alone with the general.

General Omberlis was a stocky man of no more than middle height. His keen eye and bushy grey eyebrows gave him the appearance of a wolf, one that centuries before might have preyed on a village during a lean winter. He sat with his back to the great windows that let in the golden light of Lisbon's late summer as if soaking it up.

"Pray, have a seat, Lady Daphne," he said in his unexpectedly high tenor. Daphne sat, perching on the edge of the chair.

"Well," the general said. "What excuse have you?"

Daphne touched her face, and drying mud flaked off. "I have none, sir," she said. "I lost consciousness and Major Branton is dead because of it."

"You assured me your predisposition to faint at the sight of blood would not interfere with the performance of your duties. I gave you an opportunity because I believed your dedication and desire to serve this Office were deserving of it. And now a good man is dead. Which of us, do you believe, is more to blame?"

Daphne said nothing. It was not the kind of question she had an answer for. General Omberlis continued, "By law you are obligated to give the government four years of service with the War Office. I cannot send you back to the battlefield. What, then, am I to do with you?"

That, too, seemed a question he did not expect an answer to, but Daphne said, "I can still be a courier—if I stay well away from the fighting—"

"You know the couriers go everywhere. I cannot predict where a route will take you. Lady Daphne, your desire is laudable, but you would be a liability to any officer I sent you to."

"What of the War Office itself? I might work here. Or an advance scout—"

"We have more Bounders than I have employment for. You might as well remain at home. No, Lady Daphne, it's out of the question."

Daphne bowed her head and willed the tears away. "I understand, sir."

She heard the general shift position. "I have a request from Lord Moira," he said.

That brought Daphne's head up and dried her incipient tears. "Lord Moira?" she said. "*India?*"

"He requests a Bounder to convey his lady wife and children to and from their home in England. The climate, as I'm sure you're aware, is hard on those not accustomed to it and doubly hard on children. I am inclined to send you."

"But—" Daphne's head whirled once again, and she smelled mud. "But, General, to be little more than a human chaise—"

"You are in no position to be proud, Lady Daphne," the general said in a low, cutting voice. "Your pride has cost a man his life. What I am offering is an opportunity to redeem yourself, as you cannot redeem him. The alternative is that I send you home in disgrace. Which will it be?"

His voice seemed to be coming from very far away. "I accept," she said, her own voice as faint as his. "When shall I leave?"

"Clean yourself up and pack your things. I give you leave to return home; you will likely need a different wardrobe, as your new duties will include social activities. Return here in three hours to be Bounded to Government House in Calcutta." His fierce expression softened, and he added, "This is not the end. It is still valiant service."

"Thank you, sir," Daphne said. Her heart was in turmoil, anger and despair and self-loathing all tumbled together. She hoped none of it was visible on her face.

She Bounded to her own bedroom in her parents' house, Marvell Hall, and wearily stripped off her uniform, crusted with drying mud. Should she bother having it cleaned? She no longer felt deserving to wear it. She left it piled on the floor and washed herself thoroughly, standing by habit in front of the fireplace, which on this first day of September was empty. She rinsed mud out of her blonde hair and squeezed the dirty water out onto the mat. Then she donned her other

Bounder uniform, the one she had worn when she worked for the public Bounding company Standiford's. That, at least, was one she had not disgraced.

India. The British Army had barely any presence there; it was controlled by the Honourable East India Company, traders with the remit from the British government to act on their behalf and an army of its own to defend itself. *Merchants.* She raked her fingers through her hair, straightening her tangled locks. One moment's weakness and she was to be packed off to the far side of the globe, never to have a chance to prove herself. She knew her talent to be powerful, knew herself to be the most skilled Bounder of her generation, but thanks to her weakness, no one else would ever know the truth.

You are too proud, she told herself as she pinned up her hair again. *Do you imagine your fame means anything when a man is dead because of you?* But it *did* matter. Three-year-old memories thronged her inner vision, of reasoning and arguing and pleading with the War Office to take her on early, and she burned with fury. The officials at the War Office had mocked her when they had not simply dismissed her because she was barely five feet tall and a woman, and all the greatest Bounders, Extraordinary and otherwise, were tall and strapping men, capable of carrying men twice their size. She meant to make them eat those words by becoming the most famous Bounder ever. And she could not do that in India.

She let out a deep breath, willing her anger to evaporate with it. There was no point being angry with General Omberlis or resentful of her fate, not when it was entirely her fault. She would go to India, and she would serve the Governor-General's wife, Lady Loudoun, who was a countess in her own right and by all reports a generous, kind-hearted woman. Perhaps if she were obedient and diligent enough, she would prove herself worthy of a second chance. That was an optimistic thought. She might even come to believe it, in time.

She had one trunk, a small leather-bound thing that was stiff and shiny with newness. She rarely traveled anywhere she could not Bound home from at night. She packed her favorite gowns, clean shifts and nightgowns, the stays she had learned to get into without assistance, assorted shoes, her toiletries, and shut the lid and strapped it closed.

Then she sat on her bed and stared at it. Her parents were likely home, but she could not bear to see them, to tell them what had happened. They had supported her in her attempts to join the War Office early, had given her every assistance, everything she had ever asked for, and to be banished to India felt like a betrayal of them as well. In a day or so she would write to them, and perhaps find the words that failed her now.

She picked up her trunk easily—and that was another unfairness. She had spent years practicing lifting increasingly heavy weights until she could carry a man twice her size with ease. Lady Loudoun could not possibly challenge her strength. She stifled the unworthy thought. Her pride had got her into this mess, and she needed to subordinate it.

In a breath, she was back at the War Office. She managed to maneuver herself and her trunk out of the narrow space and trudge up the stairs to the Bounder nexus, where the War Office's Bounders stood ready to convey people all over the globe. She entered the room without knocking and set her trunk on the floor, facing down the three men and one woman who turned to look at her, all of them wearing the uniform she had so longed for.

"I am Lady Daphne St. Clair," she said wearily, "and I am ready to go to Calcutta."

CHAPTER 2

IN WHICH DAPHNE RESOLVES
TO ENJOY HERSELF

Daphne clasped the infant Lady Adelaide close to her breast and—

light, breathless, floating though there is no air—

the cool air of Donington Hall's Bounding chamber, small and white, surrounded her. The all-too-familiar symbol of green and black painted on the wall facing her was by now completely unnecessary. She had made the Bound between Government House and Donington Hall, the Governor-General's English residence, so often in the last week she knew its essence far better than she did its signature. Bounding there was second nature now.

She pushed the door open and handed the child off to her nurse. The rest of the Governor-General's children had already dispersed, which irritated Daphne. It made her feel like a particularly talented servant, valued for her little tricks but otherwise of no use. And to think someday she would outrank Lady Loudoun!

Rather than Bound immediately back to Government House, or to her bedroom, she stepped into the Bounding chamber and breathed in the cool, damp air. She had never seen the Hall from the outside, but imagined it to be a great pile of stone and glass, catching the coolness of a September evening and storing it against the heat of the day. Not

8

that England knew such heat as obtained in India. And now she was stalling.

With a sigh, she Bounded back to her bedchamber in Lindsey House, her home in India, and immediately felt sweat prickle under her arms and at the nape of her neck. It had been early evening in England; here in India it was well past sunset, and the black sky was dusted with a million stars, like crystal shattered and strewn across the horizon. The air was muggy and warm even now that the sun had set. Dampness from the constant rains seeped into everything, her clothing, her few books; even the wood of the window frame felt uncomfortably mushy.

Her bedchamber, small and plainly appointed, smelled of the teak the furniture was made of and the distant scent of the boiled mutton that had been served for supper. She longed to taste the foods of India, but Miss Donnelly, the gentle tyrant who ruled the women of Lindsey House, declared such a thing was Not Done. Daphne had no idea how she managed to pronounce capital letters. It was Miss Donnelly's response to everything Daphne had proposed that might bring her closer to the real India, as she thought of it. Walking in Calcutta. Dining on Indian food. Learning to speak Hindoostani. "Better they learn to speak English, Lady Daphne, it will benefit them in the long run," Miss Donnelly had said, and Daphne, frustrated, had given up. For the moment. She might not be in India of her own accord, but that did not mean she could not make the best of it.

Her eye fell on her pocket watch, an expensive gift from her parents that told seconds as well as minutes. She was running behind the time and could not find it in herself to care. But Miss Donnelly, or one of the other residents, would no doubt knock on her door shortly, wanting to know if she was properly gowned for that evening's ball. Daphne had no desire to attend a ball, but Lady Loudoun was not to be refused, and it was not as if Daphne had anything better to do with her time. She filled her days, when she was not Bounding, with pursuing her exercise regimen, lifting the weights she had brought with her from home, and avoiding Miss Donnelly, who felt compelled to pry into Daphne's affairs. Since her idea of proper employment for the daughter of a marquess was fancy sewing, avoiding her had a certain urgency to it. Sewing made Daphne fidget.

She wearily removed her day gown and folded it away into the clothespress, then took out her second-best ball gown and wriggled into it. It was white muslin with a gauzy overdress embroidered with violets. As an Extraordinary, she was entitled to wear any color or fabric she wished, despite her age and marital status, but she liked white, even though it made her appear younger than she was. It suited her to be underestimated sometimes, particularly in social settings where she might have to fend off fortune-hunters or those interested in becoming attached to the Marquess of Claresby's only daughter and heir. She briefly touched her ear-drops, teardrop-shaped topazes dependent from round diamonds, and thought of her parents. They believed her posting to India was an honor. She could not bear to disillusion them.

A knock sounded at the door. "Lady Daphne? Are you ready?"

Miss Hanley. She was kind enough, and might well become a friend, if Daphne felt equal to the effort of making friends. As it was, the idea of sharing confidences with someone else made her shrink. This did not stop Miss Hanley from pursuing the acquaintance, and Daphne had not the heart to be rude enough to stop her. "Please come in, Miss Hanley," Daphne said, brushing out her blonde hair. "I am behind the time, I'm afraid."

"The palanquin will wait for you," Miss Hanley said. She wore rose-colored satin with matching ribbons in her chestnut hair, which framed her lovely heart-shaped face perfectly. The dark spectacles she wore day and night to protect her weak, impaired eyes gave her a sinister look, but her smile was friendly, her lips curved as if permanently on the verge of a kiss. "I have already told the bearers they are not to leave until we descend."

Daphne suppressed a shudder. She had yet to become accustomed to Miss Hanley's talent, which as an Extraordinary Speaker allowed her to send thoughts into the minds of anyone, Speaker or no. It was an eerie experience, as the thoughts sounded no different from her own inside her head, and on the few occasions Miss Hanley had turned her talent on her, she had found it difficult to remember those thoughts did not originate with her.

Daphne swiftly pinned her hair up and laid down the brush. It was not the most elegant style, but Daphne was not interested in impressing anyone at the ball. She would dance for a few hours, then excuse herself, pleading fatigue. It was even true, if one considered spiritual fatigue equal with physical fatigue. "Thank you for waiting."

"It is my pleasure." Miss Hanley trailed her hand along the wall as they descended the stairs, maintaining her balance. Daphne sometimes wondered just how little Miss Hanley was capable of seeing. She certainly seemed to manage her incapacity well. "You look rather downcast. Do you not enjoy dancing?"

"I do, it is just that it is still so very warm—the exertion of dancing cannot—though I don't mean to suggest it is not an honor to be invited to Lady Loudoun's ball, when I know she intends only to please us."

Miss Hanley laughed. "We ladies of the War Office have so few pleasures permitted us in India. We may not travel far, we may not walk unescorted in Calcutta, and the Rajas and Peshwas will not mingle with us socially. And yet—" Her voice dipped low and conspiratorial. "The officers are so *very* handsome, and so attentive."

Daphne smiled despite herself. "You are all but engaged to your young lord in Devonshire," she said. "Should you not leave the officers to us?"

"I see nothing wrong with flirting, just a little. Come, Lady Daphne, do not tell me you have *no* interest in finding a husband?"

"I intend to marry someday, yes, but only after I have had many adventures." How she was to have adventures while she was tied to Lady Loudoun's apron strings, she did not know. She had not realized how very limiting her new assignment would be, nor how pedestrian. It was an unpleasant thought, and she felt suddenly disappointed in herself. Her presence in India was entirely her own fault, and moping would do nothing to redeem herself. She resolved to enjoy herself that evening and leave her dissatisfaction at the door.

Only one palanquin remained outside Lindsey House when they

emerged. It was barely large enough for two, and painted a garish red, with curtains fluttering in the slight breeze that bore with it the silt-ridden rotten-fish odor of the Hooghly River. The bearers stood next to it waiting for them, not appearing to be impatient at their slowness, but Daphne was still not good at reading the expressions of the Hindoos. Daphne climbed into the palanquin, followed by Miss Hanley, then folded her hands in her lap as they proceeded down the muddy road toward Government House and the center of Calcutta. The night smelled of the rain that had fallen heavily all afternoon and the wet odor of the coralwoods lining the road. It was a rich, exotic scent Daphne loved, the embodiment of India as far as she was concerned, and she wished she could bottle it and take it with her wherever she Bounded.

The palanquin sped up as they entered the outer boundaries of Calcutta, its rocking gait so different from the coaches of London. Ramshackle houses lit by coconut-oil lamps piled atop one another, making a warren of streets Daphne longed to lose herself in. It was not as if she were in any danger of being waylaid, as Miss Donnelly always claimed had happened to other, unnamed women; she could Skip or Bound away from anyone who might try to apprehend her. But she was conscious of not speaking the language, of being visibly different, and feared disturbing the homes of those who had a right to be there. So she merely watched the people passing by, none of whom looked at her or the litter. They were accustomed to the sahibs making their way to and from the English part of town.

Ahead, flambeaux marked one of the great gateways into the grounds of Government House. The arched gate was topped by a stone lion, its presence a reminder of the power of Great Britain and a warning that the Honourable East India Company, though primarily mercantile, was not a force to be trifled with. Daphne privately considered it a trifle overbearing.

The long driveway leading to the yellow bulk of Government House passed through bare parkland, mostly short-trimmed lawn Daphne believed would be improved by the addition of trees. The palace itself glowed in the light of dozens of lanterns, and every window blazed with light. The bearers brought the palanquin to the bottom of the wide, shallow stairs leading to a colonnade that in the daytime would shade the doors mercifully. Daphne extricated herself from the curtains and stood with the help of one of the bearer. She had enough presence of mind not to simply Skip to the top of the stairs.

"It is a lovely building, don't you agree?" Miss Hanley said, coming to Daphne's side and putting a gentle hand on her shoulder. "Every bit as attractive as anything back home."

"Lovely," Daphne agreed, "and intimidating. Do you suppose that is what the Marquess of Wellesley had in mind when he commissioned it?"

"I wouldn't dare to try to read that man's mind—not that reading minds is possible. I know everyone is just as happy he is back in England, cruel and warlike as he was. The Company required several years to mend the damage he did." Miss Hanley took Daphne's unresisting hand and drew it through the crook of her arm. "Let us enter, and hope the air is less damp inside."

The broad, white-tiled entry to Government House had no grand central staircase to draw the eye, an omission Daphne felt spoke poorly of the architect. In all other ways, however, the man, whoever he was, had created a masterpiece. High ceilings crowned with delicate moldings shivered in the light of dozens of lamps, lending a glow to the many resplendent rooms they passed through. Most were lightly furnished in a way that appealed to Daphne's Bounder instincts. She had as yet seen little of Government House, and wished she had the freedom to explore it fully.

She and Miss Hanley ascended the narrow stairs to the second floor and passed through a short hallway to the ballroom. Several fine chandeliers dripping with crystal lozenges cast their light across the glossy floor and the pillars lining both sides of the room. An arched doorway at the far end led to another flight of stairs and an alcove in which the musicians prepared to play. The ballroom was already half-full of finely dressed women and men in formal wear or resplendent in Army uniforms. Their red coats were as bright as the palanquin. What was it about a uniform that made almost any man attractive, even to Daphne, who had no interest in forming an attachment?

"Lady Daphne," Lady Loudoun said, her sweet voice carrying over the din. Her emerald green satin gown glowed in the light of the chandeliers, which sparkled off the row of diamonds she wore around her throat. "How good of you to come. Miss Hanley, welcome."

"Thank you, Lady Loudoun, it is a pleasure," Daphne said, curtseying.

"Oh, the pleasure is all mine, I assure you. Come, there is someone I wish to introduce to you." Lady Loudoun sailed off into the crowd, and Daphne and Miss Hanley followed like beads on a string. "Lady Daphne, may I make known to you Captain Ainsworth and Lieutenant Wright, and this is Ensign Phillips. Gentlemen, Lady Daphne St. Clair."

The men bowed. Lieutenant Wright, taller than the others and with thick dark hair curling somewhat over his collar, said, "Good evening, Lady Daphne. Perhaps you will do me the honor of standing up with me for the first dance?" His bright blue eyes twinkled cheerfully at her.

Ensign Phillips had his mouth open as if he'd been about to ask the same favor. He had red hair and an attractive, cheerful face, though Lieutenant Wright was objectively more handsome. "Miss Hanley," he said instead, "would you care to dance?"

Daphne stifled a smile. The young ensign gave no hint that Miss Hanley had been his second choice, and she liked him for it. "Thank you, Ensign, I would be most pleased," Miss Hanley said, catching Daphne's eye in a way that told her Miss Hanley had seen it too, and not been offended.

Captain Ainsworth looked as if he wanted to protest—possibly he thought his rank should give him precedence—but he smiled ruefully and said, "Lady Daphne, I hope you will reserve a dance for me."

"Certainly, Captain." Daphne curtseyed. She was accustomed to having admirers, but none who were so overt about it. It was... rather pleasant, actually.

Lady Loudoun smiled and sailed off into the crowd to greet another guest. Daphne quickly surveyed the room, but could not see the Governor-General anywhere. Surely he must be present... but if not, what a relief. Lord Moira knew why she had been sent to India, and while he was always superficially polite, his politeness barely concealed disdain. He was a military man at heart, veteran of the American Colonial Conflict, and weakness of any kind was abhorrent to him. Daphne prided herself on not fearing anything, but in her secret heart, she quailed at the thought of encountering the earl.

She smiled at Lieutenant Wright, who offered her his arm and led her to where couples were forming up for the first dance. "You cannot have been in India long," he said, "as I'm certain I would remember such a lovely face."

Daphne wished she dared scrunch up her lovely face and scowl at him. The light in his eyes made his compliment sound insincere. She reminded herself that she had resolved to enjoy herself this evening and said, "Thank you, Lieutenant, I have been in India just one week."

"And how do you find it?"

"Hot. Wet. But I imagine that is what every newcomer says."

"We are coming out of the monsoon season and approaching cooler weather. I've been here three years and I am still not accustomed to it. The weather, the food, the Hindoos and Mahommedans and half a dozen other heathen types... it must be trying to your delicate sensibilities."

"I find it intriguing, actually. I am an Extraordinary Bounder and have always longed to visit new places."

"An Extraordinary? How interesting. Are you here on War Office business?"

Shame and frustration gripped her heart. "I... serve Lady Loudoun and her children. They spend a great deal of time in England, during this season, and of course it would be indelicate for a man to convey them so regularly."

"Of course, of course. I suppose we all serve where we're put, eh?"

Daphne smiled and cast about for a change of subject. "And how is India, as a posting?"

"Boring, most of the time. Much of northern India is under British protection, and while the Nawabs and Rajas are not subordinated, they rarely give us the kind of trouble that requires the battalions to move out. Not like the Marathas in the south and west."

"And is boring... good?"

Wright laughed. "I'm afraid it gets many of the sepoys in trouble. The native soldiers, that is. With nothing productive to do, they laze about or fight or gamble... I beg your pardon, Lady Daphne, I should not discuss such matters with a lady."

Daphne privately thought this was the most interesting thing he had said all evening, but replied, "I don't mind. It is good you feel you can be completely candid with me—I do not consider you at all indelicate."

Wright nodded, but when he next spoke, it was on banalities such as her title and her family, things that could not possibly cause offense and were therefore extremely boring. She curtseyed to her partner at the end of their dances and allowed him to escort her back to where they had been introduced. Daphne's exertions had left her feeling warm and she was certain her muslin gown had already wilted. Miss Hanley was nowhere to be seen. "I should not leave you unattended, Lady Daphne," Wright said with a smile Daphne guessed he used on all the young women he met.

"Oh, Lieutenant, I would not—that is, I see someone to whom I must speak, you needn't trouble yourself," Daphne lied, looking off toward the windows. "It has been most enjoyable meeting you."

"Likewise, my lady, and I hope to encounter you again soon." Wright bowed over her hand and excused himself. Daphne watched him go. He was pleasant enough, but—was that what she had to look forward to? Insincere, handsome young men with whom she might pass half an hour in meaningless pleasantries? Not for the first time, she wished herself back in the Peninsula.

CHAPTER 3

IN WHICH DAPHNE MAKES A
NEW FRIEND AND MEETS AN
OLD ENEMY

She still felt uncomfortably warm, and as soon as Wright moved away she walked to the windows beyond the pillars, where the air was marginally cooler. Fanning herself with her hand, she looked out over the dark expanse of the parkland surrounding Government House. Lights pooled on the ground immediately below, but beyond that, blackness prevailed, so complete that it might have been a starless night. She was seized with an impulse to Skip into it, away from this overwarm room and all her responsibilities, but it was an illusion, and Daphne's feet were better left touching the ground.

"Do you tire of dancing already?"

Daphne turned to look at the man standing—lounging—in the shelter of one of the pillars. He wore a red coat with captain's epaulets, and his sandy hair was ruffled as if he had run his fingers through it, disordering it. He regarded her with a steady, unreadable gaze, not admiring as Wright's had been, but not disdainful like Lord Moira, and it made her uncomfortable that she could not interpret it.

"We have not been introduced," she said, taking refuge in haughtiness.

"No, we have not," the captain agreed. "Captain Fletcher, my lady."

"You know who I am?"

"Lady Daphne St. Clair, Extraordinary Bounder. I have seen you in passing in the Governor-General's quarters."

"You are not with Fort William, then?"

"No, one of the king's men, attached to Government House." He straightened and took a few steps toward her. "Are you enjoying India?"

She wondered briefly how many people would ask her variations on that question that night. "I have not been here long enough to know."

"And you spend most of your time conveying Lady Loudoun and her children," Fletcher said.

"It does not take much—not that I am complaining, of course."

"How else do you occupy yourself?"

Now she wanted to complain, to shout her boredom to the windows and the night sky. "Well, I... there are activities... sewing, and paying calls—"

"I see." Fletcher's lips twitched in a small smile. "I beg your pardon, but that seems a waste of your time."

"I do as Lord Moira asks. I must of course always be available for her Ladyship."

"Of course."

He was still regarding her with that unreadable expression, and it angered her, as if he were in control of this uncomfortable conversation. "Why do you not ask me to dance, Captain?" she challenged him.

Amusement lit his features. "I am a Discerner, and choose not to intrude upon your privacy. I do not generally dance."

"Oh." A Discerner, capable of perceiving emotions with a touch. "Then why are you here?"

"Other than to make awkward conversation with young ladies with whom I am not acquainted?" His smile broadened. "Lady Loudoun is a firm believer in true love, and hopes to marry off all those who come within her sphere of influence. She believes I am too isolated, and requests my presence as often as I am in town. I have too much respect for her to ignore her wishes."

"Well, I have nothing to hide, Captain. You need not worry on my account."

The captain's eyebrows lifted. "You have no secrets you wish to hide away?"

The memory of Major Branton's mangled body flashed before her. "No, none," Daphne declared, willing it to be true.

Fletcher laughed and extended his white-gloved hand to her. "Very well, Lady Daphne, you have persuaded me."

For someone who rarely danced, Fletcher was an excellent dancer, graceful and smooth. Every time their hands met, he smiled, as if he had a secret he did not intend to tell. Far from annoying her, she found it compelling, and wondered what she might do to induce him to share it.

"How long have you been in India, Captain?" she asked.

"Nearly eleven years. I came out as a youth and have been back to England only a handful of times since then."

"You must miss your family—or am I assuming too much? I suppose you might not like them, and find their absence refreshing."

Fletcher laughed. "I am the sixth child of ten in my family. The question is whether they noticed *my* absence."

The idea of having nine siblings was almost beyond Daphne's comprehension. "I am an only child," she said, "and have few cousins. I cannot imagine having so many brothers and sisters. Do you like them, then?"

"I do, as well as anyone might. I am particularly close to my next older brother William. His living is in Buckinghamshire and he has a lovely wife he dotes on. His letters come with such regularity I sometimes forget we have not seen each other in the flesh in years."

"I am so grateful that the Government House post is carried by Bounder, and not by ship as it once was. I do not imagine I could bear the separation from my parents if I did not receive regular letters from them."

"And your family resides in...?"

"Suffolk, though we have houses in London and Derbyshire."

"That is lovely country."

"It is." A pang of homesickness struck Daphne. To dispel it, she said, "And since we are talking of banalities, where does *your* family reside, Captain?"

His dark brown eyes twinkled. "In Gloucestershire. My father is a baronet and we have property near the Welsh border."

"And you were encouraged to join the army because you are a younger son?"

"I rather liked the idea of going to India, and the army seemed a better fit than being attached to the East India Company."

"I understood the army here belonged to the East India Company. What does it mean that you are a king's officer?"

They took a turn going down the line, and when they came together again, Fletcher said, "The Company maintains its own forces, but mostly those are sepoys, native soldiers trained in European tactics. I am attached to the Company troops, but ultimately my orders come from England, represented by Colonel Dalhousie. Not that I would disobey an order from any of my superior officers here in India."

"I see." Daphne curtseyed to her partner as the music came to an end. "And how do *you* find India, Captain Fletcher?"

Fletcher offered her his arm, and the unusual smile touched his lips again. "Endlessly fascinating."

"You are smiling—pray tell me what is so amusing, Captain."

"Nothing amusing. I rarely meet anyone whose demeanor so closely matches her emotions. It is a pleasant sensation—though as you are not a Discerner, I cannot explain it to you any more than you could tell me how it feels to Bound."

"I understand, though I am sure it is a pity we cannot share experiences as easily as you sense emotions. Imagine how well the world would roll along if that were true!"

"I have to agree with you, Lady Daphne." He bowed, and added, "Will our newfound acquaintance support my asking you an impertinent question?"

"You put me in great suspense, Captain."

"Very well. Why are you not in the Peninsula?"

It struck her almost like a physical blow. "Why—that is indeed impertinent. I don't see why it matters to you—"

"I know your talent is strong. What brought you to play the role of carriage driver for the earl's family?"

She could not bear it. "I am... unsuited to war, Captain, and that is all I may say on the subject."

"I see. I apologize for offending you."

"I am not offended, Captain, it is—I would prefer not to speak of it. You see, it is a private matter, I would expect a Discerner to understand that—"

"I do. Thank you for your candor." He smiled that unusual smile again. "Lady Daphne, it has been a genuine pleasure making your acquaintance."

"Thank you, Captain, I have enjoyed meeting you as well." She felt unexpectedly downcast at this obvious farewell. "I see Miss Hanley—I should go to her—"

"May I escort you?" He offered her his arm, and she took it, feeling slightly uncomfortable knowing that he would be aware of her emotions; this felt so much more intimate, after the conversation they had had, than dancing. But he said nothing, merely bade her goodnight and walked off into the crowd. Miss Hanley watched him go, her mouth slack with astonishment.

"Do not tell me you danced with Captain Fletcher?" she said in a low voice. "I wasn't aware he knew how."

"He is a very good dancer, and agreeable, though I cannot see how he endures these balls if he is so reluctant to dance, not that I blame him for not wishing to." Daphne fanned herself with her hand again. "He is interesting."

"Oh, interesting?" Miss Hanley's eyebrow arched. "Is that so?"

Daphne felt a blush rise across her cheeks and wished she could push it back with her fingers. "You may stop looking at me that way, he is nothing to me, and you are terrible, to hint at such a thing!"

"I have said nothing. It is all your own conscience that makes you blush."

"I believe you must be very bored, to make matches on such slim evidence. I believe I would like a glass of punch now."

"I will take your sudden change of subject as a sign that I am right," Miss Hanley said. "In seriousness, Lady Daphne, I cannot say I have ever seen Captain Fletcher converse with a woman at one of these balls save Lady Loudoun herself. He must find you interesting, too."

Daphne recalled that odd, intriguing smile. "I cannot say I find that unpleasant."

"Lady Daphne!" Lady Loudoun appeared at her side. "Here is someone with whom you will have much in common. Pray, let me make known to you Major Schofeld."

"Lady Daphne, it is good to make your acquaintance," Schofeld said with a smile and a bow. "I am also an Extraordinary Bounder." He was tall and broad-shouldered, the very image of the perfect Bounder, and wore the uniform of the War Office, black-on-black, that she was unlikely ever to wear again.

Daphne kept a smile on her face through pure willpower. She remembered Schofeld well. His words echoed in memory: *There she is again, the Littlest Bounder come to make her plea. Does she not know how ridiculous she is?* She had seen him often at Whitehall three years ago, when she was trying to make the War Office take her on early. He had never spoken to her directly, simply mocked her behind her back while smiling pleasantly to her face. Did he believe she had forgotten him, or did he simply not know she knew what he had said? Well, he might have forgotten, but *she* never would.

With Lady Loudoun standing there, beaming with pleasure, Daphne dared not snub the man. "How nice to meet someone who shares my talent," she said. "Surely you are not posted to India, Major?"

"Just passing through," Schofeld said jovially. "Will you do me the honor of dancing with me?"

She would prefer to have nothing to do with him. "Certainly," she said, not meeting Miss Hanley's eyes. Was the woman tired, yet, of being passed over? Or did she care?

Schofeld was not a good dancer, though he seemed unaware of this. Daphne gritted her teeth and reminded herself that she need only endure for a few minutes. "I saw you dancing with Fletcher," he said without preamble. "Kind of you."

"It was no kindness; he is an excellent dancer, and I enjoyed it very much."

"Really? I've always found him a bit standoffish, myself. Not that he'd be likely to dance with me, no?" Schofeld laughed. The sound annoyed Daphne, like the braying of a tone-deaf donkey. She chose not to respond.

"At any rate, I am glad to have finally met you. Your fame quite preceded you. Your speed at Skipping, your knowledge of essences, and of course your role in the capture of Lord Endicott—I have long wished to know you."

"You flatter me, Major." More of his superficial pleasantries. What had he said about her to his fellow officers when she could not hear? "Do you come to Government House often?"

"Sometimes. I am tasked with liaison duty between Colonel Dalhousie and the War Office. I dislike India, the heat and the insects and all the rain—don't you agree?"

"I am rather fond of the place." She would have disagreed with him if he had said water was wet, but she felt defensive of India, despite the shortness of her time there.

"Oh." Schofeld looked taken aback by this, which satisfied her. "Well, at any rate, it's an enervating climate, as I'm sure you'll find. Ages a man rapidly—I would hate to see its effects on you, my lady."

"That is very kind of you."

"No kindness. I really do admire you tremendously." His expression *was* admiring, but it only made her angry. He had seemed admiring three years ago, too. She wished she had brought her pocket watch, so she could check the time and gauge how much longer she would have to spend with him.

But Schofeld settled down to ordinary talk, questions she had already answered for Lieutenant Wright, anecdotes of his Bounding activities. It was true, she enjoyed discussing her talent with someone who shared it, even someone she disliked. Had she found him appealing, she would have enjoyed his conversation despite his poor dancing skills. Instead, she could not help but compare him to Captain Fletcher, whose questions, if impertinent, had hardly been routine.

As time wore on, though, she began to feel guilty. Schofeld was so open, so friendly, and perhaps she was being too critical of him. It had been three years, after all. Suppose he had changed in that time? She had, after all, accomplished much since then that could not be dismissed. Perhaps she should be more generous of spirit.

As the music came to a close, she curtseyed. "Thank you, Major, it was most enjoyable."

"It was my pleasure, Lady Daphne." He offered her his arm. "I never expected I would be introduced to you. I have seen you before this, of course."

"Oh?"

"Yes, at Whitehall three years ago. You were much younger then, of course, but still so small—the Littlest Bounder, we called you!" He laughed. "Your appeal was so very amusing, though of course doomed to failure."

She stiffened. "I am glad to have provided you with so much amusement," she said, wishing she were a Scorcher to set his feet afire and watch him dance a tarantella of fear. He thought her amusing, like a clever dog?

He failed to hear the wounded anger in her voice. "That's all well in the past, though. I wonder that you're not in the Peninsula, a talented Bounder like you."

"I serve where I am bidden. Just like you." She released his arm and curtseyed. "Until we meet again, Major." *And may it be a long time coming.*

She wished she could leave, go to her bedchamber and pound out her anger and humiliation into her pillow, but someone would take notice of that, and Lady Loudoun might be offended. So she danced again, with affable Ensign Phillips and agreeable Captain Ainsworth. The latter was as talkative as Captain Fletcher had been reticent, passing on gossip about people Daphne did not know. "It was good of you to stand up with Fletcher," he said as they met in the figures of the dance. "He is extremely reluctant to dance—Discerner, you know."

"He told me."

"He's too isolated, I always say. But he seems to like it that way. Good thing Schofeld is so rarely here—they've bad blood between them."

This was the kind of gossip Daphne liked. "How so?"

"They were schoolmates together, rivals—or at least Schofeld felt they were; I don't know that Finn—Captain Fletcher felt the need to compete. He always took top honors, anyway. But Schofeld knows how to strike at him. He can manipulate his emotions so a Discerner can't help but be overwhelmed. I hope you don't think less of Fletcher for that."

Daphne thought of her secret weakness, and said, "On the contrary, I think better of him." So it was not just undersized Extraordinary Bounders the major felt compelled to tease. Her dislike of Schofeld hardened on Captain Fletcher's behalf.

They separated to go down the line, and when they once again clasped hands, Ainsworth said, with a wary look, "Best you not tell Fletcher I told you that."

"Why not, Captain?"

"He doesn't like people believing he's weak. He's spent years mastering his talent—it's just bad luck Schofeld can manipulate him."

"I assure you I would never consider him weak." If she thought poorly of anyone, it was this man, sharing his friend's secret with a stranger. Her interest in his gossip dried up entirely.

Tired, her feet aching, Daphne bade Captain Ainsworth goodbye and found herself once more standing next to Miss Hanley. "Have you enjoyed yourself?" Miss Hanley asked.

"I have, but I am so tired," Daphne said, "and I hope it is not too early, because I would like to retire."

"You are fortunate in that you need not wait for a litter," Miss Hanley said, stifling a yawn. "I declare it is nearly one o'clock. Lord Moira may well not sleep at all, if he intends to rise at four as he usually does."

"Let me return us both," Daphne said impulsively. "We can make our goodbyes to Lady Loudoun and be in our beds in five minutes."

"Oh, Lady Daphne, that is the best idea I have heard all evening."

Having bade farewell to their hostess, they retreated to an unused room on the first floor, and Daphne caught Miss Hanley up and Bounded them both to the left-hand parlor of Lindsey House, whose essence Daphne knew well. They ascended the stairs together in silence, but when they reached Daphne's room, Miss Hanley said, "I wish you would not isolate yourself so, Lady Daphne. People are beginning to call you standoffish. And I know Miss Donnelly's interest in keeping you occupied will only grow as you put her off."

Daphne was too tired to dissemble. "Do *you* call me standoffish, then?"

"I perceive you have a great trouble bearing down on you, and I understand how that might make you disinclined to pursue casual acquaintances. But I don't believe it does you any good to shut yourself in your room."

"I—Miss Hanley, I am simply not ready to share my burden, and I dislike imposing myself on others when my mood is so uncongenial. And I can avoid Miss Donnelly indefinitely. Pray, do not fret about me. Someday..."

Miss Hanley's smile was sad. "I see. Well, if you wish to talk about anything—"

"I will remember. Thank you."

She disrobed in the quiet darkness of her bedroom, not bothering to light her candle. She had been telling the truth; she did not care to burden others with her private pain. She had not even told her parents or her cousin Sophia the truth about why she was in India. Someday, she would be able to bear it, but until then...

Sleep eluded her, and she tossed and turned, kicking the blankets off as too warm, tangling her feet in the netting shrouding her bed. She drifted off sometime near dawn, sleeping restlessly for what seemed only a few minutes before something nudged her consciousness. It threaded its way into her dream like a wisp of smoke, tingling her nostrils, and she came awake with a jolt, fearing fire in her room.

-Lady Daphne!-

Daphne blew out a deep breath. Miss Hanley, waking her at—it was nearly 8:30, how had she slept so long!

-Lady Daphne, you must wake!-

Someone knocked on her door, a diffident sound. Miss Hanley could not bear to make a fuss by raising her voice or knocking too loudly, though Daphne thought such would be less intrusive than having thoughts inserted directly into one's brain. Daphne fought her way free of the netting and opened the door.

"Oh, good, you are awake," Miss Hanley said. "I have no way of knowing how my Speaking is received."

"Is something wrong, Miss Hanley?"

"Something urgent," Miss Hanley said. "Government House contacted me two minutes ago. The Governor-General insists you attend on him. Immediately."

CHAPTER 4

IN WHICH DAPHNE RECEIVES
NEW EMPLOYMENT

The Governor-General's quarters in Government House were
filled with morning light that drenched the ebony and gilt
furnishings in gold. In a few hours, the windows would be
shuttered against the brutal sun, but for now the corridors were, if not
cool, at least not uncomfortably warm. The place was already a
hornet's nest of activity. Lord Moira was an early riser, riding at four
o'clock in the morning, returning for an early breakfast, then settling
in for a day of work. However, Daphne had never been summoned
earlier than noon. If this were an emergency, she saw no sign of it in
the placid busyness of Government House's servants.

She strode briskly through the halls, concealing her nervousness
behind a calm demeanor. This was not a summons to convey Lady
Loudoun to England; it would be the middle of the night there, and
she would have been directed to the countess's apartment, not the official wing of the palace. Could this be the War Office's doing? No, it
was unlikely they would want her back, and just as unlikely they would
direct such an order to Lord Moira. Could they—was it her parents?
Had something happened to them? She sped up until she was nearly
running, drawing cold stares from the men she passed. Not her
parents, not her family!

The door to the Governor-General's office was closed, the antechamber empty. Daphne hovered, winding her fists into her skirts to keep herself still. Should she knock? She was reluctant to draw Lord Moira's attention to herself in any way, though he had summoned her.

She turned her attention to the portraits on the walls, former Governors-General and famous administrators of the East India Company. The Marquess of Wellesley, brother to the famous Field Marshall Wellesley Daphne so admired, had a narrow face and deep-set eyes that followed her about the room as if daring her to do something outrageous in her anxiety. He had been a military man, committed to extending English rule throughout India, but had been sent home in disgrace for overreaching himself and starting wars the Company had no interest in pursuing. Would her life in India be different if she had served under Wellesley rather than Moira? Impossible to say.

Her hands were sweating, and she was certain she was wrinkling her gown. She released her grip on its fabric and surreptitiously wiped her palms on her skirts, though there was no one to see. She ought to knock. She glanced back into the corridor, looking for someone who might give her direction, and found that no one was paying her any attention. Nervously, she rapped twice on the Governor-General's door and immediately heard a muffled command to enter.

Lord Moira was not alone in his sumptuous chamber. Captain Fletcher, once again impeccable in his dress uniform, stood opposite the door. His lips twitched in a smile when she entered. Daphne made a curtsey to the room in general and said, "My lord, your summons?"

"Lady Daphne," Lord Moira said, his heavy brow looking like thunder. "Pray, be seated."

Daphne sat in the high-backed chair someone had set before the Governor-General's desk. Normally it stood with its mate across the room, near where Fletcher stood. It made her feel like an errant schoolgirl, called to answer to the schoolmaster for some infraction. Not that she had ever been a schoolgirl; everything she knew about such things came from novels. But the comparison was inevitable.

Lord Moira sat with his hands folded together atop his desk. "Lady Daphne, are you dissatisfied with your assignment?" His brow, made more prominent by his receding hairline, furrowed further.

The high back of her chair and its position made Fletcher invisible, or Daphne would have glared at him. He dared bring their conversation to Lord Moira's attention? Her kind feelings about him evaporated. "No, my lord, I am grateful for the opportunity to serve Lady Loudoun. She is very kind and no trouble at all, though I would not complain if she were—that is, of course she is not—"

"If you recall, Lord Moira, it was *my* opinion that Lady Daphne's time is being used immoderately," Fletcher said mildly. "Lady Daphne expressed to me her enjoyment of her current assignment."

That was not true either, but Daphne felt mollified that Fletcher was at least trying to ameliorate whatever mistaken impression he had given the Governor-General. "I don't recall asking for your opinion, Fletcher," Lord Moira said. "Lady Daphne's assignment comes from the War Office itself."

"I do not mean to criticize General Omberlis," Fletcher said. Where Lord Moira's voice was the grumble of a hibernating bear prodded to wake mid-winter, Fletcher's quiet baritone sounded like water over stone, a pacifying music. "But Lady Daphne's duties are intermittent, and I am certain the general would not object to my proposal."

"It is I who must make the decision. Lady Daphne, what is your opinion?"

Daphne gaped. "Lord Moira, I have no opinion because you and Captain Fletcher have not explained what you disagree about."

"No?" Lord Moira seemed taken aback for a moment. "Fletcher, explain yourself, please."

Fletcher moved to stand next to the desk so Daphne could see him. "My duties within this government take me all over northern India," he said. "You might say I am sent to intervene when native concerns clash with the interests of the Honourable Company. At the moment, I am tasked with locating a party of missionaries who have been stirring up dissent to the north of here."

"But I thought the proselytizing of Christianity was acceptable."

"It is, with the understanding that the native population is not stirred to discontent. The Company's business cannot be accomplished if Indians are resentful of their high-handed interference and disregard for their customs. Strictly speaking, these missionaries are doing nothing illegal. But all that matters is how their actions are perceived by the Hindoos, and their activities are causing problems. I intend to take several men to locate the missionaries and return them to Calcutta, where they may take ship back to England. But the Company would prefer not to treat them as criminals. So rather than bring them back in chains, I need a Bounder who can return them instantaneously to the... custody... of Government House."

The room grew suddenly much warmer. Daphne's skin tingled. "You want *my* services?" she said, rather incredulously.

"I am not convinced," Lord Moira said. "You were assigned to Government House for a specific purpose. You must not permit other concerns to interfere with your primary duties."

"Oh, but my lord, I will not—I can be anywhere in half a breath—I am certain Lady Loudoun will understand—"

"Lady Daphne will never be in a position where she will not be able to return immediately," Captain Fletcher said. "I will take responsibility for that."

"Other Bounders—perhaps Major Schofeld—"

"Are occupied with other duties," Fletcher said. "Lady Daphne is the only Bounder attached to Government House whose skills are underused at the moment. She is a natural choice."

"She will need a chaperon," Lord Moira said, his rumbling voice subsiding somewhat.

"That will be no trouble, my lord," Daphne said quickly, though she had no idea whom she could find to fill that role. She saw freedom receding from her grasp, and added, "It would be an honor to contribute to Captain Fletcher's very important work."

It might have been overdone, but Lord Moira's brows relaxed, and Daphne judged she had chosen the right plea. "Very well," the Governor-General said. "Fletcher, I will leave the details to you, as usual. Ensure you have a Speaker attached to your party. I expect daily reports on the state of British influence in these provinces. Communicate with my Speakers before returning the missionaries here, so we will be prepared against their being... obstreperous." He smiled for the first time since Daphne had entered the room, an expression that said he rather hoped they might be obstreperous. "Lady Daphne, I hope you appreciate my generosity. This is quite outside the expectations General Omberlis had of you."

His smile became a more calculating expression, one that made Daphne's heart pound too rapidly, reminding her of the circumstances that had sent her to India. He thought so little of her, did he? She rose from her chair and curtseyed, saying, "I will do my best to satisfy, my lord."

"Lady Daphne, if you will walk with me, I will explain what I expect of you," Fletcher said, opening the door for her. Daphne exited rather rapidly, feeling Lord Moira's eyes on her as she went. In the antechamber, the eyes of Wellesley fell on her again, and she avoided them, as if it were the real man and he were as judgmental of her as Lord Moira. It was possible she might never be able to satisfy the demands of such a military-minded man as the Governor-General. She refused to consider it was impossible. Her whole future depended on proving to him that she was capable.

"Why did you do that?" she asked Fletcher under her breath. They were passing through the corridor leading back to the center of Government House. Men in civilian garb spoke with soldiers and even a few women in the black-on-black of the War Office. Probably none of them were interested in what she was saying, but Daphne did not wish to provide them with fodder for gossip.

Captain Fletcher did not pretend not to understand her meaning. "As I said, I have need of a Bounder, and based on our conversation, you are rather at loose ends. I thought to solve both our problems at once."

"I did not say I was dissatisfied."

"You did not need to. I apologize if I was presumptuous, but I'm afraid it's too late to return to Lord Moira and ask him to change his mind."

The thought of doing so made Daphne shudder inwardly. She felt a trace of irritation at Fletcher's high-handedness, but he was right, she was bored, and this was, if not the opportunity she had hoped for, at least a chance to see some of the real India. "When will we leave?"

"*We* will not leave, Lady Daphne. Chaperoned or not, you should not travel rough with a party of men. No, I will summon you when we reach our destination, some five days from now. Come to the fort tomorrow and I will have our portable Bounding chamber ready for you to learn. Then it will be as simple as Bounding—if I may say so without insulting your talent."

"No, Captain, I take your meaning, it is just—I do I wish I could see the *real* India!"

"There will be more than enough of that," Fletcher said with a laugh. "Do you truly have a companion, or was that to prevent Lord Moira from putting a stop to this plan before it has begun?"

She was about to confess her lack of a companion when an idea occurred to her. "No, that is, I shall have to ask her—but I believe she will agree, she is so, um, agreeable. And she is a Speaker, so you may communicate with her and we can leave immediately when you request our presence, unless you suppose—oh, I am saying this all wrong."

They walked down the stairs to the grand entrance, where Fletcher came to a stop somewhat out of the way of the men passing through the door in both directions. "Lady Daphne," he said, "I believe I made the right choice in making you one of my party. I take it you forgive me for interfering in your affairs?"

"Captain, I said I was not dissatisfied. I did not say I was not bored."

Fletcher laughed, hard enough to draw the attention of two uniformed men passing them on their way out the door. "You are a most unusual woman, Lady Daphne. I am already grateful to you for agreeing, and I look forward to learning more of you during this journey." He bowed, donned his hat, and left the palace. Daphne thought too late that she might have offered to convey him to his destination —*but he might have felt that an intrusion*, she decided, *and I would not for the world have him believe me inconsiderate.* She Bounded to the left-hand drawing room of Lindsey House and immediately went in search of Miss Hanley.

The Extraordinary Speaker was in Lindsey House's small library with a book held close to her eyes. "Lady Daphne," she said, "I have been on tenterhooks wondering what your summons was in regard to. Is everything all right?"

"Yes, Miss Hanley, everything is very well—are you busy? That is, I can see you are busy now, I mean to inquire of your activities next week, whether they are such that you can—oh, I am saying this all wrong."

"I have the same duties I always have, sending messages to the Governor-General and his non-Speaker staff. You seem so anxious, I must ask again, are you well?"

"I am to take a journey northward, a journey for the Governor-General's office, but I cannot travel unaccompanied—oh, but perhaps you consider this an imposition, it is not as if we are bosom friends, and we will Bound to our destination, Captain Fletcher says he will travel rough—what do you suppose he means by that? Not sleeping on the ground, surely—"

"Lady Daphne, stop!" Miss Hanley laughed, putting up a hand as if she might stem the tide of Daphne's words. "I take it you wish me to go on a journey with you? Very well, I accept."

"But—so readily?"

"I find myself curious about the country outside Calcutta. And I would like to know you better. This journey seems designed to permit both curiosities to be met simultaneously. However, I will have to insist you call me Bess, if we are to travel together."

"Is that your name? How lovely! And you must call me Daphne, I dislike being Lady Daphne when I am with friends, everyone makes it sound as if I am ten years old." Daphne sat in a chair opposite her new friend and sighed. "I should have asked Captain Fletcher what we are to bring."

"That is no trouble, I will Speak to him and request he send more information. Then *you* will tell me all about this journey. Surely there is more to it than just the need to explore India."

"No, there is more, and Bess—" Daphne sighed again, this time with excitement, "I believe it will be wonderful!"

CHAPTER 5

IN WHICH A MUCH-DESIRED ADVENTURE BEGINS

Daphne folded her War Office Bounder uniform into her trunk and closed the lid. She had retrieved it three days ago, had it brushed and sponged clean, and it looked none the worse for its encounter with the mud of a Spanish battlefield. She was still uncertain about it. At night, when she lay awake restless and anticipating Fletcher's summons, she questioned whether she still had the right to wear it. But she was still part of the War Office, even irregularly as her attachment to Government House and Lady Loudoun implied, so surely... but would it give others the wrong impression? That she had not utterly failed at her duties? Ultimately, she had decided to leave herself the option, and packed it rather than wearing it.

Instead she wore a lightweight gown of printed Indian cotton, with long sleeves to protect her fair skin from the sun, and comfortable shoes. Like most Bounders, she was bareheaded; a bonnet, while proper as well as additional protection from the sun, made her feel stifled when she Skipped or Bounded. Whether it actually interfered with her talent, no one knew, but Daphne enjoyed the feel of fresh air on her face and in her hair and was happy for the excuse.

She Bounded with her trunk to the left-hand drawing room and settled herself on the chaise longue to wait. It had been seven days since she had last spoken to Fletcher—that was two days for him to assemble his party, and five days to travel, and he ought to have reached his destination that day. Perhaps she should Bound there, learn whether he had arrived—but that would be presumptuous, and if they were still on the road, they would not have erected the Bounding chamber and she would have nowhere to go.

"I thought I might find you here," Bess said from the doorway. "I have not heard from Ensign Phillips yet."

"I have nothing to do but wait. I dislike waiting."

"You might read. You might sew."

"I am too restless for those things. Pray, ask Ensign Phillips their location?"

Bess laughed and came to sit opposite Daphne on the sofa. "I will not trouble him yet again. We Spoke this morning and he said they were within a few hours' travel of Madhyapatnam. Likely they will settle themselves at the Residence before calling for us."

Daphne scowled. "You are far too reasonable."

"*You* are far too impatient. The time will come."

"It is hardly impatience when one simply cannot bear to wait for things."

"I believe that *is* what impatience means, Daphne."

"I know. You are not the first to tell me that." Daphne leaned back and sighed. "How is it that Madhyapatnam has a Resident when there is no native ruler whose court he might be appointed to?"

"I believe there was a prince in Madhyapatnam once, but I know no more than that. They may simply call him the Resident out of habit."

"What do you suppose the Residence is like?"

"I don't know. Not as large as Government House, obviously, but it must be sizeable if it is to host all of Captain Fletcher's party and the two of us."

"And you have never met the Resident?"

"Sir Rodney attended one or two events in Calcutta society before taking his position at Madhyapatnam. He is in his late forties, rather stout, and I recall his hair was receding in front. We were never introduced, but I believe he is unmarried. I do not know if he has talent."

"Not a romantic figure, then. I understand him to be a great hunter."

"He is renowned for it. He has killed a number of tigers as well as lesser—" Bess held up a hand and tilted her head back in an attitude of Speaking. Daphne held her breath. After only a few seconds, Bess said, "We are to Bound to the Residence at our own convenience."

"Oh!" Daphne shot to her feet. "Shall I take you first, or our things? Or should I—no, that would be foolish, why would I go alone? Bess—"

"Let us go together to greet Sir Rodney, and then you may return for our luggage." Bess stood and put her arm around Daphne's shoulders. Daphne clasped Bess around the waist, lifted, and—

In an instant, the light dimmed, and the temperature dropped slightly, enough to be noticeable but not enough to be called cool. Canvas walls, greyish-tan in color, surrounded them closely. The thorny white circle of the Bounding symbol met Daphne's eyes. The portable Bounding chamber had not enough essence—it was too small and bland—so she was constrained to use its signature. Not that she minded, so long as it got her where she wished to be.

She released Bess and turned around to face the entrance. The flaps of the tiny tent overlapped securely, so no distracting glimpse of the outdoors could interfere with Bounding. Even Daphne, with all her skill, would find it impossible to Bound there if the door flaps were open on an outdoor scene. She held the flap open for Bess, then ducked through herself.

The Bounding chamber had been erected in the center of a long hallway, its floor tiled in dark blue and the walls plastered and painted a crisp white. No windows revealed the exterior of the place, and between that and the dimness of the hall, it felt comfortably shielded from the heat, though the air was still damp and smelled of mildew. Daphne had its essence almost before she registered the presence of others.

It was quite a crowd. Captain Fletcher, smiling that private smile, stood closest to the Bounding chamber, with his companions Lieutenant Wright, Ensign Phillips, and Captain Ainsworth behind him.

Beside him stood a man Daphne recognized, from Bess's description, as Sir Rodney Coote. He was taller than she had imagined, though not as tall as Fletcher, red-headed like Phillips, and his balding forehead was speckled with brown freckles from long exposure to the Indian sun. He, too, was smiling, in a pleasant way that Daphne found charming. She curtseyed to him, and said, "Sir Rodney."

"Lady Daphne. And Miss Hanley. Welcome, welcome. Such a pleasure to meet you." Sir Rodney bowed and extended his hands to both of them. Wiry red hair grew over the backs of his hands, which were as leathery and spotted as his forehead. "Be welcome to the Residence. Shall I have—you seem to have no luggage—"

"Oh!" Daphne exclaimed, snatching her hand away with what was not strictly politeness. "I forgot—do excuse me—" She Bounded back to Lindsey House, stacked Bess's trunk atop her own, and was back at the Residence in time to hear the Resident say "—traveling light, but surely—"

Sir Rodney's voice cut off mid-sentence. Then he laughed, a great booming sound that made everyone chuckle, though Daphne could not see the joke. "If this is what an Extraordinary Bounder is, then I am truly astonished!" he exclaimed. "But I will not permit you to carry your trunk here, my dear." He gestured, and a couple of Hindoos who had been standing against the wall, their faces filled with astonishment, hurried forward to take the trunks and disappear with them down the hall.

"You will share a room, naturally," Sir Rodney said, striding off after the Hindoos and forcing everyone else to trot along after him up the stairs. "It is just gone two o'clock, and I suggest you rest through the heat of the afternoon. We dine at five—I hope that is not too unfashionably early for you?"

"Not at all, Sir Rodney," Bess said. Daphne privately thought she might never eat again, her stomach was so full of excited butterflies, but she nodded in agreement.

"Then here is your room, and I hope it is to your satisfaction." Sir Rodney threw open a door at the end of the hall. It was as dimly lit as the main hall, though in this case it was because heavy shutters covered the windows, blocking out the sunlight. The air was thick and oppressive, promising rain, but despite the pervasive smell of mildew, the room did not feel damp. The Hindoos were just setting down the trunks at the feet of two European-style beds draped in the ubiquitous netting. A stand holding a basin and pitcher occupied the space between the beds, which were covered with light cotton blankets, and a fan depended from the high ceiling, motionless at the moment.

"If you wish to rest, I will send a *punkah-wallah* for your comfort," Sir Rodney said. "Anything you need, you have only to ask."

They assured him they needed nothing, and Sir Rodney gave them both a fatherly pat on the hand and a smile and retreated. Fletcher, standing in the doorway, said, "Welcome to Madhyapatnam."

Daphne glanced past him, to make certain the Resident was not within hearing, and said in a low voice, "Sir Rodney is very kind, but this cannot be all there is of Madhyapatnam."

"No, but we will discuss further at dinner, or this evening. Never fear, you will see enough of the *real* India, as I believe you put it, to satisfy you."

"I certainly hope so, Captain."

Fletcher laughed and shut the door. Bess had already opened her trunk and was rummaging through it. "I intend to read and nap," she said, "though admittedly not at the same time. Will you help me remove my gown? I don't wish to wrinkle it."

Daphne helped loose her laces, then idly pulled on the cord that set the ceiling fan, the *punkah*, waving gently back and forth. "I don't see how you can bear to nap when there are so many exciting things to see!"

"They will still be here when it is not so hot, and be the more enjoyable for it." Bess folded her gown neatly into her trunk and settled herself on her bed. "You are simply being impatient again."

Daphne flung herself onto her bed and flailed until she was free of the netting. "Then I will nap," she said, "but I refuse to enjoy it."

⚜

THE RESIDENCE'S DINING ROOM LOOKED VERY DIFFERENT FROM that of Lindsey House. The thick walls were plastered and painted white, brightening it despite how the windows were still covered even once the sun's rays were no longer so direct and hot. Rain pounded fiercely against them, filling the room with a quiet roar that forced diners to speak loudly to be heard over it. The table, however, was set with as much elegance as obtained in Daphne's parents' home Marvell Hall, and crystal chandeliers shed a sparkling radiance, and a terrible heat, over the many sumptuous dishes spread thereon. Daphne eyed a giant fish she could not identify and wondered where it had come from. The Hooghly, which ran nearby? Or some lake in distant England, Bounded here by one of Sir Rodney's household?

Daphne sat on Sir Rodney's right side, Bess on his left, with the members of Fletcher's party spread out beyond that. It was an unbalanced table, but Sir Rodney was in fact unmarried, and Daphne had not seen any other women in his household. The Residence, in fact, felt a very bastion of military masculinity, as if she and Bess were the only women who had visited it in years.

"Was your journey uneventful, Captain Fletcher?" Daphne asked.

Fletcher, seated beside Daphne, said, "I am afraid to tell you."

"Why is that? Did you have adventures?"

"No, and I fear you will disapprove of me for not being bold enough to have been attacked by dacoits or tigers."

His expression was so solemn Daphne did not at first realize she was being teased. "Captain, it is hardly—oh, you are laughing, how dare you?" But she laughed with him.

"In seriousness, it was an uneventful journey, and you need not regret not having traveled rough with us. Nothing worse happened to us than being rained on rather heavily and losing a horse to lameness. Tomorrow is when the real work begins."

"And what work is that? That is, I know you must find these missionaries. It is how you go about finding them that rouses my curiosity."

"We will go into the bazaar and see about speaking to those who have encountered them. I don't expect them to still be in Madhyapatnam, but we should be able to find a direction for their travels."

"Do you speak Hindoo, then?"

"I speak several local languages and read a few of them. I should have no trouble making myself understood."

"How is it you know so much of India, Captain?"

Fletcher paused in his eating. "I came out to India when I was seventeen. Back then, knowing Hindoostani and Indian culture were not as stigmatized in Europeans as they are coming to be now, and I was encouraged in my studies. My commanding officers found it beneficial to have someone who could communicate with the natives. And I am fond of India and its people. Terrible climate and all."

"What Captain Fletcher is not saying," said Captain Ainsworth from across the table, "is that as a Discerner, he has an advantage over the rest of us when it comes to dealing with the Hindoo."

"Oh? How is that?"

"Discernment is a common talent here in India," Fletcher said. "The Hindoo respect Discerners regardless of their race—or, I should say, respect a Discerner who bothers to respect their customs in turn. You may have noticed—no, you wouldn't have met many high-caste Indians, would you, Lady Daphne?"

"No, I have not—but pray, go on!"

"High-caste Indians, even those who are not Discerners, will not willingly touch a European. They consider us..." Fletcher tapped his fork on the edge of his plate in thought. "They dislike that Europeans' demeanors are so often at odds with their emotions. They consider it bad behavior. And many Hindoos of whatever caste feel completely justified in lying to Europeans, for that same reason."

"Makes it damned—pardon me, ladies—devilish hard to keep servants," Sir Rodney said. "Either they say they'll do something and then won't, or they'll steal the silver buttons off your coat and replace 'em with dross, or they'll cheat you on the household expenses, charge for a dozen eggs when they've only bought two. I've tried paying them better to get 'em to stop, but it makes no difference."

"They are not all so dishonest," Fletcher said. Daphne thought his tone was a trifle cool as he addressed the Resident. "But their behavior to one another is very different from their behavior to us."

"I have heard they revere Scorchers," Bess said, "but I find that difficult to believe."

40

"Because Scorchers are wildly unpredictable?" Fletcher said. "Hindoo Scorchers are very different from Europeans. They are taken from their families when they manifest talent, male and female both, and admitted to a priesthood devoted to Agni, who is god of fire. The Hindoo cremate their dead, you see, and Scorchers sanctified to the task perform that ritual before consigning the remains to the Ganges. Hindoo Scorchers are meditative and peaceful, and much honored as holy men and women."

"That is so interesting, Captain," Daphne said. "So there is nothing inherent about Scorchers that demands they behave so erratically as ours do?"

Fletcher shrugged. "Apparently not. Unless there is something inherently different about the Hindoo—which I suppose is possible."

"Of course they're different," Sir Rodney said. "We don't even look the same, do we? Pity those missionaries weren't more circumspect. I'd like to see more of these heathens converted to worship the true God, give up some of these godless customs. Like marrying more than one wife. It's unnatural. And burning widows alive—"

"That happens rarely," Fletcher said. "It is condemned by many Hindoos."

"Well, one is one too many, I say."

This seemed the sort of conversation that might become heated, so Daphne rose, prompting everyone else to follow suit. "Sir Rodney, where might we retire?"

"There is a sitting room across the hall, Lady Daphne. The servants will bring tea shortly."

The sitting room was comfortably appointed, with couches upholstered in blue narrow stripes and a number of potted trees that brought the green freshness of the garden indoors. The furniture had definitely come from England, and at great expense, because most of it was too heavy for a Bounder to carry. Daphne experimentally lifted one of the chairs. Not too heavy, but an awkward burden.

"If you are contemplating stealing Sir Rodney's chair, I will not stop you," Bess said, "because it would provide me with great amusement to see what you will do with it."

"No, I was just—it was nothing." Daphne closed the sitting room door as two servants passed into the dining room opposite. "I wish I could speak their language. Perhaps I should learn. I am passably fluent in French, but possibly Hindoostani is more difficult, especially with its foreign alphabet."

"I envy Captain Fletcher his facility with languages. I speak only Persian, and a formal Persian at that."

"Why do you speak any Persian at all?"

"To facilitate my communicating with the Mughals. Persian is the administrative language of India."

"I did not know you Spoke with the Mughals! How romantic!"

"They are not as powerful as they once were, but they did have a remarkable empire." Bess took off her spectacles and added, "India has a dramatic history, every bit as colorful as our own."

"I should say even more so!"

"War is war wherever you go. You have experienced more of it than I—you should know the truth of that."

Daphne struggled to master the feelings raging in her heart at Bess's casual words. "I suppose," she managed. "Did you never wish to serve in the Peninsula?"

"No, never. When John's regiment was called up, I was grateful that we would be separated for a time."

"Grateful, how? I do not understand how it is you and your young lord are not already married."

Bess sighed. "We grew up together, John and I, and I am very fond of him. I believe he cares for me as well. But I cannot help feeling that perhaps there should be stronger feelings in marriage than fondness. Possibly this makes me a romantic."

The door opened, admitting the gentlemen. They were laughing over some joke Daphne had not heard. It irritated her, being on the outside of someone else's humor, so she said, "How nice that you can amuse yourselves! Miss Hanley and I have not been talking of anything nearly so funny."

"We will have to amuse you, then, Lady Daphne," Lieutenant Wright said, sinking down on the sofa next to her. His smile was, as usual, charming and calculated precisely to appeal to a young woman, or so Daphne believed. She smiled at him in return and wished heartily that Fletcher had sat next to her instead.

"Oh, don't say that, Wright, you know how bad I am at being amusing," said Ensign Phillips.

"Your appearance alone is amusing," Wright said archly, with one eye on Daphne to see how she appreciated his wit. Phillips flushed, which looked odd against his red hair. Daphne ignored Wright and rose to cross the room toward Phillips.

"I enjoy pleasant conversation more than being amused," she said, and Phillips flushed again, this time with his eyes downcast. He could not be more than twenty-two, she guessed, not much older than she, but she felt so much older she wanted to pat his hand in reassurance.

"I—that is, I am not very good at conversation either," Phillips mumbled.

Two servants, dark-skinned men dressed in European clothing, brought in tea on a tray. Daphne waited for them to settle it on a nearby table before saying, "How much English do they know?"

"Enough that we should not speak badly of them to their faces," Fletcher said.

"I would not do so, even if they could not understand a word!" Daphne examined the servants closely as they left the room. They wore Sir Rodney's livery and looked extremely uncomfortable in it. Curious, that Sir Rodney would not permit them to dress in their native costume.

"I know you would not, but I imagine there are many Europeans who lack that sense of discretion." Bess poured tea and offered a cup to Daphne.

"Perhaps we ought to discuss tomorrow's activities," Fletcher said. "I intend to rise early and visit the bazaar to see what I can learn. Lady Daphne, Miss Hanley, you are welcome to join me."

"Of course we'll come along. Shouldn't go into the city alone," Captain Ainsworth said.

"Indeed, Lucian, but the bazaar is not dangerous, or I would not offer to escort the ladies. At all events, once we have discovered some hint as to our quarry's location, we will return here and make further plans."

"But surely the ladies will remain here if you have to go haring off after these missionaries!" Sir Rodney protested. "You cannot expect them—"

"But that is why I am here, Sir Rodney," Daphne said, "to assist in bringing them home to Calcutta. I must be immediately available to do so, and that means traveling with Captain Fletcher." She hoped he would not think of the obvious response, which was that she could Bound to Fletcher's presence at any time so long as he had the portable Bounding chamber.

"It's completely out of the question. Your comfort is of paramount importance—what kind of host would I be if I permitted you to leave this place for a post-house or a sodden tent in the mud?"

"Your concern warms my heart, Sir Rodney, but really, we don't mind, do we, Miss Hanley?"

"I have Spoken to Government House," Bess said, "and they are in agreement that we should stay with Captain Fletcher. But we are so grateful that this Residence is open to us should we at any time need its shelter."

Sir Rodney, his mouth open to voice another protest, shut it abruptly. Daphne hoped Bess had not just lied to him about what Government House wanted.

"With luck, the search will not take us so far afield," Fletcher said, "and we will return here in short order. Until then—" he saluted Daphne with his glass—"good luck to us all!"

CHAPTER 6

IN WHICH DAPHNE SEES THE REAL INDIA AND IS SHOUTED AT

T he curtains of the palanquin moved with the breeze and the movement of the bearers, turning the outside world into a ghost world, its inhabitants mere shadows wandering past. The illusion was dispelled by how raucously they spoke and laughed, without concern for Daphne's presence. Perhaps, behind her curtains, she was as ghostly to them as they were to her.

The faint breeze brought with it myriad competing smells. To the usual odors of rain-sodden vegetation and the distant but still faintly noxious Hooghly River were added the smoky scents of cooking meat, the aroma of vegetables roasted or boiled, and a million spices, most of whose names Daphne did not know. She drew in a deep breath and smelled as well the scents those spices disguised, the smell of waste both animal and human and the sour odor of many bodies all crammed together in one place. As the day grew hotter, the smells would grow stronger, until an evening rain washed them all away and gave the nose five minutes' respite from the assault.

Someone laughed right next to her ear, and she shied away before remembering the person could not see her. She had wanted to ride to the bazaar, but Sir Rodney had insisted on the palanquin, which was comfortable but often made Daphne feel slightly queasy. So she reclined on the cushions and considered twitching the curtains aside so she could see the passing color and life of India. She was no high-caste Hindoo woman, required to hide her face from strangers, but neither did she want to draw stares. Time enough for that at the bazaar.

She had a feeling Captain Fletcher was indulging her in permitting her to come along. He had no need of her services there, she could not speak the language, she was visibly different with her blonde hair and fair skin. Possibly she should feel insulted at his patronizing her. But her longing to see India, the real India, made her disinclined to protest. So she determined to be grateful to him rather than insulted.

The palanquin came to a halt, and jolted her slightly as the bearers set it down. She pushed the curtains aside and alighted without waiting for assistance. Behind her, Bess was doing the same. The men of their party were gathered somewhat ahead of them, dismounting and handing off their horses to native servants. Daphne straightened her bonnet, which Bess had convinced her was essential protection against the Indian sun, and took another deep breath. Finally, the adventure she had longed for!

Fletcher left the others and walked toward her. He had declined the palanquin Sir Rodney offered him, explaining that he saw more from horseback than from a litter, even with the curtains drawn back. "From here, we proceed on foot," he told Daphne. "Stay close to me, and if you become lost—"

"I cannot become lost, Captain, I am never more than a Bound away from somewhere familiar."

"True. Very well. Miss Hanley—"

"I do not anticipate becoming lost either, Captain. But I will remain close by." Her hand on Daphne's arm was the only indication Bess could not see her surroundings clearly. With her free hand, Bess tugged on the brim of her bonnet to shield her eyes more fully.

Fletcher chuckled. "Perhaps I should warn *myself* about the dangers of becoming lost in the bazaar, as the two of you seem capable of watching out for yourselves."

"We will not be foolhardy," Daphne said, "and it is not as if I speak the language. I don't wish to be separated."

"Then come with me, and let us see what we may discover about our errant missionaries." He nodded at the others, who were, like him, dressed in civilian clothes rather than their distinctive red coats. The other three men, taking separate directions, disappeared into the crowd, and Fletcher gestured to Daphne to follow him.

The road, still muddy from the previous night's rain, was thronged even at that early hour with men and women all intent on their journeys. Almost immediately Daphne felt inclined to take hold of Fletcher's hand, or even his coattails, to avoid being drawn aside and swallowed up in the crowd. She did cling to Bess's hand, and the two of them followed Fletcher into the throng and out the other side into the bazaar.

Daphne's imagination had produced, when Fletcher had first mentioned the bazaar, an Arabian Nights collection of colorful tents, with sellers hawking their wares at top voice. She had pictured elaborate displays of copper pots, tables covered in exotic jewelry, or bright silks draped across tall stands. None of it was as she had imagined. There were tents, true, but most of them were made of the same drab canvas the Bounding chamber was, or dull grey and brown cottons. None of them would keep off the rain and they would be scant protection against the sun. The overall effect was of a sea churned to pasty grey by storm or waves.

Many of the stalls were no more than squares of heavy cloth spread over the ground with wares displayed on them. Spots of brightness shone against the drab background. There were stalls selling vividly colored lengths of cloth, and one or two selling cheap brass or copper jewelry Daphne could not imagine wearing. Many stalls held sacks of spices, green and red and an eye-watering yellow-orange powder Fletcher said was turmeric. Daphne breathed in their richness and had to turn away to sneeze.

Fletcher stopped at stalls, apparently at random, and carried on brief conversations with the owners. He did not offer to translate for Daphne's sake and she felt uncomfortable asking what he had said. She stopped to examine a bracelet carved of ivory, the first truly beautiful piece of jewelry she had yet seen, and the stall's proprietor, a wizened, wrinkly old woman missing several teeth, pointed at it and said something that sounded like a question.

"I beg your pardon, I do not speak your language," Daphne said, immediately putting the bracelet back. The woman picked it up and offered it to her. "No, truly, it is beautiful, but I simply wish to admire it." The idea of owning it had already taken possession of her mind, though, and she hesitantly accepted it. The old woman smiled, took Daphne's hand, and uttered a long, complicated sentence in Hindoostani that was inflected like a question. Her eyes were set deep into her face, surrounded by wrinkles like a map of the Ganges, and Daphne started to respond before remembering she did not speak the language.

Bess said something in a language Daphne had never heard before, different from the Hindoostani the old woman had used. The woman shook her head, but held up a finger in a "wait here" gesture Daphne had not realized was universal. Perhaps she should try communicating in gestures.

The old woman called out something in Hindoostani and got a muffled reply from behind the back wall of her tent. A younger man, though still probably as old as Bess and Daphne's ages combined, emerged. The old woman spoke to him at length, making him look first at Daphne, then at Bess. He responded in the language Bess had used. Bess beamed and spoke to him, gesturing at the bracelet. The man shook his head and gestured, and Bess replied at length. Daphne became increasingly frustrated at being excluded from the conversation. She determined to learn Hindoostani, and never mind its being frowned on by people like Lord Moira who no doubt were simply jealous of those who could do what was beyond them.

Finally, Bess said, "I have argued him down to two rupees. Do you want it at that price?"

Daphne considered the state of her purse. "I do." She dipped into her purse and brought out the coins, handed them over, and slid the bracelet onto her wrist immediately. Bess said a few more words and bowed. Daphne hastily bowed as well. "Is that a good price?" she asked as they turned away.

"I imagine so. I have no idea the value of such materials and crafts-

48

manship, and likely we paid too much—but bartering is such fun, it surely makes up for all that!"

"Supposing I were poor, though, and could not afford it? We should ask Captain Fletcher's opinion." Daphne looked around. Like the others, Fletcher had dressed that morning in civilian clothing, asserting again his belief that the Hindoos would be more talkative with someone not obviously a soldier, but his height and coloring would make him stand out beside the shorter, darker natives. Even so, he was not immediately visible. "We are lost already."

Bess tilted her head back briefly. "I have told him where we are. I'm certain he will return shortly."

They waited, watching the colorful masses of travelers pass. Daphne toyed with her new bracelet, enjoying the feel of the ivory against her fingertips. It was carved in an abstract pattern that looked like flowers on fire. Did it mean something in the Hindoo culture? Perhaps something to do with that god the Scorchers were sacred to? Another thing to ask Fletcher, if he ever returned.

A hand reached out and flicked the ivory bracelet with a fingertip. "We have not been in this bazaar above fifteen minutes and already you are causing trouble," Fletcher said, smiling so Daphne would know it was a joke. "Stay close, and let us see what we can discover."

"Have you not learned anything yet, Captain? Or—that sounds like a criticism, I assure you I did not mean it as such, I simply meant that you seem to have spoken to many people and therefore—oh, it is *still* a criticism—"

"I take your meaning, Lady Daphne," Fletcher said. "I see a barber, there ahead. I intend to be shaved, and you need not wait on me. Just —stay within my sight, please? You may be capable of escaping anyone who wishes you harm, but I still experience a twinge of fear for your safety."

Fletcher did not appear to be in need of a shave, but Daphne nodded and walked past the barber's stall to a stand selling delicious-smelling morsels wrapped in bright green leaves. Bess's inquiry left them as uninformed as ever, as the stall owner did not speak Persian, but the leaves contained sticky dark-brown nuggets that smelled of spiced honey, and Daphne bought one for each of them and experimented with using the leaf to protect her fingers from the stickiness. The morsel crunched in her mouth, releasing an explosion of sweetness, tangy and delicious, and Daphne immediately asked for another. The stall owner watched her in some amusement, and Daphne guessed she was eating it wrong, but did not care about being laughed at.

"Imagine if Miss Donnelly could see us now, licking sugar off our fingers and smearing it over our lips," Bess murmured.

"She would loudly declare that such things are Not Done and that a lady would never be so common as to eat food wrapped in leaves, let alone in the middle of the street." Daphne dropped the leaf to the ground, where it joined a host of others no doubt left by other customers. "I suppose that makes me unladylike."

"I as well. How John will laugh when I tell him of our adventure!"

"*Ey-a!*"

A loud voice accosted them, sharp and biting and clearly agitated, though Daphne could not of course understand the words. She turned away from the stall to search the crowds walking past for the speaker. A woman no taller than Daphne, her eyes dark-rimmed with kohl, brandished a walking stick at her, shouting in increasing anger as she approached. Bess tried to speak to her, but either the woman did not speak Persian or was too far gone in anger to respond.

"I don't speak your language—I don't understand," Daphne said, helpless against the torrent of words.

"Perhaps we should find Captain Fletcher," Bess said, taking Daphne's arm.

The woman followed them, shouting more imprecations, and as Bess and Daphne walked, a crowd grew up around them, muttering in a way Daphne did not like. She quickened her step until they reached the barber's stall, where Fletcher was just drying his face and responding to something the barber, a tall man with an enormous moustache, had said. He caught Daphne's eye and said, "What did you do?"

"I did nothing except eat sweets from a leaf, probably the wrong way—oh, Captain, what is she saying?"

Fletcher stood and confronted the old woman, but though his stance was belligerent, his voice was calm just as it had been when he'd spoken to Lord Moira. The woman shook her stick in his face and shouted again. Fletcher shook his head and replied in the same calm tone. The woman took a step backward, suddenly silent.

Fletcher spoke again, and the woman looked at Daphne, confusion wrinkling her brow. She shook her head, said something to Fletcher, and walked away without looking back. The crowd surrounding them, still muttering, did not move. "Captain," Daphne said, feeling anxiety bubble up inside her.

Fletcher said something addressed to the crowd, then, in what Daphne could tell was a different language, spat out a couple of short, curt words. A murmur of laughter ran through the crowd. Fletcher, looking not the least bit concerned, tossed a coin at the barber, who snatched it out of the air. "We should probably move on," he said, "but you have discovered some valuable information."

"I have? But I did nothing."

"You were visibly European in a public place, and apparently that was enough. The woman accused you of blasphemy against her gods. It seems she believed you were one of our errant missionaries."

"I, a missionary? Of course I know none, so I have no idea how they dress or comport themselves, perhaps this is the kind of dress they wear—"

"Again, it was enough that you are European. That woman claims to have seen people who look like you—that is, fair-haired and fair-skinned—preaching against Vishnu, claiming he is a false god, saying words guaranteed to offend the Hindoos. It is more than I have learned anywhere else. Even the barber, who is usually a fount of gossip and information, could say only that he had heard of such stories, not that he had encountered the missionaries personally. It is very strange."

"Because no one has seen them?" Bess said.

"Because they have done a great deal of damage for people who have not been seen," Fletcher said. "That woman is the only one who has seen them, and I consider her an unreliable source. She also accused you, Lady Daphne, of performing unnatural acts I will not describe to you. That is why the crowd was so interested, and why some of them are still following us. I believe it best you return to the Residence. I will follow shortly."

"But, Captain—"

"Lady Daphne, your newfound notoriety will interfere with my ability to gather information. Unless you believe your amusement is more important?"

It felt like a blow. "No, Captain," Daphne said, successfully keeping her voice from trembling. "You are correct. I will return us immediately." She clasped Bess around the waist, lifted, and Bounded them both to their room at the Residence without asking Fletcher if he wanted her to return for him as well. The bazaar was outdoors, it would be impossible for her to Bound there, but in truth she simply did not want to face him. He thought her flighty, no doubt, impatient and selfish, and she did not know why she had ever wanted to be his friend.

"I'm certain he did not mean that the way it sounded," Bess said, removing her bonnet and tossing it onto her trunk.

"Of course," Daphne lied, "and he is correct, he cannot speak to people if he is also watching the crowds for possible assailants."

"Besides, it was growing warm, and I would have wanted to return soon in any case."

"Bess, you are too kind."

"Not at all! I dislike the heat and prefer to be indoors during the worst of it. But I believe we should return to the bazaar another time. It was rather entertaining, was it not?"

"It was," Daphne said, spinning her bracelet on her wrist, but in her heart she still felt the sting of Fletcher's words.

She did not see him again until late that afternoon. Bess decided to take a nap, and Daphne, restless and warm, did not want to disturb her. So she explored the Residence as best she could, reluctant to intrude on Sir Rodney's domain, and ended up in a little-used sitting room on the north side of the building. It was shielded from the sun by the bulk of the Residence and was almost cool in its dimness. Daphne reclined on one of the sofas and closed her eyes. She heard nothing but the distant buzzing of insects beating against the windows, desperate for the cool shade. Why they were not exhausted as every other living creature was by the heat was a mystery to Daphne.

"Lady Daphne."

She shot upright. "Captain Fletcher. I beg your pardon, I did not suppose anyone else came here."

"And you meant to have some privacy. It is I who should beg your pardon for intruding."

"Not at all, Captain, I meant that—I do not know what is appropriate for me as Sir Rodney's guest, whether I ought not be exploring the Residence and behaving as if it is mine. Please, do come in."

Fletcher took a seat on the sofa perpendicular to hers. He was once again dressed in his uniform and held his hat in both hands. "I wished to apologize," he said, "for my words today. I offended you with my suggestion that your interest in this matter is purely frivolous."

"No, Captain, it is true, I—it was kind of you to escort me to the bazaar, when you knew how I wanted to see it—I wish I could be of more assistance, direct assistance I mean, not simply by accident."

"I am grateful for your 'accident', Lady Daphne." He looked away from her, toward where the insects buzzed against the window. "I simply meant that for all of us, pleasure must give way to business. Not just you."

"I understand."

"Then you will forgive me? I would not for the world have you believe poorly of me." His eyes returned to her face, and their intensity made her breathless for a moment.

"Of course, Captain, though I believe there is nothing to forgive."

"You are a generous woman." Fletcher stretched out his legs in a casual manner and said, "Perhaps you would like to see the old palace? It is an architectural masterpiece."

"The old palace? That sounds delightful. How old is it?"

"Only about a hundred years. We call it the old palace mainly because it is unoccupied."

"I have heard there is no prince in Madhyapatnam. Why is that?"

Fletcher's expression, which had been pleasant, now went sour. "The prince died without an heir, and the Company took over the territory of Madhyapatnam."

"That seems—forgive me, Captain, you seem to dislike that, but to me it seems sensible, if the alternative is that it falls into anarchy."

"It is something the Company has done many times, and in every case it has enriched their coffers without putting them to any extra trouble. You are correct, it is better than permitting such places to lie ungoverned, or to be the focus for successional strife. I simply cannot help but feel the Company has, on occasion, behaved as if they were entitled to rule by virtue of their temporal power rather than as a reflection of the responsibility they owe the Indian people. Sir Rodney does not, but there are far too few like him."

"I believe I understand. How long ago did the prince die?"

"Some twenty years. Before my time. But I'm told the palace was once alive with light and music. You will have to judge for yourself how much of that remains."

"I would enjoy that very much, Captain. When can we go?"

"Now, if you wish. There is still daylight... if you are not averse to Skipping there."

Daphne drew in a breath. Skipping with a male passenger... it was not improper, technically, just the sort of thing Miss Donnelly would say was Not Done. But Daphne was not about to give up on an adventure for so insignificant an objection as that. It was, however, not the only objection. "Will it not be a burden on you?"

"I meant to ask you that question. Most people dislike having their emotions so exposed."

"I believe I have told you that I have nothing to hide."

Fletcher smiled, and extended his hand to her, offering to help her rise. "Lady Daphne, you are a most unusual woman. As I believe I have told *you*."

Her fingers closed over his, and his smile once again became that distinctive, secret-filled expression, the one that entranced her with its beauty. His hand was firm and strong, with clean, well-trimmed square nails, and enveloped her smaller one completely. "Then we should—we must start from outdoors," she said, feeling unexpectedly flustered, "and you will have to give me direction."

He released her hand only to tuck it into the crook of his elbow. "Lead on, Lady Daphne," he said, "and permit me to show you the real India."

CHAPTER 7

IN WHICH DAPHNE AND CAPTAIN FLETCHER EXPLORE THE OLD PALACE

Clouds, high but heavy with promised rain, obscured the sun and made the afternoon cooler, though the air was still thick and damp like wet wool. Though the Hooghly was invisible from the Residence, its sour-fish odor carried far in the wet air. "Ought we to do this another time, Captain? The rain will fall presently, not that I am averse to becoming a little wet, but with these rainstorms it is rarely 'a little' wet one becomes—"

"We have perhaps an hour and a half before the storm arrives," Fletcher said, casting an eye on the clouds. "I have faith that your talent will permit us to outrun the storm. The palace is no more than two miles away."

"Oh! In that case, it is no trouble—have you Skipped before? It can be disconcerting, not that I believe you are afraid of heights."

"I have not Skipped before, no. What do you mean, heights?" For the first time, Fletcher looked at her with trepidation.

"It is just that the higher one Skips, the farther one can travel—but if it is only two miles, I should not have to Skip very high, only it will be high enough that if you—never fear, Captain, I have never yet dropped a passenger from any height."

Fletcher laughed and released her arm. "I find that more disturbing an assertion than you likely intended it to be. Very well, I will be prepared." He swiveled on his heel, then pointed toward the tree-lined wall surrounding the Residence. "I believe it is in that direction. It is a large red sandstone building that cannot be mistaken for anything else, if that helps."

"It does." Daphne arranged her arms around Fletcher's waist and felt him drape his arms across her shoulders. This close, she was aware of the smell of the soap the barber had used that still clung to his skin, a tangy-sweet odor that left her with the desire to breathe it in more deeply. Embarrassed at her reaction, she said, "Hold on, and don't fight —you will not, I am certain, but I always warn those whose first time it is—this should only take two Skips—"

His arms tightened fractionally around her neck, and she lifted him off the ground, and Skipped—

In half a breath, they were high above the city, and Fletcher gasped. His grip on her shoulders went briefly rigid, but he made no other move that might have weakened her hold on him. Had Daphne been alone, she would have taken the brief moment before they fell to appreciate the city's color and vivacity. Instead, her eyes swept the vista, looking for the palace. She spotted it in the moment gravity asserted itself on them.

She glanced at Fletcher. He was looking at the city, his eyes alight with pleasure, and she Skipped once more, not to the ground but to the air above the palace. Fletcher laughed as they fell for a few seconds, drawing a laugh out of Daphne. She rarely Skipped with a passenger and had never conveyed anyone who seemed to enjoy it so much. Before their fall could become fatal, she Skipped once more, bringing them to the gate piercing the wall surrounding the palace.

Fletcher laughed again, somewhat breathlessly, and removed his arms from around her shoulders. Somewhat reluctantly, Daphne released him and took a step back. "It is astonishing, how lovely cities are from high above," she said.

"Indeed. I always envied Extraordinary Movers their talent, but I never realized a Bounder experiences much the same thing." Fletcher said. "I could certainly grow accustomed to such a mode of travel."

Daphne thought to offer him her talent whenever he might need it, but remained silent. *That* would be improper. It felt like such an intimate thing to suggest, which was odd because she had never thought of her talent in that way before. And it was presumptuous, since despite his words he could not be comfortable being in such close contact with another person on a regular basis. Instead she said, "At least you were not afraid—some people are afraid of heights and dislike being so high even for such a short time, but you seemed to enjoy it."

"I found it exhilarating." Fletcher offered Daphne his arm. "You should stay close, Lady Daphne. The palace is not precisely dangerous, but there are those who would take advantage of a lone woman, even a European one."

Daphne took his arm and let him lead her through the gate. "Did you not say the palace was uninhabited?"

"I said it was unoccupied, which I realize has given you a mistaken impression. There is no prince in residence, but Madhyapatnam is crowded enough that no shelter goes untenanted. There are families living inside. They unfortunately mean we cannot see the interior, as I dislike intruding on them."

"But they are there illegally."

"And I am not the Resident, with authority to clear them out. No, we will admire the exterior and the grounds. I hope that is satisfactory."

"Of course. But—does that mean the Resident ought to make them move?"

Fletcher shrugged. "Sir Rodney chooses not to disturb them. If it were criminals whose illegal activities were causing trouble, yes, but they are harmless enough—at least to anyone in this uniform."

They strolled down a pebble-strewn path that led toward a lush garden, rampant with trees whose limbs hung limp and gray-green in the afternoon heat. "I am told," Fletcher said, "this used to be a great wonder, this garden, before the prince died and his wives and household were dispersed. Even overgrown, I call it remarkable."

"I agree." Daphne ducked under one of the branches as they were swallowed up in the greenery. The trees shielded her head entirely from what little sunlight the clouds allowed through, lowering the temperature several degrees. Flowering shrubs speckled with pink and purple clustered near the path, leaving plenty of space for the trees to grow. She could hear but not see the trickling of water, a stream or a fountain flowing somewhere nearby, and felt as cool as she had been in that sitting room at the Residence.

She could see no remnants of cultivation, no signs that this had once been a tended garden. "Where did they all go?" she asked. "The wives, and the rest?"

"It was not a large household," Fletcher said, "and I believe the women went back to the families of their birth. The prince only had two children, both daughters, both too young to make a claim on Madhyapatnam even if they had been male."

"So women cannot inherit here."

"In some places, they can. There are one or two hereditary matri-archies in India. But not here." Fletcher guided her out of the garden and gestured. "There. Astonishing, isn't it?"

Daphne gasped. The building before her rose several stories tall and was covered with windows like a thousand unblinking eyes staring at her. The red sandstone of the palace seemed more real, more solid, than anything she had ever seen before, even Government House. Spires and domes, some with traces of gilding still clinging to them, thrust toward the sky as if imploring Heaven to cast its blessings upon them. An empty hole where doors had once hung gaped like a tooth-less mouth, opening on blackness. It was alien, and beautiful, and she felt she could not look at it enough.

She released Fletcher's arm and drifted toward the palace, tracing the outlines of painted arches with her eyes. Closer to, she realized about half of those windows were false, painted on the walls with such skill it was no wonder she had been fooled. The paint was half scoured off, and she felt a moment's sadness that no one had cared for it in all these years. It deserved to be treated with respect.

"How does it make you feel?" Fletcher asked from close behind her.

Daphne considered it. "Sad," she said. "It is as if it mourns its prince, though I am sure that is absurdly romantic. A place cannot mourn."

"No, I agree with you. Have you never seen a house full of children, and felt it to be happy? I see no reason why the opposite should not be true." He put his hand gently on her elbow. "Let us walk around to the other side."

They walked, arm in arm, in silence, and Daphne wondered as she had before what he felt from her. That unexpected sadness? Her pleasure at being so close to the real India? Or the tiny, furtive feeling of happiness that came from being so close to—

Embarrassment swept over her, then chagrin at feeling embarrassed and knowing *he* would know she was embarrassed. Just because she enjoyed being in Fletcher's company was no reason to feel embarrassed.

Gently, Fletcher disengaged his arm from hers. "I apologize, but you are becoming agitated, and I should not intrude," he said.

"I am not—well, there is no point lying to you, when you know perfectly well that I am—I mean that I do not *intend* to be agitated, it is just—"

"Most people live their lives in a state of mixed emotion. You are rare in that it happens to you infrequently, or at least that has been my experience in your presence." Fletcher clasped his hands loosely behind his back. "It is simply disconcerting to me. Forgive my weakness."

"It is hardly weakness if you—" Daphne began hotly, and was interrupted by Fletcher's laugh. "You are not laughing at me, are you?"

"No, just at how willing you are to leap to my defense." Fletcher shook his head. "Do you know what it is to be a Discerner?"

"By your question, it is not what I imagine it is."

"Likely not. When I touch you, I feel your emotions as if they were my own—or would if I had not had years of experience at separating the two. The more tangled your emotions are, the more difficult that separation is. It is rather like being drunk—not that I expect you to have experienced that state."

"No, though now I rather feel the lack of that, as it would make me better able to understand—and now you are laughing again!"

"You believe it is not humorous that you have just admitted regretting never having become drunk?"

59

"Well, perhaps it is funny. But you understand what I meant."

"Of course. At any rate, there is more to Discernment than the social expectation of not intruding on another person's privacy. There is also the effect on the Discerner." Fletcher put a hand on Daphne's elbow, bringing her to a halt. "Look, that is the door to the *zenana*."

"What is a *zenana*?"

"The women's quarters. Technically it does not lead directly to the *zenana*, as that would permit far too easy access to the place. It is more a secondary entrance. But the *zenana* is just within those walls."

"How do you know that?"

"I went inside the palace, several years ago, out of curiosity. It is a shame we cannot go inside. It's truly beautiful."

He took her arm once more and led her onward, and Daphne, feeling less confused, did not pull away. She had nothing to hide from him, no reason to feel embarrassed. True, she did enjoy his company, and she was beginning to feel a certain excitement when she saw him, but that meant nothing. She glanced covertly at him and saw him smiling that unusual, beautiful smile that made her wish she were a Discerner herself, to know what he was feeling.

At that moment, he looked at her, the smile falling away. "You are frustrated," he said. "Why is that?"

She felt shy admitting that she had been staring at his face. "I regret that we cannot go inside," she said, grateful that it was at least partly true and hoping it was enough true that he would not be able to tell she was lying.

They were coming up on the front of the palace again. This time, a couple of men lounged in the great empty doorway. They stared at Daphne as if they had never seen a woman before. The man on the right, clean-shaven as most Hindoo were not, and very handsome, looked away first, casually shifting his weight as if her stare had made him uncomfortable. The man on the left had unexpectedly light-colored eyes that caught the diffuse sunlight and glinted as if made of glass. His gaze weighed on her, challenging, and she glared back at him without remembering that she was a stranger in their country and ought not be so impertinent.

Fletcher glanced once at them, then dismissed them as not a

threat. "They would take it as a kindness if we did not intrude," he said. "But I regret it as well."

"You have already seen the inside."

"True. But I would like to see it again through your eyes." Fletcher put his other hand over Daphne's where it rested on his arm and squeezed it gently. "Which are remarkable."

His own eyes, dark and unreadable, met hers, and she found herself without a ready reply. She had no idea why her heart was beating faster, but his smile told her that he knew what he had said had unsettled her. Without thinking about it, she threw her arms around his waist, lifted him, and Bounded them both back to the dimly-lit sitting room in the Residence.

In the darkness before the storm, the dimness was almost impenetrable. Fletcher let out a breath at the suddenness of the Bounding, but made no move to step away, to break the circle of her arms. Daphne was conscious of how close he was, smelled again the tangy-sweet scent of his skin, and instantly she released him and stepped backward. "I beg your pardon, I should have warned you," she said.

"Not at all," Fletcher said. She could barely see his face, but he sounded amused. "Lady Daphne, thank you for the experience. Is it too brash of me to express a desire to Skip with you again?"

"No, not at all, it is enjoyable—that is, I enjoy Skipping, not that having you along is enjoyable, though I mean it is *not* as if you are unpleasant—oh, I am saying this all wrong!"

"I take your meaning." Now she could hear he was suppressing a laugh, which made her flush, not because he was mocking her—she was sure he was not—but because she was so foolish as to wish they might go Skipping right now, racing the rain together.

"I should change before dinner," she said, grateful for the darkness that kept her ruddy cheeks concealed. "I will see you shortly, Captain."

"I look forward to it," Fletcher said, clasping her hand and squeezing it gently once more. That giddy desire to put her arms around him once more gripped her, and as soon as he released her, she Bounded to her bedchamber.

"Where have you been?" Bess demanded. She was dressed for dinner already and was polishing the lenses of her spectacles with a corner of her skirt. "You were not in the Residence, I searched for you. I thought to Speak to you, but that would have been pointless as I could not hear you answer back."

"Captain Fletcher and I went to look at the old palace," Daphne said, busying herself over her trunk and praying her reddened cheeks would cool quickly.

"Really? I understand it's quite beautiful. I wish—" Bess's words cut off mid-sentence. The room fell silent except for Daphne's rustling in her trunk and the buzz of a fly beating itself against the window. "You went with Captain Fletcher?" Bess finally said. "How interesting."

Her cheeks must surely be scarlet. "It was, and he had never Skipped before, and I believe he enjoyed it—the palace is so beautiful—"

"Whose idea was this?"

"Captain Fletcher offered to take me, as he knew I had nothing to do this afternoon, and you know how I detest being idle."

"*Daphne.*" Bess's voice was heavy with meaning.

"If you insist on teasing me, I will leave this room immediately."

"I had no intention of teasing you. But—you must know Captain Fletcher never pays the least bit of attention to any woman. Until now."

"We are friends, Bess. That is all."

"I do not believe he looks at you the way he would a friend." Bess did not sound at all teasing; her voice was as serious as Daphne had ever heard her. "What I do not understand," she added, "is why the idea leaves you so distressed."

Daphne threw down the gown she had taken from the trunk and turned to face her friend. "I have no interest in becoming attached to any man," she said. "I intend to have many adventures, and I cannot have adventures if I am betrothed, or married, or have children." The declaration left her feeling hollow inside. She clung to her words like a lifeline. "So it does not matter how Captain Fletcher looks at me, can you not see that?"

Bess nodded. "I do," she said.

"And?" Daphne removed her day gown and folded it away.

"And what?"

"That sounded as if you had more to say."

"No. It is just—if John looked at me that way, my feelings for him might alter. I hope you know what you are about."

Daphne pulled her dinner gown over her head, setting her eardrops trembling. She rubbed her fingers over one of them, feeling the familiar edges of the faceted stones. "I have given it much thought over many years. I know what I want from life. Pray, do not fear for me. It is not as if I need marriage to give myself either security or consequence."

"And what of love?"

"I have my whole life ahead of me. There will be time for that, too." But she remembered Fletcher's expression, the way he had looked just before she Bounded away from him, and wondered if she were right about that.

CHAPTER 8

IN WHICH THERE IS
RECONNAISSANCE

It rained the following morning, a light patter that filled the air with the rich scent of the coralwoods growing along the roadside. Daphne settled her coat around herself and pulled the brim of her bonnet farther over her face. It was at odds with the War Office Bounder uniform she had donned that morning, feeling unaccountably shy at doing so. But she was a Bounder, she was serving in that capacity, and while she might not feel entirely deserving of the uniform, at least she was still entitled to it. Her horse's saddle was finely stitched but ill padded, and she had already had to hitch herself higher three times to avoid sliding off entirely. But it was not a palanquin, so she endured in silence.

The road wound northward just out of sight of the Hooghly River, but not out of hearing, and Daphne listened to its musical rushing and felt as if her blood was flowing in time with it. *This* was the kind of adventure she had had in mind, rain notwithstanding. Ahead, the upright backs of the men, resplendent in their red coats, matched the fiery red flowers of the trees whose names Daphne did not know. Behind, the baggage carts rumbled along the rutted road, not yet churned to mud by rain and their passage. Daphne tugged on her horse's reins to keep it from veering off to nibble at the short, soft grass that grew by the wayside. Apparently it wanted to experience India as much as she did.

"Is it too strange of me to say this is a beautiful day?" Bess said, coming up beside her. "I realize one does not usually say that of rain, but it is so cool, and the raindrops make everything seem brighter. Not at all a cold English rain."

"Yes, in England even so light a rain as this would see us indoors, longing for it to be over so we might walk." Daphne tilted her face back to let the fine droplets touch her face before laughing and wiping them away. "Though if this continues much longer, we will be soaked through despite our coats. The officers look rather damp already."

"It is still better than traveling through the heat of the day. The sun will dry us out soon enough."

Captain Fletcher, riding at the head of the procession, wheeled his horse around and trotted back toward them. "You are not uncomfortable?" he asked.

"Not at all, Captain," Daphne replied. "We were just discussing how lovely a day it is."

Fletcher laughed. "I would hardly call it that, but I appreciate your forbearance. You might have stayed at the Residence and been spared this."

Daphne glowered at him. "We might have stayed in *Calcutta* if we meant to be nothing more than transportation and an extra Speaker, Captain. Pray, do not fear for our comfort."

"Very well," Fletcher said, his eyes alight with amusement, "but I will have to insist again that you spend your nights at the Residence. The post-houses are not built for anyone's comfort, let alone two ladies'."

Daphne opened her mouth to object, and Bess said, "We appreciate that, Captain. Thank you for your concern."

Fletcher nodded, glanced once at Daphne with an amused quirk to his lips, and rode back to the head of the column. Daphne said, "We are not faint-hearted misses with an overdeveloped sense of delicacy, Bess."

"And neither do we wish to sleep rough, when we might enjoy our comfortable beds and sleep free of insects." Bess shrugged. "I apologize if that makes me faint-hearted."

"No, of course not, I beg your pardon, that was rude of me."

"I understand. It must be your Bounder uniform that makes you so daring. I have sometimes wondered what it must feel like to wear trousers and boots like a man. Is it uncomfortable?"

"A little. At first they chafe. But when I Bound or Skip, they feel like a second skin. I imagine Extraordinary Movers, the women I mean, feel the same when they Fly. No one objects to that. And yet if I were to appear in public dressed in men's clothing, not my uniform but men's breeches and tailcoat, I should feel so horribly exposed!"

"Imagine how ridiculous a man would look in a gown, too!"

Daphne pictured Fletcher in a ball gown, waving a fan, and laughed so hard she slipped in her saddle again and had to hoist herself back up. "It is too ridiculous for words. Best we stick to our own apparel—except for this uniform, that is."

The rain let up around noon, and the clouds disappeared, leaving the sun to bake them dry. Daphne removed her bonnet and held it dangling by its strings. She ought to wear it, protect herself from the sun's rays, but it was so stifling she could not bear it. Besides, it was wet almost entirely through. She tied its strings around her neck and let it dangle down her back where it could dry properly. Her blonde hair, plaited and tightly coiled around her head, felt damp as well; better to let it dry in the warm air than be confined under the bonnet.

The road curved along the banks of the Hooghly and through a forest of mangrove trees whose roots rose out of the water, tinted pale where the river had formerly flowed higher. Based on the marks, it would cover the road at its highest point. Daphne tried to imagine wading through the river, trying to follow the road, and felt grateful it was not necessary.

Now that the rain had stopped, they were no longer the only people on the road. Hindoo men dressed in drab brown knee-length trousers, leading donkeys drawing carts laden with knobby sacks, passed them headed south. They eyed the red coats dubiously, drawing well enough away from them that they occasionally left the road for a few paces. Women in bright gowns with silken shawls over their heads watched the officers more coquettishly, drawing their shawls over their faces so their kohl-lined eyes were all that was visible. Lieutenant Wright returned their glances with a cheery wave and a smile. Daphne felt certain he could not help flirting; it was in his nature.

The road left the river once more, and they stopped to eat very plain food in the shade of those red-fire trees whose name Daphne did not know, waiting out the brassy heat of noon. No one spoke; it was too hot for exertion. Daphne nibbled on soft cheese made softer by the heat and wondered when cooler weather would come. Everyone said the monsoon season was nearly over, but they had been saying that since she first arrived in India, and that day never seemed any closer.

By the time the sun fell low in the sky, she was restless and impatient to reach their destination, even if she would not spend the night there. India was beautiful, with its varied trees and vegetation and even the Hooghly with its distinctive smell, but traveling by horse was so *slow* in comparison to Skipping.

She nudged her horse out of the line and trotted forward to speak to Fletcher. "I beg your pardon, Captain, I do not wish to be impatient—"

"But you want to know when we will reach the post-house," Fletcher said with a smile. "It is about half a mile distant."

"Oh!" That was closer than she had expected. "Then... will you learn of the missionaries?"

"I hope so. They will have passed this way only a few days ago. Whoever is stationed at the post-house will know."

"The post is not carried by Bounder?"

"I believe they consider that a waste of a Bounder's talent. The *dak*, the post, is carried by native runners and riders. We passed one earlier today."

"I didn't know. And the post-house gives them a place to rest?"

"They also offer shelter to Europeans on the road, for a nominal fee. We are on Company business and need not pay."

"We may share your evening meal before leaving, yes?"

"It is rather coarse food, Lady Daphne—but I imagine that is the draw for you, isn't it?"

Daphne blushed and looked away. "I must seem so foolish to you, in disdaining the comforts of home."

"You forget, I am very fond of India. And I understand the desire to experience something new. I will never call that foolishness."

"Then I will—that is, I will not keep you longer," Daphne said, and trotted back to her place beside Bess. Bess had her bonnet drawn far over her face and her spectacles snugged up tight on her nose. "Are you well?" Daphne asked, concerned about the pinched, drawn look on her friend's face.

"The sunlight is painful to my eyes, even with my spectacles," Bess said, "and I am weary from the day's travels. I have not ridden so long and so far for many years."

Guilt gripped Daphne over subjecting her friend to such a journey. "We should have remained at the Residence," she exclaimed.

"No, I do not regret this journey one bit," declared Bess. "I can endure a little discomfort if it means seeing a country so few Europeans have. I look forward to describing it to John in my next letter."

The rain started again just as the post-house came into view. It was not at all as Daphne had expected, from Sir Rodney's dire, dark pronouncements on their poor construction and filthy condition. It was a single-story building with a wide porch surrounding it on three sides, built of native timber with a thatched roof. A second, smaller building standing some distance away looked like a stable. The fire-trees grew close around it, making its roof appear to be burning, but it seemed sturdy enough. Daphne dismounted without assistance and walked toward it, leading her horse.

"Lady Daphne, wait," Captain Ainsworth said. "We must permit the servants to take the horses."

"Oh," said Daphne. A few dark-skinned men, seemingly unconcerned about the rain, emerged from the smaller building and approached them. One held out his hand for Daphne's reins, and she yielded them to him.

"Their castes mean the division of labor is exact and minute," Ainsworth said in a low voice, as if imparting some great secret. "There will be many men attached to the post-house for that reason. A cook may not do the work of a *khansamah*, a... steward, I suppose you could call it, and neither may do the work of a *punkah-wallah*."

"Is that why the Residence has so many servants, though Sir Rodney is the only European there?"

"Exactly so. Pray, let me escort you inside."

Daphne took his arm, suppressing a twinge of disappointment that he was not Fletcher. It was foolish of her to court such feelings, and Ainsworth was a pleasant companion, if prone to gossip.

The interior of the post-house was mainly one large room, well lit by windows that at the moment stood open to the elements. They had no glass, just pairs of shutters that would shelter the room from the worst storms, but would not keep the insects out. Daphne felt a moment's traitorous pleasure that she and Bess would not be staying the night.

A low table stood at one side of the room, low enough that one would have to sit on the floor to eat at it, though there were no chairs in any case. Doors leading off to the left and the right hung crookedly in their frames, their leather hinges sagging with age. Daphne smelled hot rice and broiled fish tinged with spices she did not recognize, and her stomach growled. Ainsworth was too polite to hint that he had heard it. "Supper will be ready soon, if you're certain you wish to eat Hindoo food. It's not what you're used to."

"I know that, Captain, and I anticipate it with great pleasure."

"Lady Daphne is adventurous," Fletcher said, coming up on her other side. "Do you see now why I said—"

"Yes, Captain, you need not remind me," Daphne said with a smile. "I will remember to honor your advice in the future."

"As I am certain you will also challenge my advice in future, I appreciate your intent. But I have a request, or possibly I just need *your* advice."

"Is something wrong?" Ainsworth said, releasing Daphne.

"The *khansamah* tells me no Europeans have stopped here in the last week. He has seen no sign of our missionaries."

"They might have bypassed the house, if they were afraid of being taken." Ainsworth lowered his voice again. His eyes darted from one side of the room to the other.

"The post-house sits on the road, and Kandan is a close observer of everyone who passes by. He has seen no Europeans save us, and certainly no one who resembles a missionary. However that might look."

"Then where did they go?" Daphne asked.

"Across country, no doubt. And that is why I need your help. You are trained as a scout?"

Daphne was grateful he was not touching her, to feel how shame struck her like a blow to the face. "I was, yes. You wish me to search for the missionaries?"

"I do, if you consider it possible with the sun setting. I know little of how Bounders survey the area."

Daphne cast her gaze out the window toward the Hooghly, invisible through the trees but still audible. "A full, detailed search will not be possible," she said, "but if they have made camp somewhere in the open, I should be able to see it. When did they leave Madhyapatnam?"

"Four days ago. I realize they might be anywhere by now."

"No, Captain, we need only apply logic to the problem. They are missionaries, therefore they wish to preach, correct? So they will seek out native cities and villages. And if they travel overland, or on small roads away from this one, they will travel more slowly than we. So they cannot have got very far."

"I see you know your business. Shall we go?"

Daphne wrestled briefly with herself before saying, "Scouting is most efficient when one goes alone. I will return with information."

"Of course." He sounded disappointed, but concealed it well.

Fletcher and Ainsworth followed Daphne to the porch, where they met Bess coming the other way. "I must scout out our quarry," Daphne said. "Would you prefer me to return you to the Residence first?"

"I believe I will walk and ease my aches," Bess said. "Lieutenant Wright has offered to walk with me."

"Then I will return shortly," Daphne said. The rain had already faded to a drizzle, so she removed her bonnet and handed it to Fletcher, who looked at it with some bemusement. She took a few steps toward the road, glanced up, and Skipped.

The land lay spread out beneath her, an irregular patchwork of green and brown. Threads of dark earth crisscrossed the patches, roads of varying widths, and the Hooghly was a brown and blue ribbon on her right. She began to fall, and Skipped again, higher this time. Calmly she surveyed the landscape as she fell. There was a village a few miles to the left, but the missionaries would likely not be there—it was too close to Madhyapatnam. Orienting herself by the main road, she Skipped another twelve miles on.

Oh, it was so *good* to move, to travel freely! She had gone in the space of a breath as far as their little caravan had managed in half a day. More villages, another post-house, the Hooghly curving away to the east. One more Skip, and she saw yet another post-house. They appeared to be situated every twelve to fifteen miles along the main road. On a whim, she Skipped to earth a few dozen yards from the nearest post-house and ran up the steps, startling the elderly man who sat cross-legged at the open doorway.

"I beg your pardon," Daphne said, "I should not have been so abrupt, but have you seen any Europeans in the last few days? Other than myself?"

The man's mouth hung open in a comical fashion, and Daphne had to cough to conceal a laugh at his consternation. "No sahibs," he finally said. "Not many days."

"Thank you," Daphne said, and Skipped again.

She kept closer to the ground this time, looking for evidence of a party of travelers camping in the open. Thanks to the Hooghly forming a hard boundary to the east, she covered ground quickly but thoroughly, flicking from one point to another without rest. Even at the extremes of where she judged they might have traveled, she saw nothing out of the ordinary. She did notice, once or twice, startled travelers pointing up at her when she permitted herself a few extra seconds' worth of observation, and laughed at how astonished they must be.

Eventually she came to rest on the main road, some forty miles north of where she had left Fletcher and the others, feeling comfortably cool from all that time spent high above the ground where the breezes plucked at her clothes and hair. Wherever the missionaries were, they had gone to ground quite thoroughly. They might be in one of those villages, but would such places welcome strange Europeans preaching against their religion and traditions? That seemed unlikely. And yet she was confident they were nowhere near the road or any of the smaller roads branching off from it.

Shaking her head, she Skipped back, higher than before so as to give herself a better view of the road, and alighted just yards from the post-house entrance. The smell of food made her ravenous—she had Skipped so often in the last two hours she felt her stomach might mutiny—so she ran up the steps into the common room to find the officers and Bess conversing by the windows. "You did not wait supper on me, did you?" she exclaimed.

"*Captain Fletcher* suggested it would be impolite to eat without you, when you were performing such a valued service," Bess said. There was an undertone to her voice that Daphne had no trouble interpreting.

"It was unnecessary gallantry, Captain, but I appreciate it," she said, sounding as calm as if it meant nothing to her. "And I am quite hungry, after all my labors."

"Please have a seat, ladies, and forgive us not holding your chairs for you," Fletcher said with a smile. Daphne deliberately sat between Lieutenant Wright and Ensign Phillips. Her foolish fondness needed to be reined in. Servants dressed in comfortable-looking clothing, short-sleeved shirts and short pants and sandals, brought dishes, which they set out along the table. Daphne hesitated before the unfamiliar foods.

"Permit me to help you, Lady Daphne," Wright said, his smile charming as always. He heaped steaming rice and fish in an orange sauce onto her plate, then handed her a round, thin piece of bread. "*Doi mach.* You use the *roti* to eat the rest," he added, tearing off a piece of his own bread and using it to scoop up rice and fish. Daphne essayed a small bite. It was delicious, the rice perfectly steamed and sticky without being congealed, the fish spicy but not too hot, and she devoured her serving and helped herself to more, not thinking that it was a breach of etiquette for her to do so. European etiquette seemed irrelevant in these strange surroundings.

She could feel Fletcher's eyes on her and made herself look at him occasionally; it would not do for her to snub him entirely. But she should not encourage him if she had no intention of forming an attachment. So she smiled at him pleasantly, but did not begin a conversation, waiting for him to speak first.

"May I ask what you discovered, Lady Daphne?" he said when she was scraping the last of her fish from her plate.

"The missionaries have not visited the post-houses farther north from here, but that is as we expected. I saw no evidence that they have made camp anywhere between here and what I judged to be the farthest they might travel."

"So they have taken shelter elsewhere."

"Or did not go north."

"That seems unlikely. It was the second thing everyone I spoke to in Madhyapatnam agreed on—the first being that the missionaries had preached dissent." Fletcher pushed his plate away, signaling one of the servants to remove it. "Did you see any places they might have stopped?"

"I did, Captain, but I wonder—would those small towns, villages even, welcome missionaries intent on teaching that their religion, the natives' religion I mean, is false?"

"That does seem unlikely," Captain Ainsworth said.

"I agree," said Fletcher, "but we must kick over as many stones as possible in this search. Going back empty-handed would not look good."

"So we will travel on in the morning?" Ensign Phillips asked.

"We will take a more direct approach," Fletcher said. "Lady Daphne, if you will agree to Skip with me to the places you've made note of, I can inquire after our errant missionaries and perhaps give us more direction."

"Certainly, Captain." Daphne quelled the little leap of excitement that sprang up in her breast at his proposal. "I believe Bess—Miss Hanley and I will retire now, if you will erect the Bounding chamber so we may return in the morning."

Lieutenant Wright helped Daphne stand, though in her Bounder uniform she needed no such assistance. Captain Ainsworth did the same for Bess. "In the morning, then," Fletcher said with a smile. Daphne lifted Bess and had them back in their bedchamber in an instant.

Bess immediately made for her bed and dropped onto it heavily. "My head aches terribly," she said, removing her spectacles so she could massage her temples.

"Oh, you should not—I have been unspeakably selfish—"

"No, it was my foolishness in walking for so long, but I felt awkward, sitting inside with the officers whom I still do not know well. I will be well in the morning."

"You should remain here in the morning. I cannot take you *and* Captain Fletcher when I Skip, I am not so strong as that, and you will do me no good as a chaperon when you are with the officers and I am not."

"I do not mind waiting. Only let me sleep, and I will be well in the morning."

But in the morning, Bess's head-ache was worse. "You are staying here," Daphne said firmly, wringing out a cloth for Bess to place over her forehead.

"I do beg your pardon for being so weak—"

"You are not weak, you simply have a head-ache. I will return in a few hours to see how you are doing."

"Oh, do not interrupt your work on my account!"

"It will be hardly any interruption. I will need rest and food then anyway."

"Very well," Bess sighed, "but do not keep Captain Fletcher waiting any longer."

"I know you are unwell because you do not tease me about him," Daphne said, and Bounded away.

CHAPTER 9

IN WHICH CAPTAIN FLETCHER DRAWS AN UNEXPECTED CONCLUSION

She emerged from the Bounding chamber to find the horses saddled and the wagon ready to travel. "Good morning," Ainsworth said, for all the world as if her emergence was perfectly normal. "We are almost ready to be on our way."

"But I thought Captain Fletcher and I were to Skip ahead."

"We will," Fletcher said, trotting down the steps of the post-house toward her, "but the rest of the party will continue on toward the next post-house, for what information that will give us. Better they not sit around waiting on our return."

Daphne was not sure this made sense, but she was not in command. "Then we may start whenever you are ready, Captain."

He gestured her toward the road and an open space. "I have been in anticipation of this since yesterday, Lady Daphne—if that is not too bold of me to say."

"I admit I have never had a passenger so eager to Skip before. You are certainly unusual in that respect."

Fletcher clasped his arms loosely around her shoulders. "I am certain," he said with a smile, "it is at least in part the company."

Daphne could not think of a reply that would not tangle her words into unintelligibility. She put her arms around his waist, lifted, and Skipped high into the sky.

She glanced around, trying to bury her awareness of her passenger, and located the nearest village. In an instant, she alit on the road some few hundred feet from it and released Fletcher, who held on a few moments longer than was necessary—no, that was her imagination, surely it was. He walked toward the village, and by the time she realized he was not going to wait for her, he had entered its boundaries and was speaking to a man pushing a wheelbarrow. Daphne ran after him.

The conversation was over by the time Daphne reached him. "No luck," Fletcher said, putting his arms around Daphne's shoulders again. "They have not been here. Let's try again."

Some twelve Skips later, Daphne's arms and back were sore from lifting her passenger, and her stomach rumbled its hunger every time she touched ground. Fletcher was as chipper and alert as he had been from the beginning. It annoyed Daphne, who felt she was doing all the hard work—well, of course she was, and it was her responsibility to do so, so why should she resent it? She refused to admit it was because Fletcher, aside from his alacrity in putting his arms around her shoulders, had not treated her with the admiration and, yes, affection he had done at the old palace. She did not want him to treat her that way, so why was she so upset that he was doing what she wanted?

At their next stop, when Fletcher finished asking his questions and would have taken up his position to be Skipped, Daphne stepped away before he could touch her and said, "I am in need of rest. Just a few minutes, if you please."

"Of course," Fletcher said, sounding contrite. "I have been treating you like a vehicle and not a person. I beg your pardon."

"It is understandable, people do not realize how tiring Bounding is, probably because most people are not Bounders and have nothing to compare it to."

"Yes, but I have been in close enough contact with you that I should have realized you were reaching your limits." Fletcher took Daphne's elbow and guided her to sit on the ground beneath the spreading branches of a tree with gray-green leaves whose shadows dappled her skin. She leaned against its trunk and felt the pain in her back ease immediately.

"What kind of tree is this?" she asked.

"A tulip tree," Fletcher said, settling down beside her. "You won't see why because it is not flowering now. Its flowers are bright yellow or pink with crape-like petals, hence the name."

"It is beautiful even in this state." Daphne closed her eyes and leaned her head back. "I hope I have not led you astray, Captain."

"How so?"

"I fear I have underestimated how far our missing missionaries might have gone. I am not a very experienced scout; I was only four months with the War Office before I—before Lord Moira requested my services."

"Your search has been quite logical. I agree with your assessment as to their likely direction of travel. I believe—"

Daphne opened one eye to look at him. "Believe what, Captain?"

"Nothing. We simply need to continue until we have eliminated all the possibilities. Could they have made camp under the shelter of a grove of trees? I saw banyans on our last Skip."

"I have already examined those groves I could not see into from above. None were occupied, or showed signs of having been occupied."

"You are extremely thorough."

"The War Office's training is thorough. I was a good student."

"And yet they sent you to India."

"I believe I told you I was unsuited for war." Daphne stood and paced a few steps from him, stretching her back.

"You did." Fletcher's voice sounded meditative. Daphne kept her back resolutely toward him. Surely he would not be so impudent as to pry further. "Well, I am grateful to have your assistance now. I doubt any of the Bounders attached to Fort William are nearly so competent as you."

"Thank you, Captain."

"Please, sit. I feel quite guilty at having over-extended your reserves."

"I am well enough, Captain, I simply need to stretch." But she returned to sit beside him, leaning back and closing her eyes again.

The birds chittering in the trees above sounded, in the heat of mid-morning, limp and weary. Or possibly that was simply her own tired-ness speaking.

"You must be strong, to carry someone my size repeatedly without tiring immediately," Fletcher said, causing the birds to go silent for a moment.

"You are not very big, Captain, you are tall but not heavy, and I have practiced for years lifting increasingly heavy weights so I might be more than a courier."

Fletcher laughed quietly. "I am still larger than you."

"Most people are." She thought of Schofeld, his casual laughter mocking her, and wished she were in a position to kick him.

"That makes you angry."

Daphne looked down at her hand, resting near his. "You are not touching me."

"I am still capable of reading people's emotions the traditional way. Your face tightened up as you said that."

"Very well, it angers me, but not that I am small—that is not some-thing I can help—just that so often I have been dismissed because of my size and my sex."

"There are far too many fools in the world, if that happens to you often."

She could not bring herself to look at him, afraid of what she might see. "I resolved to make them regret it by becoming the most famous Bounder ever."

Fletcher laughed again. "And how will you achieve that?"

"Oh, by improving my Skipping time, and learning more essences—if I could be the first Bounder to Bound to an outdoor location, not just Skip there, that would be something!" Surely there was something she might discover about Bounding that would give her the recogni-tion she desired! And then it would not matter if she could not bear the sight of blood; she would be successful on her own terms.

She stood again, stretching her arms high above her head. "I am ready to proceed, Captain."

"If you're certain..." Fletcher put his arms around her shoulders. "Tell me if you again become tired."

"I will, but I consider it unlikely." Her stomach rumbled embarrassingly loudly. "I will likely need food before I need rest."

"I believe we can manage that," Fletcher said, just before she made her first Skip.

They visited three more villages before Fletcher asked her to stop. He bartered with an old woman cooking meat on wooden skewers and came away with several, which they ate sitting in the shade of her hut. It was mutton, but juicy and delicious, not at all the boiled grey meat Daphne was accustomed to at Lindsey House. She sucked meat juice off her fingers and laughed at the stories Fletcher told of his exploits working for the Company. Lighthearted and satisfied, she returned to check on Bess, who was sleeping, then went back to Skipping until, around mid-afternoon, she told Fletcher they had visited every village within the scope of her search.

"I see," Fletcher said. He leaned against the bole of a banyan tree and dug a hole in the packed earth of the road with the toe of his boot. "That... is interesting."

"I told you I was afraid I had guessed wrong about where they had gone."

"I don't believe you did." The hole became broader. "Can you return us to the party, or do you need rest?"

"I am well, Captain, but are we giving up so soon?"

"We are not giving up at all. But I wish to confer with the others."

It took only a few Skips to locate the others, still traveling along the road northward. Daphne appeared near the head of the line, causing Captain Ainsworth's horse to shy from her. Ainsworth controlled it easily and said, "You're back earlier than we expected. Did you find them?"

"No, and that's the interesting thing about this journey," Fletcher said. Wright and Phillips drew up nearer and dismounted as Ainsworth did. "I am beginning to suspect there is a reason we have not found our errant friends."

"You mean they're in hiding?" Wright asked.

"I mean," said Fletcher, "they don't exist."

Silence fell, in which the mournful cry of some hunting animal echoed across the river. "But that's impossible," Ainsworth said. "Everyone in Madhyapatnam saw them."

"In fact, no one in Madhyapatnam saw them," Fletcher said. "Even the woman who believed Lady Daphne was one of them only thought she'd seen them. Upon further questioning, it became clear that she had fooled herself into believing she had seen what others reported. They have not stopped at any of the post-houses, which would be a logical place for them to stay; they have not been seen at any of the nearby towns and villages, which would be logical places for them to preach; and Lady Daphne has not seen any sign of them along the roads. I believe we have been hoaxed, gentlemen, Lady Daphne."

"But what would be the point of that?" said Wright.

"I don't know." Fletcher rubbed his chin in thought. "Someone might have wanted us out of the way in Calcutta, but I cannot believe we are so important as to justify such an elaborate hoax."

"It need not have been a person," Ainsworth said. "Resentment at our presence—that is, the presence of Europeans in Madhyapatnam—might have simply built up over time, creating rumors that were readily believed without question."

"Except this unrest had a definite beginning, not ten days ago," Fletcher said. "That speaks to an individual or small group with intent to stir up unrest in Madhyapatnam. Even so, this is hardly the stuff of riots."

"Is it not?" Daphne said.

The men all looked at her as if they'd forgotten she was there. "Madhyapatnam was peaceful when we were there, if you'll recall," said Ainsworth.

"But there was distress, or you would not have been summoned," Daphne said. "And the woman who accosted me was extremely angry. Suppose there were only no riots because you responded with such alacrity?"

"Lady Daphne makes a good point," said Phillips. His diffidence and stammer had vanished. "Most Company officers would have traveled with a large baggage train, full camp kit and whatnot. It took us half the time, traveling rough, to arrive as such an outfit would."

"If someone meant to manufacture outrage to end in rioting

against Christians—that is something that must build over time," Fletcher said. "Our early arrival would have cut that short. But whoever it was managed also to spread rumors that the 'missionaries' had headed north, to throw us off the scent. That speaks to resources I find unpleasantly extensive."

"Then we should return to Madhyapatnam," said Wright.

"I made a mistake in sending you on farther," Fletcher said. "We have wasted time, and it is entirely my fault. Who knows what kind of mischief our adversary might accomplish while we are gone?"

"And suppose getting us out of Madhyapatnam was the point of that misdirection?" Ainsworth said.

"I can return you immediately," Daphne said.

Once again, she was the focus of several astonished male stares. "But the horses—and the baggage cart—" Phillips said.

"Oh, the drover can return the cart, and I am certain you can find someone at the post-houses to lead the horses back," Daphne said, "and if you wish, I can even return with the items of personal baggage you need. It should take no more than an hour, and we will all be back at the Residence for supper."

"Astonishing," Ainsworth breathed. "If you are certain, Lady Daphne—we would not wish to inconvenience you—"

"It is what I am trained for, and I do not mind a bit," Daphne asserted. "Now, if you would unload the things you wish returned, and someone will need to erect the Bounding chamber as we are still out of doors, I believe I should Bound ahead to give Sir Rodney warning." Without another word, she was off.

It took slightly more than an hour to return the four men and their baggage to the Residence, mainly because Fletcher insisted on her Skipping with him to the next post-house to inform them of the change in plans and to ensure there would be riders capable of returning the horses to Madhyapatnam. The cart-driver looked skeptical as they unloaded boxes and bags, but Fletcher spoke to him at length, coins changed hands, and finally Daphne and Fletcher stood in the road watching the cart and horses amble along toward the next post-house. "I suppose it would make no sense to have them turn around and start back immediately," Daphne said.

"No, they would be caught on the road after dark, and better they be comfortable at the post-house overnight and have an extra day's journey." Fletcher let out a satisfied breath. "Thank you for saving me from my mistake, Lady Daphne."

"It was my pleasure, and anyway it was a natural mistake; anyone might have made it."

"And now we must learn who started those rumors, and why."

" 'We,' Captain?"

His lips quirked up in an amused smile. "Your talent has made all the difference in this matter. I would be a fool to forget that."

"But I do not speak the language, and the last time I was in the bazaar my appearance nearly started a fight."

"You are also observant and quick-thinking. Everything else we will deal with as it comes. Will you help?"

She felt she might drown in those dark, intense eyes. "Of course, Captain," she said, accepting his hand without thinking. Fletcher's smile went from amused to that now-familiar expression of secret pleasure when she touched him, and she said, "Oh, *do* tell me why you always look that way when we are—when my hand touches yours! I feel as if you are laughing at me!"

"I assure you, I will never mock you, Lady Daphne," Fletcher said, his expression back to normal. "I simply enjoy how your emotions match your demeanor." He withdrew his hand and added, "Shall we return to the Residence?"

Feeling flustered, she wished she could demur, avoid touching him until her emotions were more in check. But that would give her away as much as physical contact would, so she put her arms around his waist and Bounded them both back, not to the entrance hall, but to the quiet sitting room she associated most closely with him. It was as dim as it ever was, and she released him, regretting that she had no excuse to Bound with him further, angry with herself for feeling that regret.

"Thank you," Fletcher said, offering her his arm.

"No, thank you, Captain, I must—it is dinnertime, and I should not dine in my uniform, Sir Rodney will not—" She Bounded to her bedchamber before she had to find a way to finish that sentence.

The room was empty. Daphne wearily shucked her uniform and donned a fresh gown, cool and light without the sweat she had raised in transporting four men and their baggage. She would sleep soundly tonight, no doubt. She draped her uniform over the trunk to let it air out and sat on the edge of her bed. She liked Fletcher, and felt certain he liked her as well, and...

She stood and straightened the blanket where her sitting had rucked it up a bit. Liking did not have to mean anything. He might be a Discerner, but he was too polite to take advantage of whatever emotions he perceived from her. Even so, she should limit her contact with him. That would be easier for everyone involved. She straightened the blanket one final, unnecessary time, and went down to dinner.

CHAPTER 10

IN WHICH DAPHNE AND CAPTAIN FLETCHER HAVE A COMMON FOE

She entered the drawing room, Sir Rodney's preferred chamber for gathering before the evening meal, and stopped abruptly. "Lady Daphne!" Major Schofeld exclaimed. "How good to see you again!"

"Major Schofeld. What a pleasure," Daphne managed. She could not help herself; she glanced swiftly at Fletcher. He appeared perfectly at ease, standing on the other side of the room from the major—surely that was no accident. "When did you arrive?"

"Just after we spoke last," Sir Rodney said. "Major Schofeld brought sensitive correspondence from Government House, and I insisted he remain for supper. I was unaware you were acquainted, but it makes sense, both of you being Extraordinary Bounders, doesn't it? And now I believe we should all go in. Lady Daphne, pray let me escort you."

Daphne accepted his arm with alacrity, fearing irrationally that she might be forced to endure Major Schofeld's escort—no, he had offered his arm to Bess, who seemed not at all unhappy about it. Well, Schofeld was handsome enough, if one did not know how he had mocked her. She took her seat on the Resident's right hand and was pleased and relieved to find Captain Ainsworth on her right. He could not disturb her calm, pleasant as he was.

"Lady Daphne, I am surprised to find you here," Schofeld said. He faced her across the table, seated between Bess and Fletcher. "Do you not have duties to the Countess of Loudoun?"

"I return whenever I am needed, but there was no one else, and I assure you I do not mind it."

"Well, I hope Fletcher appreciates your service." Schofeld applied himself to his soup. "Lady Daphne is an extremely talented Bounder. Frankly, she is wasted here in India."

"I am grateful to Lady Daphne for her cooperation," Fletcher said. "She has proved a valuable member of our party."

"Conveying all of you this afternoon—I should say so!" Sir Rodney said with a laugh. "I could hardly credit it, you know I said as much, Major."

"Yes, and Lady Daphne, you should have requested assistance." Schofeld regarded her sternly. "It is hardly proper for a woman to perform that conveyance for so many men."

Daphne wished her legs were long enough that she might kick him under the table. "You know perfectly well that War Office Bounders are expected to set aside such concerns, when needs must," she said, concealing her irritation. He was not entitled to lecture her. "And even had I known you were here, it is not as if you could have Bounded back and forth from a Bounding chamber you had never seen."

"True. I am simply concerned for your welfare," Schofeld said, unmoved by her edged words. "I wonder Fletcher is not as concerned." He clapped Fletcher on the back twice, his hand lingering on Fletcher's shoulder, the very picture of one old friend greeting another.

Fletcher's eyes closed briefly as if in pain. His face stilled, became an emotionless mask. "I believe Lady Daphne is a better judge of her welfare than either of us," he said, his voice distant and wooden. Daphne could not believe it was the same man she had conveyed all over the countryside that day. What had Schofeld done to him?

"Major Schofeld," Bess said, "I have always wondered what *your* assignment is. You appear at Government House so rarely."

"I am liaison to Colonel Dalhousie," Schofeld said, "and am particularly assigned to carry confidential correspondence all over the world. It is a position of great responsibility."

"Then I will not ask what brought you here, as I am certain you will not tell me."

Daphne shot Bess a grateful glance. Bess, as Extraordinary Speaker to the Governor-General, held a position of even greater responsibility than Schofeld's, but she had more than once told Daphne she felt no need to increase her consequence by advertising the fact. Daphne appreciated Bess's intervention; she was close to being overtly rude to the major, and defending Fletcher was not her responsibility.

"So, Captain Fletcher," Sir Rodney said, "you have not said what you learned from your journey. Why did you return so abruptly?"

"We have discovered that the missionaries who caused so much turmoil do not exist." Fletcher pushed his soup bowl aside. "My investigation therefore has taken an unexpected turn. Not only must I now discover, if possible, who started the rumors, but I must also learn *why* that person or persons wanted us to believe there were missionaries stirring up trouble here."

"Unbelievable," Sir Rodney said. "Sounds as if someone's playing games."

"I sincerely hope that is the case," said Fletcher.

"What, you're not afraid of a real challenge, are you?" said Schofeld. His smile was pleasant enough, but his eyes gleamed with malice.

Fletcher's expression went even more wooden. "Meaning what, Major?"

Schofeld looked suddenly wary. "Oh... just that it would be more difficult if this were the sign of some dastardly plan, don't you suppose?"

"I am not so foolish as to believe only the difficult assignments are worth my time," Fletcher said. Schofeld's wary look gave way, just briefly, to anger before he controlled himself. Daphne guessed she had witnessed a blow in a long-running campaign of bitterness between the two men, not that she had any idea what it meant.

"And what are we to do tomorrow, Captain?" she asked.

Fletcher shrugged. "We will make contacts within the city and attempt to discover the truth."

"You don't intend to include Lady Daphne in that 'we,' do you, Fletcher?" Schofeld exclaimed.

"If she is willing, certainly. I have great respect for her observational skills."

"An Extraordinary Bounder is above such things."

"I disagree," Daphne said, "and it is not your place to make that decision. I have already been of use to Captain Fletcher and intend to do so again."

Schofeld said nothing, merely served himself a helping of fish from the platter in front of him. He offered it to Bess, who ignored him. Her head was tilted back in the attitude of a Speaker. Daphne paused with her fork halfway to her lips to watch her friend. As Bess's mental conversation stretched out, all eating and speaking came to a halt, waiting for whatever news she had received.

Finally Bess opened her eyes and blinked. "You should not have stopped eating on my account," she said. "I do beg your pardon, had I known that conversation would go on for so long I would have excused myself."

"No trouble at all, my dear," Sir Rodney said. "Is it something you might share?"

"Yes, in fact, I am requested to let Major Schofeld know he is wanted back at Government House at his earliest convenience to convey a very important passenger. And Lady Daphne is to report as well, to convey Lady Loudoun and her children from India to England."

Daphne had not taken more than two bites of her mutton, and her stomach rumbled painfully at the delicious smells wafting from the dishes. Reluctantly, she pushed back from the table. "I should be no more than half an hour," she said. "Pray do not wait on me."

"Oh, I am certain they did not mean immediately," Schofeld said. "We have time to eat."

"You may do as you like, but I promised I would not permit this assignment to interfere with my real duties," Daphne said, dropped her napkin on her abandoned seat, and Bounded to Government House.

It was considerably longer than half an hour before she returned. The children were more than usually recalcitrant, and Daphne ended up conveying not only them, but their many nurses as well. Lady Loudoun, who waited outside the Bounding chamber for each of her children, clasped Daphne's hand when the final passenger had arrived. "Thank you for your patience," she said.

"Oh, it is nothing—it is only what is expected of me—" Her stomach rumbled loudly, making Lady Loudoun cover her mouth to conceal a smile.

"Come with us, and someone will find you something to eat," she said.

"No, it is well, I have my dinner waiting for me—please have someone Speak with Miss Hanley when you are ready to return." She waited only long enough to perceive Lady Loudoun's assent before Bounding to the cool, dim central hallway of the Residence.

Talking and laughter came from the drawing room, and light shone from beneath that door. Daphne crossed the hall to the dining room and pushed the door open, feeling unexpectedly sorry for herself. The room was dark, the table cleared—well, they could not very well just leave the dishes unattended, fair game for the billion insects that thronged Madhyapatnam. She passed through the dining room and followed the short hall to the kitchen. There, lights bloomed, and servants moved about, washing dishes and doing other kitchen-related things Daphne was unfamiliar with.

The servants all stopped in their tracks when she entered. "May I have something to eat?" she said. "I realize it is unusual, but I was forced to leave, and I am so very hungry—"

She sniffed. Something delicious was cooking over one of the fires. She drifted in that direction. One of the servants gabbled something at her, then said, "Is not for memsahib, is for us."

"Oh! I did not mean—it smells wonderful, you see—but I would not take your meal for all the world! Is there no mutton left, or fish...?"

The servant glanced at one of his fellows, a bulky man with a huge moustache and his arms folded forbiddingly across his chest. He shrugged, then opened a cabinet wherein lay the remnants of the Residence meal. Someone had made up a plate for her, and Daphne fell to. It was not as delicious as the skewers of meat she had shared with Fletcher that day, but it was still better than what was served at Lindsey House.

The servants were silent the whole time she ate, glancing at each other and occasionally muttering to each other in voices too low to make out, even if she had spoken their language. It made her nervous, and she ate faster, feeling impelled by the force of their presence to finish and exit with great rapidity. Finally, their silence became too much for her, and she set aside her unfinished plate and said, "Thank you—it was most kind—" and fled.

Safely back in the darkness of the dining room, she paused to take a deep breath and let out some of the tension coiled at the base of her neck. It occurred to her that she likely could have compelled them to serve her properly, at table, and probably should have; she would never have dreamed of eating in the kitchens at home in Marvell Hall, nor of embarrassing the servants.

India had cast a spell over her, drawing her in, stripping away her inhibitions. She needed to remember she was alien here, that the customs her people had imported lay like a veneer over a culture far older than her own. She breathed in, inhaling the leftover aromas of the meal and, fainter, the scent of whatever the kitchen staff had been cooking for their own meal. She felt embarrassed at her wish that they had served it at Sir Rodney's table instead.

She chose to walk to the drawing room rather than Bound in. Bounding to a room whose essence she knew but that was full of people was difficult in a way she could never explain to anyone but another Extraordinary Bounder. People had essence, though in a completely different way from a location, and it took skill and effort to sort those human essences from that of a room. And, of course, it was uncivil behavior to simply appear in the middle of a gathering except under emergency circumstances. She leaned on the dining room door rather heavily and trudged across the hall, only to see the drawing room door open and Captain Fletcher emerge.

His eyes gave away his surprise at seeing her, though the rest of his face was still set and wooden. Daphne felt downcast that he did not appear pleased to see her. "Lady Daphne," he said, "we seem to have abandoned you."

"Oh, it is nothing, Captain, nothing too terrible. I would have felt most unhappy had you all waited your supper on me, and I have eaten —are you leaving, then?"

"I feel unwell, and tomorrow will come early, so I thought to excuse myself."

His voice sounded as if it were coming from very far away, and he was no longer looking at her, but at something at the end of the hallway. Daphne was struck by an urge to poke him, to strike him, anything to return him from the distant land his spirit was roaming in. "Unwell? I hope it is nothing serious—shall we rise early, then, and return to the bazaar?"

"I have not yet decided. But you should remain here. Schofeld is right, this work is beneath you."

Daphne sucked in an annoyed breath. "Major Schofeld has never been right about anything in his entire life, and I wonder that you should give credence to *anything* he has to say, given how long you have known him, and I—he certainly can have no interest in *my* well-being, unless he considers himself so... so *attractive* that I might forgive him his conduct toward me—"

Fletcher's eyes focused on her, and a smile touched his lips. "His conduct toward you? You seemed rather friendly, earlier."

"You must have been too focused on your own distress not to have noticed the unfriendliness of my speech to him. Major Schofeld is not my friend, and I wish he would stop trying to be."

The smile vanished. "My distress?"

Too late Daphne remembered from what source she had heard of Fletcher's dislike of Schofeld. "I—that is, Captain—I have heard that Major Schofeld—that you and he are old... I do not know if you are enemies, but he is able to... turn his emotions on you—" The wooden look had returned, but this time it made Daphne's heart ache at being the cause of it. Curse her witless tongue! "I—it is too bad, and Major Schofeld is—he called me the Littlest Bounder and mocked me, so I know—oh, Captain, I beg your pardon, I should not have said anything!"

"You are certainly correct in your assessment of Schofeld's character," Fletcher said, without warmth, without so much as the hint of a smile. "I am very glad you are not fooled by him. I would hate to imagine him imposing himself on your good nature."

"I am much too observant for that, I am nearly as good as a

Discerner—oh, but you are a Discerner, I should not have—I meant that Discerners must be observant, and so must Bounders, but you—"

He was as wooden as he had been at dinner, as if he were containing some emotion that would otherwise overwhelm him, and the difference between that and the man Daphne was coming to know was so stark it made her want to weep.

"Please excuse me, Lady Daphne, I wish to retire. We will speak again in the morning." Fletcher nodded in farewell and made to walk away past her. Despairing, Daphne reached out and without thinking put her hand on Fletcher's arm, not trying to stop him, simply wishing she could repair the damage her careless words had done. To make him look at her again as a friend, if that was what they were to each other.

Fletcher gasped, and his eyes went wide and startled. Quicker than thought, he grabbed Daphne's wrist and tore her hand away from his arm, but rather than release her, he gripped her so tightly she squeaked in surprise and pain. "You—" he said, focusing that dark gaze on her so intently she wished she could Bound away from him. His hand anchored her to the floor; she could not Bound without taking him with her. They stood staring at each other, motionless, and Daphne wished desperately she could read his emotions as easily as he could hers. Not that she knew what she was feeling, herself. Her heart was in turmoil, shame and regret and longing all mixed together and waiting for some sign from him to tell her which should come out on top.

Fletcher seemed to realize how tightly he was holding her, and loosened his grip without letting go. "I apologize," he said. "I should not have behaved so. Thank you."

"For what, Captain?" She could have pulled away from his grasp, but she did not want to.

"For not pitying me. I despise pity, particularly from those—" He looked away, and this time he did release her. "Thank you."

"You are not an object of pity, Captain. I respect you for—oh, for so many things. You have overcome your weaknesses, which is more than I can say for myself."

He smiled, and a little of the ache went away. "I find it difficult to believe you have not conquered your weaknesses. The Littlest

Bounder, eh? I imagine Schofeld was not the only one to use that epithet."

"No, he was not, but I—" The dimness of the hall, and how close they stood, made her very nearly reveal her darkest secret, but her heart quailed at the thought. "At any rate, if you believe I would think less of you simply because Major Schofeld is insensitive, then you are foolish, and I do not suppose you foolish."

Fletcher let out a breath. "Oh, I am a fool, but not about that. Lady Daphne, you are remarkable."

"Thank you, Captain. So are you."

That made him laugh, quietly so as not to draw attention from the party in the dining room. "I wonder about that. And now I really must excuse myself. My... reaction... to Schofeld's behavior leaves me weary and makes me poor company."

"Oh! But—perhaps it is prying, but what—you seemed so stiff and even angry—"

"A Discerner's response to someone capable of imposing his emotions on him is to lock all emotions away, to effectively shut down his talent until the situation has passed. It is extremely uncomfortable."

"I should say so! But it cannot be a common occurrence."

"It is rare, yes, for which I am grateful. I have met only two people who were capable of doing it consciously."

"What of... of Coercers? Like Napoleon? Have you ever encountered—oh, but you are tired, and here I am harassing you when I am certain you wish only for bed."

Fletcher laughed again. "A Coercer's talent is different, and as a Discerner I am immune to it. And I find talking to you more relaxing even than a good night's sleep."

Daphne blushed, because the admiring, interested look was back in his eyes, and despite the part of her that shrieked a warning reminder that she had no interest in forming an attachment, she did not want him to leave. "Then you have met Coercers. I thought there were none in England."

"There are likely as many Coercers as Discerners in England. They are just very good at concealing their talent. And not all of them use it for evil." He covered his mouth as he yawned. "It seems I am in more need of rest than I imagined."

"I beg your pardon, Captain, I should not have kept you."

"As I said, talking to you relaxes me. Thank you for that." He yawned again, more widely. "We will speak again in the morning, when I have decided on a course of action."

"Of course. Good night, Captain." Daphne curtseyed to him, which made him smile and clasp her hand briefly in farewell. She watched him walk away toward the stairs before continuing across the hall to the drawing room. She paused with her hand resting on the doorknob and willed away her foolish smile. For someone who intended not to permit romantic entanglements to interfere with her life of adventure, she had been remarkably intent on restoring Fletcher's good opinion of her. Well, she could not know his heart, and probably he thought of her as a friend, and that was as it should be. Even so, she found herself hoping morning would come quickly.

CHAPTER 11

IN WHICH CALAMITY STRIKES

Daphne drew back the curtains of her palanquin, not caring, on this beautiful clear morning, that she was drawing attention to herself. Damp breezes touched her face, bringing with them the scents and sounds of the bazaar. How long would she have to remain in Madhyapatnam before they became, first familiar, and then commonplace? A small child wearing nothing but a cotton breechclout stared at her, sucking its fingers. She smiled and waved, and the child ducked behind its mother's skirt. Young Lady Selina, Lady Loudoun's youngest child but one, did the same thing when confronted with a stranger. It must surely mean something that such behaviors appeared universal.

The bearers set the palanquin down, and Daphne hopped out, unimpeded by her Bounding uniform. Behind her, Bess emerged from her own litter, shaking out her skirts. Today she wore her own uniform, a black military-style jacket trimmed with black ribbon over an ordinary blue muslin gown, signaling that she was on duty with the War Office. "You look so official, I feel I should do the same," she had said that morning as they dressed. "Though this jacket is so very warm, I almost regret the decision. Today is sure to be especially hot."

At the moment, Bess did not look overheated, merely saying, as she approached Daphne, "It is a beautiful morning, but I hope for all our sakes Captain Fletcher discovers the information he needs quickly. The clear sky suggests the afternoon will be unbearable."

"I will be happy to return you to the Residence—"

"I can endure a little heat, Daphne, and I admit to some curiosity about the truth behind our nonexistent missionaries. There, the captain is beckoning to us, we should join him."

Fletcher looked a good deal more cheerful than he had the previous night, smiling pleasantly at them both. "I feel optimistic," he said, "that we will learn much today. But I would like you both to stay close to me, and observe those to whom I do not speak. Were I an Extraordinary Discerner, I should be able to sense those who feel guilty or angry in the presence of a European simply by being nearby, but being constrained to touch others to feel their emotions, I am limited to perceiving one person at a time. Your observations may show me where best to direct my efforts."

It sounded reasonable, though Daphne still suspected he was to some degree making work for them. "We will do our best, Captain."

"The rest of you, spread out, and pay careful attention to the mood of the bazaar," Fletcher told the other officers. "We will meet here in two hours to share information and make a new decision as to our direction."

"I will remain in contact with Miss Hanley, just in case," Phillips said. The ensign spoke with calm confidence now that he had instructions and a purpose. Daphne had grown fond of him over the past few days, once he stopped blushing and stammering in her presence.

"And if for some reason Captain Fletcher changes the rendezvous time or place, I will immediately inform you all of it," Bess said.

"Agreed," said Fletcher. "Good luck to you all."

Once more Daphne followed Fletcher into the bazaar. It was, if anything, more noisy and hot and smelly than the first time, filled with people all shouting at each other in languages Daphne did not understand. They seemed on the verge of breaking into a fist fight, but Fletcher walked through the crowds unconcerned about the potential for violence, so Daphne stayed close and tried to ignore her inner sense that told her to Skip away. Beside her, Bess shared Fletcher's calm, though she could not know the languages any more than Daphne did. It embarrassed Daphne to be so lily-livered as to fear nothing more than loud conversations.

A hand tugged on her sleeve, and Daphne stopped, startled. It was the wizened, toothless woman who had sold her the bracelet. She patted Daphne's arm and said something that sounded like a question. "Oh!" Daphne said, and pushed her left sleeve up. "Yes, I am wearing it." She had not removed it since the day she had purchased it and was not sure why, except that it was beautiful and made her feel connected to this strange country she was now a part of.

The woman smiled and tapped the bracelet, tracing the outline of one of the fire-flowers and saying repeatedly, "*Agnidāha, agnidāha.*"

"What does that mean? Oh, you cannot understand me, and I cannot understand you, forgive my ignorance!"

"It means... 'fire-flame' is, I suppose, the best translation," Fletcher said, appearing out of nowhere. "It is also the word for an Extraordinary Scorcher, in Hindoostani."

"She does not suppose *I* am an Extraordinary Scorcher, does she? Simply because I purchased this bracelet?"

"I believe it is merely coincidence." Fletcher said a few words to the woman, whose smile became even brighter as she responded. "She says you are bright, like the fire, but you are no Scorcher. It seems she is a Seer, and Dreamed of you before you met the other day. She chose the bracelet for you, as a mark of your friendship for India."

"Oh! Can you tell her—give her my thanks?"

Fletcher spoke again to the woman, who patted Daphne's arm again, then pressed her palms together and bowed. She said something to Daphne, and Fletcher said, "She, ah, wishes you good health and prosperity."

Daphne raised her eyebrows. "That is not what she said."

"You *are* observant, aren't you? What she said was she wished us both happiness and, er, fertility. Apparently she believes we are married. To each other."

Daphne reddened, and made herself laugh in a lighthearted way. "That is very kind of her, don't you agree?" She put her palms together and returned the woman's bow. "I suppose it is a natural mistake."

"Of course." Fletcher bowed to the woman, then glanced at Bess, who looked as if she were suppressing laughter. "Shall we move on, ladies?"

Daphne could not look directly at Bess for fear of either erupting with laughter or bursting into embarrassed flames, thus disproving the woman's assertion that she was no Scorcher. "Certainly, Captain."

She spent the next hour surveying the crowds that surrounded them as they moved through the bazaar. Most of the faces she examined were not friendly. Though they rarely looked directly at her, their eyes and mouths stilled when the three of them were nearby, and Daphne watched their stiffened, angry bodies and wondered if she should warn Fletcher that the potential for violence was high. Fletcher seemed unaware of it, possibly because he was intent on his many conversations. As the sun rode higher in the sky, Daphne drew closer to Bess and calculated whether she was, in fact, strong enough to convey two passengers at once, should that become necessary.

She became aware of the stranger when they stopped at a sweetmeat stand for Fletcher to carry on a conversation with the owner. She had seen him earlier that day, once or twice, but this was the first time she was aware that he had been following them. He was of no more than average height, his skin darker than most, and his eyes glinted a strangely light color that in his dark face looked like glass struck by sunlight. She had the strongest feeling she had seen him before, not in the bazaar, but somewhere else.

As he turned to walk away, she remembered—he had been at the old palace the day she and Fletcher had gone there. They had stared rudely, challengingly at each other. And now he was here in the bazaar, staring at her again. Fletcher was still carrying on a conversation and sounded intent on it. She should not interrupt him for something so potentially trivial. "Bess, I will return shortly," she said.

"Daphne, where are you going?"

"I am... investigating. I promise not to go far." With that, she followed the stranger.

He did not seem to notice she was following him. It was odd, how the crowds parted for him the way they did for her, though in her case it was clearly because she was European, female, and alone. That thought almost stopped her where she strode. Fletcher had said the bazaar was not dangerous, but he had not intended that she and Bess be alone in it, and that had been before the strange dark mood had descended over most of its inhabitants. She shook off her momentary unease and kept going.

The noise was intensifying, the shouting growing harsher and louder, but the stranger continued to walk as if none of it mattered to him at all. Daphne walked faster, feeling a sudden urge to catch up to the man and force him to explain himself—though what he had to explain, she did not know, as all he had done was be mysterious and stare at her in an unfriendly fashion. Men and a few women crowded in on her from all sides. None of them touched her, but Daphne felt again fear and a need to escape. *I am not so craven*, she told herself, and at that moment discovered her quarry had disappeared.

Someone shouted, a long string of syllables that rang out above the murmuring. A crash echoed through the bazaar, the sound of glass shattering. The crowd's shouting turned into a roar, and suddenly Daphne was buffeted by grasping hands, surrounded by faces distorted with fury.

She shrieked, wrestled free of the hands trying to lay hold on her, and Skipped straight up. From five hundred feet above, the bazaar was a riot of color—no, it was a riot, an actual riot, bodies swirling and weaving in a pattern that made sense only at this distance. She Skipped again to maintain altitude and surveyed the landscape. The riot was spreading outward from where she had stood, overwhelming stalls and wreaking havoc on those poor souls whose wares were spread on the ground. She could not see Fletcher anywhere—of course she could not; at her height people were mere dots of color, moving with the tide of the mob.

She Skipped back in the direction she thought she had left Bess and Fletcher, but everything looked so different from above, and she had not paid close attention to where she was going—

-Daphne! *Daphne!*-

"Bess!" she shrieked, not that her friend could hear her.

-Daphne, it is a riot! You must return immediately. We are at the barber's stall, but we cannot remain here long.-

Daphne Skipped low, skimming the tops of the stalls, darting from place to place as she sought frantically for her friends. Finally, she saw a canvas roof she recognized, and Skipped to find herself only feet from Bess and Fletcher. Madly screaming men darted past, carrying miscellaneous items stolen from the stalls. Some of them were armed with lengths of wood or long knives and were advancing on the barber's tent.

Fletcher had put Bess behind him and stood armed with one of the tent-poles, a long and awkward weapon. "Lady Daphne!" he shouted. "You must take Miss Hanley and yourself to safety!"

"But what of you?"

"I will be—*move!*"

Daphne Skipped upward a few dozen feet and looked down in time to see Fletcher wield his ungainly weapon against a man carrying a knife long enough to be a short sword. "Go, now!" he shouted.

Daphne Skipped past him, snatched Bess up, and Bounded them both to the safety of the Residence's central hall. Bess's spectacles had slipped down her nose and her hair was untidy, and she was breathing as heavily as if they had run the distance to the Residence instead of Bounding. "You must help him," she said.

"I cannot Bound to an outdoor location!"

"Then Skip. But—" She tilted her head back. "Ensign Phillips says Captain Ainsworth has been injured. He has not seen Lieutenant Wright. They need your help, Daphne."

"Tell me where they are," Daphne said, and ran for the door.

Once in the courtyard, she Skipped to a point near the center of the bazaar, high above the peaks of its canvas roofs. It was pointless, she was too high up to see any of her friends, but it was the best she could manage.

-Daphne, Ensign Phillips says they are trapped on the north side. There is a stall with a blue roof on one side and a display of brass pots on the other, only the pots have been kicked about, so you may not see many of them.-

Daphne had never wished so fervently that Extraordinary Speakers could read minds, for her to send an answering message to Bess. She Skipped northward, then Skipped again, and again, keeping herself some fifty feet above the tallest peaks while she scanned the bazaar. Oh, if only Fletcher had permitted them to wear their red coats, so bright and easy to see! Then they... likely would have incited the riot that much earlier. Perhaps she should stop wishing for things and concentrate on finding Phillips.

There. A blue swathe of canvas, and near it, the glint of sunlight on brass. Daphne Skipped one final time and found herself behind a makeshift barricade. Phillips had concealed them well, because the rioters ignored it, shouting and screaming past it.

"There you are," Phillips said. His red hair was dark with sweat, and his shirt was torn. "Take him, Lady Daphne. Don't worry about me." He knelt on the ground, supporting Ainsworth, who lay still and unconscious. His face was—

The world spun, and flecks of light pulsed before Daphne's eyes. She found herself face-first on the ground, which felt unnaturally cool against her skin. Breathing deeply and desperately, she said, "Oh, Ensign, I cannot—his face—"

"Are you well, Lady Daphne? Were you injured?" Phillips took her arm just above the elbow and tried to pull her up. Dizzy, swaying, she closed her eyes tight and tried not to inhale too deeply.

"It is the blood—I cannot bear the sight of blood—forgive me, Ensign, I cannot!"

"Stay still," Phillips said, and Daphne focused on breathing, in through the nose, out through the mouth, though she could not remember if that was the right way round—should it be in through the mouth, and out through the nose? She heard rustling, and the movement of cloth, almost inaudible next to the shouting of the rioters.

"There. I have cleaned him as best I can," Phillips said. "Go quickly, before he bleeds again, and don't look at his face if you can help it."

Daphne nodded, her eyes still closed. She felt around until she found Ainsworth's chest, then wormed her arms beneath his shoulders and under his knees. With a grunt, she lifted him—he was a good deal heavier than Fletcher—and heard him groan in pain, then she Bounded to the Residence and set him down in the hallway, quickly and not very gently. "Bess!" she shouted. "Someone needs to care for

Captain Ainsworth!" Without waiting for a reply, she ran back outside and Skipped.

It took her only two Skips to return to Phillips' side. He crouched at the edge of the barricade, eyeing the crowds, and jumped slightly when she appeared beside him. "Where is Lieutenant Wright?" he said.

"Later," Daphne said, "we must go now." She hoisted him by the waist until she supported his weight entirely, then Bounded away. Both Bess and Sir Rodney were in the hall, along with a few of the Residence's native servants. Two of them held Ainsworth between them and were carrying him, limp and helpless, toward the drawing room. Bright blood dripped down the side of Ainsworth's face, and Daphne turned away, feeling the world whirl about her. *No, I will not succumb!* she told herself fiercely, chanting it silently to herself before looking back at Ainsworth—and the dizziness claimed her, and she sat hard on the tiles and put her head between her knees.

"Daphne. Daphne, what is the matter? Are you injured?" Bess exclaimed.

Daphne shook her head without raising it. "I am well, it is nothing." Horror pierced the weary fog surrounding her. "Captain Fletcher —I left him, I forgot entirely!"

"I will tell him you are coming. Go, now!"

Daphne pushed herself to her feet and ran for the door.

The barber's tent had collapsed when she reached it, the stool cracked into two pieces and strewn across the wreckage of the canvas. Fletcher was nowhere to be seen. The rioters had passed this area, leaving destruction in their wake. Daphne Skipped high enough to survey the area, hoping against reason to see Fletcher or Wright against the sea of humanity whose tides had swept the length of the bazaar. Wrecked tents and canopies were all that was left to the north and west of the bazaar. Rioters still smashed and looted their way eastward. Stall owners, at least Daphne presumed they were the owners, picked their way through the destruction they left behind. It was the saddest thing Daphne had ever seen, and it filled her with rage at those who had so callously smashed the livelihood of their fellows.

She Skipped lower, skimming just feet above the crowds, not caring when they exclaimed and pointed, wishing she dared fall far enough to kick some of them in their sneering, angry faces. Some of them were battered and bloody. Some of them lay motionless on the ground, their limbs contorted in ways that suggested they would never rise again. She Skipped far away from those, breathing deeply. Perhaps if she did not have to smell the blood—no, it made no difference, and she hated herself for her weakness.

She saw no one she recognized, not even the stranger with the glass-bright eyes, certainly not any Europeans. After crossing the bazaar twice, she Bounded back to the Residence and hurried to the drawing room door. The air was thick with the smell of an oncoming storm and the sharp coppery smell of blood, leaving her dizzy and in need of clear, fresh air. "Bess?" she called out, not daring to enter the room.

"You did not find them?" Bess said, coming to the door. "Daphne, you look very unwell. Are you sure—"

"I hoped they might have returned here. I will search again. Tell them both—tell them to return to the Residence if they can, and if not... I will simply have to find them."

Safely in the sky once more, Daphne inhaled the fresh, damp air and felt her head clear instantly. She was beginning to tire from all the mad Skipping about, but she could not rest so long as Fletcher and Wright were not safe. She returned to the barber's stall like a pigeon returning to its roost, feeling obscurely that Fletcher would find his way here of all places, if he could return. Nothing had changed. The bits of stool still scattered across the canvas, which lay draped in great humps across the ground. Daphne could not remember what else had been in the stall to make such lumps.

She picked up a fold and shrieked. Boots, still on someone's feet. Proper military boots—

She shoved the canvas out of the way; it moved slowly, as if made of iron rather than cloth. Gradually she piled it up to one side. Fletcher lay motionless, curled on one side with his arm up to protect his head. Blood pooled around his body, saturated his shirt. Daphne cried out, and grey mist claimed her vision, clogged her eyes and nostrils with the sharp smell of blood.

CHAPTER 12

IN WHICH DAPHNE SAVES A LIFE, BUT REFUSES TO BE THANKED

She came to herself after an eternity, tears leaking from the corners of her eyes, half-collapsed over Fletcher's body. The faintest groan escaped his lips, startling her back to full consciousness. He was alive. Alive, but for how much longer? If she could not exert herself, it might not be very long.

Daphne forced herself to sit upright and breathe deeply. The stink of fresh blood was everywhere, dizzying her—no, she would not succumb, not now that she had a chance to redeem herself. Carefully, she crouched next to Fletcher's supine form and wriggled her arms beneath his shoulders and under his knees. How long had he lain there, untended, unnoticed? She had stood right next to him and never realized—well, that line of thought was pointless, and she was stalling.

She breathed out a few times, then *lifted*, and the instant she had his full weight in her arms, she Bounded, not to the hall, but to the drawing room itself. There was a moment when her sense of the room's essence distended, the presence of a dozen people distorting it, and then she was there and looking about for a place to lay her burden down.

"Captain Fletcher!" Bess exclaimed. "Daphne—"

"He is not dead, I felt him move, but—oh, he needs treatment, he will bleed to death if nothing is done, Bess, I cannot—" Daphne backed away and turned to lean against the nearest wall, resting her forehead on her arms and closing her eyes.

"I have Spoken to Government House and they will send an Extraordinary Shaper immediately," Bess said. "Daphne, were you injured?"

"No." Weariness struck her. "Where is Lieutenant Wright?"

"Still not here. Captain Ainsworth will not wake. Oh, Daphne, this is a disaster!"

"I will go."

"No, Daphne, you have already done so much. I have Spoken to Lieutenant Wright and he knows he is to return here."

"Suppose he, too, lies near-fatally wounded somewhere? I must search for him." Daphne stood and caught sight of Fletcher, lying so still and white on the sofa. Two of the Residence's native servants knelt near him, one pressing a large wad of cloth against the terrible wound in his side, the other bathing his face. The cloth obscured the blood enough that Daphne felt no dizziness in looking at him, just a horrible aching pain in her heart and shame at her weakness flooding her limbs. "Speak with me if the lieutenant returns before I do."

She could not make herself run from the room to the courtyard, she was so weary. This was much less laborious than Skipping with Fletcher the day before—had it truly only been one day?—but felt worse because of the terrible fears burdening her. Skipping low to the ground, she quartered the bazaar. The rioters had dispersed, leaving nothing but destruction behind. Some of those picking through the remnants of the stalls might have been rioters themselves, caught up in the furor and coming to themselves too late to make a difference. Daphne had never seen a riot before, had certainly never been caught up in one before, and found it was not the sort of adventure she had had in mind for herself.

After a time, she descended to earth and walked through the paths that passed for streets in the bazaar, hoping a closer look might bring her success. Her memory of Fletcher's body lying shrouded in canvas propelled her forward. How strange, that remembering all that blood did not cause her vision to cloud over the way its actual presence did.

It should have cheered her, the idea that perhaps she might someday overcome her weakness, but the missing lieutenant dominated her thoughts and made it impossible for her to feel optimistic about anything.

She thought about asking the few people remaining in the bazaar if they had seen Wright, but their dull-eyed stares and uncomprehending faces dissuaded her. No one accosted her. Her friend, the elderly toothless woman, had vanished. Daphne hoped her wares had not been destroyed or stolen. She poked around the fallen stalls, hoping to find Wright, praying she would not find him in the state Fletcher had been in. Nothing.

Finally, despair filling her, she Skipped once more, high in the sky, and let herself fall, relishing the feeling of being light as air, then Bounding back to the Residence before she struck the ground at a fatal rate of speed. No one knew why momentum did not transfer through a Bound or a Skip, and Daphne had never cared enough to experiment. Her cousin Sophia would likely have made it her life's mission to discover the truth, had she been a Bounder rather than a Seer.

The drawing room was too crowded for an easy Bound, so Daphne went to the hall instead. The door to the drawing room was ajar, and smatterings of speech drifted through the gap, too quiet and fragmented for Daphne to comprehend their meaning. She stood still in the middle of the hall and let weariness drag her down, pulling on her arms and shoulders and bowing her neck. Her eyes, dry now, stared at the floor. The cobalt tiles did not shine, but were pitted with age and the ravages of the climate. A line of ants followed the groove between two of the tiles, marching from nowhere to nowhere. She envied the ants, who at least had some direction.

She ought to enter the drawing room, learn Fletcher's condition, but if he had died... that would be two deaths to her credit, two completely undeserving deaths. She could not even blame her weakness; she had simply failed to observe what was right before her, left him lying in a pool of his own blood while she walked past. Now the tears came, but she did not know whether she wept for him or, indulgently, for herself. She wanted nothing more than to sleep, and wake to find Ainsworth and Fletcher well and Wright miraculously reappeared... no, that was too much to hope for, even for her famous optimism.

The door opened more widely, and a Hindoo servant exited, bearing a metal bowl full of pink-tinged water. Daphne's vision started to swim, but she closed her eyes and firmly told herself, *It is nothing, just red water, you will not faint!* and the dizziness subsided. The servant bowed, no more than a low dip of the head that made the water barely wobble. "The sahibs are well, memsahib, very well," he said, crossing the hall to the courtyard and beyond.

Daphne faintly heard the slosh and splash of water being tossed outside, but the pounding of her heart overrode it. Both well? She took several measured steps toward the drawing room and opened the door fully.

Someone stood just beyond it, blocking her view of the room. She realized it was Major Schofeld just as he half-turned to see who had entered. "Lady Daphne!" he exclaimed. "You should not have exhausted yourself so. I was about to leave to search for you."

"I am quite well, Major, you need not trouble yourself." His presence annoyed her—Government House could not have found another Bounder?—but that annoyance, perversely, cheered her as well, gave her something to feel that was not abject despair. "Did you bring an Extraordinary Shaper?"

"From London, actually. Dr. Feligson has been most obliging." Schofeld stepped aside and took Daphne by the hand, drawing her into the room. It was fuller of people than it had when she had brought Fletcher back. Bess stood beside one of the windows, her head tilted back. Captain Ainsworth was sitting upright on one of the sofas, submitting to having his head bathed by a couple of Hindoo servants. And Fletcher—

Daphne realized she was holding her breath and let it out before the grey mist could claim her again. Fletcher lay unmoving on the sofa, his eyes closed and his face ashen beneath his tan. His bloody shirt was cut open, exposing his chest. A lanky man wearing the black hat of an Extraordinary Shaper knelt beside him, his hand spread palm-down on Fletcher's chest, which was unmarked by wound or blood. As Daphne watched, Fletcher's eyes fluttered open and he raised one hand to cover the Shaper's. Daphne gasped. Instantly Fletcher's eyes flicked toward her. A slow smile touched his lips, so warm and intimate that the tears started flowing again. He would not look at her that way if he knew how she had nearly failed him. She could not bear it if he did.

She resolutely looked away from him and crossed the room to where Bess stood. "I could not find Lieutenant Wright," she murmured. "Please tell me he has returned."

Bess lowered her head and opened her eyes. "He has not. Daphne, do not cry. He will return, or someone will... will bring him to us."

"You mean, bring his body. I have failed him."

"It is hardly your fault that he was caught up in the riot. You have done so much, Daphne. Captain Fletcher would be dead now if not for you."

She still could not bring herself to look at him. "Despite my failings, you mean. I walked past him—I did not even see him the first time, and he—"

"Stop that immediately," Bess said sharply. "If you insist on holding yourself to a standard of perfection the rest of us cannot meet, I will never speak to you again. Your talent saved our lives. Be grateful for that, and leave off blaming yourself for what you cannot help."

"I—"

"Be grateful, Daphne."

Daphne closed her lips on another objection. "Very well," she said, tucking her private shame away, "what more can I do?"

Bess laughed. "Daphne, you have without a doubt the most overdeveloped sense of duty of anyone I have ever met! Do you not believe that perhaps you have earned some rest?"

"I am not tired."

Bess took a more careful look at her. "Daphne, you are shaking. I believe you should sit down."

"I am not—" Daphne's knees trembled, and she caught herself on the windowsill. "I should sit down," she concluded.

"Are you in need?" said the Shaper, looking up from where he was tending to Fletcher.

"I imagine I just need to rest." Daphne's stomach growled, making Bess laugh again. "And eat, it seems."

"You have exerted yourself more than enough for one day," Fletcher said. His voice was as strong as ever, though his skin still had an ashen tint to it. "I owe you my life."

"I did not—that is, please do not be grateful, it makes me feel so uncomfortable, like having a weight pressing down on me, though it is not as if I resent having—oh, please, may we speak of something else?"

"Very well," said Fletcher. "What can you tell me of the riot?"

"You expect Lady Daphne to give you information, after what she has been through?" Schofeld exclaimed. "I might have known it would be your only concern, Fletcher."

"If Captain Fletcher respects my intelligence enough to ask such a thing, I hardly imagine you are entitled to object," Daphne shot back. "I appreciate your concern, Major, but pray, do not try to protect me from myself."

Schofeld's face went ruddy with suppressed indignation. Daphne heard Bess make an indelicate sound of amusement. "I would prefer you not discuss serious matters, Captain," said the Shaper. "You have lost a great deal of blood and endured a serious Healing, and you need rest and food, not in that order."

"You rob me entirely of conversational gambits," Fletcher said. "Perhaps it would be better if I retired." He moved as if to stand, but shook so badly he could only fall back onto the cushions.

"No walking for a day," the Shaper said. "You will not be capable of it, at any rate."

"Then how am I to achieve my bed?" Fletcher asked, arching one eyebrow with a sardonic air.

"I would be happy to convey you," Schofeld said.

Daphne managed not to make a dismayed sound. "You do not know the essence of the captain's room," she objected.

"Neither do you—or at least I assume you do not know anything so improper," Schofeld replied. Daphne had no answer for that. She caught Fletcher looking at her, his expression unreadable, but she could guess what he was thinking: he had no recourse to prevent Schofeld touching him, and could not in decency request that Daphne convey him.

"I will be just a moment," Schofeld said, "if one of you Hindoos will direct me to Fletcher's room."

The two servants remaining exchanged glances, and one of them bowed and left the room. Schofeld followed him. Daphne wished she dared ask Fletcher what she should do. If Schofeld decided to torment Fletcher, just after he had been Healed, how much would that worsen his condition? Surely even Schofeld could not be so cruel. But Fletcher was looking at the Shaper, who was speaking to him in a low voice, and she could not think of a way to justify interrupting that conversation.

The door opened again. "Ah, Lady Daphne, I did not realize you had returned," Sir Rodney said. "You deserve praise for your efforts today. I had no idea the extent of your talent—my dear, are you quite well? You look very pale. Pray tell me you have not overexerted yourself."

Daphne's stomach rumbled again. "I am very hungry, Sir Rodney. Is there anything to eat?"

"I have just been having a word with the cook. Apparently food is the sovereign remedy, or so Dr. Feligson there tells me! But you should away to your bed, and I will have a tray sent up. No, no, it's no use arguing with me, the doctor will support me in this."

"But Lieutenant Wright—he is still—"

"There is nothing more you can do for him, Daphne," Bess said, laying a gentle hand on her shoulder. "Go to bed."

"I will go as soon as Captain Fletcher and Captain Ainsworth are settled," Daphne said.

"Oh, I am quite well, just a bump really," Ainsworth said, "but I'm just as happy for a rest. Don't worry, Lady Daphne, Wright is a tough nut and no mistake. I'm sure he will arrive soon."

With a faint *whoosh*, Schofeld appeared in the center of the room. "If you're ready, Fletcher, I'm prepared to convey you directly to your room," he said. Daphne watched him closely, but there was no malice in his expression, nothing sinister at all. Fletcher, for his part, looked perfectly calm.

"My thanks, Schofeld" was all he said before the major scooped him up off the sofa and vanished with a *pop*. Daphne clenched her fists tight against the impulse to run to Fletcher's room and assure herself of his safety. Everything would be well. Fletcher was alive, and her weakness had not cost any of them their lives.

"I will go now," she said, "but please do send food soon," and she Bounded to her bedchamber. It was almost more than she could handle in her weakened condition; had Bess been in the room, it might have been impossible. She lay on her bed without removing her Bounder uniform, though she would no doubt be more comfortable in her shift. Undressing felt too much like work.

A few minutes later, Bess appeared, carrying a tray from which emanated the most delicious smells. "Sir Rodney apologizes, but this is all that was immediately ready, and Dr. Feligson told him you needed to eat right away, no waiting on 'proper' food. I had not the heart to tell him you would likely prefer this." She set the tray on the bed beside Daphne, who inhaled deeply the aromas of saffron and ginger rising off the pile of rice and the bowl of thick orange stew. A stack of *rotis,* steaming hot, lay beside the plate.

Daphne snatched a *roti* up and began scooping stew into her mouth far more quickly than was good table manners. "Oh," she moaned through a mouthful of food, "I wish I could eat like this every day, it is so delicious."

"You have positively gone native," Bess teased, taking a seat on her own bed opposite. "Try not to choke, I do not believe an Extraordinary Shaper can do anything about that."

Daphne nodded, but slowed her intake only a little. Two *rotis* and half the bowl later, she said, "I feel so much less ravenous now, and more rational. Of course it is not my fault Lieutenant Wright disappeared."

"See? You can be sensible. And you saved four lives today, five if you count your own. I believe Government House can hardly object to having sent you here."

Daphne's cheeks reddened. "I did not do it to be thanked."

"No, but you should permit people to be grateful, Daphne, it creates the most terrible spiritual imbalance if you do not."

"Is that a Hindoo philosophy, Bess?"

"No, it is all my own thinking. But I will not burden you with my gratitude, if you do not wish it."

"Thank you." Daphne went back to eating, more slowly now. "I hope Captain Fletcher is well."

"He very nearly was not. Dr. Feligson performed a miracle. He is lucky to be abed for just one day."

Daphne tried not to remember how pale he had been, how still. "I am so glad."

Bess said nothing. Daphne glanced at her and said, "You are not going to tease me again, are you? Because I hardly believe this is the time."

"No teasing. I simply saw how he looked at you. Daphne—"

"You *are* teasing me!"

"How, teasing, when I believe he is falling in love with you?"

Daphne busied herself with her rice. "Then I will have to dissuade him."

"You do not know the captain as I do. He is not the sort of man who changes his mind easily." Bess stood and took the bowl away from Daphne, forcing her to look at her. "Daphne—"

"I will not tell you I have—that I do not feel an attraction. But it would mean giving up everything I dreamed of doing, to permit myself to fall in love!"

"Are you certain of that?"

"Of course I am. What husband would permit his wife to Bound all over creation, exploring new countries and having adventures while he stayed quietly at home?"

"The right kind of husband?"

"No kind I have ever encountered." Daphne set the tray on the floor. "I almost regret agreeing to this assignment."

"You do not."

"I did say 'almost.'" Daphne removed her uniform and put on a fresh shift, then lay back down on her bed, kicking the netting out of the way. "I feel I could sleep for a thousand years."

"You will sleep for two hours, at which point you will be hungry again," Bess said. Daphne, already most of the way toward sleep, waved a languid hand at her friend, then drifted off entirely.

CHAPTER 13

IN WHICH THE
INVESTIGATION IS STALLED

Daphne woke to hands shaking her. "Daphne. Daphne! Lieutenant Wright has returned!"

In her sleep-fogged state, she could not at first remember who Lieutenant Wright was or what he might have returned from. Then she gripped Bess's hands and blinked up at her friend. "Returned, or been returned?"

"He walked in not two minutes ago. He received a blow to the head that left him unconscious for a long time, but a Hindoo dragged him to safety and watched over him until he woke. Sir Rodney expressed his gratitude to the man on all our behalf, but he would not stay to be thanked." Bess sank onto the edge of Daphne's bed and clasped her hands together. "The lieutenant seems perfectly recovered, though I believe his head still aches, because he is unusually quiet."

Daphne rose and hunted through her trunk for a gown. "I must see him. I feel so—all right, I promised I would not feel guilty, and I do not, it is just that I will not be perfectly comfortable until I see for myself that he is well."

"He is in the drawing room. He expressed a desire to speak with Captain Fletcher, but I believe the captain is sleeping at present, and anyway Dr. Feligson said he was not to discuss business until tomorrow."

"I had forgotten. What time is it?"

"Nearly five o'clock. I intended to wake you for dinner in a few minutes. Oh, Daphne, what a day this has been!"

Daphne presented her back to Bess to have her gown fastened. "It has been quite the adventure, not that I wished to have adventures in which my friends are nearly killed. Is Major Schofeld still here?"

"He returned Dr. Feligson to London an hour ago. Daphne, do you feel some animosity toward the major? Your behavior to him is always unusually cold."

"Have I never told you? He mocked me cruelly three years ago, when I attempted to induce the War Office to take me on early, and he thought it the most tremendous joke that should have amused me as well. I cannot forgive him for it. And now he wishes to treat me like I am made of spun sugar, too delicate to face the challenges of Bounding for the War Office. So, yes, I feel some animosity toward him."

"Daphne! But surely it was just teasing. He always behaves toward you with the greatest civility and admiration."

"Perhaps he meant no ill, but he—they all treated me with such disrespect, as if I were nothing, as if my *talent* were nothing. I do not see how he should be forgiven that simply because his intentions were not evil."

"I... well, that is true. Can you not simply confront him, instead of permitting him to go on believing nothing is amiss?"

"I wish I dared challenge him, but I fear it would only make me sound shrewish. So I hope to avoid him, and—he is always so flattering, as if he wishes us to be friends, which is impossible."

They walked arm in arm down the passageway to the drawing room. The air was close and muggy, promising a late storm—when would these monsoons be over? Daphne felt her hair was permanently damp from the weather. "Well, I will distract him from you as best I can," Bess promised.

Daphne pushed open the door to the drawing room, interrupting a conversation between Sir Rodney and Captain Ainsworth. Lieutenant Wright sat on the sofa near them, as indrawn as Daphne had ever seen him. His face was pinched and pale, and he moved as if his head ached. He looked up when they entered, and a ghost of a smile touched his lips, brightening his light blue eyes. "Lady Daphne," he said, his voice unnaturally husky. "I understand you exhausted yourself searching for me. I apologize for giving you so much trouble."

"I am simply so glad to see you, Lieutenant," Daphne said, sinking down on the sofa next to him. "You were sheltered by a Hindoo during the riot?"

"Yes, and he refused to take any reward," Sir Rodney said. "Damnedest—I mean, most extraordinary thing, that. Not at all what these people are usually like."

"I likely would have died without his aid," Wright said. He coughed, cleared his throat, and went on in a voice more like himself, "I understand Captain Fletcher nearly did die. We were all very lucky."

"Luck and Lady Daphne," Phillips said. He leaned against the wall near one of the windows that was well-shuttered against the sun. "It was so sudden. One minute Captain Ainsworth and I were talking to a stall owner, the next we were surrounded by screaming maniacs."

"That is what I saw, Ensign," Daphne said. "I was following someone, and something broke, and it was as if a signal had gone off, sending everyone into a frenzy."

"You were following someone?" Ainsworth said. "Who?"

"I don't know. I had seen him before today, and he seemed to be following us—I have no idea what I intended to do if I caught him, as he was Hindoo and likely could not understand my language—but it was all so mysterious I could not ignore it."

"You should not have wandered off alone, Lady Daphne," Wright said. "Suppose you were attacked?"

"I *was* attacked, Lieutenant, I was in the thick of where the riot started, in case you had forgotten. War Office Bounders are taught methods of escaping captivity, in case someone attempts to hold us against our will. Not that I wished to be in a situation to make use of them. But I regret not telling Captain Fletcher about the man. Had he come with me, we might have apprehended the stranger and discovered why he was following us."

Wright massaged his temple, which bore a spectacular bruise and lump. "He might have had evil designs on you or Miss Hanley."

"Do not frighten the ladies, Wright," Ainsworth said. "More likely he did not like that we were asking so many questions. Suppose he was involved in the false rumors about the missionaries?"

"It seems unlikely we will ever know, unless we are willing to trail round the bazaar again to draw him out," Wright said. "I believe that would be unwise."

"Should we not wait to have this discussion until Captain Fletcher is well enough to join us?" Daphne said. "He is the one who most needs to know what each of us has learned."

"I believe Lady Daphne is correct," said Phillips. "No doubt the captain learned more than any of us."

"In that case, I believe we should go in to dinner," Sir Rodney said.

The meal was a quiet affair, as if conversation were too much effort. Once or twice Bess tilted her head back to Speak to someone, but only for a few seconds at a time, and she did not share the details with the others. It was not until everyone was nearly finished that she said, "Government House tells me they are sending a regiment for the protection of the Residence."

"It's about time," Sir Rodney said. "All this unrest... suppose one of these riots leads to an attack here? We've not the resources to defend the place, given the size of the force stationed here. Madhyapatnam has been peaceful until recently."

"It will take them most of a week to arrive, and Colonel Dalhousie's Speaker tells me we are to remain in the Residence until that time. The colonel wishes to minimize the risk of our faces inflaming public unrest."

"But we will never be able to determine who is causing the actual unrest if we stay holed up in here!" Ainsworth exclaimed. "There is no guarantee there will be no more rioting just because we don't show our faces in public."

"I understand that, Captain, I am merely relaying orders."

"Of course." Ainsworth subsided, chastened. "It is hardly your fault if they are senseless orders."

"It will only be for a week," Wright said. "We can endure one another's company for a week." He had filled his plate a second time; apparently he was as hungry as Daphne felt.

"I would be happy to bring books, or cards," Daphne said, though she quailed at the thought of being cooped up playing cards for a week. How tedious.

"That's true, Lady Daphne, you are not confined as the rest of us will be," Phillips said. "We should be grateful they do not order you to take all of us back to Calcutta. After this riot, I find myself more eager to discover who is behind this mayhem."

"If we can still investigate," Wright said.

"Captain Fletcher will know," Daphne said, "and tomorrow will look different."

She agreed to play cards with Bess and Phillips and Ainsworth after dinner. Wright, pleading fatigue and a head-ache, went upstairs to his room. Sir Rodney smoked his pipe, which filled the room with its smelly fumes, and commented on the play until Daphne was ready to Bound anywhere but there. Finally, after several hands, she declared she was tired again and would go to bed.

With Bess choosing to remain in the drawing room with a book held close to her weak eyes, Daphne Bounded to her bedroom and changed into a nightgown. But sleep eluded her. She lay atop the blankets, staring at where the netting hung from the ceiling in a great tent surrounding her, and tried to quiet her fevered brain. Government House could not possibly expect them all to simply stay inside the Residence, ignoring the fact that someone was stirring up mischief in Madhyapatnam—mischief that had nearly got them all killed. Well, pointing out that fact likely would get them all returned to Calcutta for their safety, or at least get Bess and Daphne returned there, so perhaps that was not the best line of argument. She wished she could speak to Fletcher, who would no doubt be able to think of a better one, but he needed rest more than he needed to solve this problem.

She remembered how he had looked at her when he woke, remembered his smile, and a shiver went through her. It had not been the smile of someone who thought of her as only a friend. To her chagrin, it was a smile she wished to see again. That was impossible. If he was, in fact, falling in love with her, it was her duty to speak gently to him, explaining why she could not return his affections. The thought made her heart ache with a dull, numb pain that made sleep even more evasive.

Finally, she rolled out of bed and sat at the room's one writing desk, took out pen and paper, and wrote *Dearest Mama and Papa, I am*—her mind stuttered to a halt. So much to say, so much she could not tell them; it would do them no good to know the danger she had been in that day. She tapped the pen nib against the paper, leaving a trail of tiny dots. *I am well. I have made many friends, and India is beautiful, though very hot.* Such a sad, tepid letter, but she could not tell her parents what was in her heart: *Mama, I am falling in love with someone you likely would not approve of. He is merely a captain and no one the daughter of a marquess ought even consider.* Yet she knew that was not the real reason; inheritance law said she, an Extraordinary and her father's heir, might marry anyone she chose and elevate his standing rather than lowering her own. And her parents, who had given her everything she had ever asked for, wanted only for her to be happy.

She looked at the bland line she had written, and a flash of passionate anger swept through her. *Mama,* she wrote, *I am falling in love when I swore I would not, and I wish I had your counsel.* She crumpled the paper into a ball and tossed it on the floor.

It occurred to her that she might Bound home, only for a few minutes, throw her arms around her mother and tell her everything. It was against the War Office's regulations; Bounders took oath not to visit their families during their term of service, so they would not be distracted from their duties. But here, so far from the War Office, no one would ever know. Her parents would never tell. And she had never felt so lost and alone as she did right then.

She kicked the crumpled ball of paper across the room. *She* would know. And if she did it once, she would be tempted to do it again, because there would always be one more excellent justification. No, she would remain in the Residence, however her heart ached.

She climbed back into bed, closed her eyes, and called to mind the symbol of the Bounding Chamber in the War Office in Lisbon. She traced it out in her memory until it was as fresh as the day she had first seen it. Next, she thought of the Bounding Chamber in Marvell Hall, disused now that she could Bound to her own bedroom and her favorite sitting room. She recalled symbol after symbol until her mind, exhausted by the exercise, allowed her to sleep.

SHE WOKE EARLY THE FOLLOWING MORNING FEELING REFRESHED AS she had not felt for days, refreshed and ravenously hungry. She dressed quietly, not liking to disturb Bess, and Bounded to the hallway rather than open the bedroom door, which stuck in the humid heat and squealed when opened wider than a crack.

Breakfast, a proper English breakfast, was already laid out on the sideboard, the dishes well-covered against insects. To her astonishment, Fletcher sat at the table, his plate piled high with food, eating with the kind of devotion normally associated with religious ecstasy. "Captain!" Daphne exclaimed. "Should you be up already?"

"I woke half an hour ago to a stomach that was persuaded it had been abandoned for a week," Fletcher said, "and the rest of my body declined to argue with it. I feel very well, in fact, just hungry."

"I feel the same, Captain—that is, of course I was not Healed, but I exerted myself to the limits of my capacity, and you know how that makes me hungry."

"I believe I now understand that state better. Eat, please, and we can converse later." He smiled, that same warm, intimate smile, and her heart turned over in her chest. She quickly moved to the sideboard and helped herself to eggs and sausage, grateful that she did not have to look at him while doing so.

She dithered briefly about where to sit—she could not sit beside him, that was too intimate, but sitting across from him left her open to the full effect of his smiles—and ultimately took the seat at the head of the table, reasoning that Sir Rodney was unlikely to rise at this hour and demand she vacate it. Fletcher continued to make inroads on his plate, so she consumed her food in silence, as painfully conscious of his presence as if he had been a tiger sprawled beside her. She had not yet seen a tiger, which was probably for the best, though she could Bound away from one before it could attack her.

Even so, they were supposed to be magnificently beautiful, and she wished—

"Ah," Fletcher said, exhaling and startling her out of her reverie. "I daresay I may never eat again. I wonder if all Shaping leaves one so ravenous."

"You feel well, then?"

"I would not volunteer to run a footrace, but I believe I can manage to remain seated for at least an hour without resorting to my bed."

"Then—has anyone told you of Government House's instructions?"

Fletcher frowned. "I have seen no one save you since Schofeld took me to my bed yesterday afternoon." A flicker of distaste crossed his face when he said the name.

"Oh! Did he—was he objectionable?"

"Only in the spiritual sense. We may detest each other, but even Schofeld has his limits. He did not intrude upon my sensibilities."

"I am so glad. I could not imagine any way—of course I should not convey you—"

"Of course not. And you should not shoulder that burden. I don't need protecting, Lady Daphne."

Daphne lowered her gaze. "Forgive me, Captain."

"You saved my life. There is very little I would not forgive you."

She was afraid to look up, afraid of where this conversation was going. "Government House has ordered us to remain in the Residence until the regiment they have sent arrives."

"No." Fletcher pushed away from the table and stood, wobbling enough that Daphne almost reached out to steady him. She remembered in time that he would find that embarrassing and refrained.

"Captain, what do you intend?" she said.

"I intend to argue with Colonel Dalhousie until he sees sense." He held onto the table's edge until the wobbling stopped, then held out a hand to Daphne. "Take me to Government House, please."

"Captain, I do not believe you are in a condition—"

"I am well enough for this. Unless you agree with them that we should hide ourselves away like children? I have learned too much to give up now."

She recognized the determined look on his face; she had seen it in her own mirror more times than she cared to count. "Very well, Captain, but you should not exert yourself," she said, stepping toward him.

"As I said, Lady Daphne, I don't need protecting."

"I saved your life yesterday, Captain, I believe that gives me some interest in your continued well-being. Unless you wish to kill yourself through over-exertion and invalidate my actions."

He laughed, and put his arms around her shoulders. "Point well made, Lady Daphne. I promise not to exert myself."

Daphne lifted him, and in an instant they were in the over-warm confines of the Bounding Chamber Daphne knew so well. "Shall I wait for you, Captain?"

"No, come with me. I may need your support. Not physically, don't look at me that way, but your actions saved us yesterday, and I may need to remind the colonel that we are not helpless in Madhyapatnam."

This cheered Daphne, and she followed Fletcher through the halls, which even at this hour were busy with men and a few women hurrying from place to place. Some of them saluted Fletcher, who returned their salutes with a breezy one of his own. Daphne wondered as she had not before why Fletcher was still only a captain, when Schofeld, whom she judged to be of an age with him, was a major. Promotion was by seniority, but surely Fletcher had that?

She had never been to Colonel Dalhousie's offices before, and discovered they looked similar to Lord Moira's, though the furnishings were of English oak rather than ebony. Fletcher rapped smartly on a door, ignoring the protests of the aide whose desk was just outside, and opened it without waiting for a response. Daphne followed him without looking at the aide, fearing if she met his eyes, he might insist on her waiting outside, and she detested waiting for things.

Colonel Dalhousie was just rising from his desk when they entered. He was a lean man of middle height, almost gaunt, with thick grey hair done in the style of thirty years previous, though it was unpowdered as such a hairstyle would have been. "I had a feeling I would be hearing from you this morning," he said, extending a hand to Fletcher, "though I had imagined you would send word via Miss Hanley first."

"I chose not to disturb her sleep, and Lady Daphne was willing," Fletcher said. "What's this I hear about you sending troops, Jack?"

"You disagree with my decision?"

"Not at all. The Residence is under-defended and Sir Rodney could use the men. But requiring me to stay in the Residence while I wait for the troops to arrive... it's poor strategy."

Dalhousie's eyes flashed irritation. "Telling me my business again, Finn?"

"You know I swore I'd never lie to you. Someone is stirring up trouble in Madhyapatnam, and I am close to discovering who that is. If I can pull his teeth—you know what will happen if you have to order those troops to attack Hindoo civilians. Give me time, Jack."

Dalhousie seemed to notice Daphne for the first time. "Lady Daphne," he said, "I understand you saved this fellow's life yesterday. Do you judge him competent?"

"Oh!" Flustered, Daphne said, "It is not as if I know—he is well, mostly, if that is what you mean—but I have never met anyone more competent than the captain, sir."

"High praise indeed." Dalhousie regarded both of them in turn. "You might just make things worse," he said to Fletcher.

"Whoever this is, he's still stirring up trouble, and that won't stop just because my people are in hiding," Fletcher said. "Me investigating isn't going to make a difference in that respect."

Dalhousie turned his attention on Daphne. "I ought to require you and Miss Hanley to return," he said. "Phillips is a capable Speaker, and I can find a Bounder to take your place—"

"I have already proved my usefulness, Colonel," Daphne said quickly. "Miss Hanley and I are in no danger, if that is what worries you."

"I would prefer to continue working with Miss Hanley and Lady Daphne," Fletcher said, as coolly as if it didn't matter to him one way or the other. "Of course, I will bow to your wishes."

To her surprise, Dalhousie burst out laughing. "Just like all the other times, eh?" he said when he finally regained control of himself.

"Go on. Get back to Madhyapatnam. And I want daily updates—me, personally, do you understand? I expect to hear from Miss Hanley regularly."

"Thank you, sir," Fletcher said formally, but with a grin that told Daphne that despite the difference in their ages, the two men were close friends. Dalhousie bowed to Daphne, who curtseyed, and she and Fletcher exited the office, once more ignoring the aide, who looked apoplectic at being bypassed.

"I did not know you were such good friends with the colonel," Daphne ventured when they were back in the hallway.

"He is my father's best friend, and my sponsor," Fletcher said. "I respect him more than any man I know, save my father, of course."

"I see." Tentatively, she added, "Your name... Finn is Irish, is it not?"

"It's short for Phineas. We are as English as they come—but that doesn't disturb you, does it?"

"I merely wondered—Lord Moira is an Irish lord, and I thought perhaps you might have things in common..." Daphne could not remember where that sentence had been going, and let it die a merciful death.

"I was named for my uncle." Fletcher steered her toward an unused room so she might have some privacy when they Bounded. She was touched at his consideration. She did not care who she conveyed, but there were those who believed it was improper for a woman Bounder to take a man as a passenger and might be willing to chastise her for it. "Back to the Residence, and then we shall make further plans."

Daphne tried not to feel self-conscious at the feeling of his arms around her shoulders. She Bounded them back to the drawing room, which was empty, and Fletcher released her and sat on one of the sofas a little too rapidly. His face was ashen again under his tan, and he leaned back and closed his eyes, breathing as heavily as if he'd been running.

"Oh, Captain, you promised!" she exclaimed.

"I am well, I just—all right, I am not well, I can feel you looking daggers at me. It was unexpected, that is all, and I simply need to sit for a while. Join me, Lady Daphne, I cannot relax while you hover."

Daphne took a seat adjacent to him, perched on the edge and prepared to leap forward to catch him if he fainted. Fletcher opened one eye and smiled at her. "I promise not to faint," he said.

"You also promised not to exert yourself. You are a terrible judge of your own condition."

"I will be more careful in future. Now, I imagine you are eager to hear what I learned at the bazaar, before the riot."

"I am not *eager*, exactly, just—I am filled with great anticipation to know your information."

"I believe that is one definition of the word 'eager,' Lady Daphne."

"Very well, if you wish to discuss linguistics rather than tell me, I shall leave this room and you will have no one to tease."

Fletcher laughed. "Thank you for putting me in my place."

"You are welcome. Now, what did you learn?"

The laughter died away. "Nothing good," he said. "I begin to suspect we are chasing a ghost."

CHAPTER 14

IN WHICH DAPHNE RECEIVES A WARNING FROM AN UNEXPECTED SOURCE

"Y ou do not mean that literally," Daphne said.

"Of course not. But our man—or group of men, it is not clear one way or the other—our man, as I say, has left very little of himself in the actions he is fomenting. I can only surmise his existence based on the events that have taken place."

"Because it would take an actual person to start a rumor as specific as European missionaries preaching in Madhyapatnam?"

"Precisely. And because a riot always has an inciting incident, usually one person performing an act of violence."

"You have seen riots before, Captain?"

"Unfortunately, too many." Fletcher's color was returning, but he looked so grim he might as well still have been on the verge of unconsciousness. "What disturbs me is that I have been unable to discover *why* someone might want Madhyapatnam in turmoil. Sir Rodney is... not *well-liked*, exactly—that would imply a measure of comradeship that rarely exists between Hindoo and Englishman—but well-tolerated, and those working for him say they are treated fairly. So as a representative of England in India, he is an acceptable one. And the Company's presence here has improved trade and enriched Madhyapatnam."

"Except that at least one person does not feel this way."

"True, and that is why I suspect whoever our enemy is has resources beyond his individual ones. I believe we are looking for one man who has power over others, to direct them to do his bidding. Starting a riot is difficult if you want to maintain any degree of control over how and where it starts. A lone man would find that nearly impossible."

"I thought you said a riot has a single inciting incident."

"Usually, yes, but simply smashing a stall in the bazaar, for example, is not enough. The crowd must be nudged toward a state of incipient violence, to the point that smashing the right stall will set them off. But it is irrelevant, now that the danger has passed."

"You suppose there will be no more riots?"

"I believe I am not in a position to thwart them if they occur. If I were an Extraordinary rather than a mere Discerner, I might be able to predict one before it starts, but that is impossible for me."

"I thought Extraordinary Discerners were incapacitated, like the king."

"They can be, if they lack the self-mastery to distinguish between their own emotions and those of everyone around them. Not that I wish to criticize the king—there is no doubt much more to it than I've implied, and it took years for his talent to grow to a point that it could overwhelm him. But an Extraordinary Discerner has tremendous power, if he remains in control. Sensing threats before they materialize, easily identifying a lie, knowing who may be most easily swayed by argument or persuasion... I can imagine what it must be like, barely."

"But you can do all those things."

"On an individual basis, and with a touch, yes. I am an experienced interrogator for that reason."

"Unless the other person—that is, I do not mean to bring up—you did say you could be overwhelmed."

Fletcher laughed. "I am not so sensitive as to feel embarrassed at the least mention of my weakness, Lady Daphne. Yes, I can be overwhelmed, but it happens rarely."

Daphne's cheeks felt hot. "I beg your pardon, Captain, I did not mean—"

"I know. You are generous of spirit to mind so much on my behalf. It is one of the many things I admire about you."

She had to look away from him, how warm and knowing his expression was. "I—thank you, Captain, but I am not so admirable as that—and pray do not take that as an invitation to reassure me, I am simply being honest. I believe most people have faults they wish they could eliminate from their characters."

"And I believe those faults should not blind us to our virtues. Though if it would make you happier, you can tell me your faults and I will properly castigate you for them."

She swiftly raised her head and caught him smiling at her, his eyes filled with wicked amusement, and she laughed despite herself. "Captain, you are teasing me again."

"I enjoy seeing you smile, so I will not apologize."

They were venturing into dangerous terrain with this conversation. Surely they were on the verge of something far more intimate than this enjoyable... flirtation, it was flirtation, how had she allowed herself to be drawn in? Her heart was pounding so hard he must surely hear it. She could not allow it to continue. "How do you know when someone is lying?" she said.

Fletcher looked momentarily confused, then the amusement faded, making him appear emotionless, and Daphne felt a pang, as if he had slapped her. "It is a matter of differences," he said. "People who are lying have a... disparity, I suppose, between word and emotion, but it is a particular kind of disparity. It is not something I can explain to a non-Discerner."

"I understand. There are things only another Bounder will understand about Bounding." She had offended him, she could tell, and she longed to turn back the clock and make a different decision—but what else could she do, and remain herself? Falling in love would only ruin her plans for fame and success. "So what will you do now? What investigation will you pursue, I mean?"

"I don't know," Fletcher said. "I will discuss it with the others, and we will make a decision. It may require some travel, if you don't mind."

"Of course not. I am always happy to oblige you, Captain."

Fletcher said nothing to that, but his lips went thin and hard as if he were restraining some powerful urge to speak. He stood, saying, "I believe I will rest a little longer. Please excuse me."

Daphne stood watching the door after he had gone. Her heart ached with a terrible dull pain she tried to tell herself was healthy. Of course it would hurt to deny herself the pleasure of those warm, intimate smiles, but it would hurt more to be denied the adventures she had waited so long for. It was for the best. For both of them, in the long run.

She wanted to see the bazaar again, to learn whether it had been rebuilt—if that was the correct word for restoring sticks and canvas to their original shapes—but did not like to go alone, and did not want to disturb Fletcher. He clearly needed rest, even if he could barely bring himself to admit it. So she sat in the drawing room, pretending to read, until Bess came in an hour later. "I did not know I enjoyed seeing the sights of India until they were forbidden me," she said, taking a seat next to Daphne. "Surely *you* are not going to simply sit still and do nothing for a week?"

"We will not have to. Captain Fletcher has persuaded Colonel Dalhousie to permit him to continue to investigate."

"He has? Meaning that you Bounded him there this morning. Well, that is something, though it still does not answer the question of what you and I can do to contribute."

"I am certain Captain Fletcher will think of something."

Bess adjusted her spectacles and leaned well over to peer at Daphne's face. "Something has troubled you."

"It is nothing. I am simply impatient for the captain's return. He chose to rest for a while—he is not fully well—"

"And something passed between you, I can tell. Daphne—"

"I tell you, it is nothing." Daphne put her book down and rose, walking to the window and pushing open one of the shutters. "The colonel expects daily reports from you to him directly."

"Do not imagine you can put me off so easily." Bess made her way across the room to stand next to Daphne. "If he—"

"Memsahib?" One of the servants Daphne recognized as a sort of porter—she did not know the actual name for his position—knocked diffidently on the door frame. "Memsahib, is visitor."

Daphne and Bess exchanged glances. "Do you mean me?" Daphne said, pointing at herself.

The man nodded. "Is visitor outside," he added, bowing and gesturing down the hall.

"How odd," Daphne said.

"I will come with you," Bess said. "Suppose it is our enemy, and he means you harm?"

"I hardly believe whoever it is would strike so directly at me." But Daphne was not as sure of that as she sounded. She was glad for Bess's companionship as they followed the servant to the grand front door. Daphne had never yet used it, having mostly Bounded in and out of the Residence and exiting through its side door. Its dark wood was carved with fanciful images, presumably Hindoo in origin, and it made Daphne curious about who had built the Residence. The building itself was so very English, but with touches that made it clear it was built for the Indian climate—not at all like Government House, which looked like a European palace with no concessions to the tropical heat.

Two people waited in the courtyard, which was shaded by low-spreading coralwood trees. Daphne recognized one of them instantly: it was the elderly Seer who had sold her the ivory bracelet she wore even now. The other woman was much younger, possibly even younger than Daphne, her hair long and braided down her back. Both wore very plain robes of brown Indian cotton and no shoes, but were adorned with elaborate brass necklaces and earrings. The younger woman wore a delicate ring in her nose; Daphne wondered how that might feel, or what she did when she sneezed.

Upon seeing Daphne, the old woman's face creased in a broad smile. She stepped forward and took Daphne's hands in both of hers, speaking rapidly in Hindoo. "I beg your pardon, I don't understand," Daphne said, reluctant to pull her hands away and offend the woman.

Bess said something to the younger woman in Persian. The woman shook her head. She looked sheepish, as if she had been dragooned into performing a service that deeply embarrassed her. She spoke to her companion—mother, grandmother? She was old enough to possibly be a *great*-grandmother—in tones that sounded urgent. The elderly woman stopped speaking and turned away from Daphne to say something insistent. The young woman shook her head vigorously and tried to pry her fingers off Daphne's.

"Wait," Daphne said. "Bess, please ask Captain Fletcher to come here."

"I have just done so," Bess said. "She seems most insistent. I hope she does not want the bracelet back."

"Unlikely," Daphne said. If her hands had been free, though, she would have pushed up her sleeve to display the bracelet. It was the only thing the two of them had in common, and why otherwise would the woman be so determined to speak with her?

"Lady Daphne," said Fletcher from behind her, "you need a translator?"

"I may need more than that, Captain, as I cannot imagine why she wishes to speak to me."

Fletcher came to stand beside Daphne, bowing politely to the elderly woman. He said something, cutting across her stream of words. The old woman turned her attention on him, though she did not release Daphne's hands. The young woman said something that sounded apologetic. Fletcher bowed again and pointed at Daphne, saying something that included her name, then introduced Bess and himself. The younger woman stopped trying to back away and gestured at herself and the elderly woman.

"She says her name is Chaaya and her grandmother is Gopika," Fletcher said. "I have invited them inside, but Chaaya refuses. Do you mind sitting on the ground?"

"Not at all," Daphne said. She sat, rather awkwardly, finally retrieving her hands from Gopika's grip. The minute her skirts were settled modestly about her, Gopika took her hands again, holding them far more tightly than Daphne would have guessed possible. Her hands were bony and age-spotted, but strong, and her skin was darker than her granddaughter's. Daphne smiled and tried not to feel nervous at how intently Gopika stared at her.

Chaaya began speaking, her eyes demurely lowered. Fletcher translated, "She apologizes for intruding on the English sahibs' house, but her grandmother insisted, and Gopika is formidable when she wants something—that last is my own assessment," he added.

"Is there something I can do for Gopika?" Daphne asked.

The question, once translated, made Chaaya squirm nervously. She responded with many pauses, as if searching for words that would not be offensive. "Gopika wishes to warn you of her Dream," Fletcher said. "She says you are bright—it means, of a fiery spirit, one who sheds light everywhere she walks—and do not deserve destruction."

"Destruction?" Daphne said.

Fletcher spoke a long stream of syllables aimed at Gopika. She eyed him speculatively, then Daphne, and asked a question. Fletcher shook his head in negation. Gopika released one of Daphne's hands to shake a finger at Fletcher, saying something that had Chaaya blushing and trying to capture Gopika's hand and stop it waving about. Gopika twisted away from her grasp.

"Captain, what is she saying?" Daphne demanded.

"She believes I am not properly respectful of you," Fletcher said, but too rapidly, telling Daphne there was something he was not translating fully. Daphne resolved to brace him with it later.

Gopika went on, overriding her granddaughter's attempts to break in. "Gopika says there are evil spirits afoot in Madhyapatnam," Fletcher said, translating as she spoke. "They are trying to disrupt the city. Someone wants... the past to return?" He asked a question to which Gopika only shrugged. "I am not certain what she means by that. It sounds as if she is talking about a restoration, like making a place fertile soil for a particular kind of seed, but in context it makes no sense."

"Does she believe we are in danger?"

"Yes," Fletcher said when this question was relayed. "The evil spirits intend us harm because we interfere with the restoration."

"And she wants us to leave Madhyapatnam."

"No," Fletcher says, "she wants us to fight. She says you, Lady Daphne, are too strong to permit the evil to overcome you, and the evil will overwhelm—no, will immerse the city like a flood. She tells everyone she speaks to, but they ignore her or are part of the evil. So she has come to you instead."

"Captain Fletcher, how is this possible? There are no such things as evil spirits!"

"Just a moment, Lady Daphne." Fletcher listened closely to Gopika, who seemed to be winding down. He spoke a few more words, to which she first nodded, then shook her head. "She says the past will not stay in the past. That if the past returns, it will bring with it new evil forces that do not care if Madhyapatnam survives. And that someone in Madhyapatnam knows the full truth, but she does not know who that person is." Fletcher spoke to Gopika again, more forcefully, but Gopika just shook her head again. She was sagging with exhaustion, leaning against Chaaya, though her grip was as strong as ever.

"Captain, she is unwell," Daphne said. "Can you not persuade her to come inside?"

"She either believes we are unclean or believes she is, and either way she will not enter." Fletcher put his hand atop Daphne and Gopika's joined ones and said something in gentle tones. Gopika smiled mischievously and answered him, then reversed her grip and put Daphne's hand into Fletcher's. It was so unexpected Daphne did not think to pull away. Fletcher's smile became that beautiful, mysterious one, and he held Daphne's hand firmly. Gopika nodded with satisfaction and spoke to Chaaya, who helped her rise. Fletcher did the same for Daphne, but did not release her when they were all standing again.

Gopika made a complicated gesture over Daphne, then again shook her finger remonstratively at Fletcher and turned to leave. Chaaya babbled something that sounded like an apology and hurried after her grandmother. "What did that mean?" Daphne said.

"She gave you her blessing," Fletcher said. He seemed suddenly conscious that he was still holding Daphne's hand and released her. "Miss Hanley, will you summon the others to the drawing room? It is time we held a council of war."

"Of course, Captain," Bess said, but rather than tilt her head back to Speak, she turned and went inside, feeling her way past the door frame. Daphne watched her go, confused at her behavior, and turned to follow her. Fletcher put a hand on her elbow, bringing her to a stop.

"Wait until they are out of sight. It is a politeness," he said.

"Captain, you did not translate everything."

"It was simply what I told you before, that Gopika believes we are married. She chastised me for not behaving to you as a husband should. I chose not to say that in front of Miss Hanley, in case it might embarrass you."

"Oh." Now Daphne did feel embarrassed. "Thank you."

Fletcher looked off into the distance, where Chaaya and Gopika had turned a corner and disappeared from sight. "Lady Daphne," he said, "you have nothing to fear from me."

"I know, Captain, I trust you completely."

"Then why—" His lips pinched tight against further words. "I apologize. You owe me no explanations, and I should not take advantage of my proximity to you." He turned and went into the Residence, leaving Daphne more confused than ever. What had he felt from her this time? She was even less certain of her heart than she had been that morning. She wished she knew what Gopika had Seen to make her believe they were married. It was unsettling, and Daphne hated being unsettled. She went inside and closed the door firmly behind her, as if she could shut out her doubts and worries so easily.

CHAPTER 15

IN WHICH AN INVESTIGATION HAS AN UNEXPECTED CONCLUSION

She entered the drawing room to find Bess and Ensign Phillips already seated there, with Fletcher pacing in front of one of the windows, his hands clasped loosely behind his back. Daphne took a seat next to Bess. There was a pale stain on the cushion—she recalled how Fletcher had lain there the previous afternoon, and tried not to feel ill at the thought. Her vision remained clear, however, which relieved her mind somewhat; at least it was only fresh blood that distressed her.

"Fletcher, so good to see you on your feet," Captain Ainsworth said as he entered the room. He strode to where Fletcher paced and clapped him on the shoulder. "That was close."

"Apparently," Fletcher said with a smile. "I'm afraid I remember little save being Bounded to the Residence."

"Well, we all survived, which I call a miracle," Ainsworth said, glancing over his shoulder at Lieutenant Wright, who had followed him in. "And now we need only convince the colonel to permit us to continue the investigation."

"I have already done so," Fletcher said. "Now, if you'll all be seated."

"You should sit, Captain," Daphne said.

"I will do so if I become unwell, thank you, Lady Daphne," Fletcher said with such politeness it stung. "Our investigation has taken an unexpected turn, thanks to your visitor."

"What visitor?" Phillips said. "Not someone wishing to speak to you, Captain?"

"It seems Lady Daphne made an impression on a local woman named Gopika," Fletcher said. "She came to warn Lady Daphne of danger."

"But she spoke of evil spirits, Captain, I cannot believe you will take her seriously."

"My physical contact with her was limited, but enough to tell me she was utterly sincere in her care for your safety," Fletcher said. "If one assumes that her reference to evil spirits was metaphorical, much might be learned from her communication."

"The Hindoos believe in all sorts of magic," Ainsworth said, lowering his voice the way he did when he believed he was spreading secrets. "It's their religion, you see. Fakirs and magicians and all that are as real to them as... as the Hooghly itself."

"That is not precisely true," Fletcher said, directing a quelling look at Ainsworth. "They believe in the miraculous in the same way we Christians give credence to claims of the apostles of old healing the blind or the sick. The Hindoos are not fools, no more than the English, and if Gopika expresses her concerns in terms of evil spirits, that is not a reason to discount her out of hand."

"But what can it mean?" Bess asked. "If she did not mean literal spirits?"

"My guess would be some force, some group perhaps, with evil intent. Someone who acts from hiding, concealing his, or their, identity and motives. I believe Gopika has confirmed the existence of our quarry."

"That's all very well," Wright said, "but it tells us no more about this man than we already knew."

"She also said the 'evil spirits' are trying to bring about a restoration of some kind." Fletcher resumed his pacing. Daphne watched him closely for signs that he was overexerting himself, but he did not look weary or ill, just intent on the carpet where he paced. "She spoke in highly figurative language—I believe she is a storyteller of some kind. Indian storytellers refer frequently to other stories, or myths, using constructions such as 'it is just as So-and-so did when facing the witch' and leaving it to the listener to know the meaning of the stories to which they refer. So my understanding of the context of her words is limited. But the imagery she used was that of a fallow field being treated with fertilizers to make it acceptable ground for a particular crop."

"Meaning that Madhyapatnam is being prepared for something," Daphne said. "Prepared to become something."

"You have it exactly." Fletcher stopped his pacing to face her. "I believe our enemy's goal is to cause disruption in Madhyapatnam. First, our man manufactured outrage at Christian missionaries that would have culminated in riots had we not arrived too soon. Then, he created an actual riot based in a general feeling that Europeans were undermining trade in Madhyapatnam."

"Is that why?" Daphne said. "I saw only that everyone seemed quite angry."

"It is the conclusion I was beginning to come to when the riot overcame us," Fletcher said.

"But that makes no sense," Phillips said. "That riot did nothing to harm us—I mean, Europeans in general, or our trade, or even this Residence. It destroyed only Hindoo property."

"Rioters are not known for their collective intelligence," Fletcher said. "I am certain the story being told today is that the damage is entirely the fault of Europeans, that honest Hindoos were tricked into rioting by those who want to see Indian trade disrupted."

"Then... is it really safe for us to remain?" Bess said. "Though I would not for the world act out of fear."

"Individual Hindoos are no more likely to attack us than anyone." Fletcher let out a deep breath. "It is the agents of our enemy we have to fear, and we don't know who they are. Whoever he is, he may pretend his cause is just, but his willingness to permit innocents to suffer and die in that riot tells me Madhyapatnam's well-being is not important to him. He wants something else, but I have no idea what that might be."

"So what do we do?" Wright said. His voice still had that husky tone to it, as if his throat were sore. Daphne examined him more closely. Normally he sat sprawled and relaxed, taking up more than his allotted space, but today he seemed closed and stiff. He might not be as recovered as he claimed.

Fletcher resumed his pacing. "The last thing Gopika said was that someone in Madhyapatnam knows the truth about the past, and that this past will not stay hidden. We need to speak with someone who knows the history of this place and hope that person can give us some idea as to what someone might want to restore."

"You make it sound as if some long-lost prince wishes to reclaim his throne," Bess said.

"That was my first thought," Fletcher said, "but there is no one left in the direct line of the last prince of Madhyapatnam to claim his place here, even were that possible."

"I can't imagine the Company letting control of this place go, even to a rightful ruler," Ainsworth said. "It's too valuable a holding."

"One of the princesses?" Daphne said. "You did say there were two daughters, Captain."

"They would be ineligible to rule," Fletcher said. "No, I believe we will have to look elsewhere for our 'restoration.'"

"So whom do we speak to?" Wright asked.

"I don't know yet. Were this Calcutta, I could think of half a dozen scholars we might approach. Here... I fear we will have to canvas the streets again, to learn the right name. And we should begin soon, before the heat of the day sends everyone indoors to rest."

"You ought to rest, Finn, you still look off your feed," Ainsworth said.

"I am well enough, Lucian, don't trouble yourself on my account," Fletcher snapped. He consulted his pocket watch. "Gentlemen, shall we return here in, say, three hours?"

"And what of Miss Hanley and myself?" Daphne demanded.

"This is not an exercise in which you may be of help," Fletcher said. It was not dismissive or cruel, just... impassive, as if he were commenting on the weather. "When we return, we can discuss further."

"But—" Daphne heard her voice coming out as a whine and shut her mouth. Fletcher was correct; she could not help him, would likely be a hindrance as she did not speak the language, but it felt so much like a chastisement she wanted to beg his forgiveness. Not that she knew what she needed forgiving for.

"We will wait, and Ensign Phillips, you will tell me if you need our assistance," Bess said, and Daphne wanted to cringe, because she did not need to be coddled or given make-work. But Phillips only nodded, and the four men left the room. Immediately they were gone, Bess said, "It is the right thing, Daphne."

"I know, but I dislike being told to wait."

"It is not for long. And I believe there is more to it than that. What passed between you and Captain Fletcher?"

Daphne thought about lying again and could not bear it. "I said something—it was rude, and I tried to apologize, except I did a poor job of it because I was not truly penitent—he thinks less of me now, I am sure, and—oh, Bess, why must life be so *complicated?*"

"He will forgive you, and it is impossible he thinks less of you. I tell you, Daphne, he cares for you deeply."

"I know. I wish I knew what to do."

"I believe you do know, and are unhappy about it."

"That is likely true. I see no good way out of this situation."

"Well," Bess said, standing and stretching, "I will read for a while, and you may join me, or you may do your mending—your uniform is sadly torn after yesterday's exertions. And when they return, we will make them include us, or... I cannot imagine a credible threat."

"I will think of something," Daphne said, "because mending is an unacceptable alternative."

DAPHNE BIT OFF THE END OF HER THREAD AND TUGGED ON THE seam. It gave only slightly. This was the third time she had set this seam, and finally it was straight. She blamed it on her distraction, wondering where Fletcher was and what he had learned. If only she spoke Hindoostani, she might have accompanied him! She would make friends with the servants, and perhaps convince one of them to begin to teach her his language. Yashpal, the *punkah-wallah*; he was young enough he might even see it as an adventure, and practice his English language skills with her.

"I take it you are finally successful," Bess said, not looking up from her book.

"How can you tell, if you are not looking at me?"

"The lack of *sotto voce* profanity."

"I do not swear, Bess, I am too well-bred for that. And besides, *you* should not know those words either."

"I have brothers who are not very discreet around me." Bess laid the book aside and adjusted her spectacles. "I should not read so long, it gives me a head-ache."

"I have often wondered why you do not have your eyes Shaped. Surely it is possible?"

"I am told that my problem is not so much with my eyes as with the nerves themselves. All the Extraordinary Shapers I have seen are reluctant to experiment on me, for fear of me losing my vision entirely."

"I can see how that would be a challenge. Do you resent it? Having such poor eyesight, I mean?"

"What is there to resent? My vision began degenerating when I was a child, and I cannot now remember what it was like to see clearly. It is simply how things are. I have a magnificent talent and many friends in my reticulum, and I have the experience of living in India—I feel it would be ungrateful to complain about my limitations. Particularly since I am assured my vision is as weak as it will ever become, and I need not fear losing my ability to read."

"You are too good, Bess."

Bess shrugged. "Today is a good day. There are others when I am not so cheerful. But for now I can be satisfied with my lot."

The creak of the front door opening, then slamming shut, brought both of them to sit alertly up. "What time is it?" Bess asked.

"I left my watch in my room. But surely it has only been an hour?"

The drawing room door, which was ajar, opened fully as Captain Ainsworth entered. "Good afternoon, ladies," he said.

"What have you learned?" Daphne demanded.

"Well, nothing *yet*," Ainsworth said hesitantly, as if taken aback by her ferocity. "It is growing too hot to remain out of doors, so I thought to return for a midday meal. Have the others not returned?"

"You are the first," Daphne said, thinking irritable thoughts about Ainsworth's appetite and lack of fortitude. Bess tilted her head back and closed her eyes. Daphne hoped she was communicating with Phillips, who might be able to tell them more.

"Ensign Phillips went with Lieutenant Wright," Bess said, not opening her eyes. "They, too, are returning. I have sent word to Captain Fletcher, though of course I cannot know his intentions."

"I will discover whether there are plans for a meal," Ainsworth said, shutting the door behind him with some alacrity.

"His appetite is remarkable," Bess said.

"I wonder he maintains his figure at all, with as much as he eats," Daphne groused. "Did Ensign Phillips discover anything?"

"He tells me he feels they should discuss it with Captain Fletcher first."

Daphne groaned and pummeled the sofa cushion. "I cannot bear waiting for things!" She stood and shook out her newly mended uniform, then retrieved the needle from where she had impaled it on the cushion. "I will put all this away, and perhaps *someone* will have returned by then!"

She took her time tidying away her sewing things, then folding her uniform neatly and stowing it in her trunk, all the while ignoring the gibbering of the impatient little voice in the back of her head. Fletcher would return—*he* would have learned something, it was impossible that he could not. Of course the other officers were capable, and all but Phillips spoke Hindoostani, but they lacked his cool competence, his knowledge of India... She made herself stop thinking of Fletcher and considered instead when Lady Loudoun might next call for her services. Tomorrow, if she followed her usual schedule. It was increasingly difficult not to consider Lady Loudoun's needs as an intrusion on what she now thought of as her true employment.

When she returned to the drawing room, Phillips and Wright had returned. There was no sign of Fletcher. "I should have gone with him," Phillips said. "He cannot possibly be fully well yet. Suppose he were to collapse?"

"I can—" Daphne began.

"You would have no idea where to begin to look, Lady Daphne," Wright said. "I am certain the captain is well." His expression was somber, though, without its usual flirtatious smile, and it worried Daphne more than it probably should.

"He would not thank us waiting our meal on him," Ainsworth said.

"Captain Ainsworth," Daphne began hotly, "if you cannot—"

"He is correct," Fletcher said, taking a few steps into the room. "You need not have waited on me."

"Captain! What have you learned?"

Fletcher's lips quirked with amusement, relieving Daphne's mind considerably, for it was the same warm, interested expression that never failed to lighten her heart. "What a pity you do not speak Hindoostani, Lady Daphne," he said. "You must be quite sick with frustration at having to stay behind."

"I can control myself, Captain, I simply dislike waiting for things."

"Then let us sit down to table, and discuss our progress."

He did not offer her his arm, but she felt as cheerful as if he had.

Sir Rodney took his midday meal at his desk, as did his aides, but the servants seemed not at all put out at having to lay a meal in the dining room. Over cold meats and a selection of cheeses, Phillips said, "We were mostly unsuccessful. We met many who knew of men who might meet our needs, but every one of them was deceased years ago."

"I was told I should speak with Kahanikar Vaachaspati, but no one would tell me how to find the man," Ainsworth said. He had stacked bread and meat atop each other and now took a large bite that made him incapable of speaking further.

"*Kahānīkār* is a title. It means 'storyteller,'" Fletcher said. "And no doubt the reason no one would tell you how to find Vaachaspati is that you are European. Vaachaspati is, according to my sources, a holy man and poet, someone who does not sully himself in casual contact with non-Hindoos. We cannot simply demand an audience with him."

"You make him sound like a nobleman," Bess said. "Does he truly know the information we seek?"

"I can't know that until I speak to him. But I am certain he knows a great deal about Madhyapatnam's history. He moves around frequently—I believe he lives like a beggar—and is difficult to find if he chooses to remain hidden. But I persuaded an old man that I might have information to exchange, and he told me where Vaachaspati will be telling stories tonight."

"So we will meet him tonight?" Wright said.

"Not we," said Fletcher. "Lady Daphne and myself."

Daphne held back a squeak of surprise and excitement. "You can't go alone!" Ainsworth said. "Who knows what kind of violence might await you, in a gathering of Hindoos, at night, defenseless!"

"Hence Lady Daphne's presence. I believe she's proved she can think quickly under dire circumstances. And my impression was that Vaachaspati is intrigued by those visibly different from himself. Lady Daphne and I, with our light coloring, are as markedly different as they come."

"Red hair is startling too," Phillips ventured.

"True, but as Lady Daphne can only convey one passenger at a time, and you do not yet speak Hindoostani, I judge it best if we are the only ones who go. But I suggest we survey the place soon, so you will know where to look for us if things go wrong."

"You do not expect things to go wrong, do you, Captain?"

Fletcher shrugged. "Lady Daphne, after yesterday's riot I assume the worst is a possibility. But no, I do not anticipate anything worse than being turned away."

Daphne clasped her hands in her lap to keep them from drumming on the table with excitement. "I hope this Vaachaspati will see us!"

"We will be as respectful of his culture as possible," Fletcher said, "and hope that and curiosity will be enough. However... I am afraid what you are wearing will not suffice."

"I brought my nicest gown from home; will that do?"

Fletcher shook his head. "For this," he said, "we should dress like the Hindoo."

CHAPTER 16

IN WHICH A STORY HAS AN UNHAPPY ENDING

The gown, if one could call it that, came in two pieces, a fitted shirt that hung to her thighs and a skirt made for someone three inches taller than Daphne. The shirt, with its short sleeves and square neckline, fit her snugly but comfortably around the waist and breasts and revealed the smoothly defined muscles of her arms. Unlike her formal English gowns, which made her look plump and round, this attire showed off the musculature she had spent years developing. To her relief, she still looked womanly, just powerfully so.

She experimentally lifted her arms; it was not so tight that the seams strained, but she would not be doing any running in it. She removed the skirt, sat on her bed, and hemmed it swiftly, not caring that the hem was not perfectly even. It was not, strictly speaking, beautiful, woven of smooth Indian cotton dyed a plain dark blue, but in Daphne's eyes it glowed with mystery and excitement.

The gown was meant to be worn with a drape, a long, wide piece of blue fabric that matched the gown. Daphne was not certain it was a good idea, since it would likely get in her way if she had to Bound anywhere, let alone with a passenger. However, showing respect was of paramount importance that evening, and she intended to be respectful. There was also a part of Daphne that knew she looked beautiful in the alien regalia and was anticipating other people seeing her. She refused to be consciously specific as to who those other people might be.

She donned the skirt again and adjusted the waistband. Now its hem brushed the tops of her feet. Much better. She brushed out her hair and pinned it up again in a workmanlike twist, something that would keep her hair from falling into her face should she be forced to Bound or Skip rapidly in succession. Not the sort of hairstyle one would wear to a social function, but this was not technically social. Though naturally she did not wish to appear slovenly. She was, in a sense, representing her country.

Bess entered and approached closely, lowering her spectacles and squinting at Daphne. "You look lovely," she said. "Strange, if I may say that without giving offense."

"No, and I feel strange, though this is quite comfortable." Daphne hitched the wrap around herself the way it had been described to her, hanging in a great loop across her body and crossing on her left shoulder. "*This* is not comfortable. It feels as if I am doing it wrong."

"The captain will know." Daphne braced herself for more teasing, but Bess said only, "I wish I might come with you, but at night I am virtually blind and would be a liability were you to need to flee."

"I wish I could communicate with you. I confess to feeling somewhat uncertain about this excursion. Captain Fletcher seems confident that we will not be attacked outright, but I cannot help remembering being surrounded by furious men, all intent on doing me harm."

"That is perfectly natural. Just remember, you cannot easily be held against your will, correct? And Captain Fletcher knows what he is about."

"I know. I feel more eager for the adventure than I am uncertain about its outcome. I am sure it will be beautiful, even if I do not speak the language!"

The wrap persisted in slipping off her shoulder as she walked down the stairs. Frustration at it kept her from feeling self-conscious when she entered the drawing room and found herself facing the admiring stares of five men. "How well it suits you, my dear," Sir Rodney said.

"Yes, you could set quite the fashion if you appeared so at Government House!" Ainsworth said with a laugh.

Fletcher said nothing, just stepped forward and did something to the wrap that halted its slide. "Thank you, Captain," she said, daring to meet his eyes, which were alight with admiration that made her feel warm down to her toes. He wore a pair of loose grey trousers and a long-sleeved shirt that matched them, with a sort of scarf hanging around his neck, and looked altogether more dashing even than in his uniform.

"We will travel by palanquin to the house where the ceremony will be held," he told her. "The skies are clear, so no fear of rain spoiling the event."

"Ceremony? I believed this to be some kind of poetry reading."

"It is, but Vaachaspati dedicates his poems to Vishnu and it is considered a holy event. I was told it would be held out of doors, in a garden belonging to his... I suppose 'sponsor' is as good a word as any."

"Very well. Shall we go, Captain?"

Fletcher assisted her into her palanquin, which was quite an effort when one considered the need to keep the wrap from flying off in every direction. Daphne settled herself on the cushions and inhaled the damp air, still warm from the day's heat. The sun had set an hour earlier, but the earth still clung to its warmth, and Daphne immediately felt sticky and uncomfortable despite the coolness of her unfamiliar gown.

She drew back the curtains and watched the landscape bob past. The roads still teemed with men and women, most of whom stared at her as she went past. She chose to ignore the stares. Lamps glowed along the roadside, blobs of light smelling of animal fat or coconut oil, illuminating the road poorly. Madhyapatnam was smaller and poorer than Calcutta, but the people did not seem to know that. They talked and laughed as cheerily as anyone in the great city might, though their talking and laughter subsided when she was near. There was no sense of incipient violence as there had been in the bazaar, but it made her uncomfortable nevertheless.

The palanquin was passing much larger houses now, the homes of wealthier Hindoos. They were not nearly the size of the old palace, but the construction was much the same: large arched doorways, ranks of windows, paint and carvings making each home a masterwork of art. Sir Rodney and his staff did not mingle socially with the Hindoos, so Daphne had never seen any of the high-caste Indians Fletcher had occasionally referred to. She leaned forward in her eagerness. Surely Fletcher would prevent them from being turned away!

The palanquin was approaching yet another of these houses, this one much better lit so Daphne could see it was of pale yellow stone, decorated fancifully in some dark color, blue or green perhaps. Just as she was preparing to lean out as far as she dared to get a better look, the bearers set the palanquin down at the side of the road. Moments later, Fletcher was there to assist her out and to help rearrange her wrap. "Now we shall see how persuasive I can be," he said, offering her his arm.

"At worst, they will simply deny us entrance, correct?"

"At worst, they will decide we have insulted their gods and their gods' servants and set an angry mob on us, and we will return to the Residence rather more precipitously than we left it."

"You do not actually believe they—surely they must know we mean no insult!"

"I believe that is unlikely. But you did ask what the worst might be." He smiled at her. "Or would you prefer the polite lie?"

"You know I will never prefer that."

"Then let us proceed, Lady Daphne, and pray for success."

Men and women, some of them dressed less finely than they were, made their way across the grass fronting the house, which Daphne saw now was lit only on the outside; no light shone from within the many windows. She and Fletcher followed them around to the side of the house and beyond, into a vast garden lined with trees that sheltered it from casual view from the road. More lights burned there, casting the trees' shadows toward them like warning sentinels. In the darkness between the lights of the road and the lights of the garden, Daphne felt more like an intruder than ever. She suppressed an unworthy urge to take Fletcher and Bound away somewhere safe and tried not to squeeze his arm too tightly.

"You have nothing to fear," Fletcher said in a low voice.

"I do not believe it is fear precisely, just... I feel we do not belong, and I cannot help wondering how these people would feel if they were invited to a gala at Carlton House."

"I understand. Tonight we will try not to be intruders."

They had nearly reached the line of trees, and Daphne could see men and women seated cross-legged on the soft grass beyond, when two shadowy figures detached themselves from the trees and came toward them. One had her arm outstretched and was shaking her head, saying something that sounded curt. Fletcher stopped and spoke to her at length, pointing at Daphne, then at himself. The woman—the first woman; both were female—shook her head again. Fletcher released Daphne and held out his hand toward her, offering a handshake.

"Give her your hand," he said to Daphne. "They are Discerners. We must establish our goodwill toward this gathering and to Vaachaspati. Tell her why we are here."

"I do not speak Hindoostani, Captain."

"Emotions are a language beyond speech, Lady Daphne. She will understand you." He clasped the first woman's hand and spoke again. Daphne immediately extended her hand to the second woman.

"My name is Lady Daphne St. Clair, and I wish to meet with your... with Vaachaspati. We intend to find out who is causing unrest in Madhyapatnam, for all our sakes," she said, meeting the woman's eyes with what she hoped was a direct, honest gaze. Well, she was being honest, and that would be evident to the woman's Discernment.

The woman stared her down, her dark face emotionless. Without breaking their gaze, she said something to her companion. Fletcher spoke, and to Daphne's surprise, both women laughed. The second woman nodded and released Daphne, gesturing to the two of them to proceed. Fletcher again took Daphne's arm. "I had not expected that," he said in a low voice, "but it makes sense that they might have ways of keeping out undesirables."

"Why did they laugh, Captain?"

"The woman commented on—it is what I have told you before, that it is rare to find someone whose demeanor so perfectly matches her emotions. I may have made a joke about how I am growing accustomed to your being more trusted than I even though you speak not more than three words of Hindoostani."

Daphne reddened slightly. "You are certainly trustworthy, Captain."

"Gopika came to *you*, Lady Daphne. I do not resent it."

The garden beyond the tree line looked very little like an English garden. An area of soft lawn filled the space between the house and another row of trees, beyond which the garden lay in shadow. Daphne could just see rows of some kind of flowering bush, their buds closed against the night, which nevertheless sent up a sweet, robust scent that made Daphne hungry for good Indian food, rice and curry and skewers of meat.

Men and women sat on the lawn, their legs crossed neatly under them. No one spoke; the only noise was the shuffling of feet and the rustling of cloth. A few stared at Daphne and Fletcher, but most had their eyes closed and their hands resting loosely on their knees. Fletcher led Daphne to a place off to one side and helped her sit. Crossing her legs in the relatively narrow skirt proved difficult, but eventually Daphne settled the wrap in a pile in her lap and was able to look about her with interest.

Two chairs, ornately carved with exaggerated human figures, stood at the far edge of the lawn, near the house, and lanterns on tall poles stood next to them. Before the chairs lay an enormous red cushion with gold tassels at each of its four corners. More cushions flanked the space defined by the chairs and the cushion. They gave the garden the appearance of an audience chamber, though one roofed by the sky and its myriad stars. Daphne tried not to stare at the man seated nearest them, but it was difficult not to, as he wore clothes like Fletcher's, but in golden silk, and his hat, which was almost a turban, was secured in front by an opal the size of a hen's egg. He looked as out of place as they did.

"Gatherings like this have become popular in the last seventy years, ever since it became clear that Discerners were becoming a large part of the Indian population," Fletcher said in the same low voice, though they were too far from anyone else to be overheard, even assuming anyone in this gathering spoke English. "You will see how emotional display is of paramount importance to Hindoos, even those who are not Discerners. They despise concealment of one's feelings—it is an affront to the gods who gave men talent."

"But they do not mind us observing their ceremony?"

"They are not so much secret as they are sacred. Those women confirmed that we did not come to mock or disrupt, and that is enough. We are outsiders, so we do not have the understanding to fully appreciate what will be done tonight. Which is, as I believe I said, a poetry recitation dedicated to Vishnu."

"And Vishnu is their god."

"One of them. If you are interested, I will explain their religion later. It is rather more complex than time will permit."

"Of course! I am very interested in India."

Fletcher smiled and briefly clasped her hand. "I need not repeat that you are a remarkable woman, Lady Daphne."

She held his hand for a moment when he would have let her go. "I thank you for the compliment, Captain." What would he feel from her —pleasure, attraction, happiness at being in his company? In that moment, she could not bring herself to rebuff him.

A jingle of bells, the high-pitched tapping of a paper drum, drew Daphne's attention from the captain to the entrance to the garden. A man and a woman, both dressed in silken finery, approached the two chairs slowly. It looked like a processional for some religious service, which it probably was. Daphne realized she was holding her breath and let it out slowly, so as not to draw attention to herself. The man wore a hat like the other gentleman's, only fastened with a spray of peacock feathers. The woman wore more gold jewelry than Daphne had ever seen in one place: a necklace of many lengths of chain, large ruby and gold earrings, a nose ring connected to one earring by more chain, and several heavy rings on her fingers.

They took their seats in the chairs without speaking or looking at one another. A third person, this one a gangly youth dressed in red silk robes that flowed around his knees, came to stand in front of them. He bowed his head and extended his arms to each side. The lanterns flared high.

"A Scorcher, sanctified to Agni," Fletcher whispered. "That was a symbolic act declaring this evening sacred to the gods."

The Scorcher bowed, said something to the man in the chair, and backed away. Musicians carrying strange-looking stringed instruments or drums or bells filed in and took their seats on the smaller cushions. They did not make any of the sounds Daphne associated with musicians preparing for a performance, and except for the high-pitched jingling of a few uncontrolled bells, everything was as silent as before. The seated figures were as still as if they were no different than the carved figures on their chairs, though Daphne was certain the woman's eyes flicked her way once.

The silence went on for what felt like hours to Daphne, though there was so much to look at she was never conscious of being impatient. Finally, another man approached through the trees and stood in front of the man and woman. He was not tall, perhaps only a few inches taller than Daphne herself. His beard was much longer than any Daphne had seen on a Hindoo man thus far, and streaked with white, though his bare head revealed dark hair that curled around his ears and neck. He wore a long white robe with a deep neckline that revealed his narrow chest, and his feet were unshod. Surprisingly, his skin was not very dark for a Hindoo, only a few shades darker than Fletcher's tanned skin.

The man and woman stood and bowed to the man. He inclined his head and said a few words, which the man responded to. Daphne wanted to prod Fletcher for a translation, but was afraid to break the spell the man had cast over the proceedings. Everyone surrounding them was as intent on the newcomer as she was. He had to be Vaachaspati.

Vaachaspati turned to face the audience, spreading his arms wide and high above his head. He said a few quiet words. Everyone except Daphne, even Fletcher, responded in a grand chorus that sounded like a flock of birds winging past overhead. Vaachaspati lowered his arms and took his seat on the commodious cushion, settling with his back to the man and woman. If they were his patrons, surely that was an insult? Daphne resolved not to make judgments about a culture she barely understood.

Silence fell again. After a few moments in which Daphne felt the tension in the air might make her scream, Vaachaspati spoke, and the musicians struck up a tune in a key Daphne could not recognize. The funny stringed instruments wailed like women weeping for their lost children, yet somehow it was not sad. It was not merry, either, but some emotion Daphne had no name for.

Vaachaspati's voice was powerful, a warm baritone much like Fletcher's, and although Daphne could not understand his words, she knew a master storyteller when she heard one no matter what language he spoke. She was so caught up in the sound of his voice it took her several minutes to realize she had no idea what he was saying. "Captain?" she said quietly.

"It is the story of a woman, the daughter of a *wazir*, and the prince who falls in love with her," Fletcher whispered. "Their love is forbidden, and she must disguise herself as a man to save her life."

The audience suddenly drew in a breath as one, and wails went up from the listeners. "The woman and the prince are waylaid by bandits, and the prince's head is lopped off," Fletcher said. "It is a dramatic moment in the original language."

"Dramatic in translation, too," Daphne whispered. Very likely this was the sort of tale proper young Englishwomen did not listen to. She leaned toward Vaachaspati, wishing she spoke his language.

The men and women surrounding them wept openly, as if their grief were immediate and personal. Vaachaspati paused in his tale, his eye falling on Daphne. He spoke a few more words, and cheering erupted.

"The god has restored the prince's head," Fletcher said.

"Then the story is over? That did not seem very long."

"It is only the beginning of the young woman's trials."

Daphne listened intently as, with Fletcher's murmured translation, the poet's tale came alive. When the young woman, still disguised as a man, rescued her love from the witch who transformed him into a ram, she cheered with the others, laughing at how caught up she had become in a story she could barely understand. Once more, the poet's eye fell on her, quelling her. He alone in the crowd was somber, as if he had performed some terrible duty only he understood the meaning of. She wondered if he were a Discerner, if he were sanctified to his role the way the Scorchers were.

The music came to an end, and the exuberant cheering died away. Vaachaspati stood and paced around the cushion, not speaking. Finally, he said something, addressing the ground, that sent the musicians scrambling for a new melody. Fletcher went very still beside Daphne. "This is a new tale," he said. "He has never told it before tonight."

Daphne shifted her weight. The dampness of the ground had seeped through her skirt, and her posterior ached, but leaving was impossible. "Is that... does it mean something?"

"That he shares a new story when Europeans are in attendance—I cannot believe it is coincidence."

Fletcher moved closer, putting his head near Daphne's so his warm breath caressed her ear. "I will translate as I can," he said quietly, "but I may not be able to keep up."

Daphne nodded. The lanterns had begun to flicker as if their fuel were gone, and a young woman dressed in red silk brought fresh ones and lit them with the power of her talent. Vaachaspati ignored her, speaking clearly to the crowd.

"There was a prince," Fletcher said, "who ruled from the sea to the sky. He was wealthy and wise, and all came to bow before him. He was... this does not translate, I apologize."

"It is all right. Please, continue!"

"His dominion was great, and much envied by other princes, but he was powerful, and defeated all who would conquer him." Fletcher paused when Vaachaspati did. The entire garden fell silent. "But the prince had a weakness, and it would be his downfall.

"The prince had two wives, both as beautiful as the sun. The first became big with child, and when the ten moons were complete—it is how they measure time to confinement—she was delivered of a daughter. The second, too, had a daughter. The prince doted on his daughters, but longed for an heir so his dominion would not pass into obscurity.

"One day a foreign ruler came to call. This ruler was unlike the others; he claimed he did not wish to conquer, but to live in harmony, trading at the prince's cities and sharing his vast wealth. The prince Discerned that this ruler was as honest as he claimed to be, and welcomed him as a brother."

The garden echoed with moans. "What have you not said?" Daphne exclaimed.

"It is—I cannot explain, except that the Discernment—I will have to tell you later. It is a sad twist in the tale, and I am falling behind."

Daphne nodded. She could not take her eyes off the poet.

"The foreign ruler promised many things, but the most compelling was a promise to ensure the prince's dominion never failed. The foreign ruler had many great magics at his command, and the prince believed he could give him the heir he so longed for.

"So the prince began giving the foreign ruler gifts. First, gifts of money and jewels. Then properties. Then he gave him the *diwan*, the principal trading concession. But still his wives did not conceive. The prince, his heart breaking, took to his bed, begging the foreign ruler to have pity on him. To his very last breath, he believed if he were only faithful, he would see the son he so longed for."

Vaachaspati fell silent once more. His eyes were locked with Daphne's. Looking away was impossible. She felt a great knot in her chest, a powerful ache at the prince's pain. "The prince died, and the foreign ruler took his lands," Fletcher said, his voice flat and emotionless. "His people and his wives were dispersed, his property claimed by the foreign ruler that the land might not fall into destruction."

"Oh," Daphne said. "I thought... the other had such a happy ending..."

"Not all stories end happily," Fletcher said. "But—he says this is not the end. The prince's dying wish was granted. The younger of his wives gave birth to a son, five months after his father's death. And—now he is speaking in a metaphorical way—someday the son will restore what the father has lost."

"Restore?" Daphne said.

Fletcher looked impassive. "Indeed."

CHAPTER 17

IN WHICH BESS DEMONSTRATES AN EXTRAORDINARY SPEAKER'S TALENT

More moans went up from the listeners, and a few people were weeping. "But if he is to restore—"

Fletcher shushed her. He was listening intently to Vaachaspati's words. "War, between the foreign ruler and the son, but... the son has dark forces at his command, and the story ends with a warning. It is the strangest story I have ever heard."

Vaachaspati took a seat on the cushion. He looked utterly exhausted. The man in the chair stood and clapped his hands. Immediately the audience began rising, dusting themselves off and making their way past the tree line toward the road. "But—is that all?" Daphne said.

"It seems so," Fletcher said. He helped her rise and gave her his arm. "Let us see if we may speak to him directly."

They had only taken a few steps toward the seated poet when the Discerners came out of nowhere and intercepted them. One of them said something even Daphne could understand was a no. Fletcher spoke to them in his calm voice, making them both hesitate and glance over their shoulders at Vaachaspati, who didn't seem to notice their presence at all. Finally, the Discerner said a few words, making Fletcher nod, and he and Daphne proceeded toward the road.

"What did you say?" Daphne asked. "It did not sound like a rejection."

"We are permitted five minutes' conversation once the poet has recovered," Fletcher said. "We are to wait by the road until we are summoned." Behind them, the lamps went dim, and the garden was swallowed up in darkness, lit only by the sliver of waning moon that sailed high overhead and one low-burning lantern. Daphne glanced back and saw the poet, still seated on his cushion, his head bowed as if in prayer. The Scorcher finished trimming the lamp and walked toward the house.

Daphne was grateful for Fletcher's arm as they navigated the garden to the more well-lit front of the house. "That story was for us," she said.

"Undoubtedly. The prince of Madhyapatnam, dying without an heir, has his lands taken by the East India Company so they will not fall into anarchy. Some elaboration, naturally, but that is the essence of it."

"But how could Vaachaspati have known what we were looking for? And a lost prince? It seems too coincidental for words."

"We were not subtle in our search this morning. Anyone might have told him what facts we were looking to confirm. We must speak with him. If his story is true, and there is a lost prince, he might be the one behind the unrest Madhyapatnam has faced."

"But what does it mean, that the son has control of dark forces?"

"I do not know. Something to ask Vaachaspati. The story certainly lacked the animosity toward the Company one might expect. But Madhyapatnam has flourished under Company rule, so perhaps it is not so surprising."

Daphne jigged from one foot to the other. "When will they summon us?"

"Patience. He is not going anywhere."

They stood in silence, watching the rest of the audience members flow past them down the road. They all appeared to be on foot, even the ones dressed in silks the way Vaachaspati's patrons had been. Daphne wondered if that were some kind of ritual, as well, humbling themselves before the representative of God. She considered asking Fletcher, but their silence was so companionable she hated to break it for anything so irrelevant as that.

"Investigation aside, I have enjoyed this evening," Fletcher said abruptly. "Seeing India through your eyes is refreshing."

"I have always longed for this kind of adventure," Daphne said. "I no longer regret leaving the Peninsula, as I would never have had this opportunity there."

"You did not leave by choice." Fletcher's voice was quiet, and Daphne dared not look at him, for fear he would see her shame written on her face.

"I did not," she said simply.

"Ensign Phillips told me. You lose consciousness at the sight of blood."

"Yes, I do."

"That would make serving on the battlefield difficult."

"It is why—mostly why—I am in India, Captain."

Fletcher was silent. She glanced quickly at him and saw he was looking off into the distance, not at her. "Then your service yesterday was truly extraordinary, if you were able to convey me in the condition I was no doubt in."

"Please do not be grateful to me, Captain, I feel I do not deserve it."

"Something else happened in Spain, did it not?"

She let out a long, weary breath. "I failed in my duty, and a man died. You very nearly died. I cannot—it was luck—"

"It was not luck. It was sheer perseverance." Fletcher took her by the shoulders and turned her so she had to look at him. His eyes were fierce even in the lamplight. "Lady Daphne, I honor you for what you have overcome. We all of us who serve in war have deaths on our consciences. Do not permit this one to rob you of your victories."

"I hate being weak. It feels so much like failure, and if I am to fail I want it to be on my own terms, not because my body has betrayed me."

"I understand. My talent is strong, but it is also the source of my greatest weakness. It is humiliating, feeling that loss of control, and I feel such shame—"

"Captain, you have nothing to feel ashamed of! I—you are laughing at me, how dare you?"

"Lady Daphne, listen to yourself. If you will not permit me to feel shame at my weakness, how can you possibly justify it in yourself?"

It felt like a light went on inside her heart. "I—but it is different—"

"Only because you insist on making it so. Forgive yourself, Lady Daphne, and move forward."

His eyes were so intent on her, his hand rested on her forearm, and she felt a sudden urgency to put her arms around him, not to Bound with him but to take comfort in his embrace. She could tell the moment he became aware of her desire, because that slow, mysterious smile spread across his face. He took a step toward her, clasping her other hand with his free one.

A scream shattered the night. Fletcher's head whipped around to stare at the darkened garden. He released Daphne and ran for the tree line. Daphne took three staggering steps after him, said an unladylike word, and Skipped past him to alight just inside the garden.

The red-clad Scorcher woman knelt beside the cushion, supporting Vaachaspati in her arms. Daphne Skipped to her side and helped her hold the man up. His head lolled to one side, his body a dead weight. The woman gabbled uncontrollably at Daphne, then screamed again, and again, words in Hindoostani Daphne was certain no one could understand.

Footsteps pounded across the lawn toward them. "Give him to me," Fletcher said, taking the poet in his arms without waiting for the woman to respond. He supported Vaachaspati so his head tipped back, shifting his beard to expose his throat, and Daphne bit back a scream. A long, lurid line of bruising circled the man's throat. His eyes were wide open and staring. Fletcher placed his cheek close to Vaachaspati's mouth. "He's dead," he announced, then repeated himself in Hindoostani.

The woman screamed again, this time a horrified wordless wail. More footsteps, and shouting, came toward them. The woman shoved

Fletcher away from the body and lit the lanterns with her Scorcher talent. Fletcher rose and took Daphne's hand. "We have to leave. Now," he said.

Daphne lifted him and Bounded them to the Residence's entrance hall, where they stood clinging to each other, not out of desire but from a mutual need for reassurance. Daphne could not help seeing that still, staring form whenever she closed her eyes. Finally, she stepped away from Fletcher, and said, "Should we not have stayed? To help?"

"Europeans near the body of a respected holy man? That Scorcher woman might tell them we had nothing to do with it, but she was out of her mind with grief and it is not something I wanted to rely on. We would just have been accused of murder." Fletcher let out a deep, pained sigh. "We may be accused of murder anyway, depending on how stricken that Scorcher was."

"But we were nowhere near!"

"Irrelevant. They will be looking for someone to blame." Fletcher shook his head. "Let us see who is still awake and discuss our next step."

There was no one in the drawing room. "I did not realize the time," Fletcher said when he observed the mantel clock. "You should retire, and we will discuss this in the morning."

"I cannot possibly sleep after that. Was he killed to prevent him talking to us?"

"I can see no other interpretation. Vaachaspati was well-loved and respected, and as far as I can tell had no enemies. His death benefits only our enemy, who could not permit him to share whatever information he had. When we capture this man, I will take great pleasure in bringing him to justice."

"I feel rather bloodthirsty about it. What are we to do, Captain?"

Fletcher took a seat and gestured for Daphne to sit near him. "We must verify the existence of a missing third child of the Prince. An heir. Someone must know... though I do not know why I am so certain of that, given that we have heard no mention of him in all the investigating we have done."

"If we knew where the wives went, we might ask there."

"True. That may be the next best step."

"Or..." Daphne drew up her legs, not thinking that it might be immodest. Her Indian clothing left her feeling so much freer than her normal garb. "Suppose some of the Prince's household is still in Madhyapatnam? They might know of the child. You have no doubt been speaking with the men of the city—well, what about the women?"

"That is a clever idea, Lady Daphne. And your friend Gopika might be able to lead us in the right direction." Fletcher yawned. "You may not be able to sleep, but I certainly feel the need. Good night, Lady Daphne, and thank you for your company this evening. I regret that it had to end so horribly."

"So do I. I felt as if I knew Vaachaspati, despite never once speaking to him. Such a tragedy."

"We will solve this mystery, and bring him justice."

Daphne nodded and Bounded to the dark security of her bedroom.

She undressed, folding her Indian clothing away into the depths of her trunk, and donned a nightgown, then stood before her window, brushing her hair. Who could have done such a thing? What could possibly be worth taking a man's life to protect? She thought about the house, about the garden, and wondered how the murderer could have slipped past the Discerners. Her last sight of Vaachaspati had shown him sitting alone. Someone might have made his stealthy way around the far side of the house, silently walking up behind the exhausted poet, flinging a cord around his neck—Daphne shuddered and put the image far from herself. Dwelling on it would not bring the man back.

She heard a door open and shut elsewhere in the Residence, more a vibration than a sound. Someone else was wakeful at this hour, though likely not plagued with a dead man's memory. She set down her brush and climbed into bed. Morning would come early, and with it a new direction. Could they find Gopika? She would likely be in the bazaar. More to the point, would she know the information they sought?

In the darkness of the nearly invisible moon, sounds became louder: the chirruping and buzzing of night insects, the mournful cries of hunting birds, the creak of the netting as it twisted gently on the hook from which it was suspended. Daphne closed her eyes and tried to picture her home back in England, the bedroom that had been hers since she left the nursery, but images closer to hand intruded: Government House's Bounding chamber, the post-house where she had eaten a meal seated on the floor. She drifted off to sleep with memories of the bazaar filling her mind.

It seemed only moments later that she woke again to someone shaking her. "Daphne, you must wake," Bess whispered. "Something is happening outside—please, wake!" She was in her wrapper, as if something had interrupted her dressing. The grey light of dawn suffused the air, as cool as it would be hot in only a few hours.

Groggy and aching as if she had again spent the day Bounding passengers hither and yon, Daphne sat up and pushed her hair out of her eyes. "What is it?"

"I can see nothing, only hear—*listen*, Daphne!"

She came fully to consciousness and became aware of a low roar like the tide, ebbing and rising somewhere nearby. A moment later she recognized it for what it was: a large crowd of people, all talking at once, but at such a distance that she could not make out words. They were not shouting. *Not yet*, her inner voice insisted.

Daphne looked out the window, but could see nothing. "They must be at the front door," she said.

"They sound angry," Bess said. "What happened last night?"

Daphne hurried to dress in her Bounder uniform. "It was beautiful —but it was awful," she said, and quickly recounted for Bess the events of the previous night. Bess gasped when Daphne came to the murder, but did not interrupt. Finally, Daphne said, "Captain Fletcher said it was possible they would blame us for the murder. It sounds as if he was correct."

Bess donned her blue muslin gown, which was somewhat wrinkled, and said, "We should go down. I refuse to cower in here like a frightened child. You did nothing wrong, and we will convince them of that."

"I hope you are right." The noise grew as they dressed, and privately Daphne feared even Captain Fletcher's powers of persuasion would not be enough. But Bess was correct: cowering was the wrong reaction.

They met Ensign Phillips on the stairs. He was haphazardly

dressed, without his coat, and looked harried. "Ladies, you should remain upstairs," he said, in a tone of voice that suggested he knew his advice would be ignored.

"You know we cannot," Daphne said. "Do you know what has happened?"

"They accuse us of having murdered their holy man. I have sent word to the barracks, but Fletcher insists he be permitted to handle this matter. He and Sir Rodney are arguing about it now."

"Why should the soldiers not come? It is their duty to protect the Residence," Bess said.

"Because these are grieving, frightened people who are simply mistaken as to where to lay blame," Daphne said, though she could hear the mob better now and did not quite believe her own words. "If Captain Fletcher can convince them of the truth, no one need be hurt."

"Grieving people can nevertheless be dangerous," Bess said. "How far are we willing to permit them to go before we are entitled to defend ourselves?"

Daphne had no ready answer for that. "Let us speak to the captain and Sir Rodney, and perhaps they will have a better solution."

"I believe not, Lady Daphne," Phillips said. "They were arguing hotly before I left to investigate the rear exit. We may have to leave in a hurry."

Another tidal roar, this one much nearer to hand, echoed down the cool central hallway of the Residence. "—have to make an example!" Sir Rodney roared. "If we do not put up a firm resistance, we show them that we are weak and easily toppled. I won't stand by and watch this place go up in flames!"

"It will not come to that," Fletcher said. His voice was calmer than Sir Rodney's, but with an edge to it that told Daphne he was by no means relaxed. "I will speak to them—"

"It's a damned mob, Fletcher! There's no reasoning with that!"

"They are guilty of nothing more than a desire to see justice done."

"To this point, yes, but they are working themselves up to violence!"

"All the more reason for me to speak to them now, before that happens."

Sir Rodney's face was as red as his hair. "You have until the soldiers arrive from the barracks," he said. "And if they kill you, let the judgment not fall on my head."

"Agreed," Fletcher said, and strode off toward the front door. Daphne followed him, trailed by Bess. "Lady Daphne, this is not the place for you," he said without looking at her.

"But if you—I should stand ready to Bound you away—"

"I will not have you put yourself in danger of being stoned. You will do no one any good if you are wounded before you can escape—or am I wrong, and a Bounder's talent is not impaired by extreme pain?"

Daphne ground her back teeth. "You are not wrong."

"Thank you for your willingness, but this is a thing I must do alone." Fletcher paused before the carved front door, laying his hand palm-first against the wood as if in prayer, then pulled the door open and had it shut behind him before Daphne could glimpse more than the courtyard, sun-dappled in the dawn's first light.

"I cannot hear him," Bess said. "The door is too thick."

"I hear *them*," Daphne said. "Oh, Bess."

They stood, hands clasped, listening to the angry ebb and flow of the sea of words. "I have told the soldiers to move out," Daphne heard Phillips say, some distance behind them. "They will be here in minutes."

"Captain Fletcher's a fool," Wright said.

"He can also sell snow to the Esquimaux," Ainsworth said. "He'll do it."

"I don't suppose you'd care to wager on that?" Wright said.

"On all our lives? Don't be daft, man," said Sir Rodney.

The crowd's roar grew louder, and now Daphne could hear Fletcher shouting. "It's not working," she said.

Bess gripped Daphne's hand more tightly. "Step back," she said.

"Why?"

"Just—give me space." Her eyes behind their smoky spectacles were closed, and her chest heaved with slow, deep breaths, in through the nose, out through the mouth. "There is something I can do."

"What—"

Bess's eyes flew open. In a deep voice, she intoned a few syllables of Hindoostani, each sounding like a death knell. The roar outside turned to panicked screaming, high-pitched and terrified. The door flung open, and Fletcher scrambled inside and slammed it shut. His breath came in quick, short gasps, and his startled eyes were wide. "What did you do?" he whispered.

Outside, the screams were fading into the distance. Bess closed her eyes once more, trying to calm her breathing, which had become as rapid and frantic as Fletcher's. "It is... a last resort," she said. "We are taught to Speak to a crowd... all at once... in a way that terrifies. For breaking up small mobs before they riot." She opened her eyes and smiled, a shaky expression. "I apologize, Captain, for including you in its effect. It is not a precision attack."

"I had no success with them," Fletcher said. "You may have saved their lives. I cannot resent you for it."

"I believe I should sit now," Bess said, fumbling her way toward the drawing room. Daphne took her by the elbow to steady her. "I have never done that before. It was far more effective than I expected it to be. I wish I could have been of use like that in the bazaar, but that was far too large a crowd."

Daphne helped her friend find a seat, then sat next to her. "Did they truly disperse, Captain?" she asked.

"I have no idea. I was too busy obeying the command to pay attention to them. But if it was as effective on them as it was on me—"

"What command?"

" 'Go home,' in Hindoostani. I thought you did not speak the language, Miss Hanley."

"A few phrases only, for use in that circumstance." Bess's hands were shaking, and Daphne clasped them to still them. "Do not fear for me, Daphne, it is simply the aftereffects—it rings through me as if I were a bell."

"We cannot know if they will return," Sir Rodney said. "I am going to station men around the perimeter of the Residence."

"That is a wise decision, Sir Rodney," Fletcher said. "And we will seek out Gopika and hope she can tell us what we need to know."

"Gopika? What did you learn last night?" Ainsworth asked. "And what was that mob about?"

Fletcher exchanged glances with Daphne. She was eager to reach the bazaar, but it seemed explanations were in order first. "Breakfast," Fletcher said, "and we will tell you a story."

"One without a happy ending," Daphne said.

CHAPTER 18

IN WHICH WOMEN'S KNOWLEDGE PROVES VALUABLE

Daphne and Bess stood next to the sweet-seller's stall, eating morsels and dropping the bright green leaves on the ground. "Nothing," Daphne said. "Gopika seems to have disappeared."

"At least we have not been accosted, or threatened," Bess said. "I can imagine how these people might grieve over such a death as that. Grief can make one irrational."

"I am afraid for Gopika. Suppose the murderer draws the same conclusion we did and tries to kill her?"

"How could he? It is not as if he knows of her existence."

"He might. I am beginning to be afraid of what our enemy is capable of."

Bess sucked her fingertips clean, then wiped them on her handkerchief. "He is still just a man, albeit one with resources. I have told Captain Fletcher and Lieutenant Wright where we are—is Captain Ainsworth still nearby? I find it difficult to pick our officers out of the crowd when they do not wear their coats."

"He is conversing with an old man just across the way. I imagine he is inquiring about the possibility of food rather than the location of Gopika."

"At least he is consistent in his passions. I worry about Lieutenant Wright. Does he not seem different since his head injury? Perhaps we should request an Extraordinary Shaper for him, after all."

"He is quieter, and he has stopped flirting—but I believe he has simply become more serious now that we face a serious challenge. I like him better now." He still moved oddly, less freely, and Daphne had nearly resolved to suggest he see a doctor, or an Extraordinary Shaper, but she did not like to interfere in the life of someone who was barely more than an acquaintance. Wright no doubt knew his own business.

"I hope his seriousness is not because of pain." Bess adjusted her spectacles and squinted against the indirect light filtering through the heavy cloud cover. The day was hot and muggy, the air oppressive on Daphne's skin. She had changed into a gown at Fletcher's suggestion that they not draw undue attention to themselves, though she felt she was alien enough that the difference between a gown and a Bounder uniform would not make an impression on the Hindoos.

Daphne licked the last hints of sweet stickiness from her fingers and, like Bess, wiped her fingers on her handkerchief. Her mother would no doubt be horrified at her lack of good manners. Her father, on the other hand, would laugh and ask her to show him how to eat the still-unnamed morsels. Then he would tease her mother into trying some, and in the end her mother would be sucking her own fingers clean. Lord and Lady Claresby were not typical examples of the nobility—only observe their treatment of their only daughter, who had been indulged in her every whim and had managed not to grow up spoiled. A pang of homesickness struck her, and she blinked tears away.

"Memsahib?" A thin brown hand plucked at her sleeve. "Memsahib?"

"Oh!" Daphne exclaimed. The girl was small but fine-featured, and Daphne guessed she was nine or ten years old despite her size. "I do not—" Fletcher had warned her to be careful of the beggars to whom she gave coin, that generosity could start a mob centered on her purse. "Here, here is something, but—"

The girl shook her head and pushed the coin away. "Memsahib, follow," she said, carefully enunciating the word in a way that suggested she did not know its meaning. She tugged on Daphne's sleeve again.

"Daphne, what does she want?" Bess squinted at the girl's face.

"She wants us to follow her—oh, Captain Ainsworth, what should we do?"

The girl backed away as Ainsworth hove into view. "Is she disturbing you, Lady Daphne?"

"No, she simply—no, wait!" The girl backed away farther, and Daphne took a few steps in her direction. "She wants me to follow her."

"She's leading you into a trap," Ainsworth said. "No doubt her brothers are waiting to offer you insult, or worse." He directed a stream of Hindoostani at the girl, who shook her head violently and replied.

"What did she say?" Daphne asked.

"That you and the memsahib are to follow her, and she will not tell me why. Lady Daphne, ignore her. It is a trap."

"What if she knows something? Ask her if she knows Gopika."

Ainsworth scowled, but repeated the question. The girl's eyes widened, and she nodded. "You see?" Daphne said. "Captain, Bess and I must go."

"Then I will accompany you, if you insist on this mad venture."

The girl had stopped backing away and was waiting, not very patiently, it seemed to Daphne. She glared at Ainsworth and said something, then repeated, "Follow."

"She says she will go nowhere if I am present," Ainsworth said. "My lady, this is incredibly dangerous."

"I can Bound away if necessary," Daphne said, which was an oversimplification, but not one she was prepared to argue with the captain. "Bess will relay our journey to Captain Fletcher, so you may all follow us if necessary. But I feel this is the right path. Please, Captain, wait here."

Ainsworth scowled again. "If you are wrong, my life won't be worth a brass shilling," he said. Daphne had already turned away from him and held her hand out toward the girl, who nodded and scampered away into the crowd.

Daphne kept a tight hold on Bess as they scrambled to keep up with the girl. Once or twice they lost sight of her, but only for a few seconds before she returned, beckoning as if they were chickens she was herding. Not that Daphne knew whether chickens were herded. Possibly she was thinking of sheep.

They were completely lost now, in terms of knowing where they were in relation to the Residence or the sweet-seller's stall or any other landmark Daphne knew. The noise of the bazaar was deafening as the day rolled on toward noon, buyers and sellers arguing at top volume as if by sheer noise they might win out over each other. Daphne smelled roasted meat, spicy and delicious, and her stomach rumbled a complaint. Perhaps she had been too hasty to judge Ainsworth's appetite.

The girl took them by routes Daphne was sure no European ever saw, past stalls and blankets watched over by hard-eyed men and women, offering items for sale far nicer than those displayed along the main "streets" of the bazaar. If they had been on their own, she would have stopped to admire them... though had they been on their own, they would likely have had to worry about their safety rather than having time to admire. Daphne eyed the stall owners and prayed she had not been flippant with Ainsworth about how easily she could Bound away from an assailant. She could be held, true, but only by someone heavier than she who could prevent her from lifting him, and her reflexes were quick enough that such a thing never happened. Not even a Mover could hold a Bounder against her will. Even so, she remained alert to her surroundings even as she kept a close eye on their little guide.

The girl approached, not a stall, but a tent, its dark mouth agape and shielded against the sun. Daphne and Bess slowed. The girl turned and beckoned to them, then ducked inside the tent. "Now I am uncertain," Bess said. "Anything could be inside."

"Can you not tell if there are people? Minds? How did you know to Speak to the mob this morning?"

"It does not work that way. I cannot explain it to you, a non-Speaker." Bess bit her lip. "We might simply return."

"And never learn what message the girl brought?" Daphne squared her shoulders, then stepped forward and crouched to enter the tent.

She could feel Bess close behind her but saw nothing ahead. The tent smelled of a sweet incense, cloying to the nostrils, that gave Daphne the beginnings of a head-ache. She closed her eyes and listened. Her own breathing was ragged, edged with excitement, but there were at least two other people in the tent, both calmer than she. Bess fumbled about for her hand and squeezed it.

"Memsahibs, sit," said the girl, again with that intonation that spoke to a memorized phrase. Daphne felt about for a chair, but found only a soft rug, gritty with dirt. She sat cross-legged on it and opened her eyes. Now she saw three indistinct figures, one much smaller than the others —the girl. A tiny gleaming ember burned like a star off to one side, and the movement of air told Daphne it was the source of the sweet odor.

The other two were little more than bright eyes in the dimness. Daphne thought they might be veiled, their mouths covered and only their eyes exposed. She folded her hands in her lap to still them and said, "We thank you—why have you brought us here? We do not speak your language."

"I speak yours. Not well," said a woman's voice from the shadows. Another voice, higher-pitched and creaky with age, said something in Hindoostani. "You the one Gopika saw. The bright one. Bright hair, bright... spirit."

"You know Gopika? Where is she?"

The shadow woman waved a dismissive hand. "Not here. Not ever. Danger, there is."

"Someone killed Vaachaspati last night, we believe because of the questions we asked. There is danger for you as well."

"We are protected. But do not find us again. We not here."

"I understand." She was not entirely certain that she did, but she certainly understood that drawing attention to these women by retracing their steps to this tent might be fatal for them. "Do you know what we intended to ask Gopika?"

A shifting of weight, a rustle of cloth. "You seek to know of the prince."

"Yes, we have heard the old prince might have—there was a third child, was there not?"

Silence. The creaky voice spoke at length. "We do not give our words free," the woman said.

Daphne fumbled with her purse, hesitated, then withdrew a single coin. "We do not pay for nothing," she said. "This is to show we respect you. More if your information is valuable to us."

The woman plucked the coin from her hand and made it disappear into the shadows. "This is my mother, nurse to the prince's second wife," she said. "She went with her to her father's house, after the death." She spoke quietly to her companion, who responded with a lengthy stream of syllables. "She says the prince's wife was with child. She gave birth in her father's house and died soon after."

"What of the child?" Daphne asked.

The woman spoke again in Hindoostani, and the old woman responded. "The child, no... inheritance. The father, his mother's father, raised him as his own."

"But he should have been prince of Madhyapatnam, correct? Had his father not died?"

"Sahibs took the land. Mother's father believed they would kill the boy if they knew."

"They would not have killed him," Daphne said.

The woman shrugged and spoke to her mother. The old woman hesitated, then said something short and curt. "She says the past will not be the past. But the heir knows it not. And he has allies who care nothing for Madhyapatnam. He will take his heritage and see us destroyed."

"I don't understand." She wished with all her heart Bess could read this woman's mind—but her thoughts would likely be in Hindoostani, and mind-reading was impossible.

The woman spat out a harsh syllable Daphne thought might be profanity. "The heir wishes to bring back the past. We are all in danger."

"Danger, from the heir?"

The woman nodded. Daphne jerked in surprise as the old woman grabbed her hands the way Gopika had and squeezed them. "The sahibs' house will be empty, the redcoats bloodied."

Bess said, "But forcing those of us at the Residence to leave—even if that were possible, the Company has tremendous resources. They would send more regiments to defend Madhyapatnam."

The woman shrugged again. "The heir strikes from hiding. He has men and guns. He will not stop until he has what is his, no matter what it does to his people."

"Where? Where is he hiding?" Daphne said.

Again, the two women conferred. "We know not. Not in Madhyapatnam. Ghost. You go now."

Daphne took out a few more coins, choosing them by feel. "Thank you. Will you be safe?"

"Go your way, *kūdne vālā*, and do not return. This place not be here."

Daphne stood and helped Bess to her feet, then lifted her friend and Bounded back to the Residence drawing room. "Please tell the others where we are, and ask them to return," she said. "I hope what we have just purchased will make a difference."

"It will not matter," Ainsworth said. "It's not as if the Company is going to return Madhyapatnam to the Hindoos. The revenues alone—not to mention setting a poor precedent—"

"I doubt this missing heir is much moved by what the Company policy is," Fletcher said. "He is likely to strike at us until we retreat or are destroyed."

"But we have no idea what kind of resources he has," Daphne said, "aside from how he can start riots and have a man murdered. Would he not need an army to face ours?"

"The Residence troops are not much of an army, and he might have his forces concealed in plain sight, among the people of Madhyapatnam," Fletcher said. "If the unrest persists, he might turn a low-grade feeling of dissatisfaction into full-blown revolution. That is not something we can stand against."

"Should we perhaps discuss this with Sir Rodney present?" Bess said. "It is his Residence, after all, and he is responsible for the defense of the territory."

"Madhyapatnam is his province, true, but the investigation is ours," Fletcher said, "and it is I who will ultimately bear the responsibility for ending this unrest. We must find this missing heir before he can cause greater violence. If those women are correct, and the man cares nothing for the people of Madhyapatnam, thousands of innocents will suffer. That is unacceptable to me."

"The women said he does not care what happens to the people, so long as he has what is his," Bess said. "Surely the people of Madhyapatnam will not heed him, if they know he cares nothing for them?"

"If he can fool them into believing his claim is legitimate, and that they will benefit more from his rule than from that of the Company, they may believe him just long enough to restore him to his place," Daphne said. "What can we do to prevent it?"

"We know there's a prince—an heir, anyway," Wright said. "We know he intends to drive the Europeans, us, from Madhyapatnam. But we don't know where he is, except that he isn't in the city."

"Nicely summed up, but it gets us nowhere," Ainsworth said. "We have to find the sprog before anything else goes wrong, and we have no idea where to start."

"We will get nowhere if we continue with such pessimism as the two of you display," Daphne said. "Surely there is *some* way to track the young man down."

"If his goal is to encourage us to leave, or to kill us," Fletcher said, "we must search out rumors centered on destruction of the Residence. Not everyone in Madhyapatnam will support the young man's bid for power, believing rightly that his plans will throw the entire district into turmoil and cause many deaths. They may be persuaded to, if not come to our aid, at least not permit us to suffer from his plans."

Daphne sighed. "You are about to tell me I must remain behind."

A muted laugh ran round the room. "Lady Daphne," Fletcher began.

"Oh, I understand, I simply dislike the prospect. But as Miss Hanley and I have provided key information today, I am not resentful."

"You have both contributed marvelously. Those women would never have spoken to a man," Fletcher said.

"It's unfortunate we did not see where you went," Wright said. "More information about those women might have given us some idea of where else to look."

"Their safety was more important." Daphne resisted the urge to tuck her feet comfortably under her bottom. "Suppose our man, or his assassin, followed us? I could not bear the thought of that child being killed simply for what she might have told us. Which was nothing, as she did not speak our language."

"There is yet time to search the neighborhood for rumors," Phillips said. "I believe we should do so before night falls."

"I agree," said Fletcher. "And tonight I will confer with Sir Rodney. I hope to be able to give him good news."

Daphne turned to address Bess, who had her head tilted back. Everyone waited politely for her to finish her communication, even Wright, who had his hand on the doorknob. "Oh, I beg your pardon," Bess said after a moment. "Government House requests Lady Daphne's presence to bring Lady Loudoun to India."

"It seems we will all have some occupation this afternoon, save Miss Hanley," Daphne said, rising from her seat. "Good luck, gentlemen, I shall return shortly."

It took her only half an hour to convey Lady Loudoun and her belongings, as the children were remaining behind that night. To her surprise, the countess took Daphne by the arm and drew her along after her toward her apartment in Government House. "There is to be a gala tonight, and I wish you and Miss Hanley to attend," she said. "You must be so bored in Madhyapatnam."

"Oh, my lady, we are not—that is, sometimes we are bored, but you must not believe—it really is quite exciting, when it is not dull."

Lady Loudoun laughed and patted Daphne's arm. "Nevertheless, you must not isolate yourselves. I insist on your being present. There are so many pleasant young men I intend to introduce to you. Though I regret Captain Fletcher is on assignment. You seemed to enjoy one another's company, when you met...?" Her tone was one of inquiry blended with gentle suggestiveness.

Daphne successfully kept from blushing. "Captain Fletcher is... very agreeable, and I have enjoyed spending time in his company in Madhyapatnam."

"Well, he will simply have to do without you for an evening. Eight o'clock, and be prepared to dance!"

Daphne left her at the entrance to the Governor-General's wing of the palace and trudged back down the stairs, looking for a private room she might Bound from. A gala would be pleasant, true, but she found the thought of dancing with strangers enervating, as if Lady Loudoun had asked her to Skip around the world instead. No doubt it was merely that Fletcher had not been invited; dancing with him was truly pleasurable.

She Bounded back to the drawing room and found it empty. Likely Bess had retired to their room for a nap before supper. Well, it was not as if she had anything better to do. Bess might be even more bored than she was—no, Bess could never be bored so long as she had her reticulum to communicate with. In fact, Bess frequently forwent conversation with other Speakers in favor of keeping Daphne amused. Daphne felt slightly guilty about monopolizing her friend's time like that.

She Bounded to her bedroom and dropped heavily onto the bed. Bess lay still on her own bed, fully clothed, her spectacles neatly folded and set on a nearby windowsill. "Lady Loudoun has invited us to a gala tonight. Well, I say 'invited,' but it was more—"

"Daphne," Bess said, "John is dead."

CHAPTER 19

IN WHICH AN
INTERROGATION ENDS BADLY

She could not at first remember who John was. Then it struck her. "Oh, Bess, *no*," she exclaimed, crossing the room to take Bess's hand in hers. "Did you just learn—when was it?"

"He was shot," Bess said. "It was a battle somewhere in Spain. They told me, but I was not listening at that point." Her eyes were open, staring at something Daphne could not see, and her fingers gripping Daphne's were unnaturally cold and dry. "Daphne, he is dead."

Daphne wished she dared put her arms around Bess, but her friend was wandering in a distant land, and she did not know how to bring her back. "Do you need me to take you somewhere? I can return you to Portugal, or... I know places in Spain, except you said you did not know—Bess, tell me how I can help you!"

"There is nothing you can do." She blinked, slowly, as if her body had forgotten how and she had to will each eyelid to move. "Daphne, why did I not marry him? Then I would have some right—he died three days ago, and they buried him today, but no one thought to tell me sooner than this. I should have—" She closed her eyes. Tears leaked down the sides of her face.

"You did not know you loved him until now?"

Bess shook her head. "I feel no more fondness for him than ever I did, and yet—if I had loved him better, he might not have been in Spain, he might have been in India with me and safe from that rifleman's bullet. Daphne, what have I done?"

Daphne pushed her to one side so she could lie curled up next to her friend. "You are not to blame," she whispered fiercely. "Should you have married him despite your feelings, and been unequally yoked? This is the fault of whoever shot him, and not yours at all. Bess, you must not think this way."

"But perhaps love would have grown between us—"

"*Bess.* You cannot dwell on what might have been. Mourn John, yes, but stop making things worse. You cannot bring him back."

Bess shook her head, and a tear struck Daphne's cheek. She put her arms around Bess and held her while she cried, and wept a few tears in sympathy. When Bess's tears ran dry, Bess wiped her face and said, "Thank you."

"I cannot imagine how you must feel right now. Shall I give your excuses at the dinner table and have them send up a tray? And of course Lady Loudoun will understand."

"Yes, please. I cannot face company right now." She hugged Daphne hard, and said, "I still have a letter, half-finished—that is what I cannot bear, all the things I will never be able to say. His poor parents. Oh, Daphne, what a nightmare war is."

"I pray it will be over soon," Daphne said, and slipped downstairs.

BESS WAS NEVER FAR FROM HER THOUGHTS THAT EVENING AS Daphne danced and drank punch and even managed to laugh. The officers and Government House officials Lady Loudoun introduced to her blurred into one long stream of red- or black-coated men, interrupted once by Major Schofeld. Daphne could not understand how he could continue to be pleasant to her after all the set-downs she had given him. He was so pleasant and polite that if not for her knowledge of how he had treated Fletcher, she might have been willing to forgive him what he had said about her. But she was fiercer in her defense of her friend than she was of herself, and spoke politely but without warmth to Schofeld during their two dances.

Just after one o'clock, weary and with aching feet, she bade farewell to the countess and found a quiet room she might Bound from. Her exertions had left her feeling hungry, so rather than Bound directly to her bedchamber, she went to the central hallway of the Residence. It was quiet and dark and still smelled faintly of supper, which had been a delicious pork roast, among other things; Sir Rodney never had fewer than two removes no matter who was dining with him.

Daphne waited a few moments for her eyes to adjust to the darkness, then made her way through the dining room and down the hall to the kitchen. The fires had been banked for the night, the ovens were cool to the touch, and a warm red glow from the embers brightened the dark room. Daphne fumbled her way to the cabinet where the cold meats were kept, and helped herself to slices from the roast, which she ate with her hands. She was too weary to provide cutlery and a plate for herself and too hungry to care what a spectacle she must look.

A shadow passed the window that looked out over the small kitchen garden, and Daphne went still, irrationally fearing being seen. A second shadow went past. They had been large, man-sized, and Daphne set her meal aside and walked noiselessly to the kitchen door. A murmur of voices drifted to her ear, unintelligible. She pressed herself against the window frame and peered out. No one tiptoeing around the Residence at this hour could have legitimate business there.

At first, she saw nothing out of the ordinary. Then one of the shadows shifted, became recognizable as human. Daphne held her breath. One—no, two men, creeping around the Residence. Without considering that she was wearing her best ball gown, she Skipped just to the other side of the window and held still again. Whatever they had in mind, she intended to stop them.

The scent of smoke reached her nose. Red light flared, went orange and then gold, lighting the men's faces. She recognized neither of them, but they were Hindoo, if unusually large for Hindoos. The flames caught, blossomed, and the two men stepped back. They had lit a fire, one that was growing rapidly—

They were trying to burn the Residence down.

Daphne Skipped forward and shoved one of the men hard, hooking his ankle with her foot to make him fall screaming into the fire. She Skipped sideways out of his partner's grasp to a position behind him, grabbed the man around the waist and lifted him off the ground. In an instant she was high above Madhyapatnam, struggling to maintain her hold on the now panicked would-be arsonist. She Skipped repeatedly, as rapidly as she dared, until the man stopped struggling, then dropped him on the roof of the Residence and left him clinging to it, screaming in fear or fury, she could not tell which.

The first man, the one she had burned, had staggered out of the fire and fled. Daphne began hauling the fire apart, pulling the unburned ends of sticks away from the Residence and stomping on them. Her gown caught fire, and she Skipped to the banks of the Hooghly to douse it, then returned. Finally it dawned on her that she need not fight this alone. "Help!" she screamed, Skipping upward and pounding on the nearest window before she fell. "Help! Fire!"

A dark figure came racing around the far end of the Residence. "Lady Daphne!" Wright exclaimed. "What are you doing out here?"

"Fighting the fire—what are you—there is a man on the roof, Captain Fletcher will want to interrogate him—"

"A man on the roof?" Wright dismissed this as lunatic talk and said, "They set fires all around the outside—who knows how they managed to pass the perimeter guards. I have extinguished another. Good luck for us we were both sleepless tonight, eh?"

"Indeed, Lieutenant." More dark shapes rushed past, presumably the perimeter guards. Some brought water from the cistern, others had shovels with which they poured dirt over the flames. Daphne watched, feeling drained, until the last fires were doused. Wright stood beside her, as still as if he were hunting prey. It was an odd image, and one she could not determine why it had occurred to her. "Lieutenant, are you quite well? You have seemed out of sorts since your head injury, and so serious."

Wright jerked. "Am I... yes, Lady Daphne, it is simply that I feel...

frivolity has no place in an investigation such as this. The attempted arson only proves my point, I believe."

"I understand. I hope this does not mean you have lost your native good cheer permanently?"

Wright laughed, his voice once again husky, as if he had inhaled the smoke of the aborted fire. "We shall see."

A tall figure came around the corner of the Residence. "Lady Daphne, are you hurt?" Fletcher said, approaching her and Wright at a run.

"I am well, Captain, but I fear my best ball gown is ruined."

Fletcher laughed. "Quite a loss, but it might have been much worse had you not raised the alarm. Wright, you did well. It's a pity we did not capture any of them—"

"Oh, I forgot! Captain, Lieutenant, will you help me retrieve my captive?"

The man had worked his way around to the eaves and was dangling halfway to the ground when Daphne, Fletcher, and Wright came upon him. "Astonishing," Fletcher said. "Shall we wait for him to fall, or would you like to bring him to earth rather sooner than that, Lady Daphne?"

Daphne Skipped to balance on the roof above the man and hauled him up by the wrists despite his struggles, then Skipped back to the ground and handed him off to Wright. "Take him inside," Fletcher commanded. "Let's see what he has to say for himself."

Daphne followed Wright as he dragged the struggling man into the drawing room and bound his wrists with the curtain tie-back rope. "You need not stay for this, Lady Daphne," he said.

"No, I am quite interested, and I feel a measure of responsibility for him." Daphne seated herself near the man, whom Wright had forced into a kneeling position in the center of the carpet. He had long, greasy black hair and an unshaven face, and wore only a dirty pair of pyjama pants. His bare feet had untrimmed toenails that were grimy and black. He was the least appealing person Daphne had ever seen, but she felt some sympathy for him, being Skipped all over creation and then left to dangle off the roof.

Wright said something to the man in Hindoostani. The man

snarled, but said nothing in return. "Should we not wait for Captain Fletcher?" Daphne asked.

"I merely asked him how he liked being abandoned by his compatriots," Wright said. "I probably should not taunt him, but he nearly burned us all to death in our sleep, so I feel a little taunting is deserved."

The door opened, and Fletcher entered, trailed by Ainsworth and Phillips. All wore nightshirts, though Phillips had had the presence of mind to don his uniform breeches, into which his nightshirt was hastily crammed. Fletcher looked as serene as if he were wearing full court attire. "The fires are all extinguished, and the arsonists have fled," he said. "All but this one. Very quick thinking, Lady Daphne."

"Thank you, Captain. I regret that I let the other one get away, but I did not believe I could handle two at a time."

Fletcher's lips quirked with amusement. "I will make note of that in your record." The smile fell away from his face as he regarded the captive. The captive spat at Fletcher's bare feet and missed. "I wonder if our man here speaks English," Fletcher mused. He walked around behind the man and splayed his hand across the man's right cheek, then grabbed hold of his hair with his left hand when the man tried to jerk away from his touch. "Ainsworth?"

"Do you speak English?" Ainsworth said. The man glared at him but remained silent.

"He does," Fletcher said. The man jerked, tried to turn to look back at Fletcher, but Fletcher's hand held him tightly. "Continue."

"Were there more than five of you involved in this attack?" Ainsworth asked.

Again the man was silent. "Yes, and I believe there were more than ten," Fletcher said. "We will have to have strong words with the perimeter guards."

"Two of them were found dead, their throats slit," Phillips said. "It left a hole the attackers entered by."

"Interesting," said Fletcher. "Tell me something, man—do you take your orders directly from the new prince, or is there an intermediary?"

The man snarled. Fletcher pressed his right hand more closely against the man's cheek. "He has actually spoken with the young man," Fletcher said.

"*How do that?*" the man roared.

"I am a Discerner and fully intend to intrude upon your privacy," Fletcher said. "I will get the information I want from you, whether or not you choose to speak. But it may go easier on you if you choose to answer verbally."

"Let go, bastard!"

Fletcher yanked the man's head back into position. "There is a lady present, and you will watch your language," he said coldly. "Ainsworth, will you continue? I shall need my full concentration for this one."

"Of course." Ainsworth took up a parade rest position in front of the captive, comical in his nightshirt. His stern face was anything but amusing. "Do you know where the... the prince is hiding?"

"No!"

"He does," Fletcher said. "Or, I should say, he did. His uncertainty tells me the prince will have moved on by now."

"Were you meant to survive this raid?" Ainsworth said.

"Yes," the man ground out. "My lord Amitabh wastes no men."

"True," Fletcher said.

"Who slit the guards' throats?" Ainsworth said.

"Not a good question," Fletcher said. "Better stick to yes or no."

"Did you slit the guards' throats?"

"No," Fletcher and the man said as one.

"Do you know who did?"

"No."

"That is a lie," Fletcher said, "but irrelevant to us. Continue."

"Were we all meant to die in the fire?"

"Yes."

"To drive the Europeans out of Madhyapatnam?"

"Yes."

Ainsworth took a step back and raised his eyebrows at Fletcher in inquiry. "Does... Amitabh... know there are more soldiers coming?" Fletcher asked. The man was silent. "Are there many of you?" Silence. "Hmm," Fletcher said. "It seems my lord Amitabh has amassed quite an army. Our friend here has no fear of the soldiers on their way, which means either he is stupid, which despite appearances he is not, or he believes they have numerical superiority. You will show us where the prince is—where he was until recently."

"No," the man said.

"You will, or you will suffer." Fletcher wrenched the man's head around again.

"Suffer worse if I betray him." The man's voice was choked, as if Fletcher had his hands around his throat instead of his face.

"I wonder if you will continue to believe so as you fall a thousand feet to your death. Lady Daphne?"

Startled, Daphne jerked to her feet. "Captain?"

"How far up can you Skip?"

She could see his face as the captive could not, saw him lower an eyelid in a slow wink, and played along. "I do not know, Captain, I can Skip as far as I can see, which is very far when one is looking up. How far would you like?"

The man began struggling, enough that Wright had to pin him to the ground. "No!" the man shouted. "I will show!"

"Very good decision," Fletcher said. "Wright, keep him secured while the rest of us dress. Lady Daphne, will you accompany us?"

"I must change—do not leave without me, Captain—" Daphne Bounded to her bedroom, where to her surprise Bess lay still sleeping, undisturbed by the ruckus. There was an unfamiliar, bitter odor in the air, strongest from Bess's lips and the bedside table. A small brown glass bottle was the source of it. Daphne picked it up and sniffed it. Laudanum. Bess would have needed something to calm her nerves, but this appeared to have knocked her unconscious. Well, if it meant she woke rested and perhaps less distraught, she was welcome to it.

Daphne struggled out of her ruined gown and into her Bounder uniform and returned to the sitting room, Bounding in and startling Wright. She was the first to descend, as the only two people in the room were Wright and the captive. Wright had released him and sat on one of the sofas, watching the man carefully with a loaded pistol held in one hand. "If you wish to change your clothing, I will watch him," Daphne offered.

"I believe Captain Fletcher would skin me alive were I to take you up on that," Wright said, his blue eyes flashing with amusement.

"Nevertheless, I could—I know his essence now, and it might permit me to track him, should he escape."

Wright frowned. "I thought essence belonged to a place. That is, it is not as if I know anything about Bounding but what I have heard from you."

"No, that is true, but people have—it is not essence in the same way, but—oh, perhaps you had better just take me at my word that it is possible." Describing how she identified people to exclude them from her sense of the essence of a place seemed beyond her. It was something she barely understood herself, something an Extraordinary Bounder did by instinct rather than intellect. "At any rate, I—"

With a roar, the captive launched himself at her, hands impossibly free.

Daphne shrieked and Skipped to one side. "Kill you," the man shouted, reaching for Daphne's throat. An explosion rattled Daphne's skull, the sound of a gunshot going off close enough to feel. Bright red blood erupted from the back of the man's skull, spattering Daphne's face with its hot wetness.

Daphne saw Lieutenant Wright's horrified face just before her vision clouded over. "Lieutenant, I cannot," she began, and the grey mist claimed her.

She came to herself only seconds later, or so it seemed. Lieutenant Wright knelt over her, rolling her onto her back, wiping her face with a rough cloth. "Lady Daphne, are you injured? Can you sit? I didn't hit you, did I? Please, Lady Daphne, say something!"

"I am well," Daphne began, then saw the body of the arsonist collapsed with his upper body lying on the sofa. Half his head was missing. "Oh," she said, and wrenched away from Wright's supporting hands. "Oh, he is dead, how did he free himself, you shot him, I believe Captain Fletcher will be displeased." She sucked in a deep breath, then regretted it, for the air was full of the smell of blood.

She heard heavy footsteps running down the hall. "What in the—" said Captain Ainsworth. "*Lady Daphne!* She's injured!"

"No, she is well, Captain, I—I was forced to shoot the captive, and Lady Daphne—"

Fletcher shoved Ainsworth aside and dropped to his knees beside Daphne. "Are you well?" he murmured, putting a gentle hand on her arm.

"I am well, it was just all the blood," Daphne said. She was afraid to sit up again, afraid of what she might see.

"Remove the body," Fletcher said. "Wright, you had better have a good explanation for this."

From Daphne's perspective, Wright was little more than a pair of nostrils and a strong chin. "The captive escaped and attacked Lady Daphne, sir—"

"You let that happen?"

"I must have tied him improperly, sir, I—I'm sorry, I'm sorry, it is all entirely my fault!"

"And you could not subdue him?"

"I panicked, sir. I thought he was going to kill Lady Daphne."

"Lady Daphne can take care of herself. She should not be forced to do so. On your honor as a gentleman." Fletcher turned his back on Wright. "Help Ainsworth with the body. And give me that pistol. You've lost the right to carry one."

"Yes, sir."

Daphne had never heard anyone sound so defeated, and her heart went out to him even as she cursed him for a fool. They had lost important information thanks to his carelessness.

When Ainsworth, Wright, and their gruesome burden had left the drawing room, Fletcher said, "Can you sit?"

"I imagine so, Captain." Daphne kept her eyes averted from the mess on the sofa. "I believe Sir Rodney will—"

"What is going on down here?" Sir Rodney bellowed. He was haphazardly dressed, but commanded the room as if perfectly groomed. "First arson, now gunshots—my word, Lady Daphne, there is blood on your face!"

That was not the kind of reminder Daphne needed. She swayed, and Fletcher's strong hand gripped her upper arm and kept her upright. "An unfortunate accident," he said. "Our man was shot while trying to escape."

"Fletcher, this is too much. I'm inclined to send you all back to Calcutta and barricade this place until the regiment arrives."

"You will not be able to hold out," Fletcher said coolly. "The missing heir, Amitabh, has extensive resources and some kind of secret army. Our best hope for surviving this is to find him before he strikes at us."

"If he has such a large army, why hasn't he come after us before now?"

"I don't know." Fletcher's voice was tense and angry. "I thought he intended to build up support for a popular revolt, but then he attempted to burn this place down, making a direct attack. Yet if he is capable of that... What is he thinking?" He sounded as if he were speaking to himself.

"Well, the ladies at least should—"

"I am needed in case the worst happens, and we must evacuate," Daphne said, quickly heading off that line of thought. "And I cannot stay here alone, so Bess must remain with me."

"Sir Rodney, keep your men close, and let me handle the rest," Fletcher said. "Now, I will help Lady Daphne to her room. She has received a couple of nasty shocks today."

"Of course, of course. This room looks like an abattoir. I will have the ruined furniture removed at first light. Take care, Lady Daphne."

To her surprise, Daphne's legs wobbled too badly for her to stand unsupported, and she gratefully leaned on Fletcher as they walked down the hall toward the stairs. "I can Bound, Captain," she said in a low voice.

"I am afraid you might collapse upon arrival," Fletcher said. "Humor me."

He sounded so grim Daphne only nodded. "At least blood does not show on a War Office uniform," she said.

"Your capacity to see the best in the worst situations astounds me."

"I find that there is almost always a bright way to look at things, and I prefer to be cheerful than gloomy. Though sometimes I am wrong... poor Bess. I do not believe there is anything positive to be seen in her circumstance."

"She was very attached to the young man?"

"Yes, but not the way you imagine, it was not romantic love... I cannot share her secrets with you, Captain."

"You're right. Forgive me for prying."

They reached the top of the stairs, and Daphne opened her bedroom door. "Thank you, Captain. I will be well in the morning."

"It is nearly morning now. Try to sleep a few hours."

"What will you do, now that you no longer have a prisoner to guide you?"

Fletcher shook his head. "I am too exhausted to think. Things may look better once I have slept."

"Something else troubles you, though."

"I forget how observant you are. It is nothing I wish to trouble you with."

"Please, Captain, let me share your burden. Perhaps I will see something you do not."

"Very well. How did the prisoner break free to attack you?"

"I—well, Lieutenant Wright did not secure him properly. We were all in a great hurry, and I suppose he was careless."

"I wonder."

"What else could it be?"

"That is the question. What else *could* it be?"

"You cannot imagine the lieutenant meant for that man to escape? But why?"

"I cannot imagine. But Wright is a good officer. I've never known him to be careless like that, especially when others' lives are at stake. And he has been behaving strangely." He blew out his breath. "It weighs on my mind. Clearly I need rest if I can consider such wild thoughts."

"Sleep well, Captain."

"And you, Lady Daphne." He caught her hand before she could turn away. "I apologize for putting you in danger, however inadvertently."

In the dimness of the hall, his eyes were two dark pools she might drown in. "You said it yourself, Captain," she said, trying for a light tone, "I can take care of myself."

"Nevertheless." He squeezed her hand, then released her. "Good night."

Daphne slipped inside the room, wincing at how the door squealed, but Bess did not sit up, demanding to be told what was happening. She closed the door and wearily stripped off her uniform, then bathed her face and hands, hoping she had got all the blood off. In her nightgown, she lay on her bed and let her aching muscles relax. To think she had come to India longing for adventures. She was beginning to have her fill of them.

CHAPTER 20

IN WHICH TIME IS RUNNING OUT

B ess was still sleeping when Daphne rose a few hours later. She looked peaceful, as if nothing bad had ever troubled her. Daphne examined the little brown bottle of laudanum more closely. It smelled horribly bitter, not like anything edible. She set it down and wiped her fingers on her gown, deciding against waking Bess. Surely sleep could only help her.

She heard the argument when she was halfway down the hall from the dining room. Though the dining room door was closed, the sound was loud and unmistakable. Daphne approached with trepidation. Sir Rodney's booming voice warred with Fletcher's baritone, normally a calm sound, but now furious. She hesitated with her hand on the knob, decided her presence might have a calming effect, and entered.

"I have a responsibility to the Company, damn you!" Sir Rodney bellowed.

"A responsibility—" Fletcher roared, then registered Daphne's presence and visibly contained himself. He dropped into his chair and glared at Sir Rodney. "You do not have a responsibility to incite public revolt," he continued in a quieter, though no less intense, voice.

"Can you guarantee that any given Hindoo on the streets is not a member of this Amitabh's army?" Sir Rodney said.

"I cannot. But that is irrelevant. What you propose will inflame public opinion against us and will increase Amitabh's power. If you shut down the bazaar, we may be facing more than a simple riot."

"They won't dare strike at us. Our men are still better armed, better trained—"

"There aren't enough of them. Sir Rodney, see sense. We must find Amitabh himself and prevent him from taking advantage of the current unrest."

Sir Rodney still had not taken his seat. His fist curled around his fork as if he meant to use it on Fletcher. "You were the one who informed me that Amitabh's forces were mingled with the general populace. The bazaar is a natural place for them to meet and induct others into their ranks. I cannot permit it to remain open, for everyone's safety."

"You will play directly into his hands!" Fletcher shouted, slamming both hands palm-down on the table and standing. "Why can you not see this?"

Daphne cast a quick glance around the table. Wright was not present. Ainsworth sat with his fork, laden with sausage, hovering over his plate. Phillips' mouth hung open with astonishment, and his eyes went from Sir Rodney to Fletcher and back again, following their conversation like a tennis match. She was afraid to do anything so normal as fill her plate or even shut the door, for fear of tipping the balance between them.

"What I see," Sir Rodney said in a low, gravelly voice, "is someone who has forgotten where his duty lies. I am Resident here, and I will remain Resident long after you and your men are gone. I am the one who must live among these people, Captain Fletcher, and those who might rise up against us require a strong reminder of who the governing power in this vicinity is. This is a temporary measure until the regiment arrives, no more. They will understand that."

"You underestimate the level of bad feeling against us in Madhyap-atnam," Fletcher said, matching Sir Rodney's low voice, though his sounded like water over stone rather than rough gravel. "If you ever bothered to step outside this Residence—"

"Don't you dare try to teach me my business, boy," Sir Rodney roared. "You may have the Governor-General's warrant, but that means nothing compared to what I do every day to maintain the Company's presence here! You intend to swan about—"

"I misspoke. I apologize," Fletcher cut across Sir Rodney's near-apoplectic explosion. "You are the authority here. But I have a mandate, as you say, from the Governor-General, and I am responsible to him first and foremost. The Governor-General has instructed me to prevent an uprising in Madhyapatnam. I cannot do this if you persist in ignoring my recommendations."

"Recommendations? You've all but told me how to wipe—" Sir Rodney glanced at Daphne and appeared to substitute words in his head. "You dare to give me orders, in my own Residence?"

"Not orders. I merely point out the weakness in your strategy. I appreciate your concern for Company business, but surely you must see we both want the same thing—to keep Madhyapatnam from falling into civil unrest. If you close the bazaar, the people will see it as an imposition of European strength, and will act accordingly. Please, Sir Rodney, do not act hastily."

"This isn't hasty decision-making. I've been considering this step for the last two days. Lady Daphne and Miss Hanley's experience made me realize how easy it would be for an enemy force to conceal itself among the people within the bazaar."

"Oh, but Sir Rodney," Daphne exclaimed, seeing an opening, "surely our experience shows how safe the bazaar is! We were not molested or even challenged, despite being well outside the places Europeans normally go. If this Amitabh truly had a secret army concealed there, would that not have been an ideal time for them to attack us, when we were at our most vulnerable?"

"Your safety is in my keeping, Lady Daphne," Sir Rodney said, his high color fading. "You should not go outside the Residence at all, while times are so uncertain."

"And we have not. But I have faith that Captain Fletcher and the others are close to apprehending our foe. They cannot be successful if everyone hates them because the bazaar is shut down."

Sir Rodney pursed his lips in thought. He glanced from Daphne to Fletcher, holding the latter's gaze for a long, taut moment. "One more assault," he said, "one more incident of violence against us, and the soldiers will shut the bazaar down. More than that, and I will institute martial law in Madhyapatnam. Is that understood?"

"Perfectly, Sir Rodney," Fletcher said. He took a seat and said, "Good morning, Lady Daphne. I trust you slept well?"

Daphne gaped at how swiftly his anger and frustration disappeared. "Very well," she managed, and walked around the table to the sideboard to help herself to breakfast.

She ate swiftly, afraid of another argument breaking out, but no one behaved as if anything untoward had ever happened. Bess appeared when Daphne was nearly finished, impeccably turned out in her most somber gown. She was even smiling, though Daphne noticed her smile did not quite reach her eyes. No one was so callous as to press her for details. Daphne thought the men seemed uncomfortable around Bess and her grief. So long as no one, and by no one she particularly meant the garrulous Sir Rodney, tried to jolly her along, they could be as uncomfortable as they liked.

When Sir Rodney excused himself, the mood of the room brightened considerably. "I thought you might have us evicted," Ainsworth said to Fletcher.

"I should not have been drawn into the argument," Fletcher said. "The problem is so obvious I could not believe Sir Rodney didn't see it. At any rate, we are back where we started, gentlemen, ladies—we have an invisible enemy whom we cannot find, with an unseen army of which anyone we meet might be a member."

"You make it sound as if it is impossible," Daphne said.

"Not impossible, just very difficult. I have not yet given up hope." He did not sound very certain.

"Should we fear for another attack on the Residence?" Phillips asked. "I know Sir Rodney said he had increased the military presence here, but they might not be able to withstand a full-on riot."

"I believe not," said Fletcher. "The purpose of last night's attack was to make us panic and react punitively against the people of Madhyapatnam, increasing, as I told Sir Rodney, feelings of hatred toward Europeans. Amitabh wants the people to be his army—second army, at any rate. However, people can only be manipulated so far.

Already I imagine there is resentment building toward Amitabh, that he has disrupted the city, and he has shown himself canny enough not to permit that to come to a head."

"So what are we to do?" Daphne asked.

Fletcher directed an ironic look her way. Daphne scowled. "I know what you will say. Ought I to be grateful that you do not simply send Miss Hanley and me back to Calcutta?"

"You will have enough to do later," Fletcher said. "Once we have more information, I wish you to reconnoiter the locations where Amitabh may have gone to ground."

"Fletcher, you can't send her into danger like that!" Ainsworth exclaimed. "Suppose they capture her?"

"Lady Daphne has been trained to do exactly that," Fletcher said, "and I have faith in her and her talent. We will inquire after Amitabh, gentlemen, discreetly and with great subtlety, and we will find him."

"And then what?" Bess asked.

Fletcher looked as if he had forgotten she was there. "Then we will take him into custody and see him tried for his crimes. Without him as a figurehead for this movement, it will surely fall apart."

"I admit to feeling some sympathy for him," Bess said. "Had he been born a year earlier, none of this would have happened."

"Sympathy, yes, but not enough to permit him to continue to disrupt the lives of ordinary people in pursuit of his lost heritage," Fletcher said. "Ordinary people who have lived in amity with the Honourable Company for twenty years." He laid down his knife and fork and stood. "Let us gather in the drawing room—the *other* drawing room, I believe—in half an hour, and we will decide on a course of exploration."

Daphne followed him out into the hall. "Is Lieutenant Wright ill?"

"Lieutenant Wright is avoiding me," Fletcher said. "At least, that is how I interpret his behavior since last night. It is probably for the best, as I have not forgiven him his failure, and I am certain he knows it."

"But it was a simple mistake. Anyone might have made it."

"A mistake that put you in danger. And suppose his shot had missed and hit you?" Fletcher looked like someone who had seen a glimpse of a future filled with horrors. "He will have to prove himself before I am willing to trust him again."

"I... understand. It is just that he did so much to defend the Residence, I am inclined to be generous with him. I was not injured, after all."

Fletcher held the door of the drawing room, the quiet one she thought of as theirs, for her and followed her inside. At this hour, it was even dimmer and cooler than usual. Fletcher went around the room, opening shutters and letting the morning light inside. "You are far more forgiving than I."

"I once needed forgiveness when none was forthcoming, and therefore could not forgive myself. I deeply appreciate the effects when such a burden is lifted." She took a seat and watched him pace before the row of windows. They looked out over an overgrown patch between the Residence and its outer wall. Trees and shrubberies grew in wild profusion, unchecked by Man's taming hand. Daphne could imagine a tiger stalking there, concealed by the trees and the shadowy stripes cast by the early sun.

"I will remember your words," Fletcher said. He turned to look out on the garden, if one could call such a wildness "garden," standing with his hands clasped loosely behind his back.

The door opened, admitting Bess, who took a seat next to Daphne. "It appears I missed all the fun last night," she said. "Did our enemy really try to burn down the Residence?"

"He did, and we learned more of him from someone I captured," Daphne said, though remembering the man's head half blown away made her pleasure at having contributed feel diminished.

"Colonel Dalhousie's Speaker tells you, Captain, that you are to exercise caution in your pursuit," Bess went on. "The regiment will be here in a few days, and he prefers that you have their support if the man sends his forces against us."

"Please give the colonel my thanks, and assure him I will be cautious," Fletcher said with an amused smile. "Though Jack knows me well enough that such an assurance will give him little relief."

"What assurance?" Ainsworth said, entering the room, followed by

Phillips. He carried his hat in his hands and his coat was buttoned crookedly. "Is Wright not joining us?"

"I believe he felt unwell after last night's exertions," Fletcher said smoothly. "I judged it better to let him rest."

Ainsworth shrugged. "That will reduce our effectiveness considerably, but it can't be helped."

"Indeed," Fletcher said. "Ainsworth, Phillips, you will canvas the bazaar and the north side of town. I will take the south. We will meet here at noon to share results."

"Are you entirely certain there is nothing I can do to aid you, Captain?" Daphne said.

"Regretfully, no. Though if Wright's... condition improves, you might tell him where we have gone and ask him to search the west side of Madhyapatnam."

"I will do so, Captain." Daphne tried not to sound disappointed. Fletcher had certainly gone out of his way to give her employment, and the knowledge that it was essentially make-work no longer angered her.

When the men had gone, Bess said, "Now you must tell me every detail of your evening, beginning with the gala. I need something to give my thoughts direction other than dwelling on poor John."

"I would have told you last night, but you slept so soundly I hated to wake you. It was past one o'clock, at any rate."

"I feel much rested. Sir Rodney insisted I take a little laudanum, and I did not like to refuse, he was so kind. It made me sleepy enough that I could lay down my burdens—it is such a relaxing feeling. Though I do not believe I need more of it."

"Oh! I wondered... anyway, the gala was pleasant, though... actually it was somewhat tedious, as I danced with no one exciting and was forced to endure Major Schofeld's company for half an hour."

"How unfortunate that you had no partner more to your liking." Bess's eyes glinted with wicked amusement.

"I thought you had agreed not to tease me again!"

"I remember no such agreement. Besides, it was a small thing, and I only say it because I know *you* know it is true."

"Very well. At any rate—"

"I beg your pardon, Daphne, I am being addressed." Bess tilted her head back, and Daphne went silent. After only a few seconds, Bess said, "You are to return to Government House. Lady Loudoun has need of you."

Daphne sighed. "At this hour? I suppose she will have been up for hours already, but I do not know how she manages to dance until past midnight and still rise with her husband to ride before dawn."

"It is something to do, anyway," Bess said, "and will keep you too busy to repine after what you may not have."

"I fear it will simply make me more impatient," Daphne said. She stood and Bounded away.

Lady Loudoun's request was for Daphne to Bound her to the Governor-General's country residence at Barrackpur, to ready the house for Lord Moira's arrival later that day.

"I admit I prefer it to Government House," she confided to Daphne, "and the air is so much healthier than in Calcutta, don't you agree?"

Daphne, for whom the smells of Calcutta meant adventure, nevertheless concurred. "It is more cozy a dwelling," she said, though the Barrackpur residence was still enormous by any standard. "Shall I bring your children here?"

"No, they are suffering from a slight ague, and Dr. Horrocks insists on treating them at home. It will make this house so much quieter." Lady Loudoun sighed. "I am sometimes overwhelmed by all of them at once."

Daphne could not think of anything to say to this that might not be construed as a criticism, so she merely smiled and nodded.

She made a few more Bounds between Calcutta and Barrackpur, conveying the countess's essential belongings, then Bounded back to the Residence and found the drawing room empty. Rather than Bound to her bedroom to see if Bess were there, she wandered into the hall and stood for a moment, contemplating her options. All the books were in the abandoned drawing room, which might or might not have been cleaned, and Daphne had no desire to return to the scene of such gory events. It was growing too warm to walk in the garden, and she could not go to the bazaar unaccompanied. She would likely be safe, but Fletcher would be furious, and she did not wish to upset him. That he was so concerned for her safety made a warm tingle spread through her chest.

Someone pounded on the door—the rarely used front door, carved with fanciful Oriental creatures. Curious, Daphne stood where she was and watched one of the servants emerge from the dining room and open it. She could not see the person beyond, but whoever it was addressed the servant in urgent Hindoostani. The servant recoiled and looked around, rather frantically Daphne thought. His eye fell on her, and he left the door, coming toward her hastily and gabbling so fast Daphne did not at first realize he was speaking English. "I don't understand," she said.

"Memsahib, come, is for you," the man said. To her shock, he took hold of her hand and tugged her toward the door. "Is terrible, must see."

"For me?" Her first wild thought was that Gopika had returned with some dark pronouncement that would mean all their dooms. She hurried after the man and discovered the visitor was not Gopika, but a Hindoo man, tall and gaunt with his hair slicked back with grease. He started at her appearance and said something urgent to the servant, who shook his head and pointed at Daphne. The man glanced over his shoulder fearfully. He again spoke to the servant, less urgently, and the servant replied, pushing Daphne forward with a gentle insistence. "What is going on?" she demanded.

"He has brought a body," the servant said. "A sahib."

It was Daphne's turn to recoil. "A body? Of a European?"

The man had already turned away. Daphne looked past him to see an oblong bundle wrapped in old cloths drifting toward them, floating off a rickety cart that looked as if it might fall apart given the right provocation. So, the man was a Mover. Would have to be, since the Hindoo faith had strict guidelines for how dead bodies should be handled. Only a Scorcher would touch a body, and that only to perform the funerary rites and begin the cremation ritual.

She watched the bundle drift closer. She ought to retreat inside, find Sir Rodney, but she felt fixed to the spot by an inarticulate need to see this through to the end. The Mover set the body down on the flag-stones just outside the door and stepped back.

"Who... is it?" she whispered. It was a ridiculous question, and one the Mover could have no answer for even if he spoke her language.

The servant had taken a few steps back, away from the body, and said something to the Mover. Without touching the body, the Mover lifted the cloths at one end of the bundle with his talent, unfolding them as if peeling the skin back from a banana. A tremendous stench wafted up from the thing, and Daphne gagged, covering her mouth to hold back the reflex. The face revealed had already begun to decompose in the brutal tropical heat, and Daphne had no way of knowing how long ago the man had died. But there was still enough flesh left that she recognized him immediately.

It was Lieutenant Wright.

CHAPTER 21

IN WHICH DAPHNE MAKES A SHOCKING DISCOVERY

Her shocked, horrified brain seized on this fact and let it whirl round in confusion. Lieutenant Wright? Had he been killed that morning? But surely this body had been dead longer than that. So how...?

"We must arrange for his burial, or cremation, I do not know what is to be done," she said faintly. If this was Wright, then who had helped her prevent the burning of the Residence the previous night? "You should bring him around to the back, we cannot have a corpse on the front doorstep."

She turned away without waiting to see if they would obey her somewhat incoherent instruction. Sir Rodney must be told, and then... but who had they... Her mind, reeling with confusion, kept returning to that one awful question.

Footsteps sounded on the stairs, and Lieutenant Wright came pounding down them, his red coat unbuttoned and his hair awry. "Lady Daphne, forgive me, I overslept," he said. "Where might I find Captain Fletcher?"

She stared at him, mute. In the dimness of the hallway, he was a dark figure, his skin dusky. His blue eyes were the only bright thing about him, and they glinted at her like glass. Like glass. Memory struck like a sledgehammer. The bright-eyed Hindoo at the palace, his expression challenging her. The same man, spotted here and there in the bazaar, the crowds parting for him to pass until he disappeared from sight. Yet that man had looked nothing like Wright, and Wright, facing her now, looked nothing like that man, except for the glass-bright eyes in a dark face.

"Lady Daphne, are you well?" Wright said, walking toward her. She looked back over her shoulder at the grisly lump on the threshold. She was utterly certain the dead man was Wright, which meant... what? Daphne felt rooted to the spot, horror stunning her. It was impossible, but true. This was not Wright. Someone had taken his place. Someone who might alter his body to play the part of a dead man. A Shaper.

Wright looked past her. "What is that?" he said, taking a few steps past her. She grabbed his coat to stop him. Her mind was still too stunned for rational thought, but in her heart she knew she could not permit him to see the body.

"A... delivery," she blurted out. "It is nothing—come with me, Captain Fletcher left instructions—"

He pulled free of her grasp and kept walking. She knew the moment he realized what it was when he stopped abruptly and half-turned toward her. "A body?" he said. "Lady Daphne, did they bring it to you? You should not have had to witness such—faugh, it stinks!"

She examined him as thoroughly as she could, backlit as he was by the sun shining through the doorway. He was a good substitute, almost perfect except for the eyes, which, now that she was looking at them, now that she knew what to look for, were a paler blue than Wright's. But then, eye color could not be Shaped. And the man she had seen at the palace and later in the bazaar, the one she had pursued, was the right height and build to imitate Wright. All he had had to do was change his skin color and the shape of his face, and any Shaper was easily capable of that.

Wright stepped back toward her and took her arm. "You are in shock," he said, "you should lie down."

"Yes, I—come with me, and they will remove the body," Daphne said.

The servant who had insisted on Daphne coming to the door ran back toward them, but skidded on the tiles, staring at Wright. He turned back and looked at the corpse, then at Wright. "*Rakshasa*," he whispered, then screamed something else in Hindoostani and fled in the direction of the front door. He skidded again before reaching the body, reversed direction, and slammed through the dining room door.

"What? Why does he believe I am a demon?" Wright turned a confused look on Daphne. He looked so normal. It simply could not be true. Such things only happened in stories. And yet—

On an impulse, she reached out to touch his cheek. "Remarkable," she said, not thinking to be afraid in her astonishment. "Who are you?"

Wright's brow furrowed. "Lady Daphne?"

"You must have—it was the day of the riot, was it not? And you captured poor Lieutenant Wright, and—who *are* you, and what do you want?"

The false Wright's eyes flicked again to the body but now focused more intently on it. In a flash, his pleasant, confused expression transformed into something hard and cruel. Without a word, he shoved Daphne and sprinted for the door.

The pain of hitting the floor broke Daphne out of her reverie. She cursed herself. She should have pretended ignorance, kept the Shaper there until the officers returned and could capture him. Cursing again, she Skipped to the courtyard and looked around. The Shaper was already out of the Residence walls and diving into the crowd of people thronging the road, no doubt Shaping his legs to be as fleet as a deer. She took a deep breath and focused on following his essence, but it was already distorting out of recognition as his Shaping altered his body. Daphne Skipped again, higher this time, and surveyed the crowd. She could still find him visually. There he was, dodging down an alley. She Skipped to a point just in front of him and planted herself to stop him.

The Shaper kept running. Just before he would have plowed into her, he leaped, an impossible jump, over her head. Daphne spun around and Skipped after him, throwing herself at his legs. They were long and thin under his uniform trousers, and his boots had swelled and split from the force of his calves distending for that jump. The Shaper kicked her hard in the jaw, making her cry out and release him.

Blinking away tears of pain, she stood and ran after him, her face hurting enough that she could not yet concentrate for a Skip.

He ran as if his life depended on it, which was probably true. Daphne's short legs ached with the effort of trying to catch him. She followed the sound of outraged cries as the Shaper shoved men and women out of his way. The bright sun beat down upon her as she ran, sweating from heat and exertion. Her jaw throbbed, and she rubbed it fiercely, willing the pain to diminish and permit her to Skip once more. She tripped over a beggar seated cross-legged directly in her path, spat a hasty apology over her shoulder, and pushed herself to run faster.

Finally, she Skipped and got ahead of him again. She staggered into a couple of men who grabbed her and held her upright. "Let me go!" she shrieked, struggling against their grip. The Shaper turned a corner and disappeared. She wrenched free of their helping hands and Skipped high above the streets, searching for her quarry. There, turning another corner. She Skipped to the air just above him, timing it so she fell the last few feet and struck his back, knocking him down with the momentum of her fall.

He shouted in surprise and twisted, taking Daphne with him. "You will return to the Residence with me, and Captain Fletcher will learn the truth!" she shouted. The Shaper responded with a gabble of Hindoostani, struggling against her hold. Startled, Daphne took a better look at him. He was the right size, and his hair was black, but he was not the Shaper.

With an oath, she was high in the sky again, searching for the Shaper. People gaped up at her, pointing, as she Skipped repeatedly to keep herself in position, almost hovering above Madhyapatnam. Everyone had black hair. Half of them were men. She had lost him.

Wanting to weep with rage and humiliation, she Bounded back to the Residence hallway, startling Sir Rodney. He swore, apologized, and said, "What is this about a body?" Men in dark civilian coats rushed past, giving the impression of ants hurrying to rebuild their nest.

"We have been cruelly tricked," Daphne said, "and Captain Fletcher must return immediately."

"Very well, but who is dead? Lady Daphne, you should have sent for someone. You should not have been subjected to such a sight."

Footsteps sounded on the stairs, such a perfect echo of the Shaper descending only moments before—surely it had not been more than fifteen minutes?—that Daphne's heart raced. "Is anything the matter?" Bess said.

"Everything," Daphne said. "You must call the officers back. We have been tricked, and I do not know what to do next."

Sir Rodney, who had gone to crouch next to the body that still had not been removed, straightened with a surprised oath. "Lieutenant Wright!" he exclaimed. "But this man has been dead for at least three days!"

"I cannot explain it now, Sir Rodney, but the man we believed was Lieutenant Wright was an imposter. A Shaper." Daphne felt even wearier than her exertions could account for, weary and filled with irrational guilt over not having realized the trick sooner. "It must wait for the others to return. Please, have someone care for the lieutenant's body? I cannot bear to look at it longer."

"I should say not," Sir Rodney said. Men in red coats, soldiers from the battalion, stood grouped around the body as if they had never seen one before. Daphne turned and walked with slow, weary steps toward the drawing room where Fletcher had assured her, only hours before, that Wright was simply avoiding him.

How had the Shaper done it? Making himself look like Wright was one thing; aping his mannerisms and knowledge was surely impossible. She thought back over the days since the Shaper must have taken Wright's place. He had been quieter, had not flirted with her or Bess at all, had spent the evenings in his room rather than socialize... she had noticed the difference, but put it down to the lingering effects of his injury. He had succeeded primarily because none of them had even considered the possibility he was not who he appeared to be. After all, why would they?

"Daphne, sit, you look as if you might fall down if you do not," Bess said. "I have told Captain Fletcher and Ensign Phillips to return, that... how is it possible that Lieutenant Wright is three days dead? Daphne?"

"A Shaper took his place," Daphne said, sinking into a seat by feel, "and I cannot imagine our enemy Amitabh did not have something to do with it. Please, do not ask me, Bess, I do not believe I can repeat the story twice."

"A Shaper!" Bess fell silent, for which Daphne was grateful. She was angry with herself for not having captured the man, and had to remind herself that no guilt attached to that failure. She had done her best, but the Shaper knew Madhyapatnam as she did not, and could alter his body to become anything he wanted: the perfect runner, the perfect fighter, the perfect imitation. She should not castigate herself for not apprehending him.

Even so, her failure burned beneath her skin. How much might Fletcher have learned from interrogating him? Instinct told her as reason could not that the Shaper was connected to Amitabh—had likely been sent by him, to do... what? Spy on them? That seemed reasonable. The more she thought about it, the more facts fell into place. The Shaper had known where to find Vaachaspati because Fletcher and the officers had sought out the house where he had told stories in case she and Fletcher needed assistance. And those two soldiers whose throats had been slit last night—they would not have suspected any evil of a comrade. The Shaper's guise had been perfect.

She groaned, and Bess said, "Is something amiss?"

"No, it is just... I cannot believe that Shaper lived among us for three days without us knowing it."

"I still do not understand. Surely even a Shaper could not have effected so perfect an illusion? There must be some other explanation."

Daphne shook her head. "It was just our bad luck that among our number we had one whose physique and coloring were enough similar to the Shaper's that he needed only a few alterations. A Shaper may even alter the sound of his voice, did you know that? I attended a performance once in which a singer, a singer who was also a Shaper, sang in thirteen different voices in a single night."

"It is astonishing," Bess said, and once more fell silent.

The door opened. "What the devil is going on around here?" Ainsworth said. He and Phillips entered the room, both of them red-faced and sweaty with running. "Your message was quite cryptic, Miss Hanley."

"We must wait for Captain Fletcher—"

"Miss Hanley told us Wright is dead," Ainsworth said. "You must tell us *something*, Lady Daphne, or I for one will run mad."

Daphne regarded his desperate, frustrated face, and could not find it in her to deny him. "Very well," she said, "but you must sit quietly, and not ask any questions until I finish, or you will simply confuse things further."

She intended only to gloss over the events of the morning, but found herself adding details for clarification, and in the end told Ainsworth and Phillips the whole story, including her conclusions about what the Shaper had done in Wright's form. "Now if only Captain Fletcher would return," she concluded, "we might begin devising a plan to mitigate this disaster."

"Disaster indeed," Phillips said. "That Shaper knows all our plans. If he is employed by Amitabh—who knows what damage he might do?"

"We must assume Amitabh knows we are hunting him, and that we know his hiding place," Ainsworth said. "He will be prepared to repel an attack. Surprise was to be key to our assault, and we no longer have that."

"Then you know where he is?" Bess said.

"We learned of an abandoned estate, on the outskirts of Madhyap-atnam northward, that would be an ideal hiding place for anyone seeking to conceal an army." Ainsworth paced beneath the windows, exactly where Fletcher had that morning. "We were returning when Miss Hanley summoned us back."

"But the Shaper does not know that," Daphne said. "He fled before your return."

"It is irrelevant in any case," Ainsworth said. "Amitabh will surely move as soon as the Shaper reports he has been exposed. He will disperse his army into the populace to hide until he calls them up for an attack."

"I may still explore—"

"*No*, Lady Daphne," Ainsworth and Phillips said as one. "It was one thing, you risking yourself in reconnaissance when we thought we were acting in secrecy," Ainsworth went on. "But the Shaper knows of that plan. You would simply be walking into a trap."

"So there is nothing for it but to make a new plan," Phillips said, "as soon as Captain Fletcher returns."

"But—" Daphne said, then subsided. Phillips was correct; there was nothing else to do but wait.

"Let us eat something," Ainsworth suggested, "and then I propose to search Wright's room, in case the Shaper left anything of himself behind.

It was a good idea, though Daphne had to stifle some unworthy thoughts about Ainsworth and his appetite. She herself could only pick at her meal, straining to hear the sound of the outer door opening and Fletcher's quick stride crossing the hall. She longed to see him, and not for the usual reasons; she felt she would not be truly comfortable until he told her, himself, that she was not to blame for losing the Shaper. She told herself it was foolishness, that she did not need his good opinion, but she thought of his smile, and the comforting touch of his hand, and knew her heart was utterly lost.

CHAPTER 22

IN WHICH THE PRINCIPLES OF BOUNDING LEAD TO ANOTHER DISCOVERY, LESS SHOCKING

A fter the meal, Daphne and Bess retreated to the drawing room, closing the shutters against the noon sun. Bess soon became engaged in Speaking, and since Daphne felt it would annoy her for Daphne to ask repeatedly to whom she was Speaking, she reclined on one of the sofas and watched dust motes dance in the currents of air flowing from somewhere near the ceiling. She felt bone-weary and emotionally drained, too tired to join in Ainsworth and Phillips' search, too tired even to read. Eventually she nodded off and dreamed of dancing with Wright, surrounded by a thousand faceless men in uniform. In the dream, she was as tall as he, and they danced a dance she had never heard of in the waking world. As they danced, Wright's face grew darker, began to rot, and she dragged herself out of the nightmare just as the flesh slipped from his skull.

Nothing appeared to have changed. Bess still sat with her head tilted back. The room was sufficiently shielded from the sun that with its northern exposure she could not immediately guess what time it was. Daphne stretched and tried to put the horror of her nightmare behind her.

"Are you rested?" Bess said. She still sat in the attitude of a Speaker, her eyes closed, but Daphne knew her hearing was acute. "You seemed to need sleep badly."

"I suppose I did. What time is it?"

"I don't know. After four o'clock, I believe."

Daphne sat up straight. "And Captain Fletcher has not yet returned?"

Bess opened her eyes. Her expression was tense and strained. "We would have woken you if he had."

"But—you did tell him to return?"

"I have Spoken to him five times since you first asked me to summon the officers back. I have no way of knowing if he hears me, or what might account for his delay. I stopped Speaking to him an hour ago in fear that I might be interrupting some delicate negotiation. I am certain there is a good explanation for his absence, Daphne."

"Something is wrong. I am certain of it. I cannot imagine anything more important than the news that one of our own has been murdered and replaced by an imposter." Daphne rose and immediately felt light-headed. "We must search for him."

"How? Madhyapatnam may not be as large as Calcutta, but it is still enormous."

"I do not know, yet. Where are Captain Ainsworth and Ensign Phillips?"

Bess sighed. "Out searching for Captain Fletcher. They do not believe it is impossible either."

"I am so glad. I will change my clothing and join them."

She ran to her room, not even thinking to Bound there in her agitation. Whatever had happened to Fletcher, they would find him, she was certain of it. Swiftly she donned her Bounder uniform and secured her hair more carefully. They would find him, and he would think of some way to defeat Amitabh and his Shaper. There was no reason to fear for him—he was a capable officer and strong—but tendrils of doubt crept into her thoughts. She stomped them out ruthlessly and ran downstairs. Perhaps she should have Bess call Ainsworth and Phillips back, so they could coordinate their search—but no, if they had made progress she did not want to ruin it. She would find them herself, and proceed from there.

At the bottom of the steps she stopped, startled. "Major Schofeld," she said, a little breathlessly. "I did not know you were here."

"Delivery for Sir Rodney," Schofeld said, smiling pleasantly. "How nice to see you, Lady Daphne. May I join you in the drawing room? I am invited for dinner, and I would enjoy talking to you until then."

Daphne suppressed a shudder. "No, Major, I must—of course I would enjoy—but I am on an errand and may not stay."

"Oh? Is it anything I might help with?"

"No, I—wait, *yes*, Major, you will be of great help!" Schofeld might dislike Fletcher, but he could not wish any real harm to come to him. "Captain Fletcher is missing, and there are only three of us to search. Will you help?"

Schofeld made the tiniest expression of distaste before his features smoothed into affability once more. "Missing? For how long?"

"Oh, perhaps five hours? But—"

"Five hours is not long enough to worry. I am certain he will return in time for dinner."

"No, Major, he was summoned back and has not returned, and there is such news that I know he would have returned had he been able. I fear something has happened to him."

"Even so, Lady Daphne, Madhyapatnam is large—there is no point in searching for one man in a sea of men." Schofeld laughed. "You needn't fear for Fletcher's safety. The man is wilier than a greased cat. He never met a problem he couldn't scheme his way out of."

Daphne bristled. "That is uncharitable."

"I have known him for twenty years. It is nothing but the truth." Schofeld's brow furrowed. "Lady Daphne, he has not imposed himself on you?"

"I do not know what you mean. We are friends, certainly."

"Then he has imposed on your good nature." To her shock, Schofeld took both her hands in his in a rather paternal gesture. "I assure you, Lady Daphne, whatever lies he has told you—"

Daphne pulled her hands away. "Do not speak to me in such a way," she said. "Captain Fletcher is an honorable man who has *never* lied to me, and certainly would never mislead me. I do not know what animosity is between you that you would believe so, but I hardly expect someone like *you* to understand that, since you are the kind of man who thinks nothing of taunting others for his own amusement."

Schofeld's mouth fell open. "Lady Daphne," he said, sounding stunned, "what did I say to deserve that?"

"You do not remember? You thought it funny to mock my size and my eagerness to serve, to pretend to admiration when your private words said otherwise, and you expect me not to hate you for it? Did your humor at my expense make you the darling of your comrades, or was it simply for your personal pleasure?"

"The—but that was three years ago, Lady Daphne! And I meant no harm by it. I admired you—"

"That was a terrible way to show your admiration. I cannot believe you expect me not to be offended simply because *you* meant no harm. I have no respect for anyone who takes pleasure in others' pain."

Schofeld pinched the bridge of his nose, his eyes squeezed closed against the onslaught. "I had no idea," he said. "I—yes, I can see how you might have been offended, but I never mocked you to your face. How can you believe I am the sort of man who enjoys hurting others? I have never behaved other than with perfect politeness to you."

"You cannot possibly believe I should forgive you simply because you kept your cruelties concealed from me? It was dishonorable behavior, Major, and as I knew of it regardless, you can hardly claim I was not injured."

"You are correct," Schofeld said, drawing himself to attention. "Lady Daphne, I behaved abominably. I should never have spoken ill of you, even in private, and you are right to be angry. Please, accept my apologies."

He seemed sincere, but Daphne, warming to her subject, was disinclined to back down. "And am I to ignore your treatment of Captain Fletcher? I have seen the deliberate pain you inflict on him." She took a step forward and enjoyed seeing Schofeld back away from her as from a dangerous animal. "There is nothing you can say about your antagonistic relationship with him that can possibly justify that."

Schofeld's formal air of entreaty gave way to confusion. "I don't know what you mean."

"Of course you do. You deliberately inflict your emotions on him to overwhelm his talent. I have seen it. How do you justify *that*? Some admiration for the captain hidden so deep even you are not aware of it?"

"Lady Daphne," Schofeld said, shaking his head, "you are overwrought. Fletcher has lied to you to gain your trust and make me look like a monster. I have never done anything more to him than tease him, and he deserves it, I promise you he does."

"I fail to see how you are entitled to determine what punishments others deserve. I have seen the effects with my own eyes, Major. Captain Fletcher becomes ill after your so-called teasing. It shuts down his talent entirely. Lie to yourself if you must, but do not attempt to lie to *me*."

"Ill?"

Too late Daphne realized what a weapon she had just handed Schofeld. "I have nothing more to say to you," she said. "I must search for the captain. If you wish to be of help, you can aid me. Otherwise, let me alone."

"Lady Daphne, wait." Schofeld's hand hovered over her arm, but he did not quite dare to touch her. Wise of him, Daphne thought, considering she might just bite his hand off if he did. "I cannot—I apologize for causing you pain. Please believe I intended no harm."

"I may be able to forgive you someday," Daphne said, "and..." He looked unexpectedly miserable, and despite herself she felt a pang of remorse. "I believe that you did not intend to insult me. But Captain Fletcher is my friend, and—"

"Fletcher and I have known each other since before our talents manifested," Schofeld said. "I can offer you my apologies for the wrong I have done you, but I will not justify myself to you. I assure you that you are mistaken, because contrary to what you believe, I have never caused deliberate harm to Fletcher." His words were bold, but there was uncertainty in his eyes.

"That is something you will have to discuss with the captain," Daphne said. "And now I truly must go."

"Let me prove my sincerity by helping you search," Schofeld said. "Where did Fletcher go missing?"

"To the south. We might quarter the city, but if he is trapped somewhere—"

"You have reason to believe he might be trapped?"

"If he has not returned, I assume it is because he cannot."

"Then searching for him visually is pointless. Pray, do not rip up at me again, Lady Daphne, I say only what seems obvious to me."

Daphne sighed. "No, you are correct. But I cannot stand by and do *nothing*."

"It is a pity there is no way to Bound to a person the way an Extraordinary Speaker Speaks to a distant mind." Schofeld pinched the bridge of his nose again. "It is not as if people do not have a unique essence."

"Yes, and I can certainly identify him," Daphne began, then fell silent as Schofeld's words set her to thinking. *Was* there a difference between a person's essence and a location's?

"We can attempt the search if you wish. I simply do not want to waste our time, if there were something more productive we might do."

"There is," Daphne said. The essence of a place, cluttered by the essence of a person... to Bound to such a place, one must exclude those human essences and encompass the pure uncluttered clarity of the location's essence... "Suppose I Bound, not to a location, but to a person?"

"That is impossible. The essence of a person is the wrong kind of essence."

"So far as anyone knows. Who has ever tried it to find out for certain?"

Schofeld shrugged. "Then try the experiment. You will likely just fail, and go nowhere."

"You will not dissuade me?"

"I was not aware Lady Daphne St. Clair could be so easily discouraged, once she set her mind to a thing." Schofeld smiled, his eyes twinkling, and Daphne, caught off-guard, smiled back, a real smile. Perhaps Schofeld had some redeeming qualities, after all.

"Then I will try."

She considered going to the drawing room for privacy, but the idea had taken hold of her to such a degree she did not want to postpone the attempt. Bounding to a person rather than a place... Why had no one ever thought to do that before? Excitement took the place of her anxiety and fear for Fletcher. She was certain it was possible, and she would be the first to prove it. What a difference this would make to the War Office!

She closed her eyes and relaxed her breathing, in through the nose, out through the mouth, shutting out her awareness of Schofeld standing nearby. The momentary conviction that Schofeld would not mock her for failure startled her, then she shut that away too and focused on Bounding.

Essence. For an Extraordinary Bounder, it defined a place, comprising its shape and texture, the way the sound echoed off its walls, the smells that lingered just outside human perception. Places filled with too many things, or too much movement, had no essence, or, more specifically, had an essence too fractured for a Bounder to connect to. Places containing people ought to fit that definition, but for the fact that humans all had an essence of their own that an Extraordinary Bounder could easily exclude from the essence of the place. It was those latter essences Daphne sought now—specifically, one essence.

She knew him so well now that her memory of what made him himself sprang instantly to mind: his quick smile, his ready laugh, those dark eyes that saw her so clearly it was as if he knew her essence as well. She drew on those memories, then turned them outward, searching for the man in a sea of other men.

She felt herself try to Bound almost immediately, but only to the drawing room, where she had last seen Fletcher. Instead she held herself poised, caught between the present and the future, a sensation like being pulled gently in all directions, and made herself search. Focused as she was, she became aware of others first: Schofeld, immediately to hand, then Bess and Sir Rodney, still close by. Other essences presented themselves, all feeling as if they were as near as her own hand, even the ones like her parents that she knew were thousands of miles away.

Then she found him, quivering in her other senses like a butterfly trapped in jelly. Before she could lose either her sense of him or her precarious Bounding position, she Bounded to him.

Agony shot through her, white-hot burning pain that consumed her. She screamed, and tried to Bound away. Something held her, and for a moment she was two people and could not remember which of them was her. The burning pain intensified, so hot it felt cold at the same time. Screaming again, she wrenched herself free of the fierce grip, struck something hard, and everything went black and still.

CHAPTER 23

IN WHICH DAPHNE IS AN
IMPROPER YOUNG LADY

S he came to herself on a hard, cold surface that smelled of dust
and dry wood, fragrant like old cedar. Her head hurt as if
someone had pounded it with a hammer. She tried to raise her
hand to feel her skull, to learn whether it was as shattered as it felt, but
her arm ached numbly to the point she could not move it. Distantly,
she heard herself moan, but could not feel her throat vibrating with
the sound.

Footsteps sounded somewhere nearby, and someone knelt beside
her. "Try not to make noise," Fletcher said. "We cannot let them know
you are here."

A dozen questions sprang to Daphne's mind, but no sound came
out when she opened her mouth. "Can you sit?" Fletcher said. "You are
clearly in too much pain to Bound." He put his hands under her shoulders and eased her upright. A spike of pain shot through her skull, but
when she was sitting, the aching eased considerably. She opened her
eyes and blinked away tears. Fletcher's blurry face hovered about a foot
from hers, his expression tense. He let her go, and she wobbled, but
managed to stay sitting up.

The only light came from tiny round windows high in the walls like
a dozen lidless eyes. The dimly lit room smelled disused and was

completely devoid of furniture. The hard, cold floor was made of wooden tiles, interlocked like a puzzle box. A riot of colored mosaics in abstract patterns covering the walls gave the impression of a rose garden left to its own devices for a decade. Fletcher had stood when he released her and walked, somewhat stiffly as if his body ached, to a square doorway to one side of the room. He disappeared through it without saying anything else. Daphne tried to rise, but that black numbness has taken hold of her legs as well, and they refused to obey her.

Shortly, Fletcher returned to kneel in front of her, a slow, tentative movement. "How are you here?" he asked in a low voice. "You cannot possibly know this place to Bound to it."

Daphne worked her mouth and swallowed to moisten her throat. "I Bounded," she creaked, cleared her throat and tried again. "Bounded to you. To your essence." Memory was returning. She had Bounded, yes, and it had hurt more than any pain she had ever known, which was certainly unlike Bounding—

"Oh," she said. "Oh, that was stupid. I have been luckier than any Bounder ever deserves to be."

"What do you mean?"

"I located your essence and tried to Bound to it. But when one Bounds, one travels to *within* the essence of a place... and I believe my body tried to merge with yours."

"It certainly hurt enough for that to be possible. What possessed you to do anything so reckless?"

His sudden anger startled her. "I... you were missing, we could not find you, it was all I could think of—"

"And your death would have helped locate me?"

Guilty shame flooded through her. She had been so caught up in the potential glory of her discovery she had not thought it through. She might have killed Fletcher as well. "I did not know it could kill me. Major Schofeld thought it would simply fail."

"Schofeld encouraged this? I thought you had better sense than to pay any heed to that fool." Fletcher stood, unfolding one slow joint at a time, and turned his back on her. "And now we are both trapped here."

"I can Bound us—I just need to recover—"

"They will return for me at any moment." Fletcher swore explosively and did not apologize. "I was in a position to escape until you... arrived. Now it is hopeless."

Her heart ached as much as her body. "Then you should go—I will recover soon, and Bound away—you need not wait on me."

Fletcher laughed, a short, bitter sound. "I am certainly not going to leave you, helpless as you are, simply to gain my freedom. They will search this place when I do not appear immediately. No, you will hide in here, and when you are recovered, you will Bound back to the Residence and send troops. And pray Amitabh doesn't have me killed outright before that."

"But... where?"

"We're locked in the *zenana* of the old palace. Amitabh has been hiding here the whole time. All that nonsense about him being outside Madhyapatnam was... well, nonsense. It is so much worse than we believed."

"How so, Captain?"

"Amitabh is not trying to restore his birthright. He is here as an agent of Napoleon, intent on bringing Madhyapatnam under French control. Napoleon wishes his empire to exceed that of Alexander the Great, you know, and conquering India would both accomplish that and weaken Great Britain's power. Amitabh cares nothing for Madhyapatnam, just as the women said; he is using it as a pretext for doing his master's bidding."

Daphne's mouth fell open. "But... how can he convince the people of Madhyapatnam to agree to it? This will bring nothing but bloodshed!"

"The palace is full of French soldiers, waiting for their moment. And there are those in Madhyapatnam who believe they will be rewarded in the new regime if they are loyal now. Perhaps some of them genuinely believe Amitabh deserves to rule, but I believe most of them are as opportunistic as he." He let out a pained sigh. "I have done Wright's memory a grave disservice. I thought at first, when I saw him standing with Amitabh, that he had been suborned. Miss Hanley's message about the Shaper was a complete surprise."

"It was a surprise to all of us, Captain. We could not have known."

"I knew he was behaving strangely. I should have pressed him harder."

"I do not see how we could have guessed at the reason for his strange behavior." She had so longed for his reassurance that his anger was another spike of agony through her heart. She wiped away a tear, furtively, ducking her head so he would not see her weep. "Have they... hurt you?"

He laughed that awful, bitter laugh again. "No need. Amitabh is a Discerner—an Extraordinary Discerner. He has been... interrogating me. I have been resisting. At some point, he will decide I am more trouble than I am worth, and then I will partake of Lieutenant Wright's fate."

"Then you must escape, Captain! I will be well enough on my own."

"Don't be more of a fool than you already have been. I can withstand long enough for the troops to storm this place."

"But I—"

"That is an *order*, Lady Daphne!" Fletcher shouted, the words echoing off the walls, then closed his mouth hard as if he could take the explosion back.

Daphne found the strength to rise and face him. "Do not shout at me, Captain," she said as coldly as she could manage. "I have done what no other Bounder ever dreamed of doing, and yes, it was a mistake that might have killed us both, but I could not bear to leave you captive, or hurt, or... I did not know what to believe, when you did not return, except that you have never failed to come when I needed you, and if something terrible had happened, I could not simply sit still and not know!"

They faced each other, the few feet between them filled with bitter acrimony. More tears slid down Daphne's cheeks and she refused to wipe them away, feeling obscurely that the action might give them power over her.

Fletcher lowered his head and let out a deep, despairing breath. "I apologize," he said quietly. "I should not have spoken so to you. I am angry with myself for falling into Amitabh's clutches and by extension involving you. Of all the people I know, you are the last I would want to share my confinement with."

It was the worst blow of all. Reflexively, she tried to Bound away from him, but her body still hurt too much to do so. "I realize I am useless," she said miserably, "but I did not believe you would be so cruel as to remind me of it."

Fletcher's head snapped up. "Lady Daphne, *no*," he said, crossing the distance between them in two long strides. He raised his hands as if he wanted to shake her but let them fall without touching her. "If Amitabh were to learn what he could force me to do, simply by threatening you... I would not be able to bear it if he chose to torture me through you." He raised his hand again and brushed her cheek, the lightest of touches, but it made him tremble and close his eyes briefly. "I deserve your anger," he said. "Please, forgive my hasty words. My fear for you... I spoke carelessly, and I regret it more than I can say."

Daphne blinked up at him, at his anguished face, and her anger evaporated. Her heart swelled within her, misery and love threatening to overwhelm her if she did not find the right words to tell him she would forgive him anything. Or... perhaps she did not need words. She reached out and took his hand, letting her heart speak for her.

Fletcher's eyes widened. His hand closed firmly over hers, his skin warm and pleasantly dry. His mouth opened, but no sound emerged. He looked so stunned Daphne could not help but smile. It prompted a smile from him, the warm smile that said he knew a wonderful secret, the smile, Daphne realized, he only ever shared with her. "Daphne," he said, "oh, my love," and bent to kiss her.

His kiss left her breathless, speechless, sending a rush of joy through her that set her whole body tingling. He gasped and pulled her close to him, kissing her again and again until she burned with the longing for more. They had been this close before, when she Bounded or Skipped with him, but it had never felt like this, his body against hers, his arm circling her waist. She released his hand to put her arms around his neck and returned his kisses, feeling utterly wanton and not caring one bit. If this was something no proper young lady would ever dream of doing, she did not want to be proper.

A scraping sound, an ancient key in a rusted lock, broke them apart. Fletcher brushed one last kiss across her forehead, then gently pushed her away. "Hide back here, and when you are recovered, Bound back to the Residence," he whispered.

"But—"

His eyes blazed a warning. "Just go!" He turned and disappeared through the square opening. Daphne heard a deep voice address him in French, heard Fletcher reply in a tone that did not suggest he might be going to his death, and then the door ground shut again.

Daphne backed away from the opening, into a corner where she could not possibly be seen from the door, and sat against the wall. Her pain was fading, but not enough, and she closed her eyes and cursed, quietly. She was doing so many improper things today she felt hardly entitled to call herself a lady. If only Bess could read her mind! They could send the soldiers immediately, and not wait on her recovery. Not that she wished Bess to know what she had been doing only moments before.

The thought of Fletcher alone, facing down Amitabh, filled Daphne with wordless terror. She tried not to imagine the kind of suasion an Extraordinary Discerner might use. Fletcher had said he was resisting, and as a Discerner he was certainly aware of how his emotions would appear to another Discerner, but who knew how long he might be able to hold out? He needed help immediately.

She stood and walked to where she could peek around the opening. The room beyond was as bare as hers, and as intricately decorated. A door with a grille in its center stood opposite the opening. Daphne jerked back into hiding, but no one exclaimed, and the door did not open. She peeked out again, then carefully made her way across the room to the door and looked out through the grille. The door opened on a short corridor, not nearly so colorful as the *zenana*, and dimly lit at both ends by lamps that gave off a smoky, bitter smell. It was empty.

Daphne rested her hands on the grille and tried to picture where she was with regard to the outside world. She remembered the door Fletcher had showed her in the palace wall, the one he had said led to the *zenana*, if indirectly. It was no doubt locked, but suppose she could open it, permit the soldiers access to the palace at two points instead of just the one gaping hole at the front? If she could get free, she could do that, and by the time she was finished, she would no doubt be recovered enough to Bound to the Residence.

She pressed her face hard against the grille, straining to see where the hallway went. At both ends, it made a sharp turn away from the *zenana*, presumably toward the center of the palace. That did her no good. She needed more information. She stepped away from the door, her hands still resting on the grille, and the door moved fractionally toward her. She tugged harder, and it groaned quietly as it swung inward on its ancient hinges. Of course. With their prisoner no longer within, there was no point in locking the *zenana*. Daphne silently said a swift, incoherent prayer of thanks and pulled the door open enough for her to slip through.

Tiptoeing, she hurried down the corridor to the right and peeked around the corner. The new hallway was wider, tiled in vivid blue and scarlet and deep green, and its ceiling came to a peak high above. It, too, was lit by more smelly lanterns, and it extended into the distance with no sign of any other exits. Daphne backed away quietly, though she saw no more movement there than before.

To the left, around the corner, another hallway extended into the distance. This one had doors along its length, most of them on the right, one larger one on the left. The right-hand doors had to lead deeper into the palace, but that left-hand door... it must be the one she sought. Daphne listened, straining to hear movement, then ran for the door. It did not appear to have a lock at all, just a heavy iron bar slung across it preventing her opening it. Daphne put her weight under it and heaved. It gave slightly, perhaps an inch, before falling noisily back into place. She quickly looked around to see if the noise had summoned anyone, but the hall remained unoccupied save for her.

She examined the bar more closely. It did not simply sit in its slots; one end of it was fastened to a fat iron pin it might swivel around. Naturally, this was the end Daphne had pushed on. She switched to the other end of the iron bar and heaved on it. The pin squealed as the bar pivoted around it, up and into brackets on the wall beside the door. Daphne shoved hard on it until she was certain it was secure and would not come swinging back down into place. Then she pressed down on the latch, one slow inch at a time, until the pin engaged and the door swung inward a few inches.

Cheering silently, she sat and removed one of her boots, then peeled off her stocking and jammed it into the latch mechanism. Now the door would close without latching, and the soldiers need only push on it to enter the palace. Hopping on one foot, she put her boot back on and leaned against the door, breathing a little too rapidly from her exertions. Excitement and fear for Fletcher's life made her blood pulse harder than it should. She would return to the *zenana* to rest just a few more minutes, and then Bound away and tell the soldiers where to go.

When her heart had stilled somewhat, she ran back along the corridor. The lamps stank badly; they would be unbearable in cramped quarters. But they gave off enough light to guide her feet—

—and to show her the face of a tall, muscular soldier just as she rounded the corner and ran into him.

She Skipped out of his reach, or tried to; a stabbing pain went through her head as she attempted it. The man's reflexes were better than hers, and he grabbed her arm before she could flee the traditional way. In French, he said, *"Where did you come from?"*

"Let me go," she replied in the same language. His grip was like a vise, but she tried to pull away anyway.

He regarded her with puzzlement, then swept her up over his shoulder and walked away down the right-hand corridor. *At least he will not see what I did to the door*, she thought wildly.

She fought him with every ounce of strength she possessed, but might as well have been a kitten fighting to free herself from the coils of a python, for all the good her fighting did her. Finally, her captor silently slapped her across the face, a ringing blow that dizzied her and momentarily sapped her strength. Despairing, she sagged, thinking perhaps this would fool him into relaxing his grip and letting her slip away. But if anything, he held on tighter. Not that it mattered; her head and body still hurt, and Bounding eluded her.

She heard noises now, the sound of many men together in one place, laughing and talking at too great a distance for her to make out the language. A chill went through her, fear at being helpless and surrounded by her enemies, and she began to make plans for getting away that did not depend on her Bounding talent. There were horribly few of them, and all of them were founded on her captors being stupid, or arrogant—not things she could depend on. She felt tears come to her eyes and she dashed them away angrily. Crying would not save her.

The noises grew louder, and she craned her head to see where the man was taking her. She caught a glimpse of a large room that stank of the lamps and unwashed bodies, heard a dozen conversations in unrefined French, and then, to her surprise, they went past it and into an empty chamber where her captor's footsteps echoed. This one had a high, vaulted ceiling, with more of the tiny round windows near the top, and the ruddy light told her sunset was coming. If she had not been so foolhardy, the soldiers might have been on their way now. Instead, she was a captive, and Fletcher would be furious—

The man pushed open a door that creaked in a high, thin wail. Daphne caught a glimpse of another high ceiling, and tiled walls that flickered with what looked like real gold. She raised her head and saw in the lamplight men in French military uniforms lining the walls, all of them armed with swords and pistols thrust through their belts. Their stern visages regarded her dispassionately, as if they knew she was small and helpless and no threat. She glared back at them, though her heart was pounding again, this time with terror.

"*What is this interruption?*" someone said angrily.

"*I caught her in the hall. I do not know how she entered,*" the man replied in a gruff voice. He swung Daphne off his shoulder, setting her roughly on the floor and giving her a shove so she staggered forward. Angrily, she turned on him, fists raised, though she had no idea what she intended to do to someone his size—batter his toes into submission, possibly? He looked briefly startled before bursting into laughter and prodding her shoulder, making her stagger again. He grabbed her by the shoulders in a painful grip and turned her around.

Fletcher stood there, some ten feet away from her, looking more impassive than she'd ever seen him. He was not bound, but stood stiffly, as if he were afraid to move. Another ten feet from them, forming the point of an equilateral triangle, was a dais that rose three steps above the floor. Upon it stood a throne carved of pink marble, its arms and back decorated with elaborate human figures that appeared to be dancing. It would have been unspeakably gaudy anywhere but India. A red velvet cushion rested on its seat, trimmed with gold cord and tassels, but no one sat upon it.

Seated on the dais in front of the throne was a young Hindoo, clean-shaven and extremely handsome. It took Daphne only a moment to remember that she had seen him before, lounging in the door of the palace with the Shaper that day she and Fletcher had visited. Then, he had looked away as if embarrassed to be caught staring. Now he gazed at Daphne with fascination. It was the look of an entomologist who had discovered a representative of a new species of bug and was considering how best to dissect it. She stared back at him coldly, refusing to be intimidated.

Movement distracted her eye. Behind the throne, the Shaper, still in the guise of Lieutenant Wright, leaned against its tall back. She expected him to smile maliciously, to taunt her with having escaped her grasp, but he merely looked at her the way he might a dog, or a horse—some creature that might prove useful, but whose opinion he would not even consider entertaining. It was a more terrifying look than the one the young man wore, so she returned her gaze to him and tried to pretend the Shaper was not in the room.

The young man shifted his position, bringing his knees up and resting his chin on them. It was such a youthful gesture Daphne realized that he could not be much older than she. "You are disturbed," he said without taking his eyes off her, yet she was certain he was not speaking to her. "Interesting." His English was precise, French-accented but easily intelligible.

"You have been battering at me for hours. I believe 'disturbed' is an understatement," Fletcher said, his voice calm. Daphne was afraid to look at him, for fear her eyes might give her heart away.

"It is not that. Something has changed." The young man stood in a lithe movement and came down the steps of the dais to stand in front of Daphne. "I wonder."

Daphne tried to project emotions, wishing she knew Schofeld's trick—anger, determination, fearlessness. The young man's eyes widened briefly. Then he laughed, a merry sound such as any schoolboy might utter. His hand darted out, quick as a snake striking, and grabbed Daphne's chin, so that if she had not already been looking at him she would have no way to look elsewhere.

"I believe," said Amitabh, "you deserve my full attention."

CHAPTER 24

IN WHICH A CONFRONTATION LEADS TO A TERRIBLE ULTIMATUM

"I believe you are a troublemaker," Daphne said. "Let us go."

"And lose the opportunity to learn more of you, fearless girl? You whose demeanor matches her words so perfectly?" Amitabh's grip grew painfully tight, making Daphne close her eyes. Her body no longer ached, the pain in her head was bearable now, and if she were not held tight by the enormous soldier, she might have Bounded back to the Residence as Fletcher had ordered. She looked at him, at how controlled he was, and her heart ached at the thought of leaving him behind. She had to find a way to bring them both out of this safely.

"Ah," Amitabh said, releasing her with a twist of his hand that rocked her head back. "You care for him. But he… I believe you may be doomed to disappointment, girl. Or do you know this already? Your misery pours off you like steam from a boiling cauldron."

"The others believed he cared for her," the Shaper said. He sounded less like Wright now, his voice husky and with the faintest hint of a French accent.

"He shows no sign of it." Amitabh drew a fingertip along the line of Daphne's cheekbone, making her flinch. Had not Fletcher once said high-caste Indians would not willingly touch a European? Why was Amitabh so different?

"Take care," the Shaper said. "She is *kūdne vālā*, and will escape if you give her room."

"Is she? Interesting." Amitabh made a gesture, and the hands clamped down harder on Daphne's shoulders, pressing her into the ground. She clenched her teeth hard to prevent a cry of pain from escaping. Fletcher did not need any such distractions.

"You came seeking your captain, did you?" Amitabh continued. "How did you bypass my guards? They are ever vigilant."

"Not vigilant enough," Daphne said. "It was easy."

The blow caught her by surprise, rocking her head back again. She swallowed, tasting blood. "I will not tolerate lying, certainly not from a European woman. You did not enter by the front door. I ask again, how did you bypass my guards?"

Daphne did not dare look at Fletcher. "I Bounded to where he was."

"You do not know the... is it signature? You have never been inside this place. How is it done?" Amitabh sounded genuinely curious, not at all angry. Daphne wished she were free to return blow for blow—or better yet, to Skip with him through the palace until she could see sky, then drop him from a thousand feet up.

"It is essence," she said, "and you would not understand how it is done unless you are also an Extraordinary Bounder."

He slapped her again. "Try."

She glared at him. "Can you explain to me how you know when I lie? There are things only one who shares your experience can understand. I followed Captain Fletcher's essence and Bounded to it and very nearly lost my life. It is not a thing I will do again."

Amitabh shrugged and turned away, apparently losing interest as rapidly as he had pounced on her. "Then you cannot teach my Bounders."

"If they are Extraordinaries—but I would teach them only to kill themselves, and I do not believe you want that."

"Unfortunate." Amitabh walked up the steps of the dais and once again seated himself before the throne. "Perhaps you will be more forthcoming than the captain. Tell me, how many troops are stationed at Fort William?"

"I do not know. I am not a soldier."

"How many troops defend Government House?"

"Again, I do not know."

"Lady Daphne is with the War Office and as such is little more than a courier," Fletcher said, in an impassive voice that matched his demeanor. "She knows nothing of war."

"And yet she traveled with you. Patenaude, what do you know of her?"

The Shaper stood upright and let his fingers trail across the marble of the throne's tall back. "She is far more than a courier," he said. "Her reputation as an Extraordinary Bounder is unparalleled. I do not know why she is in India and not the Peninsula, but I presume it is a punishment for some misdeed. She is required to return to Government House on occasion to convey Lord Moira's wife and children, so she knows its interior well. She might be a better choice than Fletcher."

Daphne risked a glance at Fletcher. He was still impassive, his eyes fixed on Amitabh, who in turn had his gaze on Fletcher. They had the focused look of two men engaged in a wrestling match, which Daphne had once seen when she was intended to be elsewhere. There had been a moment when the wrestlers stood poised, each gripping the other, muscles distended and taut, neither giving way. She was reminded of that moment now.

"You will give in to me," Amitabh said, his voice tense. "I do not see why you persist in fighting."

"I will not," Fletcher said calmly. He gave no hint of the struggle raging between them. "Your efforts are pointless. I am far more experienced at this than you. Release us, and I will see that your grievances are heard."

Amitabh laughed, throwing his head back and roaring with delight. "Will you? How generous, when we both know the Honourable Company has nothing resembling honor when it comes to its treatment of its... subjects. They will never give up Madhyapatnam—its revenues are far too great."

"They will recompense you for your loss. You will not be prince, but you will not be impoverished. You need not throw in your lot with the French."

"I need not sense your emotions to know that is a lie, if a well-meaning one. I will even do you the courtesy of believing *you* believe it."

"I would not make such a promise were I not capable of fulfilling it. My word means much to those who matter."

"You are so very *earnest*, Captain, so determined to see this poor Hindoo treated fairly. Madhyapatnam means nothing to me. I am French, not Hindoo, and the place stinks of poverty and filth. It is the means to an end only. I will take Madhyapatnam in the emperor's name, and he will drive the English from India, and *then* I will have my reward in the drawing rooms of Paris."

Amitabh gestured, and Fletcher slowly rose off the floor. His arms and legs remained as still as if they were bound. Daphne looked around wildly, hoping to identify the Mover who had Fletcher in his power, but none of the men in the room seemed to be paying attention to the conversation. Fletcher still did not seem ruffled by this turn of events.

"Angry again, girl?" Amitabh said. "You dislike seeing your captain treated this way. If he tells me what I want to know, I will release him."

"What do you want to know?" Daphne asked.

Amitabh gestured again. Fletcher flew across the room to impact with the wall above a soldier's head with a sickening thump. Daphne cried out and struggled against her captor, and got perhaps a fraction of an inch away before his hands settled on her shoulders firmly. "No!" she shouted. "This will not get you what you want!" They had not hurt him before, Fletcher had said; this show was for her benefit, to convince her to give in so Fletcher would not be tortured. But she had no idea what Amitabh wanted.

The unseen Mover brought Fletcher back to stand in the same place. His head wobbled as if he could not quite hold it up. Daphne wiped a tear from her cheek and said, "If you simply delight in causing others pain, I refuse to have any sympathy for you."

"As if you had sympathy before," Amitabh said.

"I did. Vaachaspati told such a story... it was so sad, and I could understand why you would be angry at being denied your inheritance

—how can you not care for your people, and start riots that get them killed? I do not understand you at all. Did your Shaper kill Vaachaspati? We thought he did."

"Vaachaspati knew the truth about my plans. He would have told you far too much about me. I could not permit that."

Daphne glared at the Shaper. "It was a cruel, horrid deed to kill a holy man. I wish I had caught you so you could hang for his murder."

Amitabh laughed. "The Company cares not for the murder of Indians. They would simply consider it one less stupid Hindoo to trouble the world."

"That is not true. And I would not have permitted that."

"And again we come up against the question of who you are, girl." Amitabh's eyes narrowed in thought. "Your confidence comes from... what? Your talent? Your rank?"

"She is the daughter of a marquess, and his heir," the Shaper said. "I tell you, she would be ideal."

"Ideal for what?" Daphne asked.

"Leave Lady Daphne out of this, Amitabh," Fletcher said. "She will not do as you ask."

"Even to save your life?"

"Even then."

"What are you talking about?" Daphne demanded.

Amitabh walked toward her. "My men are poised to attack the Company in Madhyapatnam. They need only a... distraction. Something to disrupt the Company's presence here. An assassination."

"Assassination? Sir Rodney?"

"No." Amitabh smiled. "The Governor-General."

Daphne was struck breathless. "You cannot assassinate the Governor-General," she said when she regained the power of speech. "You would never be able to reach him. He is too well surrounded by loyal men."

"*I* would not, true. But one of his own loyal men could. Or... women."

Daphne drew in a deep breath. "I will not do such a monstrous thing."

"Not even to spare the life of the man you love?"

Daphne glanced at Fletcher, swiftly, then once more glared at Amitabh. "He would never forgive me if I did."

"I can make him suffer. It would be on your head."

"It would be on *your* head, you... I do not know a word awful enough for what you would be if you would do such a thing, but do not believe I am so foolish as to be swayed by that threat."

"Just imagine, girl... you might Bound there from here, shoot the Governor-General through the heart, or the throat, and Bound back, and I would allow the two of you to go free!"

"Stop it," Fletcher said. "She will never agree to it. I am the one you need, Amitabh."

Amitabh stopped, inches from Daphne's face. "You slipped," he whispered. "I felt it. You slipped."

Fletcher's face shone with sweat. "I did not."

"Yes, you did. I felt it. Fear, and..." He walked toward Fletcher and gripped his chin as he had Daphne's, holding his head in place. "It is gone now."

"You are imagining things," Fletcher said coldly. "Lady Daphne and I will never agree to participate in your plot."

Amitabh tilted his head. His lips curved in a smile. "Say her name," he said. Fletcher said nothing. "Say it, or I cut you."

Fletcher's face was still and impassive. Amitabh smiled more widely. "Say it, or I cut *her*," he said.

"... Lady Daphne," Fletcher ground out.

"Again."

"Lady Daphne."

"*Again!*"

"Lady... Daphne."

Amitabh released him with a crow of exultation. "I felt it!" he shouted. "It is in the way your voice caresses your beloved's name, even as you struggle to hide from me. She is in my power, and now... oh, now, brave captain, I believe you will do as I tell you."

The impassive look vanished, and Fletcher's head sagged. Daphne's eyes burned with unshed tears. So she was to be a pawn, a hostage against Fletcher's good behavior, and what would he not do to prevent harm from coming to her? Amitabh looked her way, his smile triumphant, and she knew he could feel the despair and anger rolling off her in waves. If only she had not tried to be a hero!

Amitabh laid his palm against Fletcher's cheek, a gentle parody of a lover's touch. "Can you feel that, captain?" he said. "Feel that pleasure? Your despair is like sweet wine. You will do as I tell you, or she will suffer. You know I do not lie to you."

"I know," Fletcher said, his quiet voice echoing with the despair Daphne felt. "I will do whatever you ask. But you must release her."

"Not yet. She will ensure your compliance. Kill the Governor-General, and she goes free in that hour."

"That is not enough. You must swear that no one will touch her. No harm will come to her. Or I will bring the army of Fort William down upon you and disembowel you myself."

"You believe you are in a position to make demands?"

The soldier holding Daphne was paying close attention to this exchange. She realized his grip was loosening. Carefully she maintained her feelings of despair, nurturing them, never giving conscious space to her awareness of her growing freedom. Just a few moments longer... but it would require careful timing, and all her strength.

"This is a negotiation," Fletcher was saying. "You want something from me. I have conditions under which I will do that thing. She is my condition. Hurt her in any way, and I swear I will hunt you down and make you suffer. Tell me I am lying."

"You are not lying, but we both know a Discerner can be defeated by one who genuinely believes an untruth. Even so..." Amitabh lowered his hand and took a few steps back. "Very well. I believe you. How will you do it?"

"You must cause your men to withdraw. The unrest in Madhyap-atnam is what keeps me here. I cannot leave until it is settled." He was back to impassivity again. "I will return to Calcutta and make my report to the Governor-General, and while reporting, I will kill him. You will learn of it, I judge, within a day. And Lady Daphne will go free."

She wanted to scream at him to stop, to refuse to go along with Amitabh's evil plan, but she could not risk them remembering she was in the room. True despair filled her, and she let herself indulge in it, not allowing herself to think of anything else.

"Your plan does not include your escape," the Shaper said. "Have you no care for your own life?"

"None, so long as hers is in jeopardy," Fletcher said.

The hard hands gripping her were barely touching her anymore. Daphne watched, and waited for her moment. *Step back again, Amitabh, just a foot more...*

"Will not your people wonder where she has gone?" Amitabh said. He had halted a few feet from Fletcher, still too close, close enough that he might lunge forward and grab her if she Skipped to Fletcher's side. Daphne wanted to scream with frustration, but she dared do nothing that would draw attention to herself. She waited, barely breathing, waited for her opening...

"I will return with a story that will convince them," Fletcher said. "I will tell them her last Bound killed her. There is another Bounder there who will confirm that is plausible."

It sounded reasonable, so reasonable that Daphne for a moment forgot it was all a lie. Surely Fletcher would not commit murder simply to save her? Amitabh appeared to have forgotten all about her. He turned, stepped toward the dais. Two steps. Three.

Daphne wrenched free of her captor and Skipped to Fletcher's side, startling exclamations of surprise from the watching soldiers. She flung her arms around his waist and Bounded.

Pain lanced through her body, not the pain of trying to meld with another person, but an agony as if she were being torn in half. It felt as though part of her had Bounded successfully and the rest of her had remained behind. The Mover. She had forgotten the Mover who had Fletcher in his grasp. He still held Fletcher tightly with his talent, anchoring him to the ground.

She stopped trying to Bound and found herself back in Amitabh's throne room. Fletcher was stiff as a plank in her arms, unable to give her even the slightest assistance by putting his arms around her shoulders. Amitabh was screaming for his men to advance. Some of them were very close, and in another couple of seconds they would be upon her. Drawing in a deep breath, Daphne changed her grip from Fletcher's waist to below his knees. With a scream of defiance, she heaved upward, felt something tear, and Bounded away.

The stinking lights of the throne room gave way to the cool dimness of the Residence hall. Daphne dropped Fletcher, who landed hard on the tiles and groaned. She fell to her hands and knees and then lowered herself to the ground, unable to support herself on shaking arms and legs. Her chest and stomach burned as if they had been shredded, and she could not seem to catch her breath. Shuddering, she lay still, willing the pain to go away, but it was growing worse, and the dim lights of the hallway were dimming further.

Fletcher coughed, and she felt rather than heard him roll onto his side and push himself up. "Daphne," he said in a voice that sounded raw, as if he had been screaming, "are you well?"

She tried to answer him, but breathing was so difficult. She could barely manage to draw a thin stream of air through her nostrils, and when it reached her lungs, it hurt so badly she wished she had not bothered. Her stomach convulsed, and she rolled back onto her hands in time to vomit all over the tiles. Even in the dimness, the bright red of blood was obvious. She waited for her vision to cloud over, staring at all the blood—surely there should not be so much of it?—but it remained clear, though the stench of blood and bile made her want to vomit again.

I am going to die, she thought, *but at least I am cured of my weakness.* She could hear Fletcher from very far away, a strange effect since she could see him crouched next to her, but could not understand his words. Then he lifted her, cradling her like an infant, and she let her head loll back to look at him, his face once more impassive. Surely that was unnecessary now they were free of Amitabh's presence? His lips moved soundlessly, not that she could hear anything over the sound of the blood rushing in her ears. Just as the rushing sound stopped, she felt herself transferred to someone else's arms. She wanted to protest that she did not want anyone to hold her but Fletcher, but at that point she ran out of air, and fell into a painless unconsciousness.

CHAPTER 25

IN WHICH DAPHNE LEARNS
THE LIMITS OF HER TALENT
AND SUFFERS ACCORDINGLY

Daphne woke to the sound of distant murmuring and the crackle of a fire burning nearby. She tried to open her eyes, but they felt heavy, weighted down by a gentle but inexorable pressure. After trying a few times to get them to obey, she gave up. She lay in a soft bed, not the one at the Residence nor her bed in Lindsey House back in Calcutta, yet so very familiar... she breathed in the scent of violets, and realized she was in her own bedroom at Marvell Hall. She was warm, but not over-hot as she had become accustomed to in nearly a month living in India, and the smell of burning wood comforted her.

She had... what had happened? She tried to piece memory together, like a puzzle with half the pieces missing and the other half blank white. She remembered going to the bazaar and speaking with those Hindoo women, learning about Amitabh—

Amitabh. The palace. Hard hands, holding her in place.

Fletcher.

She tried to rise, but her body did not obey her any more than her eyelids had. "Is someone there?" she croaked, a horrible raspy sound that did not resemble her voice at all. She cleared her throat and tried again, this time producing only a reedy whistle. Tears came to her eyes that she could not wipe away because her arms were too heavy to lift.

A door opened, and the distant murmuring grew louder, distinguishable as human speech, though still too quiet or far away for Daphne to make out words. "She's awake," a woman said After a moment's thought, Daphne recognized it as her mother's voice. Someone took her hand and laid a cool hand on her brow. "Daphne, can you hear me?"

"I need water," Daphne croaked.

The hands were removed, and shortly someone helped her sit and held a glass to her lips. Daphne swallowed gratefully and immediately felt better. "Thank you," she said, in a voice more like her own.

"You have slept for two days," her father said. "After a Healing that took half a day. You... it was a near thing, Dr. Courtenay said."

Daphne concentrated, and managed to open her eyes, though it was hard not to let them close again. Her parents were a couple of man-sized blurs in her vision, and she wondered briefly if this was how Bess saw the world. "Did anyone tell you what happened?"

"Major Schofeld has been here three times to inquire after your condition," Papa said. "The second time, he gave us what I believe is the full story, though he had it second hand. You will have to tell us how correct it is. You Bounded with someone who was being held by a Mover? Daphne, did you not know such a thing is impossible?"

"Not impossible, only very difficult and apparently dangerous, but I could not leave him, Papa, truly I could not, he would not leave me behind even though he could have escaped and left me to recover— and at any rate I did not realize he was being held until I had already Bounded the first time, and I was desperate. Did Major Schofeld tell you I Bounded to his essence, Captain Fletcher's I mean?"

"No, but is that not impossible as well?"

"It seems it is just a very bad idea. Well, perhaps Major Schofeld does not know what came of that experiment, as he was not there. I have done so many impossible things this week, Mama, Papa, and I feel lucky to be alive."

"You are lucky," Papa said darkly. "I wish you were young enough for me to confine you to your bedroom. It would be good not to worry about what mischief you were up to again."

"Oh, my dear, Daphne is sensible, and I am certain she did all of those things for a good reason." The sound of Mama's voice suggested that she wanted to hear the story behind Daphne's adventures. Daphne smiled, but it was interrupted by an enormous, jaw-cracking yawn. "Daphne, you are not tired already? You must stay awake long enough for Dr. Courtenay to arrive. She wished to examine you when you woke. I am certain she will be here soon."

"Perhaps if you help me sit, I will be able to stay awake," Daphne said.

Papa not only helped her up, he picked her up in his arms the way he had when she was a child, and Mama arranged pillows to support her when he set her down. She discovered she was wearing her own nightgown, and that made everything seem real in a way that even the smell of her bedroom had not. Mama gave her another drink of water; it was cool and sweet and tasted nothing like the water of India, and she felt an unexpected twinge of homesickness. Surely she would be able to return to India soon. India, and Fletcher—she missed him terribly, and wished he had been there when she woke.

Dr. Courtenay had been Daphne's physician since she was a tiny, prematurely born infant, and just the sound of her voice, booming and deep for a woman's, calmed Daphne no matter how much she hurt. The Extraordinary Shaper was a beautiful, perfectly proportioned woman of late middle age, though her unlined face made her seem younger, and she made the black cap look stylish. When she saw Daphne sitting up, her only remark was, "You had better not be pushing yourself into an early grave, young lady. It will look bad on my references."

"I am too tired to move, Doctor," Daphne said, trying once more to raise her right arm and failing. "I do not believe I can push myself anywhere."

"Fortunate for all of us," Dr. Courtenay said, stripping off her satchel and setting it on a nearby chair before sinking onto the bed beside Daphne. "Did Lord and Lady Claresby tell you what happened?"

"That it took half a day to Heal me, but they did not say why."

"It is perhaps just as well you do not know the details." Dr. Courtenay laid two fingers on Daphne's wrist, feeling for her pulse. "You tore most of your internal organs trying to Bound with someone who was being held by a Mover. It took three of us to repair the damage. Never do that again."

"I will not. I did not know it was so dangerous, Doctor, but I could not help it—" A horrid thought struck her. "Captain Fletcher is uninjured, yes? If I injured myself—he was the one being held—"

"Calm yourself, Lady Daphne. I don't know this Captain Fletcher, but if he had been as badly injured as you were, I would have heard about it, whether or not he survived the Healing."

"Major Schofeld said he was well," Papa said. "You should not fear for him." He averted his eyes, casually appearing to look out the window, but she had known him all her life and was familiar with his expressions. Her throat tightened with fear.

"What is wrong with the captain, Papa?" she asked, pretending her whole heart was not caught up in the answer.

"You are too ill to worry about anyone but yourself," Mama said.

"You have just guaranteed I will make myself sick with fear. Please, tell me what has happened?"

Mama and Papa exchanged glances, and Papa said, "Dr. Courtenay?"

The doctor looked up, her eyes glassy with the distant look of someone Healing another. "Lady Daphne is correct; it will only hurt her to permit her imagination to run rampant. She cannot go running off for the next few days, in any case. Go ahead and tell her."

Papa sighed. "The Residence in Madhyapatnam is under siege by French and Indian troops," he said. Daphne gasped, making Dr. Courtenay hold her wrist more tightly. "Major Schofeld, on his last visit, said they were holding out admirably. Sir Rodney chose not to abandon the Residence, fearing that retaking Madhyapatnam would be more difficult if there were not a European presence there. The Company sent a regiment to reinforce them, and they need only hold out for a few more days."

"But they will need—I must go there!" She tried to stand and discovered her legs would not respond.

"You cannot Bound yet, and you must recover from the Healing," Dr. Courtenay said, unmoved by her struggles.

"Then I should recover there. Bess—my friends—"

"We will send word by Major Schofeld that you are awake. That will have to be enough. Daphne, you nearly died! Lay down your responsibilities for a few days." Mama's eyes were bright with unshed tears, filling Daphne with guilty misery. And yet—how many days was it, yet, before the regiment arrived? She had lost track entirely, but surely it was more than a few. If her friends were killed, if Fletcher died and she were not there... it was unthinkable.

"Very well," she said. "I am simply eager—we have come through so much together—" She could not tell her parents she had fallen in love, not when Fletcher's life was in such jeopardy. Memories of kissing him made her heart race, causing the doctor to look at her strangely, and she made herself think of something else, something less disturbing to her calm. "May I speak with Major Schofeld when he returns?"

"If you are awake, certainly," Papa said. "Very personable young man, that."

This time her father's expression said he was weighing Schofeld's qualities as a potential future son-in-law. He was far more eager than her mother to see her happily married; Daphne suspected him of harboring a secret wish for a regiment's worth of grandchildren. Daphne considered telling them Schofeld was the one who had originated the Littlest Bounder epithet and decided against it. She was not sure she forgave him for it, but she could not help feeling that he genuinely had meant no harm, and she did not want her father having him beaten for it, nor her mother turning her Moving talent on him to dangle him from the eaves of Marvell Hall.

Dr. Courtenay let go her hand and stood. "You are in perfect condition," she said, "as perfect as Healing can make the human body. No hidden weaknesses, all your organs are fully repaired. But, Lady Daphne—" She leaned in close and put a hand on Daphne's shoulder. "You were incredibly lucky that you were in a position to be Bounded to the hospital and that there were enough Extraordinary Shapers present to put you back together again. You cannot count on that luck holding. Do not take such risks, and do not experiment any further with Bounding."

Daphne swallowed. "Yes, Doctor," she said quietly. "I beg your pardon, I should not—"

"That was not a request for an apology, young lady. I want to see you live to grow up and, if God is just, have seven Bounder children who give you as much grief as you give your poor parents." She straightened, and smiled at Daphne to take away the sting. "I will return tomorrow. She must rest, sleep as much as she can, and eat as much as she likes. Speak to my assistant if you have any concerns."

"Thank you, Doctor," Mama said, escorting the doctor out. Papa stood next to Daphne's bed, looking out the window again. Daphne saw that he, too, was holding back tears.

"You will have to tell us of your time in India," he said gruffly, "before you go back to the War Office."

"But you do not mean—surely I will return to service with Lord Moira?" Fear gripped her. To leave India... she had three and a half years left of her service, and was she to spend it elsewhere?

"I don't know. General Omberlis suggested that your term of service with the Governor-General might be up—something about the earl and his lady wife changing their permanent residence. But it's nothing you need worry about now. Rest—unless you would prefer food?"

She had not realized she was hungry until that moment. "Food, please, and lots of it," she said, making her father laugh.

The tray the kitchen sent up bore half a cold roast chicken, seven slices of roast beef, a loaf of rich, nutty bread she ate without bothering to slice it, and a pot of hot, delicious tea. Daphne ate as if she had never seen food before, having to consciously make herself chew slowly and thoroughly so she would not choke. She felt certain Dr. Courtenay would be bitingly sarcastic with her if she were called in to resuscitate her after choking on her meal.

Daphne, she thought, wondered why she was thinking her own name, and realized she was being Spoken to. -Daphne! If you are awake —oh, we are so glad! Captain Fletcher has been so distraught, blaming himself for your condition. Major Schofeld will come to you soon, and you must tell him to tell the captain not to fear. Daphne, he loves you so devotedly, it hurts me to see him in pain. I sincerely hope, if you are determined not to marry, that you may be gentle with him. We are well, and it has been very exciting, but I have asked the major to tell you what has happened so I do not continue to disturb you. You are better off where you are, I assure you, but I will not be perfectly comfortable until I can see for myself that you are well. I will Speak to you again once you have seen Major Schofeld.-

The communication ended, and Daphne realized she had a mouthful of food she had forgotten to chew. She swallowed and pushed the tray away, her appetite gone. It had not occurred to her that Fletcher might blame himself, but now she came to think on it, it made sense. She wished she could Bound to the Residence, reassure him, perhaps find a quiet corner for more kissing... no, that would be inappropriate, if utterly wonderful. But at the very least he needed to stop taking on guilt that by all rights belonged to Amitabh and his Mover. It did not seem the kind of message she could send via Schofeld.

A knock sounded at her door, and Mama entered. "Daphne, Major Schofeld has arrived and would like to speak with you. I believe, if you are capable of sitting, you might receive him in the blue drawing room."

"I am, but I do not believe I can walk," Daphne said. She made the effort anyway, but her legs only quivered before losing strength entirely.

"I will carry you," Papa said. "Here, here is your dressing gown."

Her father's arms were as strong as she remembered from her childhood, and he picked her up as easily as if she were that long-ago child. "You are not as plump as you look," he commented as he carried her down the stairs.

"No, it is mostly muscle now. I have worked so hard to become strong, I could likely lift *you* were I not so weakened."

Papa laughed. "You will have to prove it, another time." He pushed the door to the blue drawing room open with his toe and helped her recline on a sofa. Mama covered her decorously with a soft blanket. "I will tell Major Schofeld he may enter," she said. "We are all anxious for the latest news. We have never met your friends, but we are quite concerned for them, thanks to Major Schofeld's reports."

When Mama had gone, Daphne said, "Has he told you much about them?"

"He says Miss Hanley is nearly blind, but a talented Extraordinary Speaker, and Sir Rodney is a crack shot, as is Captain Fletcher. It is unfortunate he is a Discerner, and prone to being overwhelmed."

"That is not true," Daphne said hotly. "Captain Fletcher uses his talent to good effect. I have seen him very nearly read the mind of a villain who attempted to burn the Residence down—it is just Major Schofeld's spitefulness that would cast him as a weakling."

"The major did not suggest he was weak," Papa said, raising an eyebrow. "But I wonder about that, given that you were forced to rescue him."

"That is only because he was too gallant to leave me behind when I was incapacitated! He is a true friend, and I—of course I do not regret saving him from Amitabh, who likely would have killed him when he knew the captain would not do what he wanted, and he would have done the same for me."

"Indeed," Papa said, his expression inscrutable in a way that made Daphne blush and look away. "I believe I would like to meet him, since you speak so highly of him."

"Perhaps when this is all over," Daphne said. How much had she given away? She simply felt incapable of telling her parents the truth.

The door opened, admitting Mama and Major Schofeld. He did not look as if he had been in a siege, not that Daphne knew what that would look like. But, then, it was likely he had merely conveyed supplies to the defenders of the Residence, and not stayed to be shot at. He smiled broadly when he saw her. "Lady Daphne! What a pleasure to see you awake! I look forward to conveying the good news to the Residence. I believe they could use a boost to morale."

"Thank you, Major, I feel very well," Daphne said, though in truth she was becoming tired. "Is everything well? Being besieged... it does not sound promising."

"The Residence is very defensible, though they do not have many troops." Schofeld took a seat near Daphne's head. "The regiment will arrive in just two days, and then it will be over. With Bounders like myself providing supplies and ammunition, they really are in very little danger."

Daphne doubted it was as rosy a picture as he had painted, but decided to let it go. "Did the people rise up, or was Amitabh left with only his secret army?"

"I have no knowledge of a public uprising. Fletcher says the army is more than enough. They have been hard-pressed, but I do not believe they have lost many men."

"That is a relief. Do you go there often?"

"Whenever Miss Hanley Speaks to me requesting supplies. I wonder at her. She ought to permit me to Bound her to safety, as she is a lone woman surrounded by soldiers, but she insists that this is where she is needed."

"Oh, I do wish I could be with her! Perhaps—"

"Major Schofeld is not going to Bound you to the Residence in your condition," Papa said. "You would be a liability, Daphne, and you do not want to put your friends in danger from having to defend you as well as themselves, do you?"

Daphne scowled. "I will be well soon."

"Then you can go Bounding into danger soon." Papa's growl was belied by the twinkle in his eyes. It lightened Daphne's heart to know she had a father who was not inclined to coddle her, even after she had nearly killed herself with her talent.

"Yes, Lady Daphne, you would distress us all if you returned before you are ready," Schofeld said. "In fact, you look rather tired, and I will leave you to your rest. Have you any messages you wish me to convey?"

Daphne wished at that moment she had thought to write a message to Fletcher, though of course that would look very suspicious. What could she say to him that would not sound bizarre in Schofeld's mouth? She wanted so badly to reassure him of her love, and urge him not to despair, but that was impossible. "Please tell them I am entirely well, and I will return soon," she said, "and... tell Captain Fletcher, exactly, that he is not to feel guilty, and if he does insist on blaming himself, he should remember the *zenana*. Will you remember those exact words?"

All three of them were looking at her as if she had gone mad, but Schofeld nodded and stood. "I will remember. Good day, Lord Claresby, Lady Claresby, Lady Daphne."

When he was gone, Mama said, "Daphne?" in a helpless, questioning tone of voice that said she had not been at all fooled by Daphne's attempt at circumspection.

Daphne blushed hotter. "I feel tired," she said, half-truthfully. "Will you return me to my bed, Papa?"

Mama trailed behind them as they ascended the stairs and tucked Daphne in just as if she were a child. "You know, you used to tell me everything," she whispered, brushing a lock of hair away from Daphne's forehead.

"There is nothing to tell, not yet," Daphne said, "but I promise there will be soon."

It was not yet dark, and although Daphne's body ached with tiredness, her mind was not yet sleepy. She watched birds circle and dip outside her window, which her mother had left open at her request despite the coolness of the late September evening air. How soon would she be capable of Bounding? She did not want to injure herself, but her desire to return to India was a physical thing, pulling her inexorably eastward. At the Residence, it would be just after sunset, she judged. Would they have respite from the battle now it was dark, without even the light of the moon to guide their shots? She hoped Schofeld's arrival was a relief to them. She hoped Fletcher would heed her words.

She shifted her weight and discovered she could roll onto her side, though her legs still shook when she tried to stand on them. She lay on her side with her hand curled under her cheek and closed her eyes. She had been such a fool, so eager to prove herself and her talent by discovering a new use for Bounding, and had she not been lucky, she and Fletcher would be dead now. Risking herself was one thing, but endangering another... her fame was not worth that. Certainly not when the other in question was the man she loved.

She let out a deep breath. So. She had fallen in love, against all her promises to herself. Promises aside, she did not regret it. But it meant she needed to review her desires. Fletcher would never permit her to

Bound into danger; he would be devastated if she returned injured or, worse, did not return at all. But she was only twenty-one, and that was far too young to simply settle down.

And what of the War Office? She wished she had thought to ask Schofeld what he knew of the possibility that Lord Moira and Lady Loudoun might not need her services anymore. If it was true that she no longer fainted at the sight of blood—something she ought to verify —General Omberlis would likely want her back in Spain, and that would separate her from Fletcher rather definitively. It surprised her to discover that the thought of returning to the Peninsula did not thrill her as it once would have. Perhaps it was the new soberness nearly being killed by her talent had instilled in her, but the idea of becoming famous for her Bounding skills no longer had the same appeal. And when she thought of her future, it was her friends that came to mind, not the accolades of men.

She sighed deeply, appreciating as she had not before how smoothly her lungs worked, how easily they drew breath and expelled hot, moist air. Perhaps she was being premature. Fletcher had not said anything, there had been no time, and possibly he did not want to marry her. The thought gave her a pang that surprised her. She had never given any thought to marriage, certainly not as something that meant anything to her, and here she was feeling sad because a man she barely knew had not yet proposed marriage to her. It was ridiculous, and she needed to stop being a fool.

She remembered how Fletcher had looked, there in the *zenana*, that smile that made her heart flutter, remembered his kisses, and another rush of pleasure suffused her. Oh, how she longed to see him again, to ask him a million questions, to speak her love as she had not been able to do before. He loved her, she was certain of it. She tried not to remember the danger he was in at that moment. That only made her heart ache more.

-Daphne! I hope you are not asleep. I wish I could hear your thoughts, because we are all dying to know the meaning of your message to Captain Fletcher. He developed the most unusual smile when Major Schofeld relayed it to him, and he has been so much more cheerful since. Thank you for that. It has been painful to watch him, he does not—did not smile, and was curt with all of us. I will not disturb you longer, but I thought you should know. If it was a way of declaring your love, I applaud your sneakiness.-

Daphne smiled. Bess certainly seemed in good spirits. She found she could draw her legs up to her waist, and wrapped her arms around them and hugged herself. She had made him smile. She fell asleep with that knowledge warming her heart.

CHAPTER 26

IN WHICH DAPHNE RECEIVES
NEW ORDERS, AND RESENTS
THEM

She woke in the darkness and sat up before she remembered she could not. Carefully, she extended her legs and tried to stand. Oh, how they ached! But they supported her weight, if in a rather wobbly way, and she left her bed and walked to her window. It took more than a minute for her to cross the short space, feeling at every moment that her legs might desert her. If only she had a walking stick... but pushing herself in this small way would no doubt strengthen her, and the sooner she was back to Bounding, the better.

She leaned out of the open window and watched the skies. Her War Office training told her it was around four o'clock in the morning. It would be full daylight in India, they would have finished breakfast and settled in for a day of being besieged. She could not remember what Major Schofeld had said about how soon the regiment would arrive to relieve them. Two days? Three? Not soon enough.

She tottered back to her bed and made herself sit primly on the edge rather than fall face-first into it as she wanted to do. Control, that was what she needed, because that would lead to strength, and strength would lead to stamina, and at that point she would be able to Bound again.

Her stomach pointed out to her that it was empty, had been empty for far too long, and would she kindly see to filling it? She felt around for the bell pull, but changed her mind before she could summon a servant. She needed practice walking, and this was as good an excuse as any.

She fumbled her way into her dressing gown and put on a pair of slippers, but kicked them off after a few trial steps told her she needed direct contact with the floor if she did not want to fall down. Trailing a hand along the wall, she left her bedroom and made her slow, halting way down the hall to the stairs. There, she found her balance was sufficiently off that she was forced to sit and bump her way down, one shallow step at a time. Halfway down, she wondered why she had not lit a lamp for herself, but this night had a mystical quality she did not want to banish with tawdry, ordinary light. She reached the first floor with an abrupt jolt and sat motionless for a time, gathering the strength to stand.

The house at night seemed a living thing, breathing so slowly it was imperceptible. The usual smells of roses and furniture polish were muted, as if light amplified them, brightened them as it did everything else. Denied sight, Daphne became aware of sounds: the creaking of the floorboards, which Daphne had never heard before; the ticking of the clocks, and there were more clocks than Daphne had ever realized; and the sound of her own breathing, which had a rough edge to it. Perhaps she was not as recovered as she had thought.

The stairs to the ground floor were steeper than the others, which surprisingly made it easier for her to slip from step to step. Or possibly she was just growing adept at maneuvering with her posterior. Once again she sat, somewhat breathless, until her heart rate slowed, then used the wall to pull herself up. She leaned on it for a few seconds, then felt her way along toward the kitchen. She could smell her destination; the scents of roasted meats and fresh, pungent cheeses hung in the air like the ghosts of a thousand dinners. She felt her way to the pantry and found most of a meat pie, probably destined to be her father's midday meal in a few hours. She helped herself to a knife and fork and dug in, sitting on the pantry floor and eating as if Papa might appear and snatch it away from her.

When the pan was empty—she heroically refrained from licking it

—she set it and the knife and fork in the apron sink and searched for something else. Oranges, Bounded fresh from the Americas, filled the air with their tangy scent. She made a basket of the skirt of her dressing gown and took two, and a handful of apples, and a banana, which she did not normally like—the seeds were so large—but in her hunger everything sounded good. Thus laden, she made her careful way back to the stairs, which she managed to climb without dropping her load or falling on her face. So much easier to Bound. At the foot of the second set of stairs, she tried Bounding, just as an experiment. A quiver went through her, but nothing else happened. It occurred to her that it might have injured her to Bound in her weakened condition, and fear struck her, fear of having almost broken her promise to Dr. Courtenay. She shuddered, and climbed the stairs the traditional way.

Back in her room with her loot, she lit a lamp and ate her way steadily through the stash, making a pile of peels and cores on the little table next to her bed. Sucking orange juice off her fingers, she finally felt full, her stomach distended comfortably. She lay back without extinguishing the light and stretched, enjoying how easily her body moved. She had feared, when her legs did not at first obey her, that she would need to revise her exercise regimen to regain muscle, but it felt now as if she were waking from a deep sleep, one body system at a time. She already felt stronger.

Pink light tinged the horizon, seeping across the sky like a water-color painting. Daphne watched the line grow and deepen until the bright sun peeped across the line, making her eyes water. She no longer felt sleepy; she felt eager to be up and about. She rolled out of bed and opened her clothespress. Her Bounder uniform, the War Office uniform, lay folded neatly atop her other clothes, the ones she had left behind upon going to India. Someone had sponged it, and it did not smell of blood and vomit, just of clean fresh linen. She gave it only a moment's thought before removing her nightgown and donning the uniform. If she were to regain her strength, she would need to exercise, and she could scarcely do that in a nice muslin gown.

When Mama entered the room two hours later, Daphne was engaged in a strength-building exercise that had left her rather sweaty. Her muscles burned pleasantly with exertion, her mind was clear, and she was not expecting her mother's pained exclamation and the words "Daphne! You are meant to be resting!"

Daphne dropped the lead weight and turned, stretching out her arms. "I do not feel tired, just restless. I thought this would help me more than lying in bed thinking dangerous thoughts would."

"Dangerous thoughts? And what would those be?" Mama sat on the edge of Daphne's bed.

"Oh... contemplating how I might induce Major Schofeld to Bound me back to India. Those kind of thoughts."

"Dangerous indeed." Mama interlaced her fingers and rested them on her knee. "General Omberlis sent word that he will visit you this afternoon, if you are well enough. I take it from this display that you are."

A chill passed through her despite the warmth of her exertions. "Why is the general visiting?"

"He did not give specifics. I imagine he wishes to see for himself that you are well. Your condition... there was rather a lot of speculation about you, and whether you would recover fully."

"Why should I not recover fully? Mama, was there a chance..." She did not know how to finish the sentence.

"No. Dr. Courtenay assured us if you recovered at all, it would be a complete recovery. The speculation was more about whether you would still be a Bounder, let alone an Extraordinary."

Daphne staggered to the bed and sat on it. Her legs were not as strong as she had supposed. "But... why would I not? Mama, surely Dr. Courtenay would not have given me false hope, if there were—Mama, tell me it is not true!"

Mama put her arms around her and hugged her close, rocking her gently. "Speculation only. Your talent caused your injury, after all, and there were those who supposed that meant your talent might be in danger. You are still an Extraordinary Bounder. But those rumors spread widely, and the general is a cautious man."

Daphne clung to her mother as if she were once again three years old and crying out against her first thunderstorm. "I would almost rather be dead."

"Never say that, darling."

"I did say 'almost.' I tried to Bound earlier without guessing it might hurt me, but I simply could not. Are you certain—"

"Certain. An Extraordinary Shaper has ways of knowing. Now, I believe you should nap for a few hours, if you can. General Omberlis can be overwhelming."

Daphne nodded and let Mama help her into bed without removing her uniform. She was asleep moments later.

⚜

"IT IS GOOD TO SEE YOU WELL, LADY DAPHNE," GENERAL OMBERLIS said, extending his hand for her to shake. "I trust this visit does not inconvenience you."

"No, sir," Daphne said. She was sitting up on the sofa rather than reclining, and at General Omberlis' request they were alone. Daphne tried not to feel unnerved at that. If this were merely a social visit, he would not have asked Lord and Lady Claresby to leave. The general had something on his mind, and Daphne would not be comfortable until he came out with it.

"You are fully Healed?" General Omberlis said. "There are no... side effects?"

"I am Healed, and in possession of my talent, though I am not yet capable of using it."

"Forgive my bluntness, but if you cannot use it, how do you know you still have it?"

"There was no reason to believe it would be lost simply because it was the cause of my injury, General. And Dr. Courtenay assures me it is intact. In a day or so I will be back to Bounding as usual."

"Ah." General Omberlis leaned back in his seat and fiddled with his hat, which rested on his knee. "That is good. You are a valuable part of the War Office and I would hate to lose that."

"Lady Loudoun certainly considers me valuable." Daphne did not believe she sounded bitter. She liked the countess, and did not mind conveying her and her children. It was simply not the same as being a courier, or a battlefield Bounder, or even having Major Schofeld's position. She felt the general was patronizing her, and it made her irritable.

The general cleared his throat. "Lady Loudoun has decided to bring her household permanently to Calcutta. She sees herself as a leader of society, and believes she will be better positioned to fill that role if she does not have one foot in England."

"But what of the children? Lady Loudoun has told me often that she believes the climate is not a good one for children."

"I understand Lord Moira and Lady Loudoun have decided they would prefer to keep their family intact, even if there is an increased risk to their children's health. They intend to hire an Extraordinary Shaper to attend on their household, for that reason."

Daphne made herself breathe calmly, in through the nose, out through the mouth. "Then she will have no more need for me. Will I instead be attached to Government House in general?"

"Possibly. They already have many Bounders, Extraordinary and otherwise. We may assign you elsewhere."

Daphne fought a brief and bloodless battle with herself. "General, I believe... my condition no longer troubles me."

"Your condition?"

"My predisposition to faint at the sight of blood."

He raised his eyebrows. "This is not a ploy to change my mind, is it?"

"No, sir. I cannot be certain, it happened when I was dying, so I intend to make a trial and verify my claim. But I thought you should know, so as to best determine where I may be useful." To think she had once longed to be free of her weakness. Now she could only imagine how it might take her farther from Fletcher. "But... if I may, General... I am very fond of India."

"Are you? I was unaware anyone was fond of India."

Daphne remembered Fletcher eating *doi mach*, sitting cross-legged on the floor, and how natural he had looked doing it. "Some of us are. If... if my wishes are at all relevant, I should prefer to remain there."

"Lady Daphne," General Omberlis said, "if you are capable of serving on the battlefield, I am inclined to put you there. We have a great need for battlefield transportation and for couriers. But I will consider your request."

"Thank you, sir."

They both fell silent, though Daphne was certain the general had more to say. She clasped her hands in front of her and waited, not very patiently. Finally, the general said, "Who is this Captain Fletcher who nearly got you killed?"

"He did not—General, that is not at all what happened, it was my fault, the captain was being held and I did not realize it was impossible to Bound with someone being held by a Mover. He is a king's officer attached to Government House, if that is what you mean."

"He seems to have inspired great loyalty in you, for you to risk your life for him."

You have no idea, General. "We are friends, sir. He would have done the same for me, in fact he did, he could have escaped but it would have meant leaving me behind—"

"That is enough, Lady Daphne. I did not mean to criticize. I merely wish to know your assessment of him as an officer. I have heard his name in a variety of contexts and would like your opinion."

Daphne gaped. "I... he is a good officer, I believe. His men listen to him, and he does not unnecessarily risk their lives. He knows India well and the people respect him, which is not usual. I do not know why he has not been promoted."

"He is not in my chain of command, so I cannot answer that, but I imagine that will no longer be the case when this Madhyapatnam business is finished." The general tapped his fingers on his hat. "Very well, Lady Daphne, thank you for your candor. You will return to India?"

"Very soon. As soon as I can Bound."

"The War Office will be in contact with you shortly. It will take Lady Loudoun some time to complete the movement of her household, so you should consider yourself attached to her until further notice."

"I understand, sir."

"You are not to return to Madhyapatnam."

It was like a blow to the face. "Sir?" she said, closing her hand on the arm of the sofa.

"You are too valuable to risk there, and your first duty is to Lady Loudoun. Major Schofeld has been temporarily assigned to the Residence."

"But—General, I have been a part of—they are my friends, they depend on me—"

"There is nothing you can do for them. If for some reason the Residence needs to be evacuated, Schofeld will call for your assistance. Otherwise..." He spread his hands wide, indicating the discussion was over.

Daphne had to concentrate on her breathing again. "Yes, sir."

The general rose. "We are all very grateful for your survival, Lady Daphne. You have many friends at the War Office who were concerned for your health."

"Thank you, sir." She could not imagine who at the War Office might be concerned about her, save in the sense that humans are drawn to the sight of great disasters. She was too angry to say more than that.

"Do not stand, please," the general said, though Daphne had made no move to rise. "Rest well, Lady Daphne."

She stared blindly at the door once it shut behind him. She had not expected that. Cut off from Madhyapatnam, for no other reason than that General Omberlis thought her weak enough to have been disabled by her Bounding. He had not even had to say it. Daphne felt she might scream, but it would frighten her parents, and they had already been frightened enough.

Without thinking, she Bounded to her bedroom, and realized what she had done when she startled a maidservant tidying her dressing table. She made a hasty apology and Bounded back to the blue drawing room, where she again sat on the sofa and tried to calm herself. She was well, she might go anywhere she liked in the space of a breath, but she was bound by her promises and her oath to the War Office not to go to the one place she longed to be. It was so unfair... but no, fairness had nothing to do with it. To think how she had been so eager to join the War Office, and now she resented its control over her.

She stood and stretched. She might be capable of Bounding again, but she did not feel equal to carrying a passenger, and her legs and arms still felt rubbery if she exerted herself too long. She would walk to her room, and then she would write a letter to Bess, explaining it all. She could not write to Fletcher and the others; how odd that would look, a young woman writing to a group of men to whom she was neither related nor engaged. But perhaps she might confide her feelings in Bess, who could pass on her message to Fletcher: *I would not leave you for all the world, but duty drives me*. She would have to leave it to him to come to her. She hoped she was right, and he still wanted to.

CHAPTER 27

IN WHICH DAPHNE IS CALLED INTO ACTION

Major Schofeld came late that evening, after supper, when Daphne had begun to feel weary and in need of her bed. "Do not be alarmed, Lady Daphne," he said. "I apologize for coming so late, but I thought you would want news of the siege."

Daphne caught sight of her parents exchanging glances. "Not bad news?" she exclaimed.

"No, of course not, everyone is quite well. That is," Schofeld cleared his throat, "the battle is rather more heated than it has been. But there is no need to fear. The regiment is almost there, and it will break the siege, I am certain of it."

"Major," Daphne said, trying to keep from shrieking at him, "I would prefer not to be told a comforting lie. How bad is it, truly?"

Schofeld cleared his throat again. "Sir Rodney is still confident in his men. He has not yet ordered an evacuation."

Daphne shot to her feet. "But you will call on me if that happens, will you not? Major—"

"Daphne, do not exert yourself," Mama said. "If Sir Rodney is not afraid, you should not be."

"That is precisely true, Lady Daphne," Schofeld said. He looked relieved to have Lady Claresby's support. "I have not been instructed to bring you in—"

"General Omberlis said I might return if you called on me to help with an evacuation. Please, Major, do not try to protect me, I am nearly fully recovered."

"Daphne—"

"Mama, I *am*, I feel quite well!"

"You are also enthusiastic in your desire to help your friends, which is laudable," Papa said, "but you cannot help anyone if you injure yourself further."

"I promise I will not do so! Do you imagine I wish to weaken myself?"

"I believe you are sincere in that promise, but your evaluation of your capabilities might be... flawed." Papa looked as serious as she had ever seen him, and she flinched away from his gaze.

"Then how else am I to know when I am capable? It is not as if anyone else can sense beneath my skin. I ran up and down the stairs this afternoon, and I feel no tiredness from Bounding throughout the house. I am certain I am ready to return to India."

"One more night here," Mama said, "one more hearty breakfast. You may well return in time to meet your friends in Calcutta, if the regiment arrives soon enough."

"I am prepared to carry any messages you might have," Schofeld said. Daphne's parents looked at her expectantly, as if hoping she might come out with more cryptic utterances. Daphne Bounded to her bedroom for her letter to Bess and returned immediately, putting it into Schofeld's outstretched hand.

"Please give everyone my best wishes," she said, "and promise me you will—"

"I understand, Lady Daphne, but I truly believe the Residence can hold out one more day," Schofeld said. Daphne examined him closely for signs he was exaggerating, or telling her a comforting falsehood, but he seemed the same jovial man he always was. She nodded, and he vanished.

"Daphne," Mama said, then let out a deep sigh and shook her head in resignation.

"What is it, Mama?"

"You are an adult, and an Extraordinary, and we do not wish to pry," Papa said, "but we wish you would tell us what you are not saying about your time in India."

"I—there is likely much I have not told you—"

"If you have formed an attachment, I believe it is not unreasonable for us to wish to know about it," Mama said. "You are simply too eager to return to Madhyapatnam for anything so commonplace as friendship. But if you don't trust us—"

"Oh, Mama, that is low," Daphne exclaimed. "Of course I trust you, it is just that... everything is so uncertain, and nothing is settled... I feel I should not speak until... actually I am not certain—"

"Daphne," Papa said, laying a gentle hand atop hers, "if you fear we will disapprove, I assure you we have the highest opinion of Major Schofeld."

Daphne gasped and jerked her hand away. "*Major Schofeld?* Papa, he is the last person—Captain Fletcher is so far superior to him, if you knew him you would—"

She stopped. Her mother had averted her gaze. Papa had a hand over his mouth to conceal a smile. "Oh, you—you have *tricked* me, that is a terrible thing to do to your own child!"

"As terrible as a child concealing her feelings for a man her parents do not know?" Mama said. "Come, Daphne, tell us the truth. You are in love with your Captain Fletcher, are you not?"

Daphne sighed. "I did not believe I would—Mama, you know I swore I would not form an attachment for years to come, it is just that he—I do have the warmest feelings for him, and I promise you he is worthy of me. It is just that it seems so wrong talking of love when he and Bess and the others are in such danger, I did not want to tell you."

"We dislike you forming an attachment to someone who is a stranger to us," Papa said, "but with you in India, it hardly seems fair to expect you to drag home every man you have an interest in. And... is this not rather sudden? You have not been in India a full month yet. You can speak with such confidence of your attachment to a man you have known for three weeks?"

Daphne scowled and looked away toward the clock on the mantel. "It has been nineteen days. But they were a very *intense* nineteen days!"

"I fell in love with your mother in twelve," Papa said, a reflective smile touching his lips. "It took rather longer to convince her of my sterling qualities. I assume Captain Fletcher returns your affections?"

Daphne had to stop herself smiling in giddy memory. "He does, Papa—of course he is very respectful of me, you have nothing to fear on that account."

"Then I believe we should meet him," Mama said, "as soon as possible. Where is he from? Who are his parents?"

"They live in Gloucestershire, near Wales—his father is a baronet, and he is sixth of ten children—do you not consider that remarkable, ten children?—I cannot recall their names—" Daphne blushed. Falling in love when she barely knew anything of his family—she had well and truly thrown over all sense of decorum, had she not?

"Daphne—" Mama began, then pressed her lips together to capture the rest of her objection. "We have faith in you," she substituted, "but promise me you will be circumspect in the promises you make."

"I have done nothing to betray your trust in me, Mama." *Except daydream about his kisses.* "And I believe Captain Fletcher is more conscious of my reputation even than I am."

"Well, that is one thing," Papa said. "Now, off to bed, and sleep well. Try not to fret about your friends. Major Schofeld would not tell you an untruth about their situation."

"I know, Papa." She flung her arms around her father and felt her mother's arms go around them both. "I truly have the best family in the world."

"Of course you do," Mama said. "Never forget that."

⊗⊰⊗

DAPHNE DRESSED IN HER WAR OFFICE UNIFORM THE NEXT morning before coming down for breakfast. It felt like armoring herself against her parents' possible objections that she might not be ready to return to her duties. Not that her duties were onerous enough to try her returning strength. She had not attempted to Bound with a passenger yet, but she felt certain she was capable of it. Her arms and legs no longer shook from exertion, and she had gone Skipping over the countryside early that morning, just to test herself.

"I admit to being loath to let you return to India," her father said, seating himself next to her. "We missed you terribly, and having you home... perhaps I should not have insisted you recuperate here, if it would make us miss you more when you left."

"I am so glad you did, Papa, I know I recovered more quickly for being in familiar surroundings." Daphne took a bite of eggs, savoring their richness. Even so, she longed for a taste of real Indian food. How difficult would it be to teach the cook to make *doi mach*, when this was all over and her service was finished?

She scooped up another bite, and an ear-piercing scream shattered her calm. The fork fell from her nerveless fingers. Numb, she stared at her father, who seemed not to have heard the noise and was eating placidly. *-Daphne!* I apologize if you are already awake, but I could not risk—oh, Daphne, Major Schofeld has fallen, we are evacuating the Residence and we need you *now!-*

Daphne shoved back her chair. "They are evacuating—please forgive me, Papa, but I *must* go!" She Bounded away without waiting for a response.

The quiet peace of the breakfast room gave way to the most tremendous noises of rifle fire and men screaming. Daphne ducked reflexively, but the sounds followed her. She had Bounded without thinking to the Residence's primary drawing room, which was still empty of furniture that had been removed covered in gore. Aside from her, there was no one present. "Bess!" she shrieked, and darted out of the room into the hall. It, too, was empty. The rifle fire seemed louder from upstairs, so she Bounded to her bedroom—where was everyone?

She ran from the bedroom, listening for some clue as to where the inhabitants of the Residence had gone. Surely if Amitabh's men had overrun it, she would have seen them?

-Daphne, you must come! Major Schofeld is seriously injured and cannot Bound!-

"Where are you?" Daphne shouted. A door flew open, and Bess leaned out. Her hair was a flying mess and her spectacles were missing.

"Oh, thank goodness!" Bess said. "Hurry, Daphne, I believe he is dying!"

Daphne shoved past her into a bedroom, she did not know whose. Two men with rifles stood at the windows, taking aim at unseen targets below. One shot and ducked out of sight, reloading rapidly. Daphne did not know him, but the other was Captain Ainsworth. Major Schofeld lay on the bed, his chest heaving. Bright blood saturated his uniform trouser leg, which was wrapped tightly in a makeshift bandage. Daphne took hold of him and hoisted him over her shoulder, staggering under his weight. She Bounded, feeling the distortion of a dozen human essences in her destination, and appeared in the main hall of Government House, far enough from the windows that the outdoors was not a distraction.

"The Residence at Madhyapatnam is being evacuated!" she shouted, laying Schofeld down as gently as she could manage. "This man is seriously injured—somebody help! Bring Bounders, and I will convey them there!" Without waiting to see if anyone heeded her words, she Bounded back to the Residence, this time to her bedroom —there was too much out of doors exposure in the room where she had found Bess. When she emerged at a run, she found Bess in the hallway.

"Sir Rodney left to lead a sortie against the attackers," she said. "Captain Fletcher and Ensign Phillips are on the other side. Daphne, I do not know what to do next!"

"You are leaving," Daphne said, snatching Bess up and Bounding back to Government House. "Do not argue with me. I need you to organize these people because we will need more Bounders than just myself to bring back as many soldiers as possible. If Sir Rodney led an attack, they will be difficult to retrieve. Do you understand? Get someone to bring as many Bounders here as possible." Bess nodded, and Daphne Bounded away again.

She ran into the room and found the unfamiliar soldier reloading and Ainsworth taking aim from cover. "Which of you should leave first?" she shouted over the mayhem.

"We are covering Sir Rodney's assault," Ainsworth said. "We cannot leave."

"That is not true, Captain, if he has engaged the enemy you cannot fire at Amitabh's troops without risking hitting one of our own." Daphne resolved to haul one of them out bodily if Ainsworth persisted in being recalcitrant. "Tell me, or I will choose for you."

Ainsworth cursed. "Take Dockery, then return for me."

Daphne waited for Dockery to sling his rifle around his shoulder before Bounding him away. The Government House hall was almost too crowded for Daphne to reach, all those human essences interfering. She released Dockery, then found Bess. "You must have everyone but the Bounders leave, or I will not be able to return here. *Are* there any Bounders?"

Bess said, "Yes, but they do not stay close enough for me to distinguish them—Daphne, please forgive me!"

"It is not your fault. Clear the room, and it will be enough. If you are a Bounder, come to me!" she shouted, and two men ran toward her, pushing through the throng. She grabbed one of them around the waist and released him half a breath later, in the bedroom.

"Downstairs," she gasped, "and outside. You know how to evacuate a riot?"

"Yes, ma'am," the man said, saluting her.

Daphne choked on an inappropriate giggle. "The Bounding Chamber is beneath the stairs in the main hall. Go, now!" She steered the man toward the stairs, then ran to fetch Ainsworth. Aside from feeling a trifle out of breath, she felt good, strong, capable of carrying anyone who might need it.

Ainsworth did not argue, but threw down his rifle and stretched out his arms to her. "What else may I do?" he asked when they arrived at Government House. The hall was practically empty save for Bess and five or six men, one of whom was approaching with his hand outstretched.

"Help Bess," Daphne said, and took up the second Bounder in her arms.

Having sent the man downstairs with quick instructions, Daphne ran through the first floor of the Residence, alternately shouting Phillips' and Fletcher's names. She searched room after room, frustrated at how many of them there were. Surely Sir Rodney did not need so many bedrooms?

She was so accustomed to finding empty bedrooms she almost shut the door on the occupied one. Fletcher and Phillips were engaged in shooting from the open window as Ainsworth and Dockery had been, taking careful aim and then reloading rapidly. Fletcher glanced up from his work and saw her. He was filthy, his hands and face covered with black powder. "Take Phillips," he said curtly, "and hurry."

"But—" Phillips protested. He took aim once more.

"That is an order, Phillips!" Fletcher roared. Phillips fired and threw down his rifle, ran toward Daphne and nearly bowled her down. She released him in the Government House hallway and bent over, panting, waiting for the next Bounder.

"That is all, Daphne," Bess called out. "There are no others available."

Daphne cursed and Bounded back. Fletcher had the rifle to his shoulder and was taking aim. "Let me return you, Captain!" she shouted.

"Sir Rodney is hard pressed, and I dare not leave him," Fletcher said. He took his shot and dropped to the floor, reloading. Daphne ran to the window and pressed herself to the wall beside it, peering out. "Lady Daphne, do not go so close!" Fletcher shouted.

She waved him off and peered out the window. The fighting was too fierce for her to make out individual fighters, just masses of red coats and beige or gray shirts. "You cannot possibly know whom to shoot at," she said, "so I will take you back and return to retrieve any soldiers—"

"That is madness," Fletcher said, pausing in his reloading to glare up at her. "You will be overwhelmed, or shot. We must leave this place."

"I brought two other Bounders who are involved in the evacuation, and Sir Rodney is still out there. I cannot leave them!"

Fletcher scowled and finished reloading his rifle. He stood, slinging it over his shoulder, and held out his hand to clasp hers. "You will stay close to me, and if I say it is hopeless, we leave, understand? Let us see if we can find Sir Rodney."

His hand felt grimy and sweaty, but it was still so familiar it sent a rush of confidence through her. She followed him into the hall and down the stairs to the coolness of the tiled central hall. The noise was greater there, a sound she remembered so horribly from that battle in Spain that had seen Major Branton dead. Shouts of anger, higher-pitched screams of pain, the thunderclaps of rifle fire, and a deep rumbling she could not identify filled the air, and had she not been holding Fletcher's hand, she might have put her hands over her ears to block the sound.

They ran to the side exit, and Fletcher pulled the door open cautiously at first, then rapidly, and he pulled her outside with him. The noise redoubled when they left the Residence, but Fletcher seemed unaffected by it. The side door opened on a narrow space between the Residence and its low outer wall. No one had got this far, and Fletcher drew Daphne along the wall, moving slowly and motioning her to press as close to it as she could. Its roughness plucked at her uniform and her hair, urging her to slowness as well.

Suddenly, the cries of rage became triumphant, and a great cracking sound split through the furor. "The gate," Fletcher said. "It's too late. We must leave."

"But the others—"

"Daphne, you swore to obey!"

His hands on her shoulders gripped her tightly, his eyes were fierce, and wordlessly Daphne lifted him and Bounded back to Government House.

CHAPTER 28

IN WHICH A DEFEAT
REQUIRES A CHANGE IN
PLANS

Bess had done her work well; the hall was virtually empty. A few injured men, none hurt too badly to walk, limped toward the distant front door. Fletcher released Daphne, and a second later she stepped away from him, wishing she dared hold him longer.

Bess stood some distance away, talking to Ainsworth. "Bess, did the other Bounders return—did anyone find Sir Rodney?" Daphne cried.

"Oh, Daphne, I am so glad. I was about to call you back." Bess made her halting way toward the sound of Daphne's voice. "The other Bounders returned just moments before you did. They could not make their way through the melee, and neither of them saw Sir Rodney."

"Lady Daphne, are you quite well?" Ainsworth asked.

Daphne realized she was breathing heavily from exertion and made herself take several deep, calming breaths. "I am well," she said, "and in a moment I will go after Sir Rodney."

"I told you that is madness," Fletcher said, gripping her shoulder tightly as if to anchor her in place. "Sir Rodney is either dead, or captured, and in either case you would simply get yourself killed trying to rescue him. You will stay *here*, Lady Daphne."

"But—" Fletcher's face was set and tense, but his eyes betrayed his fear for her, and that stilled her more than his hand did. Once more she longed to put her arms around him, though whether for reassurance for him or for herself, she did not know.

She heard heavy footsteps on the stairs, and looked up to see Colonel Dalhousie and Lord Moira descending together. "Then we send more soldiers," Lord Moira said, sounding as if he were at the last of his patience. His eye fell first on Fletcher, then on Daphne, and she had to struggle not to look away from his irritated glare. "Where is Sir Rodney?"

"Sir Rodney led the Residence troops against Amitabh's army," Fletcher said, overriding Daphne. That was probably for the best; she had had no idea what to say, and likely would just have babbled. "He was in the thick of things when the gate was breached. We assume he is either dead, or captured."

"Then Madhyapatnam is lost to us," Lord Moira said. "We will have to attack with greater force if we are to recover it."

"The regiment is within hours of Madhyapatnam. We should permit them to attempt to retake it," Colonel Dalhousie said. He, too, sounded frustrated, as if this were an argument he had already had five times over.

"They will simply waste their strength against the occupying forces," Lord Moira said. "Better for them to wait on reinforcements. I only want to fight this battle once, Dalhousie."

Daphne had to admit it was a sound strategy, much as she disliked the earl. "Very true, my lord," Fletcher said, sounding not very deferential, "but waiting will permit Amitabh to dig in with his forces and convince the people to support him as rightful ruler of Madhyapatnam. The regiment has a chance if they can act swiftly."

"The people know better than that, according to your own reports, Captain Fletcher," Lord Moira said. "Or were you mistaken when you wrote they disliked how Amitabh represented instability and unrest?"

"No, my lord, that is true. But Amitabh can make defeating the Company look like a divine mandate to occupy and restore Madhyapatnam, and convince many that his lies are truth. We may end up facing a popular uprising as well as Amitabh's French army."

Daphne held her tongue. So far, no one seemed to remember she was there, and she was glad of it. "I intend to send a large enough force to make the issue moot," Lord Moira said. "Thank you for your opinion, Captain Fletcher."

"Very well, my lord," Fletcher said, inclining his head.

Lord Moira turned his attention on Daphne. "You were not to go to Madhyapatnam," he said.

"My lord, General Omberlis said I was only to go if Major Schofeld called for me." Daphne wondered if Schofeld was dead and hoped he was not. "I enlisted other Bounders as quickly as I could, but the assault overwhelmed all of us."

Lord Moira harrumphed. "That's as may be. Clean yourself up, and report to Lady Loudoun. She will keep you very busy over the next several weeks."

Daphne's heart sank. "Yes, my lord," she said. Back to being a human chaise... well, she had saved most of her friends, that was something. She brushed at a damp spot on her uniform and realized as her fingers came away sticky that it was Schofeld's blood. She had seen any amount of blood that day and not felt the least bit incapacitated. Apparently the shock of seeing her own blood in such quantities had cured her. She chose not to dwell on it too deeply, for fear of cursing herself again.

"My office in one hour, Captain Fletcher," Colonel Dalhousie said, "for a full report." He followed Lord Moira through the hall toward the front door, casting one look over his shoulder at Daphne as if he wished he might order her to report as well. Then the hall was silent, and empty save for Daphne, Bess, Ainsworth, and Fletcher.

Ainsworth cleared his throat awkwardly. "It's a pity about Sir Rodney. I'd grown fond of him."

"We do not know he is dead," Daphne said, but her words felt hollow, echoing harshly in her ears.

"Better for him if he is," Fletcher said grimly, and that put an end to that line of conversation.

Bess rubbed her eyes and forehead. "My head aches so, though I feel awful complaining of such a small pain when so many others were wounded grievously. I did not see what happened to Major Schofeld, except that he was taken away by two men. I hope he was not too badly injured. There was so much blood..."

"Let me take you to Lindsey House, Bess," Daphne said. She glanced at Fletcher, who was studying the floor. She could not imagine any excuse that would leave them alone together, leave her free to tell him everything that was in her heart. "Unless you would prefer... though I cannot imagine where else you might go..."

"Yes, Lindsey House. Thank you, Captain Fletcher, Captain Ainsworth. It has been most enjoyable despite the ending." Bess smiled and put her arms around Daphne's shoulders. Daphne cast one last look at Fletcher, then Bounded them both to Lindsey House's left-hand drawing room. Bess immediately stepped away from Daphne and said, "Do not move, do not say a word." She flung her head back in the attitude of Speaking to someone.

Daphne, bewildered, did as she was told. Bess's conversation lasted for perhaps half a minute, during which time Daphne examined the drawing room. It did not appear to have changed in the week and a half since she had Bounded away from it to Madhyapatnam. A few books lay on the table in a manner that suggested someone had finished reading them but had not bothered to put them away. The room still smelled of furniture polish and old sunlight, trapped in the heavy curtains.

"There," Bess said, lowering her head. "You are to Bound to Government House's Bounding chamber in one minute. Really, life would be so much easier if I could hear the responses to the communications I make." She laughed and threw her arms around Daphne. "Oh, I am so pleased for you! Am I permitted to tease you about your inconstancy of resolution, swearing you would not fall in love, or will that simply annoy you?"

"Bess—"

"Very well, I shall refrain, but it is exceptionally difficult. It is just as well we have been under siege, because Captain Fletcher would have driven us all to distraction with his impatience to see you again. Not that anyone but myself knew that is why he was impatient, he is very circumspect, but to me it was clear he could not bear your separation. Do tell me about the *zenana*! No, there is no time." She hugged Daphne again, and said, "You must go. We will speak more later."

Daphne, her head whirling, obediently Bounded to Government

House. The still, over-warm confines of the Bounding chamber rose up around her. She could hear nothing but the sound of her own breathing. Tentatively, she opened the door and peered out. The long, windowless hall was empty—no, someone had just turned the corner at the far end.

Fletcher.

She Skipped to meet him, unable to contain herself. He looked worse than she had originally realized, his eyes reddened, his skin black with powder residue, his hair disordered, and he smelled of sweat and black powder, but to her eyes he was utterly beautiful. He regarded her impassively, unsmiling, and her own smile faltered. It was not the way she had pictured their reunion.

"I could not tell Miss Hanley not to send you, as I cannot imagine a place where we might have some privacy," he said, his voice low, "and perhaps for the sake of your honor that is just as well."

"I consider myself the keeper of my honor, and I trust you, Captain." Why would he not smile? She ran through a list of places she knew to Bound to, came to a rather unorthodox one, and said, "Do you trust *me?*"

He raised his eyebrows. "Of course."

Daphne put her arms around his waist and waited for him to put his arms around her shoulders. She smiled up at him and was rewarded with the beginnings of the warm, wonderful smile he kept for her alone. She Bounded—

and Fletcher exclaimed in surprise. "Why are we in Jack's office?" The room was dark, the windows well-shuttered, and it smelled unexpectedly of incense that masked the dank scent that pervaded every Company structure Daphne had ever visited. "I did not know you knew its essence."

Daphne did not release him. "Well, most of the places I know are either not very private, or are far too private, if you take my meaning, and I did not believe you would be comfortable in any of my bedrooms. And Colonel Dalhousie did imply he meant to be gone for a while."

Finally, *finally*, Fletcher laughed, a hearty, amused sound that warmed Daphne's heart. "Oh, my darling," he said, "I had nearly convinced myself you were a dream. That you did not love me, that I had imagined it all."

Daphne took a step closer, and his arms lowered from her shoulders to her waist. "And now?"

Fletcher embraced her, pulling her close so her head rested on his shoulder and he could stroke her hair. "You may be the only real thing in my world," he said, "and I hope Jack stays away for a year."

Daphne laughed. "I believe we will have to settle for twenty minutes."

"You are well? Daphne, when I learned what had happened to you —that I was the cause of it—"

"That is foolish talk, and you will stop that right now. Amitabh's Mover was the cause of it, and you are not in any way to blame. And I am perfectly well. I will certainly never try that again, though I still believe it might be possible to Bound to a human essence, not *to* it, of course, but near it—"

"I believe my hair is turning grey just imagining it. Please, promise me you will not be reckless again."

"I promise to be very careful. I believe there may be a way to experiment without actually Bounding, would that satisfy you?"

"I am coming to learn that protecting you from all harm is a fool's errand, given that you have spent years becoming the sort of woman who thinks nothing of risking herself to help others." Fletcher shifted his hold on her so he could look her in the eye. "But you should know I am the sort of man who cannot easily send the woman he loves into danger, if he cannot be by her side."

"I never want to leave you again." She remembered General Omberlis, and sorrow and anger touched her heart.

"That was an unexpected emotion," Fletcher said. "What troubles you?"

"It is just... I still owe the War Office three and a half years of service, and General Omberlis has threatened—I am certain he did not mean it as a threat, but that is—I may be sent back to Spain."

Fletcher's arms tightened around her. "Leave India? Surely you are needed here."

"Not as much as I may be needed there, according to the general. I do not know what to do."

"It is a difficulty. I could ask to be transferred, but... I am too valuable to the Company, trained as I am in the language and culture here... Daphne, it is too soon to worry about that."

"I suppose." She tilted her head. "I love you."

"I know."

"I mean that I did not actually say those words, and I thought perhaps I should."

Fletcher kissed her, his lips lingering on hers. "I will always love hearing them," he said, kissing her again and making the world spin around her, "but standing here, touching you—what you feel for me fills me to overflowing, and I wish I could share it with you."

"Kiss me again, and that will be enough," Daphne said.

⚜

TWENTY MINUTES LATER DAPHNE BOUNDED BACK TO HER BEDROOM in Lindsey House and flopped gracelessly onto her bed. How strange life was, and how beautiful. She felt warm inside, and happier than she could ever remember being. They had kissed, and talked, and Daphne had not wanted to leave, she felt so content in her love's arms, but Colonel Dalhousie could not return and find them there together. "Will he not wonder why you are still so filthy from the battle?" she had asked. "Surely he meant you to take this hour to clean yourself up."

"I will have time to change my clothes and wash my face at least," Fletcher had said. "Jack is accustomed to my eccentricities when it comes to my military service. I once reported to him dressed as a Hindoo beggar and he did not bat an eyelash."

Now Daphne took the opportunity to change her own clothing, stained with grime and Schofeld's blood. How might she find out what had happened to him? Surely she had been in time to save his life. She sponged off her face and hands and her shoulder where the blood had leaked through her uniform to her skin, then donned a clean gown and wished as she never had before that someone had bothered to provide her with more than one uniform.

~Daphne?~ Someone knocked on the door.

"Enter, Bess," Daphne called out.

Bess had found another pair of spectacles and had also changed her clothes and tidied her hair. "So, tell me everything," she said, taking a seat on the edge of Daphne's bed. "What happened in the *zenana* that made Captain Fletcher smile so?"

"It would be indelicate of me to elaborate," Daphne said primly, then smiled and threw her arms around her friend. "But I am rapturously happy, even if I cannot show it openly."

"Whyever not? It is not as if he is ineligible. Or—it is rather sudden for a declaration of love, I suppose."

"Almost no time at all. Bess, he behaves as if he is deeply attached to me, but he has not said anything about... about marriage, or the future. Yet he knows as no one else could how I feel about him." Daphne released her and drew in a deep breath. "I choose not to dwell on it. My future is still uncertain, anyway. I may be sent back to Spain."

"But—you cannot!"

"I can, if my service to Lady Loudoun is at an end. She intends to bring her household to India."

Bess's lovely mouth drew up in a scowl that with her spectacles made her look positively villainous. "They have need of Bounders in India."

"General Omberlis says they have a greater need for Bounders on the battlefield." Daphne sighed. "It is another thing I choose not to dwell on, since I cannot do anything about it."

"Wise, and I applaud your strength of will." Bess held up a quelling finger and tilted her head back. Her merry expression gave way to one of dismay. "We are summoned to Lord Moira's office," she said with her eyes still closed. "To make our report."

Daphne heart beat faster. "You do mean 'we' as in myself as well?"

"Lord Moira's Speaker was very clear." Bess opened her eyes. "Do not fear. You were positively heroic. The Governor-General can have no reason to complain of your service."

Daphne thought privately the Governor-General needed no reason to complain of her. "Very well," she said. "Though I was there hardly any time at all."

"Time enough to rescue us." Bess arranged her arms around Daphne's shoulders, and in half a breath they were in the Bounding chamber at Government House. "I have not heard word of Major Schofeld's condition," Bess went on, "and I feel great concern for him. I know he offended you, Daphne, but he has performed admirably, brought us news of your condition—he has even been cordial toward Captain Fletcher."

"I feel I may be able to forgive him, as he has been so penitent, and I believe he meant no harm—though I do not believe one ought to be forgiven the worst of sins simply because one did not mean to commit them. The harm has still been done, after all." Daphne did wonder about Schofeld's treatment of Fletcher, though. She had inadvertently told the major the effects of his torment of Fletcher, and had expected him to rather redouble his efforts to hurt him. Cordial toward Fletcher? Perhaps she had misjudged Schofeld, after all.

They climbed the stairs to Lord Moira's office, ignored by the men in uniform they passed despite their being gowned in their nicest daywear and appearing completely out of place in that bastion of male privilege. Daphne was accustomed to being stared at and felt oddly naked at receiving no attention. She resolved to ignore the officers as well. It was getting on toward noon, and the air grew stiflingly hot as the windows were shuttered against the sunlight. Government House was beautiful, but Daphne wished it had been built with the heat of an Indian climate in mind.

Lord Moira's door was open. Daphne and Bess entered to find the windows were open, letting bright, hot sunlight into the room. The Governor-General sat behind his desk, facing Fletcher, who had as promised changed into a clean uniform and washed his face, though the shadow of black powder still lingered on the curve of his throat and around his ears. Captain Ainsworth and Ensign Phillips stood behind him, similarly cleaned up and looking rather uncertain. Colonel Dalhousie stood behind Lord Moira and to his left, his face impassive.

In the face of all that military force, Daphne hesitated just inside the door, but Bess kept moving, halting only when the corner of the desk brought her to a stop. "Come in, Lady Daphne, and close the door," Colonel Dalhousie said. "Captain Fletcher has already told me everything."

For a moment, Daphne's heart beat faster before she realized he did not mean her relationship with Fletcher and the kisses they had stolen in Dalhousie's office. "You are all to be commended for your work, particularly since it took a turn no one could have anticipated," Dalhousie continued. "Lady Daphne, you did not return before you were fully well, did you?"

"No—that is, yes, I am fully well," Daphne stammered, conscious of Lord Moira's baleful eye on her, "but I would have returned anyway, as I could not bear to desert my friends."

"There is no place for sentimentality in the military," Lord Moira said. "You would put your fellows in jeopardy by returning when you were not fit for duty, and force them to take special care of you?"

"Lady Daphne's spirit is laudable, but it leads her to a certain inaccuracy of speech," Fletcher said. "She could not have Bounded to Madhyapatnam were she not fully recovered. And her performance at Madhyapatnam was exceptional, proving that she was far from a liability. She and the Bounders she brought in rescued everyone left in the Residency and several of its defenders."

"But not Sir Rodney," Lord Moira said.

Fletcher was standing with his hands clasped loosely behind his back. Only Daphne saw him close one hand tightly enough that his knuckles went white. "I forbade Lady Daphne to attempt to rescue Sir Rodney, my lord. Criticism for that decision should be on my head."

"All reports suggest that Sir Rodney was in the thick of the fight, my lord," Dalhousie said. "It is unlikely anyone could have got through to save him."

"That sounds like Sir Rodney," Lord Moira agreed. "Very well. I commend you all for your actions in Madhyapatnam, given that your initial remit went so far astray. It is unfortunate you could not prevent this Amitabh from taking control, but I'm disinclined to criticize after your valiant defense of the Residence. I—Miss Hanley?"

Bess had her head tilted back, but as Lord Moira spoke, she opened her eyes and focused on him. "My lord, I apologize, but I have just received an urgent message concerning Sir Rodney."

Lord Moira's eyebrows went up. "Is he not dead?"

"No, my lord. Would you like to receive the message in private?" Bess sounded shaken.

Lord Moira nodded. "All of you are dismissed."

Daphne followed Fletcher out of the office and crowded with Ainsworth, Phillips, and Dalhousie in the antechamber. She caught Lord Wellesley's portrait's eye; it glowered at her much as Lord Moira had done. She glared at it, daring it to take issue with her actions in Madhyapatnam. That had been a grudging commendation, Daphne was sure, at least as far as her own portion of it was concerned. It would not matter that she had overcome her weakness; she would always be a liability to Lord Moira.

"You know the Governor-General is sparing with his praise," Dalhousie murmured. "As far as I am concerned, every one of you deserves a true commendation for your actions. Lord Moira knows it."

"We didn't do it to be thanked, Jack," Fletcher replied.

The office door flew open, startling them all with its abruptness. "Lord Moira would like to speak with you. *All* of you," Bess said, looking meaningfully at Daphne.

Bewildered, Daphne trailed along at the end of the line and took up her place near the back of the room. Lord Moira had looked irritated before; now he looked positively apoplectic. "Reprehensible," he was saying to Bess as they entered. "Utterly beyond the pale." He turned his attention to Dalhousie. "Miss Hanley's message was relayed to us by Amitabh's Extraordinary Speaker," he said. "Sir Rodney was taken alive in the siege. Amitabh refuses to trade for him on any terms."

"That cannot be all," Dalhousie said.

"It's not." Lord Moira spat out the words as if they were poisoned. "Amitabh intends to demonstrate his superiority over the Honourable Company by executing Sir Rodney tomorrow at dawn."

CHAPTER 29

IN WHICH CAPTAIN FLETCHER COUNTERMANDS AN ORDER

"Execute?" Daphne exclaimed, then wished she had not when Lord Moira's furious eye fell on her. She knew he was not angry with her, but it was hard to bear nonetheless.

"He will cause the people to rise up in his favor if he goes through with it," Fletcher said. "It is a potent symbol and may well convince them he is destined to rule Madhyapatnam. You cannot permit it."

"I am aware of that, Captain," Lord Moira said drily. "And there is the small matter of not permitting a servant of the Company to die in such an ignominious fashion."

"We are prepared to leave for Madhyapatnam immediately," Fletcher said, ignoring the Governor-General's sarcasm. "I will need a few more men, my lord."

"I dislike having my orders anticipated, Captain." Lord Moira tapped his fingers on his desktop. "But you are correct. I intend to send you and a few other handpicked men to rescue Sir Rodney. I assume from what Colonel Dalhousie has said about your other missions that you need no more direction than that?"

"I already have some ideas, my lord."

"Good man." Lord Moira cracked a dry, dusty smile. "Miss Hanley, would you summon Major Schofeld? I wish to give him his orders myself."

"My lord, Major Schofeld is still recovering from a major Healing. His injuries nearly cost him his left leg," Dalhousie murmured, as if he were Ainsworth telling a great secret. Daphne felt her heart begin to beat faster once more. She did not wish Schofeld ill, was glad to hear he was not dead, but...

Lord Moira cast a quick glance at Daphne, then said, "Corporal Broome, then, or Lieutenant Fisher. They participated in the evacuation of the Residence and can Bound to Madhyapatnam."

"Broome and Fisher know only the Bounding chamber at the Residence," Fletcher said. His head was held high and he appeared to be staring at a spot on the wall above Lord Moira's head. "It is almost certainly under Amitabh's control. In fact, my assessment of the man suggests that he will have made the Residence his headquarters."

Lord Moira's face darkened. "Lady Daphne," he ground out, "it appears you will be needed for this adventure."

"Yes, my lord," Daphne said, trying not to sound inappropriately cheerful.

"You are to Bound Fletcher's men there, and Bound them back again, no more than that. I do not wish you to be anywhere you might be incapacitated. You will not endanger good men's lives, do you understand?"

She wanted to protest that she was cured, but his expression told her he would not believe her and did not care if she were. "I understand, my lord."

"Very well. Fletcher, you are to leave as soon as possible, but take no unnecessary risks. What we do not need is multiple executions come morning." Lord Moira pushed back heavily from his desk and stood. "Dalhousie, continue your preparations for the troops to move out. No matter what happens tomorrow, we march on Madhyapatnam in two days."

"Understood, my lord," Dalhousie said. He exchanged unreadable glances with Fletcher that made Daphne wish she knew what meaning had been conveyed between them. She followed the others out of the office and watched Lord Moira and Colonel Dalhousie walk away down the hall. Had she not been so tremulous with excitement, she would have found it amusing how everyone stepped out of their way, like ducks bobbing out of the wake of a ship. She opened her mouth to ask a question, and without looking at her, Fletcher held up a hand for silence. That either spoke to some preternatural ability or the fact that he simply knew her too well.

When the two men were fully out of sight, Fletcher said, "You know of no Bounding locations you can safely go to within Madhyapatnam, is that true?"

"Yes, but I did not like to say so in front of Lord Moira, in the event he decided this was too dangerous an adventure."

"Very wise." He flashed a quick smile at her. "We will have to move fast. Ainsworth, choose three men, preferably ones who have worked with us before. Phillips, assemble native costume for six men and one woman, and weapons enough for all. Miss Hanley, go with Captain Ainsworth and make the acquaintance of the three men he chooses; you may need to Speak to any of us." Fletcher held out his hand to Daphne. "Lady Daphne, can you Bound to the first post-house we stayed at?"

"If the shutters are closed, yes, Captain."

"One moment." Bess tilted her head back. "I have Spoken with the *khansamah* and asked him to close off the post-house to the outdoors. Give him five minutes."

"Thank you, Miss Hanley." Fletcher fixed each of them with his eye briefly. "This is certainly not what any of you expected," he said, "but Sir Rodney is a friend, and he is depending on us. Let us not disappoint him."

Daphne nodded with the rest. Fletcher slung his arms around her shoulders, and she lifted him and Bounded away.

THE SMOKY LIGHT OF A COCONUT-OIL LAMP MADE THE TINY SHACK look dirtier and smaller than it likely was. Daphne sat cross-legged on the packed earth floor and traced patterns on it with her fingernail. Its walls were stained from decades of monsoon weather, its roof was a thatched mess that had had gaping holes in it before she and Fletcher had hastily mended them with scraps of canvas, and its door was nothing more than another large piece of canvas tied to the lintel with fraying ropes. Its only redeeming feature was that it was, after their ministrations, completely opaque to the outside world and suitable for Bounding. Daphne knew its essence well after hours of sitting in it wishing she had been able to go with the men.

She had Bounded Fletcher's party in around seven o'clock that evening, well after sunset. The three new men Ainsworth had chosen were Sergeant Dockery, whom she had Bounded away from the Residence only hours before, and two Hindoos, Vajra and Chirayu, neither of whom she had met before. They gave her very professional nods when they were introduced to her. Both looked so ordinary they could not possibly draw attention to themselves, and Daphne guessed this was in part why Ainsworth had chosen them.

The Englishmen did not fare nearly so well. Dockery's skin was darkly tanned, more so than Fletcher and Ainsworth's, but he still looked European. Phillips had covered his red hair with one of the peculiar hats that were not quite turbans, and Fletcher did wear a turban in the Mahommedan style. They were dressed rather haphazardly, but in the dark, the non-Hindoos would likely go unnoticed.

"You will remain here," Fletcher had told her, "and Miss Hanley will communicate with you to tell you of our progress. It is possible we will be leaving here at a run."

"You believe you can discover where Sir Rodney is being held, and free him?" Daphne had said.

"I have contacts within the city, and some of them will know the facts we need. We will assess the situation, and make another plan at that point."

"That sounds dangerous."

"Less dangerous than assuming we know all the facts and simply charging in, waving our rifles and shouting." Fletcher had flashed a smile, gripped her hand briefly in farewell, and then they were gone into the night.

Now Daphne leaned back against the wall, then thought better of it and sat up again. The low rumble of Madhyapatnam at night surrounded her, the sound of thousands of people conversing and walking through the city mingled with the more distant sounds of the mofussil, the untamed lands between settlements. She imagined she heard a tiger, but no animal would come so close to civilization as to be heard clearly. Here, humans were the superior species.

-Daphne, Ensign Phillips says they have discovered Sir Rodney is being held captive in the Residence. That must simply be adding insult to injury, don't you suppose? He says they are evaluating the approach, though I do not know what it means precisely.-

It was unfortunate she could not respond to Bess, as it would give her something to occupy herself during the long wait. She had left her pocket watch behind at Marvell Hall, and her second-best one had been at the Residence. No doubt some horrid soldier of Amitabh's had stolen it, possibly Amitabh himself. The thought annoyed her. Who knew what use they might make of her things? Her Standiford's Bounder uniform? She wished more than ever she were at Fletcher's side, so she might spit in Amitabh's eye.

She stood and dusted off her bottom, stretched her legs, and popped the joints in her neck. Phillips had found her women's clothing similar to what she had worn to Vaachaspati's poetry recital, but she had insisted on loose trousers and a long-sleeved shirt. "Suppose something goes wrong?" she had exclaimed. "I must be free to move, as free as possible, and as I cannot wear my uniform—and besides, it is not as if anyone will see me." Fletcher had sighed, and directed Phillips to bring her the clothes she desired. They were too big, the sleeves falling over her hands and the trouser legs trailing in the dust, and she had occupied herself for the first hour by hemming up the legs so she did not trip over them. They had not found any sandals small enough for her feet, so she was barefoot, a sensation she rather enjoyed.

-Daphne, Captain Fletcher is going to attempt to sneak into the Residence. Oh, I am so nervous for him! Ensign Phillips assures me he knows what he is doing, but it seems so dangerous. I can only imagine what you must feel right now.-

A chill swept over Daphne despite the warmth of the night air, centering on her heart. Sneaking in—and he thought *she* was reckless! She closed her eyes and focused on the smells in the air to keep her from panicking. The coconut-oil lamp, smoky and bittersweet at the same time. Roasting fish nearby, making her stomach growl; nerves had prevented her from eating properly before they left. Farther away, but still close enough to make her hungry, the sweetish scent of cinnamon. Someone was making those delicious spiced honey nuggets whose name she still did not know. She determined to ask Fletcher as soon as this was all over.

She leaned back, forgetting herself, and had to jerk upright once more. The wall was not as damp as it looked, and Daphne realized it had been a few days since the rains had fallen heavily. A light shower as she and Fletcher were Skipping from the post-house to Madhyapatnam was all the rain she had seen. Perhaps the monsoons were finally over. What was India like during its winter? She hoped she would be there to find out.

No one seemed to be near their little shack, which was on the outskirts of the town proper and isolated from its neighbors, so Daphne pushed the canvas door aside and stepped out. The sky was bright with a million stars, undimmed by moonlight or the faintly glowing lamps attached to a few of the nearby hovels. Nothing moved in all the darkened streets nearby; but for the distant sounds of humanity Daphne might have been alone in the world. She shivered, and ducked back inside.

-Daphne, they are returning. Ensign Phillips says they have separated and it may take them some time to come back safely. They do not have Sir Rodney.-

Though Bess's words were often indistinguishable from Daphne's own thoughts, this time Bess's discouragement came through as clearly as a fingernail against crystal. Daphne sank to the floor, her own heart aching. Fletcher must be safe, Bess would have said were that not the case, but if they were returning without Sir Rodney, it must be hopeless. She drew her knees up to her chin and sat hugging herself, wondering who would be first through the door.

Less than an hour later, or so she judged from how the lamp burned low, Sergeant Dockery and Vajra pushed through the canvas door. "We could not reach him, Lady Daphne," Vajra said, sinking to the floor next to her. "Captain Fletcher was able to sneak into the Residence grounds, but Sir Rodney is well-guarded on the first floor. He could not bypass Amitabh's men."

"But I could," Daphne said. Excitement had risen in her when he mentioned the first floor. "I might Bound to my old bedchamber, then—"

Dockery and Vajra exchanged glances. "Best you wait for the captain," Dockery said. He was a gruff-looking man in his middle thirties, with wiry black hair and a dark beard shadow.

"Wait what for the captain?" Fletcher said as he entered. He took one look at Daphne and said, "Oh, no. Lady Daphne, you would not be able to reach Sir Rodney either. There are two guards on his chamber and one within. I believe Amitabh expects us to try something like that, having met you and seen what you are capable of. You would likely get as far as the top of the stairs before you were seen."

"I am very fast at Skipping, Captain—"

"You are, but it is an unnecessary risk. I have something else in mind."

"And that is...?"

He shook his head. "Wait for the others to return."

Ainsworth entered shortly thereafter, followed by Chirayu. Phillips did not return immediately. Had Bess not relayed his messages to Fletcher, who shared them with the rest, Daphne might have gone mad with worry over the young man. Finally, Phillips entered, looking dustier and more worn-out than the others. "I beg your pardon," he said, "but I had to take a roundabout way to return here. I believe one of Amitabh's men suspected me of being a thief. But he did not guess who I really was, or there would have been a furor at the Residence."

"Very good," Fletcher said. "Have a seat, and I will tell you my plan."

Daphne sat next to Fletcher, carefully not touching him. Excitement flooded through her, setting her bones to tingling, and he did not need any distractions. "We cannot reach Sir Rodney in the Residence," Fletcher began, "and we naturally do not have enough men to assault the place directly. Our only chance is to take him as he is being escorted to the place of execution, which is the public square outside the bazaar."

"That means knowing the route they will take," Ainsworth said. "It's a big risk."

"There is only one large street from the Residence to the square. Amitabh will want the spectacle of displaying his captive as publicly as possible." Fletcher leaned forward and drew a quick sketch in the dirt. "We will go now to examine the route and determine which is the best place to make our attack, then we will position ourselves there before dawn. Ensign Phillips, at that time you will stay near the Residence and communicate Sir Rodney's condition to Miss Hanley—how many guards, how he is bound, et cetera. I expect you to follow them, continuing to Speak to Miss Hanley, until we engage with Amitabh's men."

He turned to look at Daphne, his dark eyes inscrutable. "Lady Daphne," he said.

"I know, Captain, I am prepared to wait here for your return."

Fletcher shook his head. "I intend for you to join us."

Daphne's mouth fell open. "But, Captain, Lord Moira—"

"Is not the man on the spot. If this is to have any chance of success, you will have to Bound Sir Rodney back to Calcutta while the rest of us occupy Amitabh's men. He will likely not be in a condition to flee under his own power. Are you capable of conveying him to safety?"

"I am, Captain, but... Lord Moira will be angry."

"I will take full responsibility." He smiled, the warm, wonderful smile she loved. "And if we are successful, I see no reason Lord Moira should know about this at all."

"Very well, Captain, I agree."

"Then... I'm afraid I must ask you to wait here while we reconnoiter. I doubt you were trained to sneak through the streets of a city by night, and Skipping will not provide the information we need."

"No, Captain, you are correct." She felt no irritation at being left behind. To play a real part in saving Sir Rodney...! She wanted to Skip across Madhyapatnam, shouting her excitement, which would ruin the plan entirely. So she remained seated when the men left, filing out one at a time until only Fletcher was left. He crouched beside her and laid a hand on her shoulder, and amusement lit his eyes.

"Do not be too excited, or it will make you unfit for this adventure," he said.

"I will not, it is just that I am so glad—you might have made me stay behind, where I would be safe, and it does not seem even to have occurred to you—"

"I did say I would have trouble sending you into danger if I could not be by your side." He swiftly kissed her, the briefest touch of his lips to hers, and vanished out the door. Daphne clasped her hands in her lap and practiced breathing, in through the nose, out through the mouth. How wonderful, that he did not believe she needed protecting from danger! She must take him to meet her parents, and soon—no, she ought to ask him about *his* parents—oh, there were so many things they might do to make a life together! The possibility of being sent to the Peninsula shrank into unimportance beside that.

Despite her excitement, she dozed off, leaning against the filthy wall without caring about its condition. She woke once to Bess telling her she was going to bed, and would Speak with her before dawn, then again muzzily to someone drawing her down to lie on the hard earth. *I cannot sleep in a shack with six men*, she thought faintly, but was too tired to make any more objection than that.

When she woke, she was alone. The darkness had the still, damp quality that comes just before dawn. Her heart pounded once, hard, with fear that it was too late and Sir Rodney was already dead, but it was too dark for that to be possible. They would be in time.

-Daphne, I hope you are awake. Ensign Phillips is still asleep, and you might wake him if you are able. Oh, I am so nervous I can hardly bear it!-

Daphne left the hovel and found the men scattered here and there around it in varying attitudes of sleep. It warmed her heart that they had been so considerate of her, though she supposed low minds might consider her virtue tarnished simply because of her association with them with no more chaperon than Bess's disembodied voice. Fletcher knelt crouched over Ainsworth, shaking him awake. "Wake the others," he whispered. "It is time."

The city was coming to life as they made their way through its still-darkened streets, the smells of hot rice and roasted meat making

Daphne's stomach rumble. An hour, no more, and it would all be over and she would be back at Government House, or at Lindsey House, eating her breakfast. She tried to cling to that image without letting it weaken her. Sir Rodney's life was still in danger.

Phillips disappeared without Daphne realizing it. He would be taking a circuitous route to the Residence, acting as their spy. Daphne ran over possibilities in her head to keep herself from growing too nervous. If Sir Rodney were bound to someone else, she would have to free him before Bounding him away. He might be shackled with heavy weights to prevent him running, which could make Bounding complicated; Sir Rodney was not a small man, and while Daphne was strong, there were limits to her strength. Finally, she made herself stop guessing and focused on following Fletcher to their designated spot. Phillips would tell them all soon enough, and then she could make a real plan.

The place Fletcher had chosen was a bend in the street that led from the Residence to the public square. On one side of the street, a house somewhat sturdier than the usual ramshackle construction jutted forward of its fellows, forcing the street to bow around it. On the other side, a curtained booth marked where someone sold honeyed figs during the day, based on the smell. The street narrowed between these two points. Daphne guessed Amitabh's men would have to go two abreast rather than four, and with them strung out like pearls on a string, they would be easy to pick off.

Fletcher gestured to Vajra, Ainsworth, and Dockery to cross the street and conceal themselves. He handed Daphne a length of cloth and whispered, "Cover your hair." Daphne nodded and wrapped the cloth around her head. It would fall off if she exerted herself, but if that happened, exposing her hair would likely be the last thing she was concerned with. Fletcher guided her to a spot somewhat back from the street that nevertheless had a clear view of it, then disappeared.

Daphne and Chirayu watched the street as the skies lightened and more people appeared. Chirayu was stouter than the others, but moved lightly on his feet, and he gave Daphne a reassuring smile every few minutes. Daphne smiled back, but felt she would have been more reassured if Fletcher were there. Where had he gone, anyway?

Then he was back, holding three skewers of meat. "Eat up," he said, handing them out. "We will look less suspicious if we are not simply loitering."

Daphne dug in. She was suddenly ravenous—well, it had been hours since her last meal. She finished eating and sucked the meat juice off her fingers. She would miss the food in India if she were forced to leave. She dropped the skewer on the ground and said, "It is nearly dawn."

Fletcher nodded. The crowds had grown while they ate, and although Daphne had little experience with foreign cities, she felt the mood of this one was dark, angry, and anticipatory, like a tiger seeking its next meal. It frightened her, and she made herself push that feeling deep inside, where it could not harm her. She took half a step back and wiped her suddenly sweaty palms on her trousers. It must happen soon.

-Daphne! Ensign Phillips says to tell you Sir Rodney is bound with his hands before him and led by two very large men, connected to him by ropes. I am warning everyone that he must be separated from his guards if you are to Bound with him.-

Daphne looked at Fletcher. By his expression, he had just received a similar message. He nodded at the air, then took up a casual pose near the edge of the street. Daphne resisted the urge to shelter behind his broad back and scanned the crowd, though she did not know what to look for—signs that their disguises had been penetrated, perhaps? She listened to the unintelligible conversations carried on around her. If she could convince General Omberlis to permit her to remain in India, she would learn to speak Hindoostani. Yashpal, the *punkah-wallah* at the Residence, had been willing, but she would not remain in Madhyapatnam. She would have to enlist one of the servants at Lindsey House.

-They are approaching,- Bess said. -Three guards, then Sir Rodney and his guards, then Amitabh followed by a lot of his men. Ensign Phillips estimates they are two minutes' march at their current speed from where you wait.-

Daphne saw Fletcher twitch the way he frequently did when Bess addressed him. He turned his head to look off down the street toward the still-unseen procession. Then he went still, rigid as if paralyzed. He made a gesture like cutting his throat and turned, grabbing Chirayu and dragging him away from the street. Daphne, startled, backed away from him. He took her arm with his free hand and pulled her along in his wake.

"We are lost," he said in a low voice, never stopping his swift march away from the street. "I should have guessed Amitabh would remain close to his victim."

"But—" Daphne began.

"His Discernment, do you not see? Had we remained there, he would have sensed our presence before we were in range to recover Sir Rodney." Finally, Fletcher came to a halt at the center of two narrow paths, surrounded by busy men and women who paid them no mind, and released them. "We cannot reach him. Our plan has failed."

CHAPTER 30

IN WHICH DAPHNE ONCE
MORE DOES THE
UNEXPECTED

"**B**ut we cannot abandon our goal!" Chirayu said.

"We will not," Fletcher said. His eyes were narrowed, and he drummed his fingers on his thigh. "I need time, and we have very little of that."

"Tell us what to do, Captain," Daphne said.

Fletcher bit his lip in thought. "Lady Daphne," he said, "can you find the public square? Without Skipping?"

"I believe so. It is at the end of that street—or perhaps I should stay away from the street, if Amitabh can sense my feelings—are you certain he would be able to pick us out from such a large crowd?"

"Very certain. He is skilled, for one so young, and feelings of anticipatory fear stand out like—I have no time to explain it." Fletcher laid a hand on her shoulder. "Go to the square and hide yourself on the far side. When Sir Rodney appears, the rest of us will separate his guards from him, and when that happens, you are to Bound him away immediately. No matter what else you see, do you understand? Then return to the rendezvous point and wait for us. Chirayu, with me."

He turned away, and Daphne, dread creeping over her, said, "Captain—"

Fletcher glanced back over his shoulder. "We will succeed, Daphne,

I promise you that." With a few steps, he and Chirayu were swept up in the crowd.

Daphne took a deep breath, inhaling the smell of food and animals and human beings that made up the distinctive scent of Madhyapatnam. Then she plunged into the crowd.

The rising sun tinted the sky a paler blue but was not yet high enough to give her guidance as to her direction. She followed narrow paths, staying away from the main street, praying her inner sense was enough to keep her in the right way. No one stared at her; they were either preoccupied with their own business or were flocking in the same direction she was. She realized they were going to see the execution just as she came out from between two buildings and discovered she had reached the square.

The crowds had swollen until Daphne was certain all of Madhyapatnam had turned out to see the horrid event. Did they all wish Sir Rodney dead, despite how much he had done for Madhyapatnam? Or were some of them there in protest? She pushed her way through, ignoring the cries of anger in Hindoostani, until she reached an open space. She had never been so grateful to be small and yet have the strength to shove past those blocking her view. She crouched, ducked, and broke through to the front of the crowd, then bit back a scream at the grey monstrosity only fifty feet from where she stood.

In the next moment, her eyes adjusted, and she realized it was an elephant, shifting its weight from one enormous front foot to the other. A couple of men dressed in short trousers and soft hats held halters to which its harness was attached. They ignored it, bantering and laughing with each other in Hindoostani, laughing louder when the elephant's trunk plucked the hat from one man's head.

Daphne regarded the scene in confusion. It had such a carnival, festive air that she could not imagine what role the elephant might play in the drama that was about to unfold. Perhaps Amitabh intended to take a celebratory ride around the bazaar? She noticed a block for mounting the elephant nearby. It was plain, with dark stains along its sides, and far too short to help anyone mount an animal that size.

Or... she recalled a story Miss Donnelly had whispered one night after supper, as if speaking it softly might make it less horrid. A story of how some executions were performed in India, with the victim made to kneel with his head on the block, the elephant led forward, its giant foot induced to set atop the victim's head, and then... Daphne swallowed against her sudden nausea. How symbolic, crushing the head of the representative of the Company, asserting Amitabh's dominance. It was exactly the kind of execution Daphne might expect him to arrange.

She looked away, hoping to regain her calm. The square might have been any shape, it was so thronged with people ringing it, appearing to sway as men and women did as Daphne had done and made good vantage points for themselves. The bazaar was to Daphne's left about a quarter of the way around the square, its dun and grey tent peaks already erected against the day's business. No doubt the stall owners hoped an early morning execution would whet their customers' appetites for purchasing all manner of things.

To the right, about the same distance, a gap in the wall of people showed where the main street entered the square. She could not tell, at that distance, how Amitabh's men were keeping the street clear for his macabre procession, just that no one seemed inclined to take that space regardless of how much pushing was happening. Daphne determined to make a place for herself opposite that opening, which would give her a perfect view and, possibly, put her in a position to rescue Sir Rodney.

Deciding against simply running across the square, she ducked back into the crowd and made her way around, ducking her head and slinking through the narrowest gaps between people to her desired place. She found she could not stand directly opposite the street, as that put the elephant between her and the opening, so she stood to the left of the elephant and its keepers. Had she understood Hindoostani, she would be able to follow the conversation the keepers were having, she was that close.

Someone prodded her in the back, and she half-turned to see a boy of about eight or nine, trying to do as she had done and push his way to the front. His eyes widened as he registered she was European. Daphne lunged for him, not knowing what she would do once she had him, but he dodged and disappeared into the crowd. With luck, she had scared him off and not prompted him to go looking for someone who might accost a lone European woman in Madhyapatnam. She adjusted the cloth around her head and turned around to discover she'd missed the opening moves in the drama now playing out before her.

Three guards had entered the square and separated, two pacing around the circumference of the crowd, the third approaching the elephant. All three were burly, bare chested, and bore swords and pistols thrust into their belts. Not Amitabh's French soldiers, but natives. Daphne pressed back into the crowd and ducked her head as one of them passed near her. She did not need him to identify her as a European, not now.

The men finished their sweep of the crowd, and fell back to flank the elephant on both sides. The keeper on Daphne's side was eyeing the men without staring directly at them. He looked worried that the guards might upset his enormous charge, and based on how the elephant's movements had become more agitated, he might be right to worry. Daphne assessed the distance between herself and the elephant. It was far enough that she could Skip well out of its way, if that became necessary.

Then she forgot to worry about the elephant, because two more guards had entered the square. They each held the end of a rope attached to a man they were towing behind them. Sir Rodney looked terrible. Dried blood coated one side of his face, his clothing was torn, and he was barefoot. He stumbled along as if he was unaware of his surroundings. Daphne, furious, took a step toward them—but the guards still held Sir Rodney's bonds, and she might be able to surprise one of them into dropping his rope, but it would be the only surprise she would get. She needed to wait for Fletcher's attack.

The guards marched forward, and Sir Rodney stumbled and went to his knees. The crowd roared, whether in approval or in anger, she could not tell. *Soon*, Daphne thought, *it must be soon*. She found herself balanced on her toes, ready to leap forward at the slightest warning, which was ridiculous because Skipping did not involve motion like that. Yet she waited in that precarious position anyway, letting the need for balance keep her mind focused. *Soon...*

A thunderclap out of a clear blue pre-dawn sky cut across the noise of thousands of people eager to watch a man die. One of Sir Rodney's guards jerked, blood fountaining from his chest. He sagged to his knees, the rope falling loose from his hand. Daphne immediately Skipped across the square and took hold, not of Sir Rodney, but of the remaining guard's rope. She yanked on it with all her strength, and it came flying free of the startled man's hand. Another shot rang out, then another, but she had no time to listen to rifle fire. She heaved Sir Rodney to his feet, got her arms around his knees, lifted—

—and in half a breath was in the dim coolness of Government House's Bounding chamber. "Get out of here," she gasped, pushing him toward the door, and Bounded back to the shack where she had spent the night. She rushed outside, listening. In the distance, screams and gunshots and the high, terrified trumpeting of a panicked elephant drifted toward her. Daphne swore and Skipped high into the air. She could not just wait for the men to return. She needed to find them before they were all killed.

She Skipped again to the square and immediately regretted her impulse. The crowd had dissolved into a mob, not a mass of men intent on destroying everything in their path, but a frightened, helpless wave of people all trying to get away from danger without any idea of where the danger was. The elephant's keepers had a heroic grasp of the halters, but the elephant dragged them from one side to the other, bellowing its fear. Daphne Skipped high again and shied away as a rifle ball came within inches of her head. "How dare you shoot at me?" she screamed, irrational in her fear for Fletcher and the others, and Skipped again, desperately searching the crowds.

Just as she had determined it was useless, she saw Phillips fighting his way through the crowd. In an instant she was beside him and swept him up and away to Government House. "No!" he shouted. "You must return us to Madhyapatnam. I can relay instructions—"

"You can do it from here," Daphne said, and vanished.

To her surprise, Vajra was at the rendezvous point when she ducked out of the shack. He was breathing heavily and had the beginnings of a bruise across the bridge of his nose and beneath his eyes. "Dockery was behind me," he said. "He is on his way. We fought—"

Daphne picked him up and Bounded him to Government House.

"—the rest of Amitabh's guards," he continued. "It is just a matter of taking everyone home now."

Daphne nodded and Bounded back. This time, she forced herself to wait, pacing before the shack and listening to the noise of the mob. If it came this way... where else could they go? Where else would she know to look for them?

Chirayu staggered out from between the nearest ramshackle houses, followed seconds later by Ainsworth. "Go, go, Lady Daphne!" Ainsworth shouted. She Bounded both men in quick succession. Just Dockery and Fletcher left, and they would arrive in time, she knew it.

Seconds passed, turned into minutes, and still no sign of Dockery or Fletcher. Frustrated and despairing, Daphne flung herself into the sky once more.

The mob had quieted but was still a wild mass of movement. Daphne knew instantly the chances of her finding anyone she knew were vanishingly small. Still, she cast about, quartering Madhyapatnam using her trained skills and her own intelligence. Perhaps they might see her, hovering and darting above the city like a drab hummingbird, and would find a way to return.

There were patterns to the mob, she noticed, streaks of color through the generally dull masses of brown and black. Lacking any other direction, she followed the color and immediately had to Skip out of the way of rifle fire. She rose higher. Only Amitabh's men had rifles—or, at least, if her friends had rifles, as it seemed from the exchange in the square, they would not be shooting at her. Therefore, the colorful streaks were Amitabh's people.

Pain creased her left arm, and she fell, Skipping to safety only moments before impacting with the earth. She touched her arm, and her hand came away bloody. Dazed, she let herself be jostled by the mob until the initial pain passed.

Another hand grabbed her arm, making her hiss and wince away. "What are you doing here?" Fletcher exclaimed. "You were to return to the shack!"

"I did, but you and Dockery—I had to find you—"

"You are a commander's worst nightmare," Fletcher said. "Dockery is dead. Let us go—"

Even in the noise of the affray, the sound of a rifle bolt ratcheting into place echoed, and Daphne turned to see the long, gleaming barrel of a rifle pointing at Fletcher's head. Fletcher went very still, as if he could prevent the soldier from firing through willpower alone. He said something in Hindoostani and put a protective hand on Daphne's uninjured arm. She stood as still as Fletcher. Could she lift him and Bound them both away before the rifle fired? She was fast, but it was Fletcher's life she would be risking.

Someone approached and pushed aside the rifle. "I think there is nothing you can say that will spare you," Amitabh said. "And it would be a shame to waste the elephant. I understand they are less... decisive... when they are afraid. Can you smell the fear?"

"We have stolen your symbol. Our deaths mean nothing to the Company," Fletcher said.

"Yours, perhaps. But an Extraordinary Bounder? They cannot have so many of those that they can afford to waste any." Amitabh took a few steps closer and rested his hand on Fletcher's shoulder. Fletcher closed his eyes as if in pain. "I believe... she will be the first to die. I am generous, yes, in sparing her the sight of your death?" Amitabh rested his other hand on Daphne's shoulder in a parody of comradeship. "Yes, you are far—"

Quicker than thought, Daphne crouched and put an arm around Fletcher, below his posterior. With the other, she embraced Amitabh the same way. She pulled them both close to her body, *lifted* with her legs, and with a great agonized scream, Bounded away.

Her arms, her back, and the back of her thighs hurt as they never had before, their sharp ache a counterpoint to the dull throbbing of her injury. The instant the walls of the Bounding chamber rose up around her, she dropped both men and staggered backward into the wall, closing her eyes against the pain. She heard a scuffle, a very short one, the sound of flesh striking flesh hard, and then Fletcher's voice, saying, "Daphne, are you well?"

She wheezed out, "I do not believe I could repeat that. Please tell me you have subdued him."

"I have. Do you suppose you could open the door? My hands are rather occupied."

She opened her eyes. Fletcher had one of Amitabh's arms twisted behind his back and held him up by his collar with his other hand. Amitabh appeared semi-conscious, sagging in Fletcher's grasp. Daphne opened the door and stepped back to permit Fletcher to precede her into the hall. "I would offer to Bound him elsewhere, but I do not know where I might take him. I know no locations within Fort William, which to me seems a sad oversight."

"We will turn him over to someone who can hold him—" Fletcher stopped at the foot of the stairs leading up to the main floor of Government House and gave his captive a perplexed look. "Now, why does that idea give you pleasure?" he said.

Amitabh's face went impassive, but his eyes flicked toward Daphne briefly. He looked much like a cat creeping up on a fat mouse. "He cannot have planned for us to capture him," she said.

"No, and it is the possibility of being held for a while—of time passing—that has him pleased." Fletcher resumed his march up the stairs. "I believe I should interrogate him immediately. Ah, you are less happy about that, are you? You are not stupid, whatever else you may be."

"I will give you *nothing*," Amitabh snarled.

"Please, feel free to exercise bravado if it will cheer you," Fletcher said. "Let us see—oh, I had forgot there would be a welcoming committee."

The grand entrance hall was thronged with people, among them Fletcher's men, Sir Rodney, and Bess. Colonel Dalhousie came forward with his hand outstretched, which he withdrew when he saw Fletcher's hands were occupied. "That's not—is that *him?*"

"It is Amitabh," Fletcher said, "and we owe Lady Daphne for his capture."

"Indeed." Dalhousie's smile grew. "Lady Daphne, congratulations."

"Thank you, Colonel, but I cannot—that is, Captain Fletcher should interrogate Amitabh immediately. There is a smugness about him we do not like."

"I see." Dalhousie gestured. "Then I should observe. Finn, there is a drawing room just down this hall."

The drawing room was as minimally furnished as most of Government House, with only a sofa and two spindle-legged chairs, a table, and a rug patterned in blue and gold. Dalhousie pulled one of the chairs around to face the sofa and gestured at Ainsworth, who stripped the curtain ropes from where they hung and used them to bind Amitabh to the chair. Daphne watched him closely, remembering the last interrogation she had witnessed—but then Ainsworth was not a Shaper in disguise and was unlikely to want Amitabh to escape.

Fletcher went around behind the captive and splayed his fingers across the man's right cheek. Immediately his eyes closed, and his lips went taut. "Fight me if you wish," he said, a trifle breathlessly, "but I am far more experienced at this than you, and I will learn what I want to know."

"But will you learn it soon enough?" Amitabh breathed.

Fletcher smiled through taut lips. "You should not volunteer information. You have no idea what I'll make of it. Are you waiting for something?"

Amitabh was silent. "Yes, but we already knew that," Fletcher said, answering his own question. "Hmm. Waiting for rescue? No, and you know your life is forfeit, so you are not waiting for a reprieve, either."

"You are guessing," Amitabh said.

"*You* are worried. I applaud your efforts to throw me off, but overwhelming me is not one of your talents." Fletcher drummed the fingers of his left hand on Amitabh's shoulder. "Do you have a larger force elsewhere, marching on Madhyapatnam?"

"Fool."

"So you do not. I call that fortunate for everyone."

"You will never learn my secret in time."

"What did I tell you about giving information away?" Fletcher went silent and appeared to be thinking hard. Finally, he said, "Your Shaper friend was not in your procession today. Where is he?"

Amitabh's eyes widened fractionally, then drooped closed. Fletcher gasped. "The Shaper. You have sent him somewhere, on some mission."

Amitabh jerked away, or tried to; Fletcher gripped his long, dark hair with his left hand and held his captive's head immobilized. "Where did you send him?" Fletcher demanded. "Tell me where."

"I will never tell," Amitabh gasped, "and you cannot read my mind."

"Did you send him for reinforcements?" Silence. "To ally with another prince?" Silence. Fletcher shook his head. "Not to increase the army, not to bring someone else in... what else could there be?" he mused. Amitabh laughed, a low, throaty sound Fletcher ignored. "What is a Shaper good for? For impersonating others, for sneaking where he will be unnoticed, for assassi—"

Fletcher went very still. Daphne, watching him closely, saw his knuckles whiten. "Jack," he said in a quiet, conversational tone, "do you know where Lord Moira is right now?"

CHAPTER 31

IN WHICH DAPHNE HAS DIFFICULTY GETTING ANYONE TO TAKE HER SERIOUSLY

"Lord Moira went to Fort William, to inspect the preparations for the march to Madhyapatnam," Dalhousie said, perplexed. "Why?"

"He is in grave danger," Fletcher said. He released Amitabh with enough force to make the man's head rock. "Amitabh's Shaper is coming to murder him."

"You cannot be certain of that, just from what the man does not say!" Dalhousie shook his head. "We need more proof."

"All these years, and now is the time you choose to doubt my talent?" Fletcher walked around to stand in front of Amitabh, who looked up at him with a malicious grin. "He could not have left much before the siege began, for Lady Daphne and I saw him in the old palace. But if he had left immediately after that, traveling overland, he might already be here."

"I will tell you nothing," Amitabh said. "Run about like geese, honking after every possible threat. You will never find Patenaude if he wishes not to be found."

Dalhousie turned to Daphne. "Go to the Governor-General immediately. Convince him to go to safety. We must first protect him, and then—"

"Yes, sir," Daphne said. She turned and ran for the door, skidded down the entrance hall and out the great front doors. Officers turned to watch her pass, barefoot, clad in the garments of the poorest Hindoo, but she had no time to wonder what they made of her. She reached the top of the stairs and Skipped high into the sky. Below her, the *maidan*, the enormous parkland surrounding Fort William, lay spread beneath her. She Skipped again, over the walls of the fort, and cast a frantic eye across the buildings within as she fell. She could not Skip low enough to make out individual men without falling to her death, so she alit near the front gate and ran toward the sentry waiting there.

The man did not at first see her; she approached from inside the fort, and his attention was outward. "Sergeant!" she shouted when she was near enough to make out his insignia. The man turned, startled, and brought his rifle to his shoulder. Daphne skidded to a halt and flung her hands up to show they were empty. "Sergeant, I am Lady Daphne St. Clair, Extraordinary Bounder, and I have been sent by Colonel Dalhousie to find the Governor-General. I have an urgent message for him."

The sergeant examined her closely. "Why are you dressed like that?" he said in a dull, drawling voice that suggested his intellect was as dull and drawling as the rest of him. How he had become a sergeant stymied her. Another sentry, this one a corporal, came to join his partner. Both men wore the ill-fitting uniforms that marked a Company soldier; their outfitting was contracted to the lowest bidder.

"I have been... actually, it is none of your business, and my message is extremely urgent," Daphne said, picturing this conversation going on for an hour as she tried to convince these men she was who she claimed to be. "Where is Lord Moira?"

The sentries looked at each other. Daphne could almost hear the thoughts going through their heads: *Who let the madwoman in?* In about five seconds, they would realize she had not passed them to enter the fort, and then everything would fall apart. "Never mind, gentlemen, I will find him myself," she said, and Skipped into the sky once more.

She had never visited Fort William and had no idea what each of the low, rectangular buildings was for. A church, beautiful and elegant, looked completely out of place in this setting, its spires catching the early sunlight as if tipped with gold. Soldiers in formation, probably sepoys, drilled on one of the parade grounds. She watched them for half a breath before Skipping to the ground and running across the field to where their officer stood.

"Sir," she said, "I was told Lord Moira was inspecting the troops today. Can you tell me where I might find him?"

"Who allowed you—you're a woman!" the captain exclaimed. Daphne suppressed the urge to roll her eyes. "Why do you seek the Governor-General?"

"I am Lady Daphne St. Clair, Extraordinary Bounder," Daphne said, "and my errand is urgent enough that I do not have time to explain it to you. Please, Captain, where is he?"

The captain regarded her at length. Daphne tried not to jig from one foot to the other with impatience. Finally, the captain said, "He went with Colonel Haight and General Comstock to the Arsenal. Do you know where that is?" Daphne shook her head. "West past the next two buildings, then south, and it is the third on your right. Lady Daphne—"

"Thank you," Daphne said, and threw herself into the sky. The captain's directions were clear and precise, the layout of the grounds exact, and Daphne Skipped directly to the building indicated. It was a two-story construction, plain and unadorned, with two entrances at opposite ends. Both were guarded by more sentries, also armed with rifles. Daphne's heart sank. More men to argue her way past.

-Daphne!- Bess's voice echoed in her mind. -Colonel Haight's aide-de-camp says the Governor-General is with the colonel in the Arsenal. Find your way there, and hurry!-

Now Daphne did roll her eyes. It was all very well for Bess to tell her to hurry when she was in no position to do so. Possibly the Governor-General was safe indoors, away from where the Shaper might shoot him with a rifle or pistol, but the Shaper could be almost anyone, and Daphne did not want to rest her hopes on that slim thread.

She ran lightly to the nearest door and smiled in a friendly way at the sentry, a plain-faced corporal with spots on his cheeks. "Pardon me, Corporal," she said, "is Lord Moira within?"

"What are you supposed to be?" The corporal eyed her strange garb and bare feet with confusion.

"I am Lady Daphne St. Clair, Extraordinary Bounder—" the little phrase was starting to lose all meaning—"and I have an urgent message for the Governor-General. Pray tell me, is he here?"

The corporal hitched his rifle higher. At least he had not leveled it at her. "You don't look like no lady."

Daphne wanted to scream. "My attire is irrelevant. And Lord Moira will be very displeased with you if you do not help me. You do not want to come to his attention, do you?"

The corporal's confused expression became fearful. "No, miss. My lady." He stepped aside. Daphne nodded in thanks and sprinted up the steps.

Bess's voice came to her mind. -I have Spoken to the Governor-General and explained the situation, but I do not know if he believes me. I was at my most persuasive, however. With luck, you will not have to do very much convincing.- Uncertainty tinged the message, and Daphne agreed with what Bess had not said: Lord Moira was unlikely to agree to anything Daphne proposed, no matter who it originated with or how much sense it made. Daphne gritted her teeth. She was sworn to do her best to protect this man, and she would do it regardless of his own feelings on the matter.

The door to the Arsenal opened on a dimly lit, stuffy chamber fully two stories tall. Spare regimental flags crossed near the ceiling, high above, along with a Union Jack that had seen better days. The walls were lined with rifles of all shapes, including some longer than she was tall. Men in shirtsleeves worked silently, cleaning the weapons, counting them off. A set of mobile stairs gave access to the upper racks, and a man in the garb of a Mahommedan ambled down it, making it rock.

At the far end of the long room, Lord Moira stood with two other men, both in proper uniforms despite the warmth of the room. One of the men, holding his hat under his arm, had short black hair. Panicked, Daphne Skipped the length of the room and grabbed the man's chin, forcing him to look at her. His brown eyes, initially perplexed, grew angry. "What the devil are you doing?" he said, wrenching away.

"I beg your pardon, sir, I—" No time to explain what she had been about. "Lord Moira, did you receive the message?"

"An impossible one," Lord Moira said irritably. "Explain yourself, Lady Daphne."

Daphne breathed deeply, inhaling the bitter scent of black powder and the fainter odor of old sweat. "My lord," she began, "you were informed that Amitabh, the man who attempted—"

"I know who he is. Do not waste my time."

"I beg your pardon. He has in his company a Shaper who took the form of Lieutenant Wright and lived among us at the Residence in Madhyapatnam for a time."

"I know that as well." Lord Moira's face grew stormy. Daphne swallowed to moisten her dry throat. She would not permit him to cow her.

"That Shaper—Amitabh sent him, several days ago, to travel to Calcutta, disguise himself as one of the soldiers—actually Amitabh did not say that, it is a logical supposition—and attempt to kill you, my lord. We believe he is in Calcutta now. My lord, you must permit me to Bound you to safety until he can be found."

Lord Moira continued to scowl at her. Daphne faced him down, praying her uncertainty and fear did not show. "My lord, is this true?" said the black-haired colonel Daphne had manhandled.

"Miss Hanley assures me it is," Lord Moira said. "She would not manufacture such a hoax. Apparently the would-be prince seeks to destabilize the Company so he may gain control over Madhyapatnam in Napoleon's name."

Inside, Daphne fumed. Of course Bess was trustworthy, but that he did not attach the same credence to *Daphne's* words... it was infuriating, and Daphne simply did not know how to change his mind. *Because you cannot*, the thought occurred to her, and with it came a remarkable feeling of peace. She could *not* change Lord Moira's mind, would never be able to do so, and it was irrelevant. She did not need his approval or his respect to be the woman she knew herself to be, and the thought made her able to stand up straight and face him fearlessly.

"Very well. Thank you for the warning, Lady Daphne." Lord Moira turned to his companions. "The condition of the arms is no better than it ever has been. Why are so many of them in shoddy condition?"

"It is what the Company is willing to pay for," said the other man, a general whose hair was whiter than Lord Moira's. "If they permitted us to—"

"We aren't going to change Company policy," Lord Moira said, cutting him off. "Very well. Have as many of them repaired as possible before we march. Now I want to see the troops."

"Oh, my lord," Daphne said, alarmed, "you cannot go out in the open. Please permit me to Bound you to your office."

"I have no intention of hiding in my office when there is work to be done," Lord Moira said. "I will not be Bounded anywhere." He set off down the passage, trailed by his companions. Daphne scrambled to catch up and Skipped in front of the door to bar his way.

"Please, my lord, please have a care for yourself! The Shaper could be almost anyone," she said, starting to feel irritated with his recalcitrance. "Give Captain Fletcher time to find him."

"If I permit that upstart Amitabh and his pet Shaper to dictate my movements, he has won. Let them hunt me. I am not so easy to kill as all that." Lord Moira made as if to take Daphne by the shoulders and move her aside, but thought better of it. "Stand aside, Lady Daphne."

"Oh...!" Daphne exited the building rapidly and scanned her surroundings. So many of the men walking past were of the right height and coloring! *Why* was Lord Moira so stupid? No, that was unfair, he was not stupid, just proud and entirely too foolhardy. What should she do now?

She trailed along behind the general and the colonel, torn between watching Lord Moira and trying to have eyes everywhere. Lord Moira did not order her away, so she chose to take that as implicit agreement to her presence. Perhaps she should return to Fletcher... though he was likely no longer in Government House, but searching for the Shaper in the grounds of Fort William. The desire to be in a dozen different places at once was like a physical pull making her dizzy. She closed her eyes briefly, then panicked and opened them again, feeling superstitiously that her moment of inattention would be the moment the Shaper would strike.

She became conscious of just how many men wielded rifles. There were almost none bearing pistols, which would require them to be fairly close if they wished to strike with any accuracy, and the officers' swords also seemed like unlikely weapons for an assassin. But a rifle... the Shaper need not approach to any close distance, and there were enough men practicing their shooting that aiming a rifle would not stand out.

They neared the parade grounds, or at least one of them. It was the same one Daphne had approached earlier. Lord Moira walked forward to speak with the captain, and Daphne hung back, examining the sepoys. She had been told so many disparate things about them: that they were the backbone of the Company's army, that they were prone to disorderliness, that they were the best-disciplined troops in India... she did not know what to believe. They certainly looked orderly, spread out in regimented lines, if a bit odd in sandals and short pants with the funny tilted hats.

The captain called out a command, and the sepoys halted in place, relaxing, some leaning on their guns, others examining them as if checking for faults. Daphne recalled what the general had said about the rifles; she guessed that they, like the uniforms, were contracted to the lowest bidder. That struck her as a bad idea, since the military depended on its weapons, but she was not in charge of ordnance.

She let her eyes skim over the ranks of sepoys. The Shaper would find it easy to hide there, despite his light blue eyes, for how many Europeans paid attention to the eyes of a Hindoo? She kept careful watch on those raising their weapons, sighting along the barrels—none of them were pointed at Lord Moira, thank goodness, because she was not sure what she would do if they were. Skip to block the shot? She had no desire to be wounded again, or killed, but was it not her duty?

A couple of corporals passed in front of her, both armed for sentry duty. The blond one nodded at her appreciatively, which she found amusing, given that she was still dressed as a Hindoo man. Not that anyone would mistake her for a man except at the most cursory glance. She smiled at him, but let her eyes rove on.

One of the sepoys had wandered off the parade ground, fussing with his rifle, which appeared to be jammed. The captain, deep in conversation with Lord Moira, did not notice him to reprimand or call him back. Daphne watched him walk away for a few seconds, then went back to scanning the grounds.

She saw the flicker of movement out of the corner of her eye, looked back to see the sepoy raise his gun to his shoulder, and screamed a warning before Skipping to Lord Moira's side. The shot reverberated off the walls surrounding them. Lord Moira cried out. "No, forgive me!" Daphne cried, her arms around the Governor-General too late.

"Get off me, Lady Daphne," Lord Moira said irritably. Daphne let him go. He did not sound at all in pain, just angry as he usually was when speaking to her. She turned toward the sepoy, who had collapsed atop his rifle, and Skipped to the man's side. She dropped to her knees and rolled him over, onto his back. His eyes, wide open, were a clear, glinting blue in a dark Hindoo face. Blood spread across his uniform jacket, and Daphne felt the briefest moment of dizziness before reminding herself that it no longer disturbed her.

She stood and looked around, trying to judge where the shot had come from, and saw Lord Moira and the officers coming her way. "What the devil is going on?" Lord Moira shouted. "Who shot that man?"

"My lord, that is the Shaper," Daphne said. She wished she could make a grand gesture, but her hands were shaking. She had been over-confident, having captured Amitabh and rescued Sir Rodney, and had the shooter not been faster than the Shaper, Lord Moira would be dead.

Lord Moira bent to look at him. "He looks like a sepoy," he said. "How can we know what you say is true? Someone may have just shot an innocent man!"

"I beg your pardon, my lord, but I am certain that was the Shaper," Fletcher said, running up behind them. He was out of breath and carried a rifle in one hand. "I watched him join the troops drilling after the rest were already in place, then maneuver himself to where he would have a clear shot."

"And his eyes—my lord, the Shaper's eyes are blue, it is very distinctive," Daphne said, trying to regain her equilibrium.

Lord Moira peered at the dead man's face. "Indeed," he said. "Thank you, Captain Fletcher."

"You made it possible, my lord, by cleverly trailing around in the open and luring him out," Fletcher said. He managed to make it sound like a compliment and not a sarcastic criticism.

"Very good shot," Lord Moira said. "Have someone dispose of this body, and I will finish my inspection."

"Excuse me, my lord," Fletcher said, "but with Amitabh captured, his troops in Madhyapatnam are without leadership. It might be possible for the regiment currently there to defeat them, without sending in further troops or attacking the civilian population."

"I'm of a mind to make an example of them, Fletcher," Lord Moira said darkly. "We cannot afford to have a citizenry that harbors a secret desire for a return to an earlier regime."

"My lord, Madhyapatnam is in general a peaceful place. Those who went along with Amitabh's plans did so out of a desire not to see any more bloodshed. They are also not fond of the French interlopers. I predict that were Amitabh's defeat made public, many of the natives would rise up against his remaining men, and drive Napoleon's men out for us." Fletcher looked cool, in command of himself, but Daphne could see the knuckles of his fist were once again white.

Lord Moira looked once again at the Shaper. "You ask me to take a tremendous risk," he said.

"With a tremendous reward, should my words prove true," Fletcher said.

"Very well," Lord Moira said. "Have Colonel Dalhousie pass the word to the regiment at Madhyapatnam. In fact—" He glared at Daphne. "Since you are so keen to assist, you might Bound the colonel there so he may take command directly."

"Yes, my lord," Daphne said. "Captain, may I return you to Government House?"

"Thank you, Lady Daphne, I would appreciate it," Fletcher said. His eyes twinkled with suppressed good humor.

Daphne put her arms around his waist and Bounded them to the tiny chamber, but did not let go once they were there. Fletcher let out a deep sigh and cradled her cheek in one hand. "It is over," he said.

"Oh," said Daphne. "I feel rather let down, which is ridiculous, as I should be happy that peace will be restored to Madhyapatnam and that the Governor-General is not dead."

"I always feel that way when I have completed an assignment. Being driven by a set of goals for so long leaves me at loose ends when those goals are achieved."

"I understand that." She let out a sigh to match his. "I must convey Colonel Dalhousie to Madhyapatnam, and then I should visit Major Schofeld. He was so obliging while I was recovering, I feel I ought to offer him my services. He is not so terrible as I believed."

"Schofeld and I spoke for nearly an hour two days ago," Fletcher said, "and to my complete surprise he apologized for his behavior in imposing his emotions on me. He claimed—well, it was a long conversation, but in the end we parted, not friends, but no longer enemies. I have no idea what prompted his change of heart, but I must agree with you, he is not terrible."

Daphne chose not to relate the argument she had had with Schofeld. "Then I will leave you and seek out the colonel, and speak to Major Schofeld. And after that—I do not know what will happen next."

"Nor do I," Fletcher said, "and I am afraid much of it is out of our control."

That gave Daphne a frisson of fear she could not quite suppress before Fletcher perceived it. He smiled, a little sadly, and said, "My love, I assure you I will do whatever I can to keep you by my side."

"Will you?"

"My word on it," he said, and pulled her close for a kiss.

CHAPTER 32

IN WHICH DAPHNE DISCOVERS WHAT HER HAPPY ENDING IS

Daphne sat in the left-hand drawing room of Lindsey House and pretended to read. It had been three days since the capture of Amitabh and the death of the Shaper, and during those three days it was as if the events at Madhyapatnam had never occurred. No one from Government House had so much as Spoken to Bess, summoning Daphne; no one had come asking her to Bound anyone anywhere; and Fletcher had disappeared as thoroughly as morning mist.

The last disturbed her most. She knew he must be busy, helping to restore Madhyapatnam to its pre-Amitabh state, but she had hoped he might find time to call on her, socially if not professionally. Had she not been utterly convinced of his love for her, she might have worried that their relationship had been the result of propinquity under extreme conditions. She made herself ignore the tiny twinge of doubt that had set up residence in a corner of her heart.

She nearly set the book aside before remembering it was essential camouflage from Miss Donnelly, who had been making noises again about finding a project for Daphne to fill the long afternoons. Why Miss Donnelly had decided fancy sewing was exactly the thing to

306

occupy Daphne's empty hours, she had no idea, but she did not intend to be trapped into monogramming handkerchiefs, not even for people she knew. If only someone would provide her with *meaningful* employment! Lady Loudoun was still at Donington Hall, preparing her things to be Bounded to India, and would be for another day. Then the work would begin, tedious work, but better than nothing.

-Daphne! Oh, never mind, you cannot tell me where you are.-

"I am in the drawing room, Bess," Daphne called out. She laid her book aside just as Bess pushed open the door. "Please tell me you have a message for me."

"No, I'm afraid not." Bess settled herself on the sofa opposite Daphne's. "I was simply tired of being alone with my thoughts. It is— would have been John's twenty-fifth birthday today."

"Oh, Bess. You have my sympathy." Daphne hesitated. "Are you— that is, you have seemed rather—but I do not wish to judge your emotions—"

"Have I resigned myself to his death?" Bess's lips quirked up on one side in a self-deprecatory smile. "I will never stop missing him, in a way, because we were so close. He knew me as no one else did. But my heart will heal, and I will someday be able to remember him without pain. And I no longer feel guilt at not having loved him dearly. In fact—"

"Yes?"

Bess bit her lip. "It is a terrible thing to admit, but suppose we had been reunited, and he had persuaded me to marry him despite my feelings? I would not for all the world that he had died, but... I did say it was a terrible thing."

Daphne rose and hugged her friend. "I believe it is natural to look for ways in which a tragedy is not so horrid after all. And you do not mean it. You would not have married him, regardless, and someday you will find someone you *do* love with all your heart, and it will be glorious."

Bess laughed and hugged her back. "And your heart?" she said. "I wonder that Captain Fletcher has not appeared in all this time."

"He is no doubt busy," Daphne said. "I can be patient."

"You are the very model of impatience, Daphne."

"I know." She sighed. "Tomorrow I am off for England again. We—the other Bounders and I—estimate it will take a full day to convey all that Lady Loudoun insists on having brought from England. I am so grateful I was permitted to enlist a few Bounders from Fort William, or it should have taken me two days by myself."

"Then will your service to Lady Loudoun be at an end?"

"I will be at her disposal until the end of next week. After that, who knows?" Daphne tried to sound carefree about it, but in her heart, she was discouraged and a little afraid. She felt like a man dangling over a cliff, holding a rope attached to he knew not what. That her future depended on what other people said or did or thought unsettled her.

"Surely General—" Bess went silent and held up a finger for Daphne to wait while she Spoke to someone. A peculiar expression crossed her face. "That is odd," she said when she was finished. "I had been about to say his name, and his office Spoke to me. You are to Bound to the War Office in Lisbon in half an hour."

"I am? Why?"

"The War Office is never forthcoming with details like that. But I cannot imagine it does not have something to do with your new assignment." Bess looked as wary as Daphne felt. "Daphne, if you are assigned to the Peninsula, what of Captain Fletcher? Surely the Army will not want him to leave, not with everything he understands about India?"

"You are saying things I have thought a thousand times before, Bess. I see no solution. Besides, it is not as if he has made me any promises." The tiny twinge of doubt redoubled.

"Do not talk like that! He loves you, I am certain of it."

"But we hardly know each other! And I do not know what his intentions are. If I am to go to Spain, perhaps he imagines marriage is a mistake."

"Is that what you want? Marriage?"

"Oh, I do not know what I want, Bess, except to see him again so I might ask him all these questions."

Bess rose, straightening her gown. "All will be well. General Omberlis will commend you for your actions here in India, and will permit you to choose your next posting."

"How do you know that?"

"I don't. I am simply trying to be optimistic. *You* taught me that."

⊗⊗⊗

HALF AN HOUR LATER, DAPHNE TROD SLOWLY UP THE GRAND MARBLE stairs from the War Office's tiny Bounding chamber. The last time she had done so, she had been covered in mud and disgrace. This time, her black uniform was clean and neatly pressed, her hair was tidily pinned around her head, and the whispers she could hear but not comprehend were likely speculations on her identity. Not that there was more than one five-foot-tall female Extraordinary Bounder attached to the War Office.

She approached the antechamber and smiled at the men standing in small groups, conversing quietly. Once again, the armchairs at the center of the room were unoccupied. After a moment's thought, she took a seat, ignoring the whispered commentary that went up all around. She no longer felt she had anything to prove, not to General Omberlis, not to these men, and certainly not to herself.

She leaned back and crossed her legs at the ankles, admiring the polish of her boots. They were shiny without looking new, the boots of someone who had worn them in action. She had mended a small tear in the inseam of her trousers, near the kneecap, herself. She was no longer the same woman she had been a month ago—had it truly been only a month? It felt like a lifetime. In a sense, it had been.

General Omberlis' door opened, and the same slim young man she had seen before emerged. He scanned the antechamber, and his eye fell on Daphne. "Lady Daphne, the general will see you now," he said. A murmur went up again, this one sounding annoyed. Well, if they did not have the good sense to make an appointment—or to be summoned—on their own heads be it.

General Omberlis stood at the window, looking out over the city.

309

"Have a seat, Lady Daphne," he said without turning around. Daphne sat and realized the height of the chair meant she either could sit on the edge like an eager puppy, or sit back and allow her feet to dangle two inches off the floor. She chose eagerness, reasoning that she needed the general to think of her as an adult for this conversation.

The silent moment stretched out between them. Daphne looked past General Omberlis at Lisbon and wondered what he saw when he looked at it. Did he think of Lisbon as home, after all these years? Where did Daphne call home, now?

Finally, General Omberlis turned and took his seat behind his massive desk that sat like a castle wall between them. "Lady Daphne," he said. "I am not certain what to say."

"Sir?" Daphne tried not to sound puzzled. She had no idea what to expect from this conversation, but she had believed the general, at least, would know why he had called her.

"You were sent to India to assist the Governor-General's lady wife. You instead helped to foil an assassination plot, prevented a French invasion of one of the East India Company's richest provinces, and saved a dozen lives, as well as discovering two new uses for Bounding. And all in one month's time."

Daphne gaped. "Well, to be fair, sir," she said, "I *was* also of assistance to Lady Loudoun. And those Bounding techniques are deadly, so I am not sure I should be given credit for that."

"Nevertheless." General Omberlis leaned back in his chair, his wolfish eyes assessing her. "Are you free of your trouble?"

"I am, sir. That is, blood does still make my vision cloudy at first sight, but it is slight—barely noticeable—and I never lose consciousness anymore."

"Excellent." The general smiled. It was such a rare expression on his craggy face Daphne did not at first realize it was meant as reassurance. "And your service with Lady Loudoun is at an end."

"In nine days' time, sir."

"I see. Then in ten days, you will report to this office in preparation for being sent to the front. Field Marshal Wellesley is preparing for a major push that may see our armies marching on France within the week. You will be directly under his command."

Field Marshal Wellesley. Daphne heard all the words after that name in a daze. The man she so admired—and she was to serve under him. To carry his orders—possibly himself!—across the battlefield. It was what she had dreamed of. Why, then, did the idea feel so hollow?

"Of course, General," she heard herself say, "but I... I did tell you I was fond of India."

"This is the War Office, Lady Daphne. We serve where we're sent, and fondness has nothing to do with it. Service with Wellesley will guarantee your advancement within this office and will enhance your reputation as a Bounder." General Omberlis leaned forward and lowered his voice, forcing Daphne to lean forward as well. "You suppose I don't know how you chafe under the restrictions laid upon you, a woman, regardless of your talent? Make a name for yourself here, and you will find those restrictions evaporate. No one will ever tell Lady Daphne St. Clair what she may or may not do for the sake of propriety. Three and a half more years, Lady Daphne, and who knows what you may accomplish? And India will still be there." He laughed. "It has been there for thousands of years. It is unlikely it will miss you much."

"But—" Her objections were disappearing faster than she could lay hold of them. She could not tell the general she intended to marry when Fletcher had not spoken. General Omberlis might not care if she did. He might even tell her she was forbidden to marry until her term was up; it seemed the sort of thing the War Office might expect of its Extraordinaries. And—to serve under Wellesley... the general was correct that valiant service to him would open doors she had never dreamed of. Even if they were no longer her dream.

Ultimately, it did not matter. She was not being offered a choice. "Thank you, General," she said. "I will return in ten days."

She rose when he did and shook his enormous hand when he offered it. He held onto her hand when she would have pulled away. "You are not as happy about this as I expected you would be," he said.

"I am, General, it is simply not at all what I expected."

"Better than you expected, I hope."

She smiled, and felt it strain the corners of her lips as if she had forgotten how. "Different."

She did not bother going to the Bounding nexus for privacy, but Bounded back to her Lindsey House bedroom from the general's antechamber. She sat on her bed and buried her face in her hands. What would she tell Fletcher? Would he believe she had abandoned him? Which she had, in a way. Where *was* he?

-Daphne, Captain Fletcher is here—you must come now!-

Startled, Daphne Bounded, sensing Fletcher's essence in the left-hand drawing room an instant before appearing there and startling him as well. Bess was leaving, closing the door behind herself, but she spared Daphne a wide-eyed glance that it was just as well Fletcher did not see, as her expression said clearly she intended to have the full story from Daphne later.

Fletcher wore full dress uniform and had just set his hat on a small table that was not big enough to hold anything else. "Lady Daphne," he said formally, "you are on official business."

"What? Oh. No, I have simply been in Lisbon, receiving new orders."

His face went still. "And?"

"I am to report back in ten days, for a field assignment. To Field Marshal Wellesley's command."

"Then you are leaving." His voice sounded so strange, and Daphne's heart broke at hearing it. There was none of the affection, none of the love she was so accustomed to hearing from him, even when his words were not endearments.

"I am, but..." It was all wrong. She loved him, but she was doing everything wrong. "General Omberlis tells me it is a grand opportunity, and he is right, but it takes me away from you, and—though you seem so strange today, and you have been gone so long, perhaps it is what you want—"

"What I want? Daphne, no!" Fletcher took her hand and pulled her into his embrace. She put her arms around him and breathed in the smell of warm wool and sandalwood that would forever after remind her of him. "I am too late, it seems," he went on. "My business kept me rather longer than I expected, and I was in England yesterday—"

"In England? Why?"

He detached himself from her embrace and drew her down to sit beside him on the sofa. "Because it is customary," he said, "when one intends to propose marriage to a woman, to ask her parents' blessing upon it."

Daphne gasped. "Captain—*Phineas*—"

He smiled and caressed her cheek. "You should consider carefully before accepting me, my darling," he said. "I am well aware that your social and economic status are far above my own. The benefits to such a marriage are entirely on my side. I can only promise to love you devotedly, to stand by your side through every trial life sees fit to send us, and to defend you against all comers, though admittedly you seem not to need much defending."

"But I—if I am in Spain, and you are here—"

"I don't have a solution to everything. I simply want the right to find the solution with you. Please, Daphne, say you'll marry me?"

Daphne flung her arms around him and buried her face in his neck. "Yes," she whispered, "yes, I will, and how dare you suggest that you are the only one who benefits, when I gain your courage, and wisdom, and the way you kiss me that makes me breathless—"

He interrupted her with a kiss of that very nature, and speech became impossible.

Finally, Daphne turned her face away and said, "We should not be so indecorous here, as Miss Donnelly would positively erupt were she to know about it."

"I find I care nothing for the Miss Donnellys of this world, so long as I have you," Fletcher said, though he withdrew as far as holding Daphne's hand would allow. "I meant it when I said the benefit of this marriage is all mine. Daphne, with my talent I see the very basest impulses of humanity, and I have met so many women who desired to attach me whose hearts were dark with greed and selfishness. That night at Lady Loudoun's ball... you radiated integrity and joy, and I believe I knew without acknowledging it that you were the only woman I could see myself growing old with."

Daphne blinked. "That is the most romantic thing I have ever heard."

"It is entirely true. I love you, Daphne."

Daphne stood and let go Fletcher's hand. "I will return shortly," she said, and Bounded away.

She raced up the marble steps and down the hall to the antechamber, where she startled the slim young man, who had just opened the door to General Omberlis' office. "Pray do not trouble yourself," she said, "I will only take a moment of the general's time."

General Omberlis frowned when he saw her. "Lady Daphne. I did not summon you."

Daphne shut the door in the slim young man's face. "No, General, but I must speak with you, and you will not like what I have to say, but I must say it, and when I am done it will be up to you to decide."

The general raised one bushy grey eyebrow. He gestured toward the chair, but Daphne shook her head and stood in front of the desk. "General," she said, "I did not tell you why I love India. Or, that is, I do love India, but there is also a man—he is—I love him, General, and I intend to marry him, and you can see how that would be a problem because he is a captain there and cannot leave. Although I suppose he *could* leave, it is just that he is so very good at what he does that the Army will consider it a waste to send him elsewhere, much as I'm sure it seems a waste to send me anywhere but to Field Marshal Wellesley."

The general opened his mouth to speak, and Daphne hurried on. "You see, General, I know I am bound to serve where I am bid, but if it is just a matter of building my reputation or my career, I find I am less eager to be the greatest Bounder ever because I have found something more wonderful. Do you know—are you married, General?—do you know what it is to find someone who wants you to be the very best self you can be, who does not coddle or protect you from yourself, so long as he can go into danger by your side? I did not believe there were any such men in the world, and I am so happy to be proved wrong. But now... General, as I said, I am under your command and I will do as I've sworn, and if you say I must go to Spain, I will do so. And—it now occurs to me that perhaps you have pulled strings to get me this assignment, and if that is so I am incredibly honored, and you must imagine me terribly ungrateful, but I must be honest with you, for his sake and mine."

General Omberlis' expression had gone from puzzled, to angry, to dispassionate in the course of Daphne's speech. "Lady Daphne," he said, "you would give up the assignment a thousand Bounders have schemed for, just for love?"

"I suppose I would, sir."

The general shook his head, slowly, a frown drawing his bushy eyebrows down. "Report to me in ten days' time," he said. "And I do not want to see you before then."

It felt like a blow to the face. Daphne bowed her head and whispered, "Yes, sir." Without leaving his office, she Bounded back to the drawing room, put her arms around Fletcher, and let herself weep.

⚜

FIVE DAYS LATER, THEY WERE MARRIED. DAPHNE, WHO FOUND herself indifferent when it came to considering her service with the War Office, very nearly chose to marry from the church near Marvell Hall despite regulations, but Fletcher was more sensible, and in the end the service by special license was held at St. John's Church, near Government House. Daphne broke the rules to the extent of Bounding her parents, and Fletcher's parents and brother William, to Calcutta. It was an unexpectedly cool day for northern India, and Daphne's happiness was almost enough to fill the aching hole in her heart that was General Omberlis' looming deadline.

Lord Moira and Lady Loudoun gave them the use of a suite in Government House for their wedding night, and Daphne learned there are advantages to having a Discerner for a husband that he does not share with anyone but his wife.

They set up house for the next four days in a property belonging to one of Fletcher's fellow officers who was away near the northern border. Lady Loudoun, with her usual grace, had told Daphne she had no need of her services anymore, "but you will always be a welcome guest, and I know the children are fond of you." Daphne's impression of Lady Loudoun's children was less positive, but the generous gesture warmed her heart.

On the ninth day, she sat close beside Fletcher as they trundled along the paths of the *maidan*, enjoying the rare breezes that came off the Hooghly on a late Sunday afternoon drive. The carriage, which came with the house, was not well-sprung, and Daphne found she needed to cling to Fletcher's arm to keep from being flung off on more than one occasion.

"I wish you would come with me tomorrow," she said.

"I have not been summoned. It might put General Omberlis' back up."

"Yes, but it would also show him whose life he is ruining."

"I would prefer not to be an object of pity, darling."

Daphne sighed and rested her head briefly on his shoulder; the jouncing of the carriage made longer than that impractical. "I know. Regardless, I will return afterward, and we will decide how to go on. I truly do not mind Bounding from Spain to our home in India, wherever we choose to make it."

"*I* mind being separated from you. I tell you, I can make arrangements to serve in the Peninsular Army."

"But at a loss of seniority. And you are so close to being made a major."

"I have everything I could ever want, right here. Military rank only matters because without it your father looks at me as if I am stealing away his little ewe lamb."

"He likes you. He just enjoys making people work for his approval."

Fletcher steered the carriage along the road toward their house, nodding at an acquaintance that passed on the other side. "In any case, I refuse to be the useless appendage to my famous Bounder wife. I must have *something* to do, Daphne, and if that something is in Spain, or France, so much the better." He brought the carriage to a halt and assisted Daphne down, keeping hold of her hand when she alit. "Let us not dwell on it tonight. Let us pretend we are any other married couple, and dine early, and go to bed early."

Daphne squeezed his hand. "That seems an excellent plan."

DAPHNE ROSE EARLY THE NEXT MORNING AND DRESSED WITH MORE than usual care in her War Office uniform. Then she sat, drumming her heels, in their drawing room until Fletcher fled, protesting that her anxiety was wearing on him. Daphne grumbled, because she had not been touching him for him to experience any such thing, but she had to admit privately she found herself annoying, too.

The five-hour difference between Lisbon and Calcutta meant it was well after noon when Daphne finally Bounded to the War Office. She paused on the landing to look out over the red roofs of the city. It was beautiful, and temperate, and she wished with all her heart she was back in Calcutta, where it was still stiflingly hot and the Hooghly smelled of fish guts and corpse fires.

At this hour, the War Office was barely occupied, and no one else waited in the antechamber. Daphne took a seat and interlaced her fingers on her knee. The carpet had a subtle purple sheen to its weave, not something Daphne had ever seen before. She leaned forward to look at it more closely. Where had it come from? Persia? China? Or might it have come from some market in India? She liked to imagine it was the last, and that her feet had one last contact with the place she was unlikely to see again.

The general's office door opened. "Lady Daphne," the general said. "Pray, enter."

Daphne rose and followed him, and once again sat perched on the edge of her seat. General Omberlis sank into his chair and steepled his fingers in front of him. The gesture made him look even more wolfish than usual. "So," he said. "Your business in Calcutta is finished?"

"Yes, sir, that is—yes."

"I heard you were married five days ago. Congratulations."

"Thank you, sir."

"What have you decided to do?"

Daphne decided if he were not present, Fletcher did not get a vote. "I will travel between the Peninsula and Calcutta whenever I have leave, sir."

"That will disrupt your service. Your commanding officer would prefer you be available at all times."

"But I will have leave, sir."

"Not very often. Are you certain your marriage can bear such a separation?"

"We are determined that it shall, sir."

General Omberlis tapped his fingers together, creating a rippling effect centered on his hands. "Lady Daphne," he said, "this assignment is in your best interests. It will offer you challenges you will not find elsewhere, as well as the opportunity to serve your country. You will, I judge, become the most famous Extraordinary Bounder in England. I am doing this for your own good."

"Yes, sir."

The general shoved back his chair and went to stand in front of the window. Daphne focused her gaze on his thick-fingered hands, clasped loosely behind him. He let out a long stream of breath. "It is unfortunate," he said, "that I am very bad at judging what is best for other people."

Daphne's head came up. "Sir?"

General Omberlis turned around. "I am informed that trouble is brewing near the Nepalese border," he said. "The Gurkhas have made continuing efforts to take territory properly claimed by the East India Company in the name of Great Britain. War is coming to India again, and England is in the heart of it. Major Phineas Fletcher is soon to be assigned to the negotiating team—I say 'negotiating,' but they are an advance force, no question—and he will need to be conveyed to Nepal, and from Nepal to any number of potential battle fronts. The War Office has chosen to assign you to the major for the duration."

Daphne's mouth fell open. "Sir, I—*major?*—but what of—"

"Do you wish me to change my mind, Lady Daphne?"

She shook her head. "No, sir." A broad smile spread across her face that she could not control. "Thank you, sir!"

"It is not the choice I would have made for myself," General Omberlis said. "On the other hand, I am reminded of what you accomplished when you were merely to be a human chaise. I believe I will be better off not trying to predict the future. Go."

"Yes, sir!"

In her excitement, she Bounded directly from his office to the tiny, dark room she used as a temporary Bounding chamber at their borrowed house. She ran from it, slamming the door behind her, shouting, *"Phineas!"*

Fletcher emerged from the drawing room. "Daphne?"

Happiness like the rising sun filled her, tangled her tongue so at first she could not speak. He came toward her, concern touching his face until he took her hand. His eyebrows rose in surprise, and then the wonderful smile crossed his lips. "Daphne?" he said again.

"I'm home," Daphne said.

AFTERWORD

The Honourable East India Company was significantly less benign in real history than I have made them here. Effectively rulers on behalf of the British government, they governed large portions of the Indian subcontinent and, depending on the whims of the officials, were more or less sympathetic to native needs (usually less). As a martial presence, they were unparalleled, and they unfortunately used that presence to impose their own laws on India, not always to its benefit. In my history, the existence of magical talents, which are distributed without regard for race or color, serves as an equalizer, making the EIC more of a commercial entity and less domineering.

I fear I have unfairly maligned the character of Lord Moira, who to my knowledge was historically guilty of nothing worse than being a close friend of the Prince Regent and a horrible spendthrift who left his family deeply in debt at his death. He was, in fact, a military-minded man and a veteran of the War of Independence, so I decided it was likely he would disdain someone like Daphne whose weakness might cost good men their lives. In real history, Lord Moira did not become Governor-General until October of 1813, but he was appointed to the position in November of 1812, and with the existence of instantaneous travel, I felt justified in pushing up the date when he took command at Calcutta.

Vaachaspati's story is from Kavi Ārif's *Lālmon Kecchā*, "The Wazir's Daughter Who Married a Sacrificial Goat," translated by Tony K. Stewart in the wonderful book *Fabulous Females and Peerless Pīrs*. This collection of Bengali stories is fun and exciting, and I recommend it to anyone interested in non-European fairy tales (though calling them fairy tales is a bit of an oversimplification).

ACKNOWLEDGMENTS

Once again I have to thank my stellar beta readers, Jacob Proffitt, Jana Brown, and Hallie O'Donovan for being willing to read this more than once. Sherwood Smith made a suggestion that turned out to be key to the plot, for which I am beyond grateful. They all were generous in pointing out errors and incongruities. All remaining mistakes are mine alone.

It would be impractical to list all the resources I used in writing this book. I find India endlessly fascinating, from its culture to its history to its religions, and loved the opportunity to learn more about it. For those interested in the fact behind the fiction, particularly with regards to English involvement in the subcontinent, I recommend John Keay's *India: A History* and his exhaustive look at the history of the British East India Company, *The Honourable Company*.

THE TALENTS

THE CORPOREAL TALENTS: Mover, Shaper, Scorcher, Bounder

MOVER (Greek τελεκινεσις): Capable of moving things without physically touching them. While originally this talent was believed to be connected to one's bodily strength, female Movers able to lift far more than their male counterparts have disproven this theory in recent years. Depending on skill, training, and practice, Movers may be able to lift and manipulate multiple objects at once, pick locks, and manipulate anything the human hand can manage. Movers can Move other people so long as they don't resist, and some are capable of Moving an unwilling target if the Mover is strong enough.

An EXTRAORDINARY MOVER, in addition to all these things, is capable of flight. Aside from this, an Extraordinary Mover is not guaranteed to be better skilled or stronger than an ordinary Mover; Helen Garrity, England's highest-rated Mover (at upwards of 12,000 pounds lifting capacity), was an ordinary Mover.

SHAPER (Greek μπιοκινεσις): Capable of manipulating their own bodies. Shapers can alter their own flesh, including healing wounds. Most Shapers use their ability only to make themselves more attractive, though that sort of beauty is always obvious as Shaped. More subtle uses include disguising oneself, and many Shapers have also been spies. It usually takes time for a Shaper to alter herself because Shaping is painful, and the faster one does it, the more painful it is. Under extreme duress, Shapers can alter their bodies rapidly, but this results in great pain and longer-term muscle and joint pain.

Shapers can mend bone, heal cuts or abrasions, repair physical damage to organs as from a knife wound, etc., make hair and nails grow, improve their physical condition (for example, enhance lung efficiency), and change their skin color. They cannot restore lost limbs or organs, cure diseases (though they can repair the physical damage done by disease), change hair or eye color, or regenerate nerves.

An EXTRAORDINARY SHAPER is capable of turning a Shaper's talent on another person with skin-to-skin contact. Extraordinary Shapers are sometimes called Healers as a result. While most Extraordinary Shapers use their talent to help others, there is nothing to stop them from causing injury or even death instead.

SCORCHER (Greek πϱοϰινεσις): Capable of igniting fire by the power of thought. The fire is natural and will cause ordinary flammable objects to catch on fire. If there aren't any such objects handy, the fire will burn briefly and then go out. A Scorcher must be able to see the place he or she is starting the fire. Scorcher talent has four dimensions: power, range, distance, and stamina. Power refers to how large and hot a fire the Scorcher can create; range is how far the Scorcher can fling a fire before it goes out; distance is how far away a Scorcher can ignite a fire; and stamina refers to how often the Scorcher can use his or her power before becoming exhausted. The hottest ordinary fire any Scorcher has ever created could melt brass (approximately 1700 degrees F). When she gave herself over to the fire, Elinor Pembroke was able to melt iron (over 2200 degrees F).

Scorchers are rare because they manifest by igniting fire unconsciously in their sleep. About 10-20% of Scorchers survive manifestation.

EXTRAORDINARY SCORCHERS are capable of controlling and mentally extinguishing fires. As their talent develops,

Extraordinary Scorchers become immune to fire, and their control over it increases.

BOUNDER (Greek τελεταχύς): Capable of moving from one point to another without passing through the intervening space. Bounders can move themselves anywhere they can see clearly within a certain range that varies according to the Bounder; this is called Skipping. They can also Bound to any location marked with a Bounder symbol, known as a signature. The location must be closed to the outdoors and empty of people and objects. Bounders refer to the "simplicity" of a space, meaning how free of "clutter" (objects, people, etc.) it is. Spaces that are too cluttered are impossible to Bound to, as are outdoor locations, which are full of constant movement. It is possible to keep a Bounder out of somewhere if you alter the place by defacing the Bounding chamber or putting some object or person into it.

An EXTRAORDINARY BOUNDER lacks most of the limitations an ordinary Bounder operates under. An Extraordinary Bounder's range is line of sight, which can allow them to Skip many miles' distance. Extraordinary Bounders do not require Bounding signatures, instead using what they refer to as "essence" to identify a space they Bound to. Essence comprises the essential nature of a space and is impossible to explain to non-Bounders; human beings have an essence which differs from that of a place and allows an Extraordinary Bounder to identify people without seeing them. While Extraordinary Bounders are still incapable of Bounding to an outdoor location, they can Bound to places too cluttered for an ordinary Bounder, as well as ones that contain people.

THE ETHEREAL TALENTS: Seer, Speaker, Discerner, Coercer

SEER (Greek προφητεία): Capable of seeing a short distance into the future through Dreams. Seers experience lucid Dreams in which they see future events as if they were present as an invisible observer. In order to recognize the people or places involved, Seers tend to be very well informed about people and events and are socially active. Their Dreams are not inevitable and there is no problem with altering the timeline; they see things that are the natural consequence of the current situation/circumstances, and altering those things alters the foreseen event. Just their knowledge of the event is not sufficient to alter it.

No one knows how a Seer's brain produces Dream, only that Dreams come in response to what the Seer meditates on. Seers therefore study current events in depth and read up on things they might be asked to Dream about. Seers have high social status and are very popular, with many of them making a living from Dream commissions.

An EXTRAORDINARY SEER, in addition to Dreaming, is capable of touching an object and perceiving events and people associated with it. These Visions allow them not only to see the past of the person most closely connected to the object, but occasionally to have glimpses of the future. They can also find a Vision linked to what the object's owner is seeing at the moment and "see" through their eyes. Most recently, the Extraordinary Seer Sophia Westlake discovered how to use Visions attached to one object to perceive related objects, leading to the defeat of the Caribbean pirates led by Rhys Evans.

SPEAKER (Greek τελεπάθεια): Capable of communicating by thought with any other Speaker. Speakers can mentally communicate with any Speaker within range of sight. They can also communicate with any Speaker they know well. The definition of "know well" has meaning only to a Speaker, but in general it means someone they have spoken verbally or mentally with on several occasions. A Speaker's circle of Speaker friends is called a reticulum, and a reticulum might contain several hundred members depending on the Speaker. Speakers easily distinguish between the different "voices" of their Speaker friends, though Speaking is not auditory. A Speaker can send images as well as words if she is proficient enough. Speakers cannot Speak to non-Speakers, and they are incapable of reading minds.

An EXTRAORDINARY SPEAKER has all the abilities of an ordinary Speaker, but is also capable of sending thoughts and images into the minds of anyone, Speaker or not. Additionally, an Extraordinary Speaker can Speak to multiple people at a time, though all will receive the same message. Extraordinary Speakers can send a "burst" of noise that startles or wakes the recipient. Rumors that Extraordinary Speakers can read minds are universally denied by Speakers, but the rumors persist.

DISCERNER (Greek ενουναίσθηση): Able to experience other people's feelings as if they were their own. Discerners require touch to be able to do this (though not skin-to-skin contact), and much of learning to control the skill involves learning to distinguish one's own emotions from those of the other person. Discerners can detect lies, sense motives, read other people's emotional states, and identify Coercers. Discerners are immune to the talent of a Coercer, though they can be overwhelmed by anyone capable of projecting strong emotions.

An EXTRAORDINARY DISCERNER can do all these things without the need for touch. Extraordinary Discerners are always aware of the emotions of those near them, though the range at which they are aware varies according to the Extraordinary Discerner. Nearly three-quarters of all Extraordinary Discerners go mad because of their talent.

COERCER (Greek τελενουναίσθηση): Capable of influencing the emotions of others with a touch. Coercers are viewed with great suspicion since their ability is a kind of mind control. Those altered are not aware that their mood has been artificially changed and are extremely suggestible while the Coercer is in direct contact with them. By altering someone's emotions, a Coercer can influence their behavior or change his or her attitude toward the Coercer.

Coercers do not feel others' emotions the way Discerners do, but can tell what they are and how they're changing. Many Coercers have sociopathic tendencies as a result. Unlike Discerners, Coercers have to work hard at being able to use their talent, which in its untrained state is erratic. However, Coercers always know when they've altered someone's mood. Coercers do not "broadcast" their emotions, appearing as a blank to Discerners. Because Coercion is viewed with suspicion (for good reason), Coercers keep their ability secret even if they don't use it maliciously.

An EXTRAORDINARY COERCER does not need a physical connection to influence someone's emotions. Extraordinary Coercers are capable of turning their talent on several people at a time, and the most powerful Extraordinary Coercers can control mobs. The most powerful Extraordinary Coercer known to date is Napoleon Bonaparte.

ABOUT THE AUTHOR

In addition to The Extraordinaries series, Melissa McShane is the author of more than twenty fantasy novels, including the novels of Tremontane, the first of which is *Servant of the Crown; Company of Strangers*, first in the series of the same name; and *The Book of Secrets*, first book in The Last Oracle series. She lives in the shelter of the mountains out West with her husband, four children and a niece, and three very needy cats. She wrote reviews and critical essays for many years before turning to fiction, which is much more fun than anyone ought to be allowed to have. You can visit her at her website **www.melissamcshanewrites.com** for more information on other books and upcoming releases.

For news, new release announcements, and other fun stuff, sign up for Melissa's newsletter **here**.

If you enjoyed this book, please consider leaving a review at your favorite online retailer or on Goodreads.

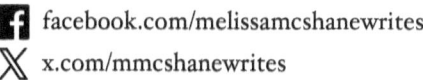 facebook.com/melissamcshanewrites
x.com/mmcshanewrites